MARK MILLAR WRITER

GREG CAPULLO PENCILLER

JONATHAN GLAPION INKER

FCO PLASCENCIA COLORIST

NATE PIEKOS OF BLAMBOT® LETTERING/DESIGN

RACHAEL FULTON EDITOR

COVERS
GREG CAPULLO WITH JONATHAN GLAPION
AND FCO PLASCENCIA

REBORN CREATED BY
MARK MILLAR AND GREG CAPULLO

NETFLIX

image

Reborn, TP. Second printing. June 2019. Published by Image Comics, Inc. Office of publication: 2701 NW Vaughn St., Suite 780, Portland, OR 97210. Copyright © 2019 Netflix Studios, LLC and Netflix Global, LLC. All rights reserved. Contains material originally published in single magazine form as Reborn issues #1-6. "Reborn," its logos, and the likenesses of all characters herein are trademarks of Netflix Studios, LLC and Netflix Global, LLC., unless otherwise noted. "Image" and the Image Comics logos are registered trademarks of Image Comics, Inc. No part of this publication may be reproduced or transmitted, in any form or by any means (except for short excerpts for journalistic or review purposes), without the express written permission of Netflix Studios, LLC and Netflix Global, LLC., or Image Comics, Inc. All names, characters, events, and locales in this publication are entirely fictional. Any resemblance to actual persons (living or dead), events, or places, without satirical intent, is coincidental. Printed in the USA. For information regarding the CPSIA on this printed material call: 203-595-3636.
For international rights, contact: lucy@netflixmw.com. ISBN: 978-1-5343-0652-3.

IMAGE COMICS INC.
Robert Kirkman: Chief Operating Officer
Erik Larsen: Chief Financial Officer
Todd McFarlane: President
Marc Silvestri: Chief Executive Officer
Jim Valentino: Vice President
Eric Stephenson: Publisher / Chief Creative Officer
Corey Hart: Director of Sales
Jeff Boison: Director of Publishing Planning & Book Trade Sales
Chris Ross: Director of Digital Sales
Jeff Stang: Director of Specialty Sales
Kat Salazar: Director of PR & Marketing
Drew Gill: Art Director
Heather Doornink: Production Director
Nicole Lapalme: Controller
IMAGECOMICS.COM

ONE

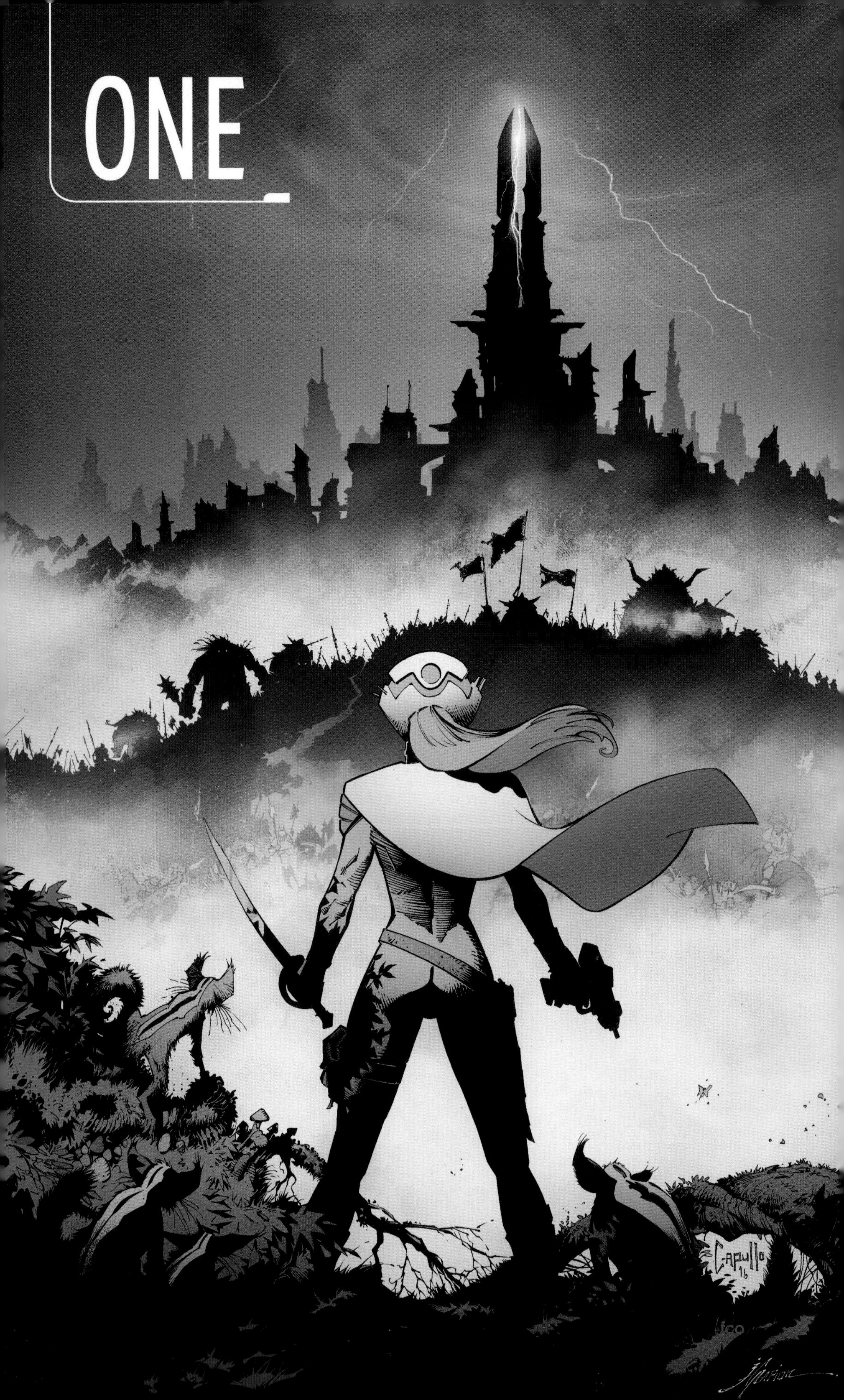

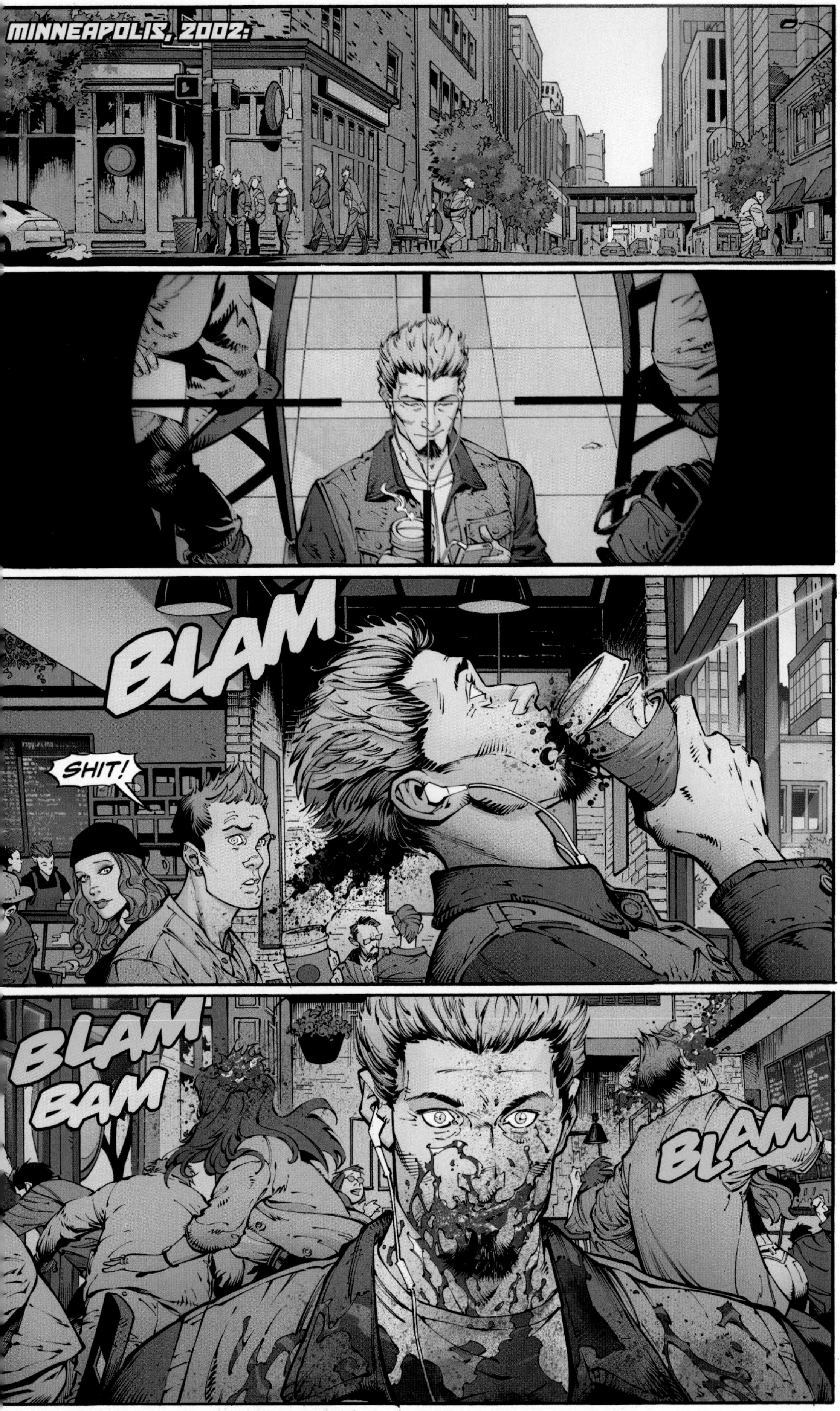

MINNEAPOLIS, 2002:
BLAM
SHIT!
BLAM
BAM
BLAM

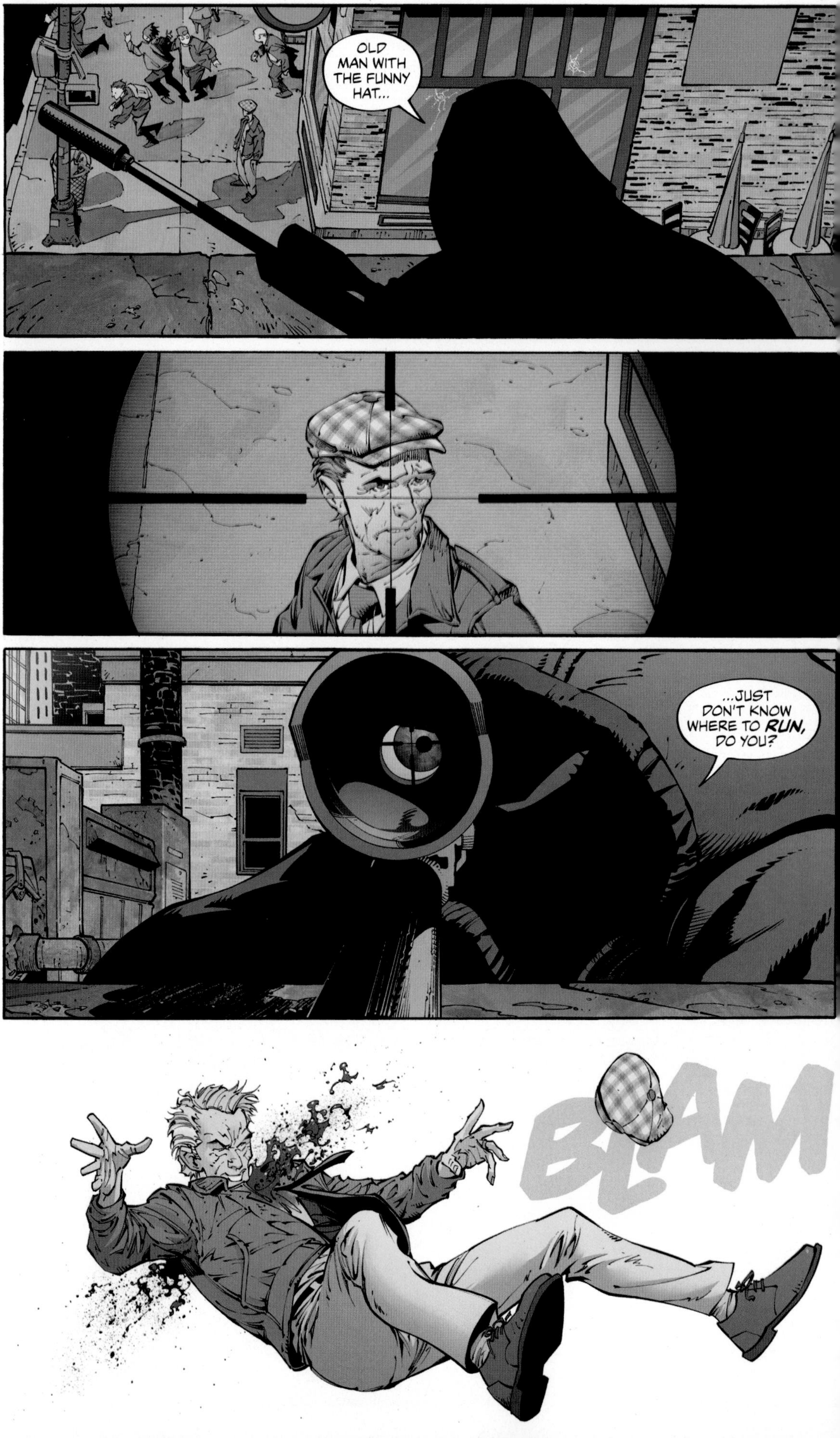
OLD MAN WITH THE FUNNY HAT...
...JUST DON'T KNOW WHERE TO RUN, DO YOU?
BLAM

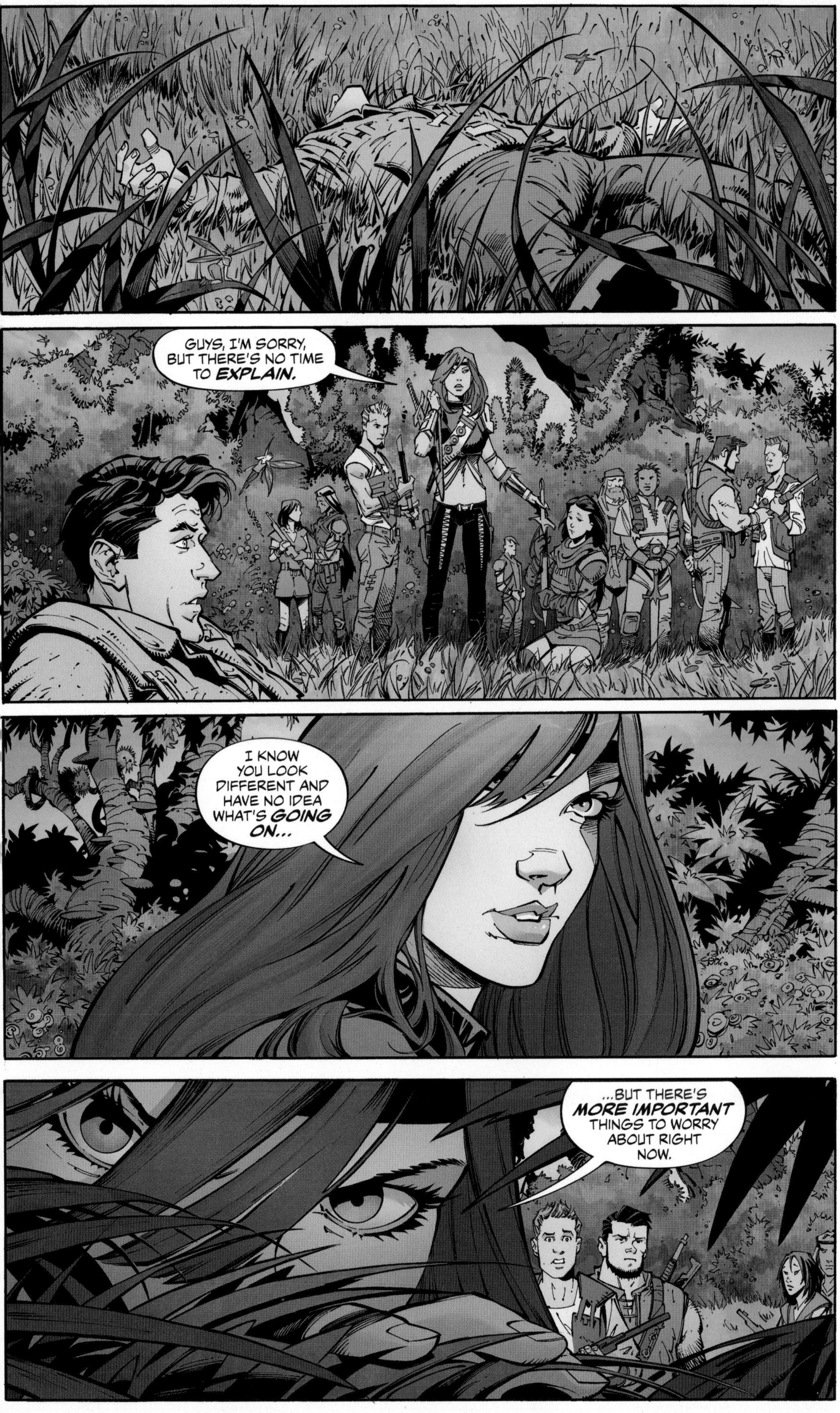
GUYS, I'M SORRY, BUT THERE'S NO TIME TO EXPLAIN.
I KNOW YOU LOOK DIFFERENT AND HAVE NO IDEA WHAT'S GOING ON...
...BUT THERE'S MORE IMPORTANT THINGS TO WORRY ABOUT RIGHT NOW.

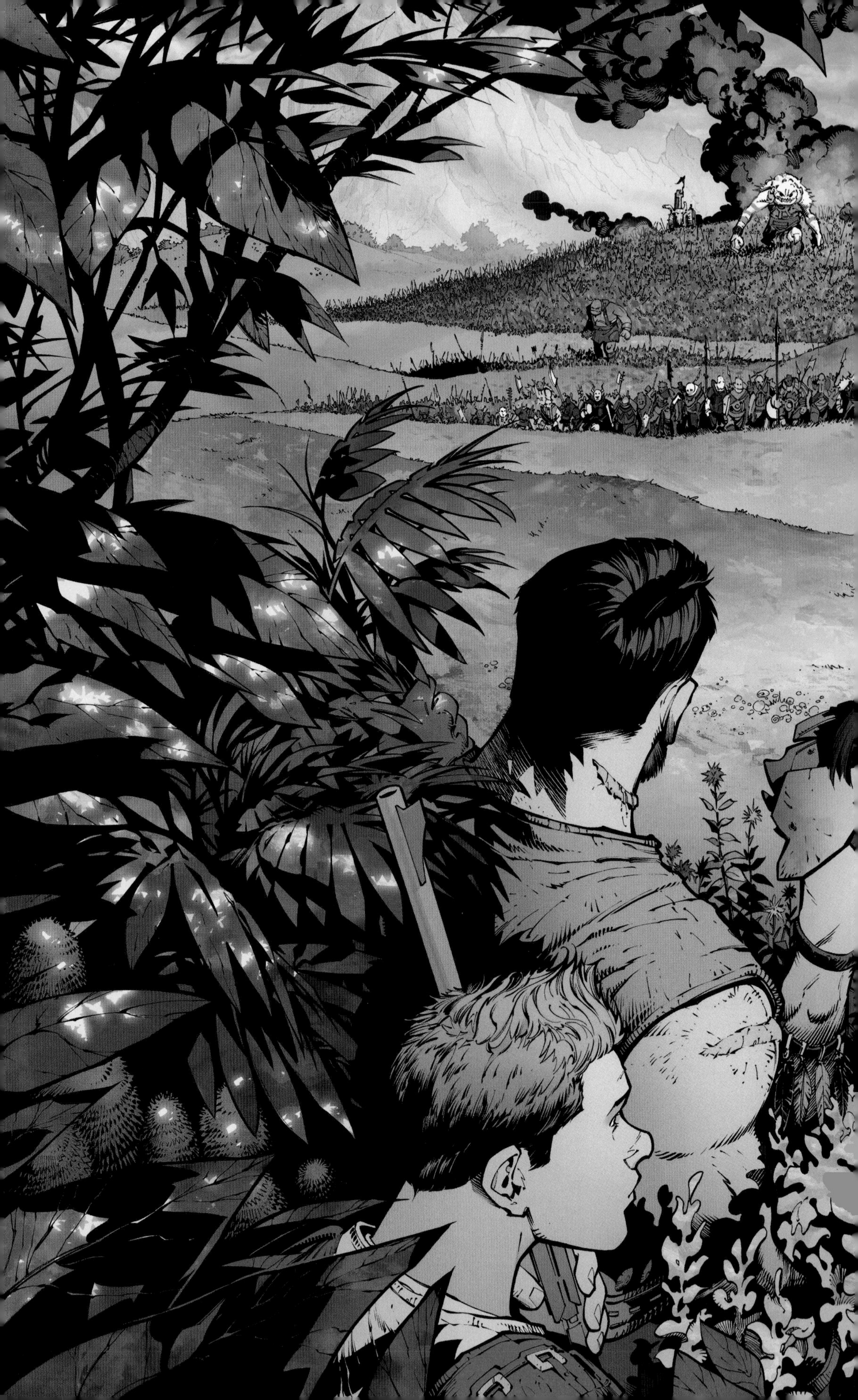

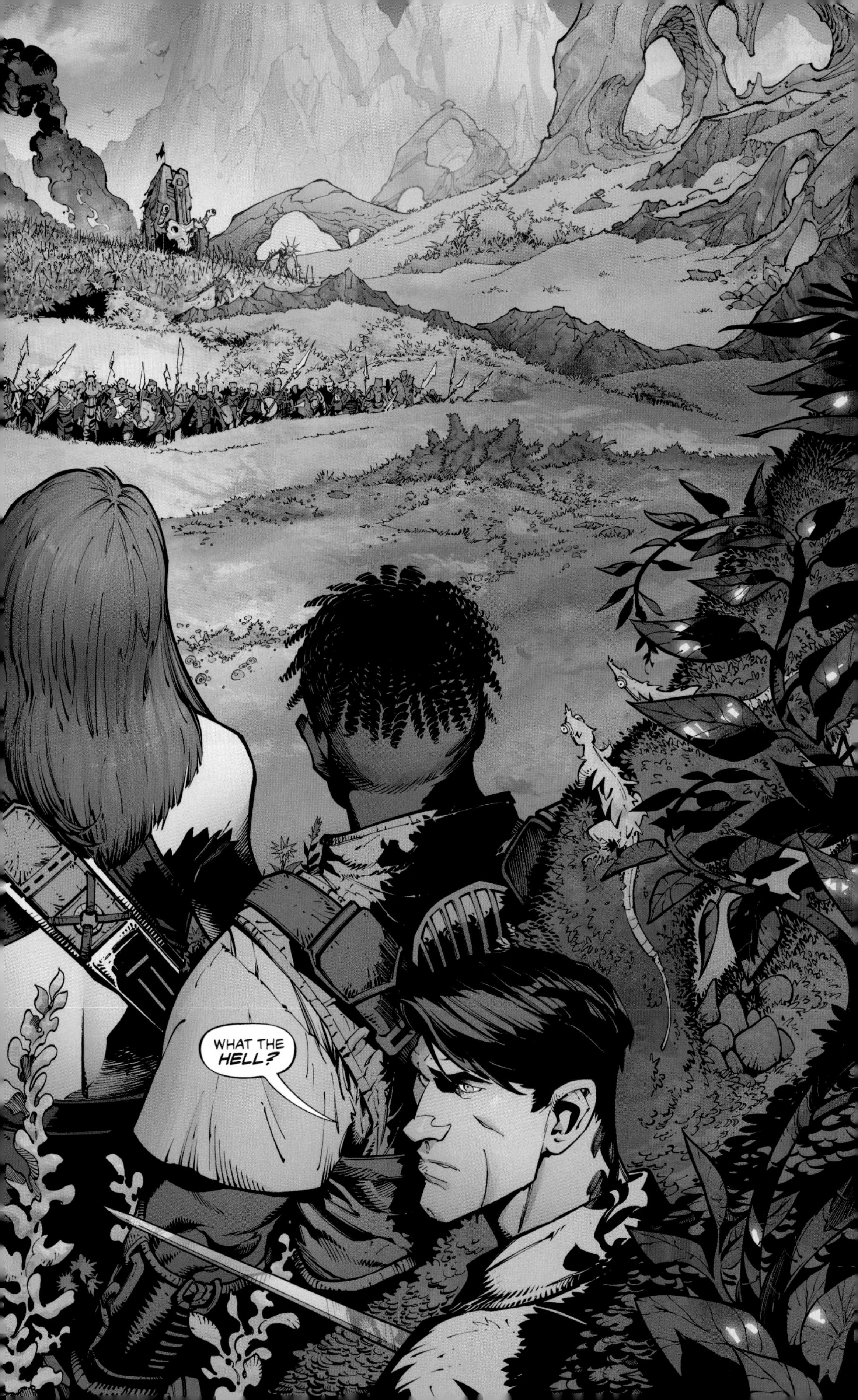
WHAT THE HELL?

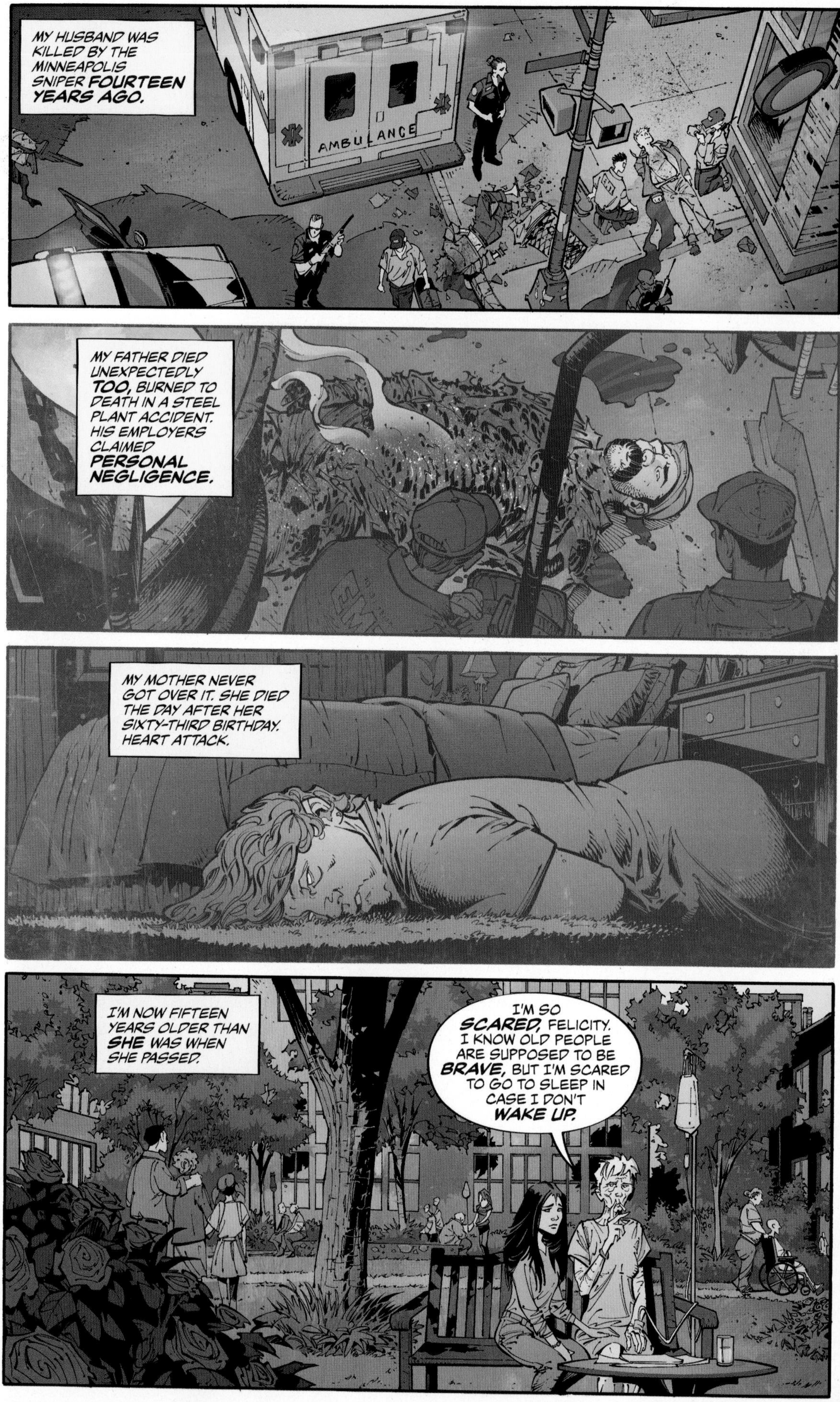
MY HUSBAND WAS KILLED BY THE MINNEAPOLIS SNIPER FOURTEEN YEARS AGO.
AMBULANCE
MY FATHER DIED UNEXPECTEDLY TOO, BURNED TO DEATH IN A STEEL PLANT ACCIDENT. HIS EMPLOYERS CLAIMED PERSONAL NEGLIGENCE.
MY MOTHER NEVER GOT OVER IT. SHE DIED THE DAY AFTER HER SIXTY-THIRD BIRTHDAY. HEART ATTACK.
I'M NOW FIFTEEN YEARS OLDER THAN SHE WAS WHEN SHE PASSED.
I'M SO SCARED, FELICITY. I KNOW OLD PEOPLE ARE SUPPOSED TO BE BRAVE, BUT I'M SCARED TO GO TO SLEEP IN CASE I DON'T WAKE UP.

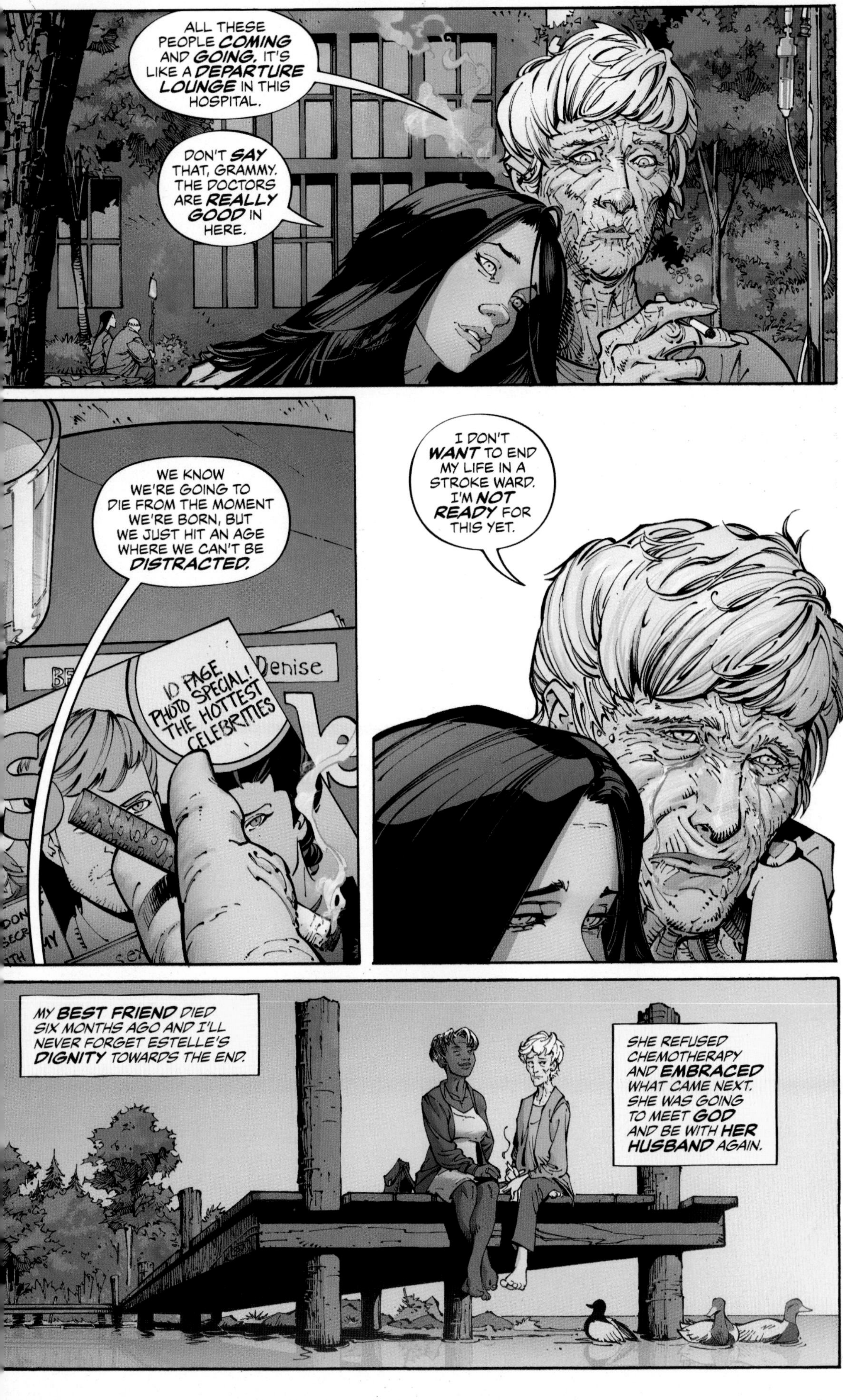
ALL THESE PEOPLE COMING AND GOING. IT'S LIKE A DEPARTURE LOUNGE IN THIS HOSPITAL.
DON'T SAY THAT, GRAMMY. THE DOCTORS ARE REALLY GOOD IN HERE.
WE KNOW WE'RE GOING TO DIE FROM THE MOMENT WE'RE BORN, BUT WE JUST HIT AN AGE WHERE WE CAN'T BE DISTRACTED.
Denise
10 PAGE PHOTO SPECIAL! THE HOTTEST CELEBRITIES
I DON'T WANT TO END MY LIFE IN A STROKE WARD. I'M NOT READY FOR THIS YET.
MY BEST FRIEND DIED SIX MONTHS AGO AND I'LL NEVER FORGET ESTELLE'S DIGNITY TOWARDS THE END.
SHE REFUSED CHEMOTHERAPY AND EMBRACED WHAT CAME NEXT. SHE WAS GOING TO MEET GOD AND BE WITH HER HUSBAND AGAIN.

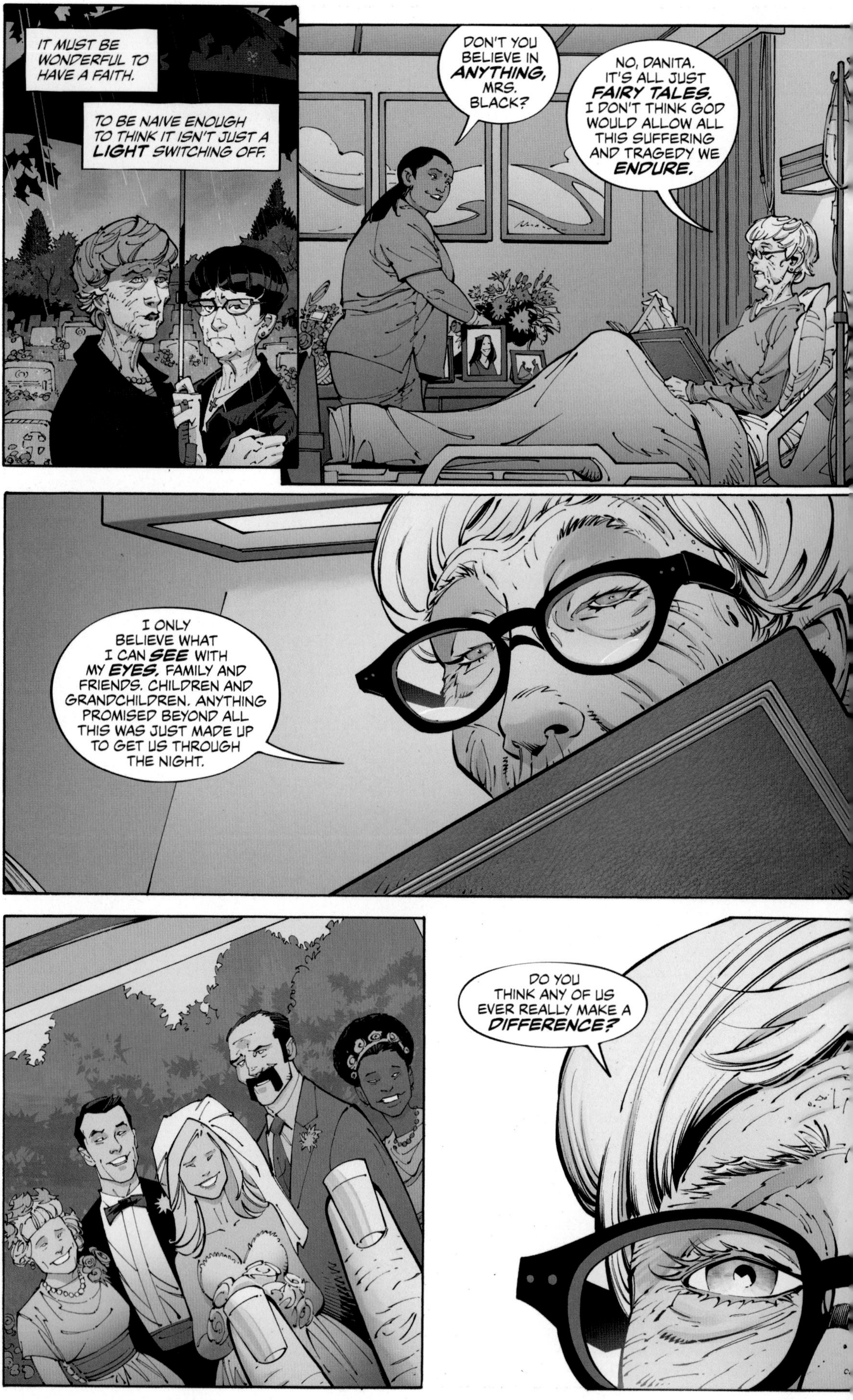
IT MUST BE WONDERFUL TO HAVE A FAITH.
TO BE NAIVE ENOUGH TO THINK IT ISN'T JUST A LIGHT SWITCHING OFF.
DON'T YOU BELIEVE IN ANYTHING, MRS. BLACK?
NO, DANITA. IT'S ALL JUST FAIRY TALES. I DON'T THINK GOD WOULD ALLOW ALL THIS SUFFERING AND TRAGEDY WE ENDURE.
I ONLY BELIEVE WHAT I CAN SEE WITH MY EYES. FAMILY AND FRIENDS. CHILDREN AND GRANDCHILDREN. ANYTHING PROMISED BEYOND ALL THIS WAS JUST MADE UP TO GET US THROUGH THE NIGHT.
DO YOU THINK ANY OF US EVER REALLY MAKE A DIFFERENCE?

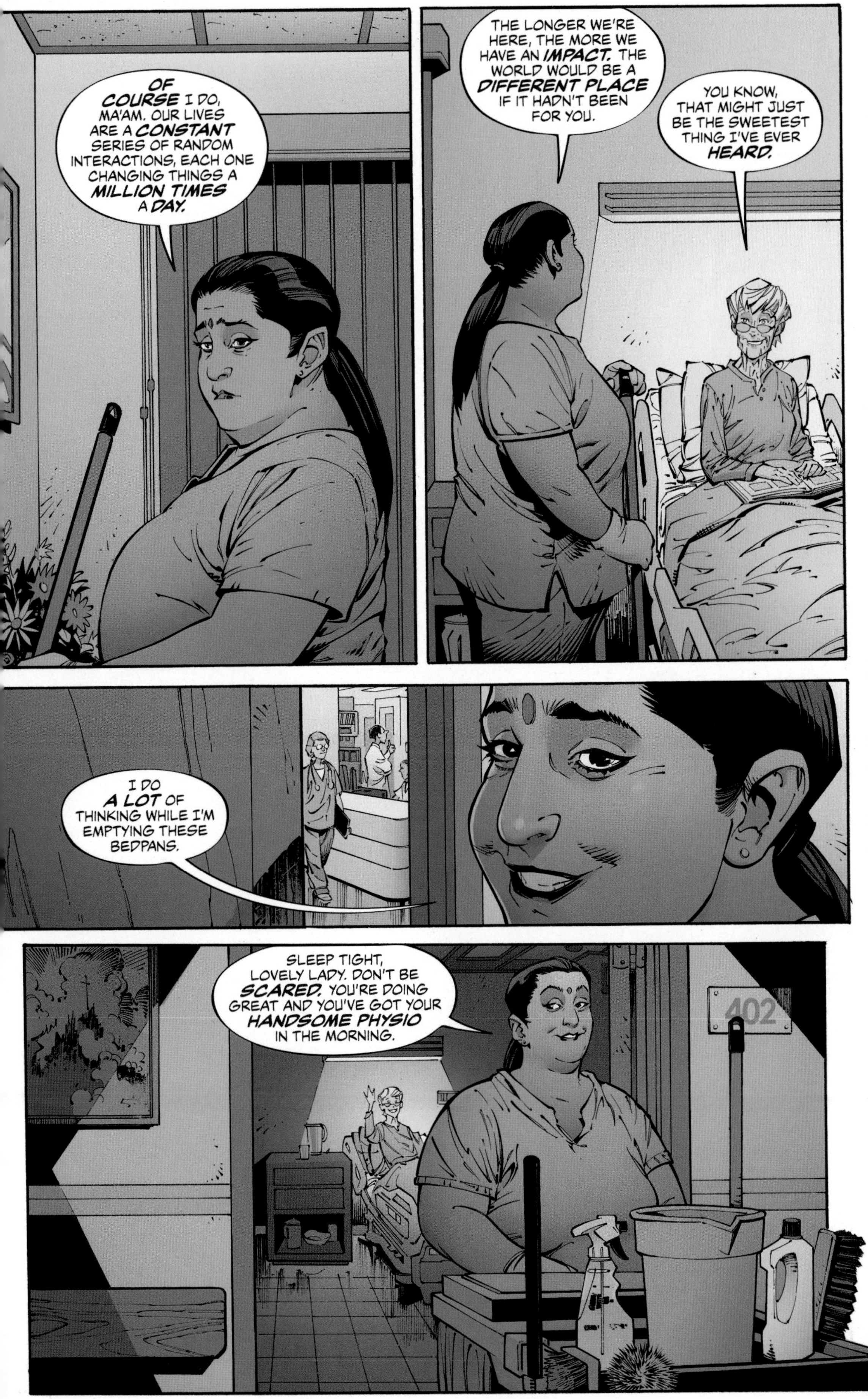
OF COURSE I DO, MA'AM. OUR LIVES ARE A CONSTANT SERIES OF RANDOM INTERACTIONS, EACH ONE CHANGING THINGS A MILLION TIMES A DAY.
THE LONGER WE'RE HERE, THE MORE WE HAVE AN IMPACT. THE WORLD WOULD BE A DIFFERENT PLACE IF IT HADN'T BEEN FOR YOU.
YOU KNOW, THAT MIGHT JUST BE THE SWEETEST THING I'VE EVER HEARD.
I DO A LOT OF THINKING WHILE I'M EMPTYING THESE BEDPANS.
SLEEP TIGHT, LOVELY LADY. DON'T BE SCARED. YOU'RE DOING GREAT AND YOU'VE GOT YOUR HANDSOME PHYSIO IN THE MORNING.
402

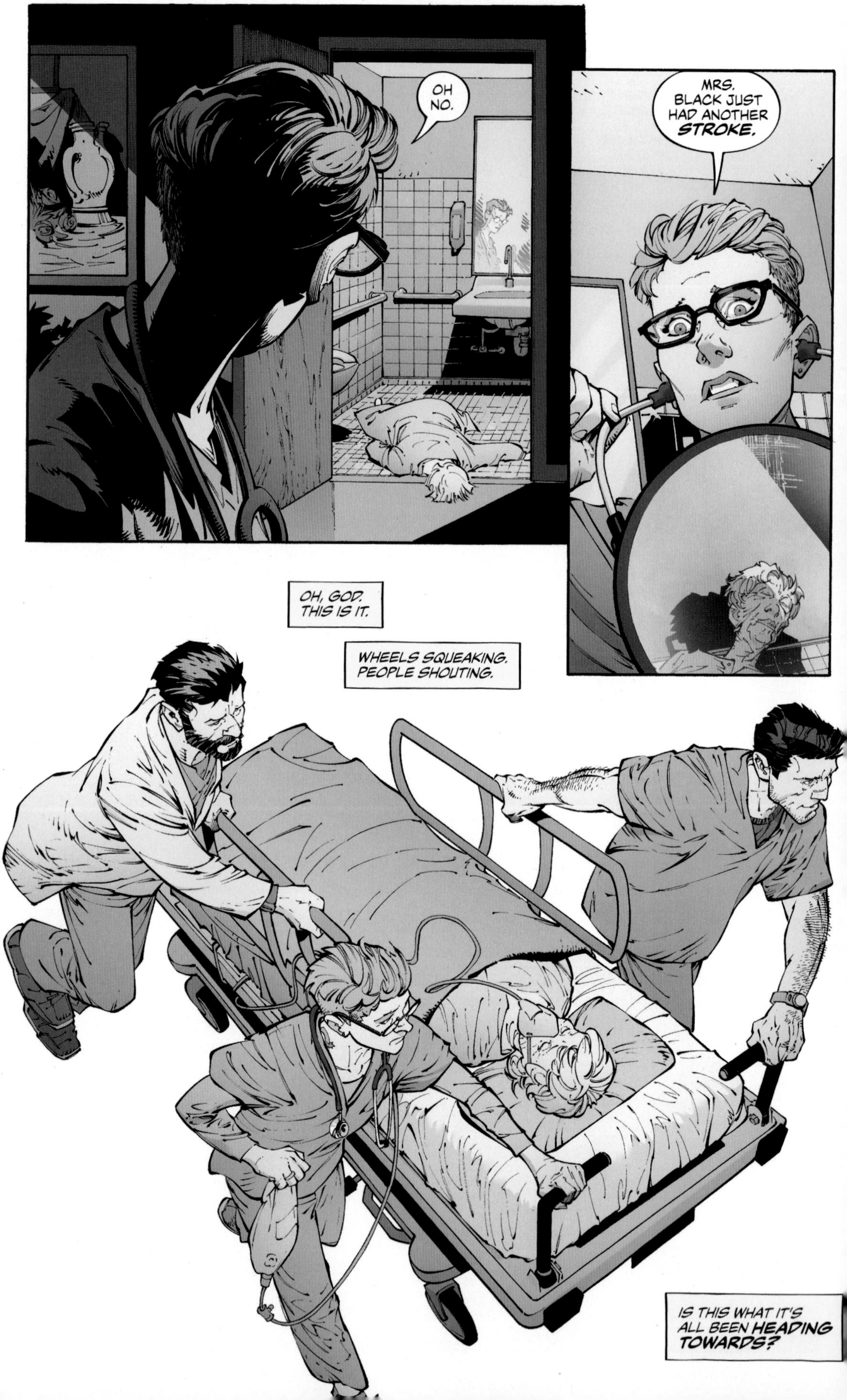
OH NO.
MRS. BLACK JUST HAD ANOTHER STROKE.
OH, GOD. THIS IS IT.
WHEELS SQUEAKING. PEOPLE SHOUTING.
IS THIS WHAT IT'S ALL BEEN HEADING TOWARDS?

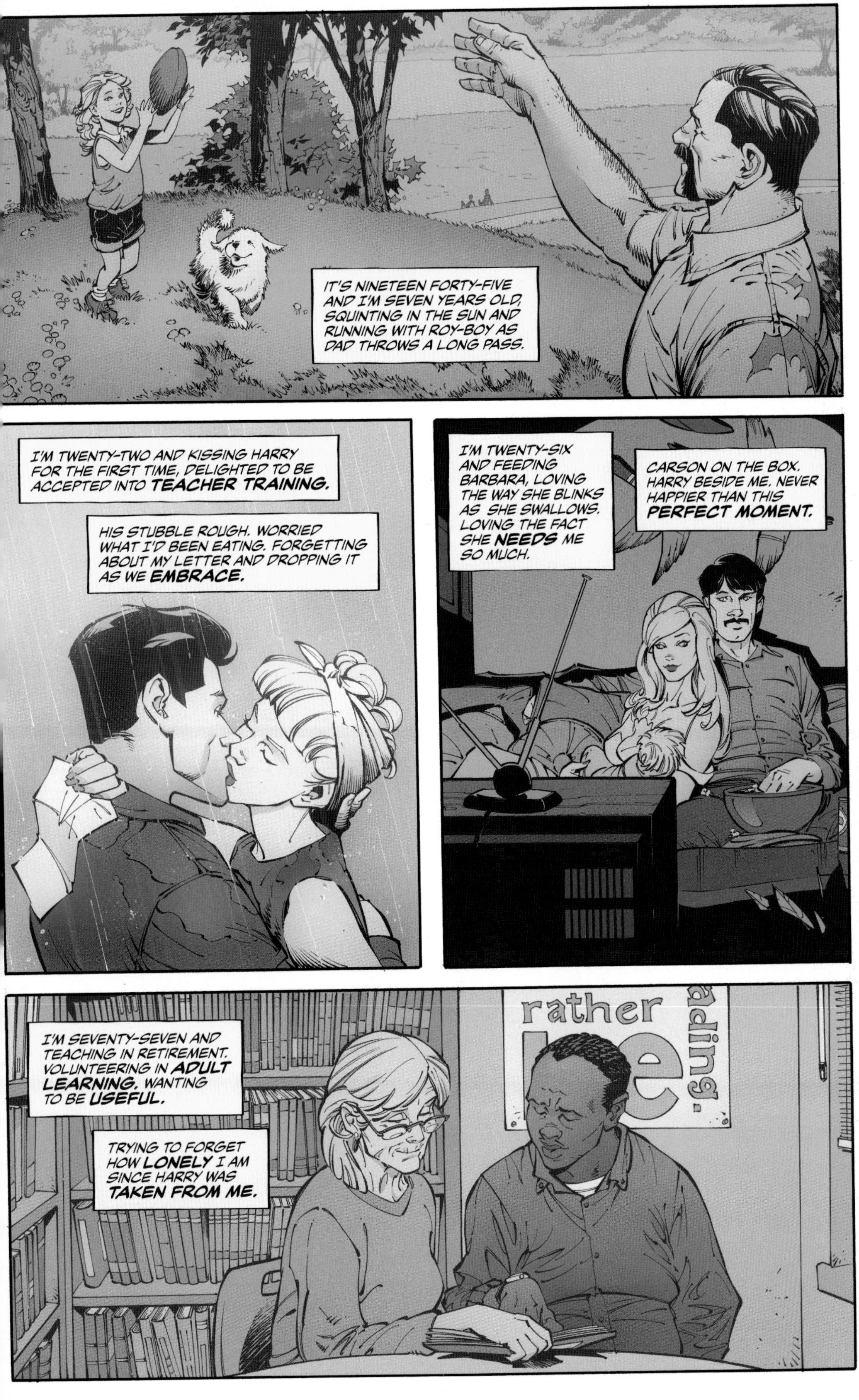

IT'S NINETEEN FORTY-FIVE AND I'M SEVEN YEARS OLD, SQUINTING IN THE SUN AND RUNNING WITH ROY-BOY AS DAD THROWS A LONG PASS.
I'M TWENTY-TWO AND KISSING HARRY FOR THE FIRST TIME, DELIGHTED TO BE ACCEPTED INTO **TEACHER TRAINING.**
HIS STUBBLE ROUGH. WORRIED WHAT I'D BEEN EATING. FORGETTING ABOUT MY LETTER AND DROPPING IT AS WE **EMBRACE.**
I'M TWENTY-SIX AND FEEDING BARBARA, LOVING THE WAY SHE BLINKS AS SHE SWALLOWS. LOVING THE FACT SHE **NEEDS** ME SO MUCH.
CARSON ON THE BOX. HARRY BESIDE ME. NEVER HAPPIER THAN THIS **PERFECT MOMENT.**
rather
I'M SEVENTY-SEVEN AND TEACHING IN RETIREMENT. VOLUNTEERING IN **ADULT LEARNING.** WANTING TO BE **USEFUL.**
TRYING TO FORGET HOW **LONELY** I AM SINCE HARRY WAS **TAKEN FROM ME.**

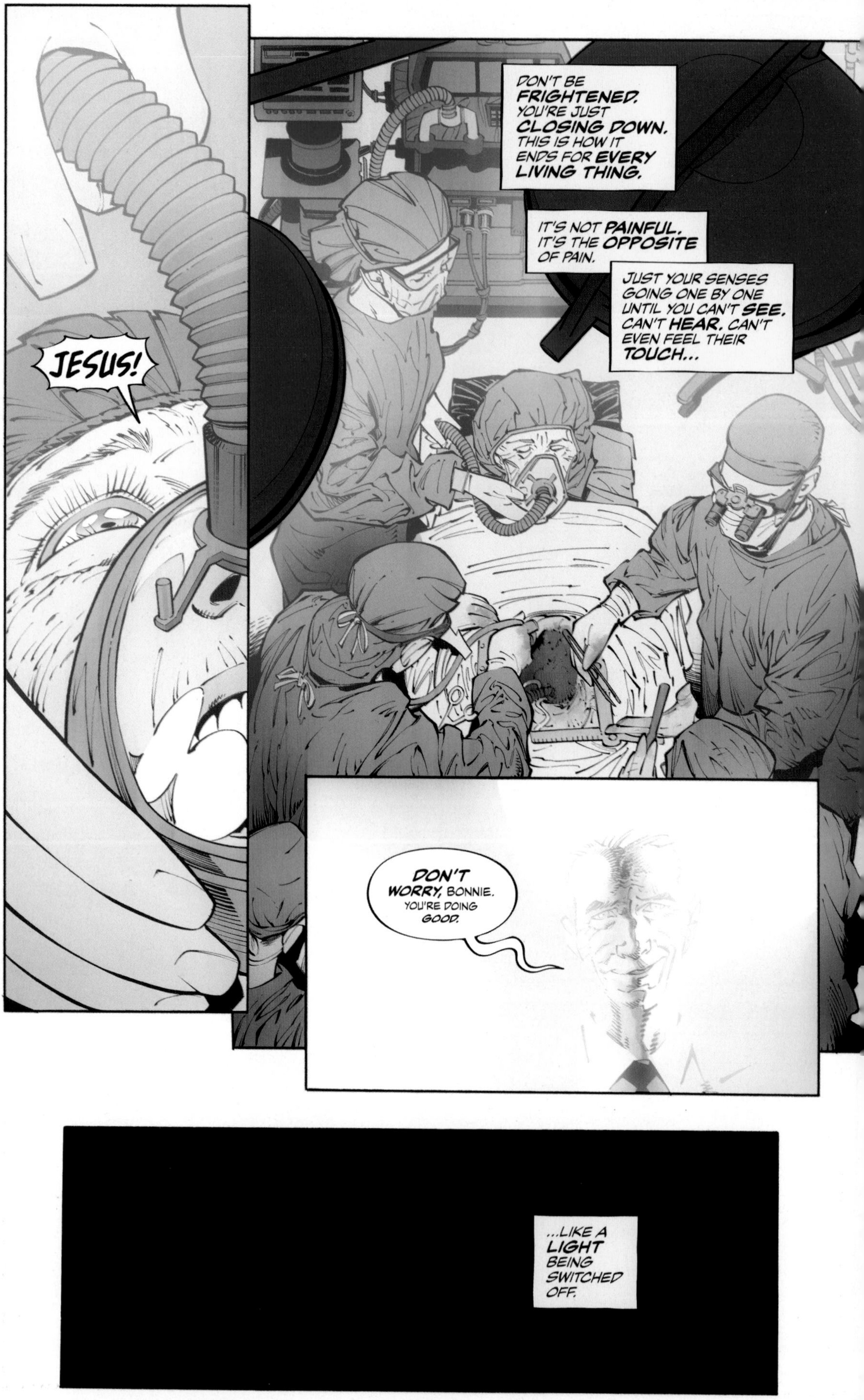
JESUS!
DON'T BE FRIGHTENED. YOU'RE JUST CLOSING DOWN. THIS IS HOW IT ENDS FOR EVERY LIVING THING.
IT'S NOT PAINFUL. IT'S THE OPPOSITE OF PAIN.
JUST YOUR SENSES GOING ONE BY ONE UNTIL YOU CAN'T SEE. CAN'T HEAR. CAN'T EVEN FEEL THEIR TOUCH...
DON'T WORRY, BONNIE. YOU'RE DOING GOOD.
...LIKE A LIGHT BEING SWITCHED OFF.

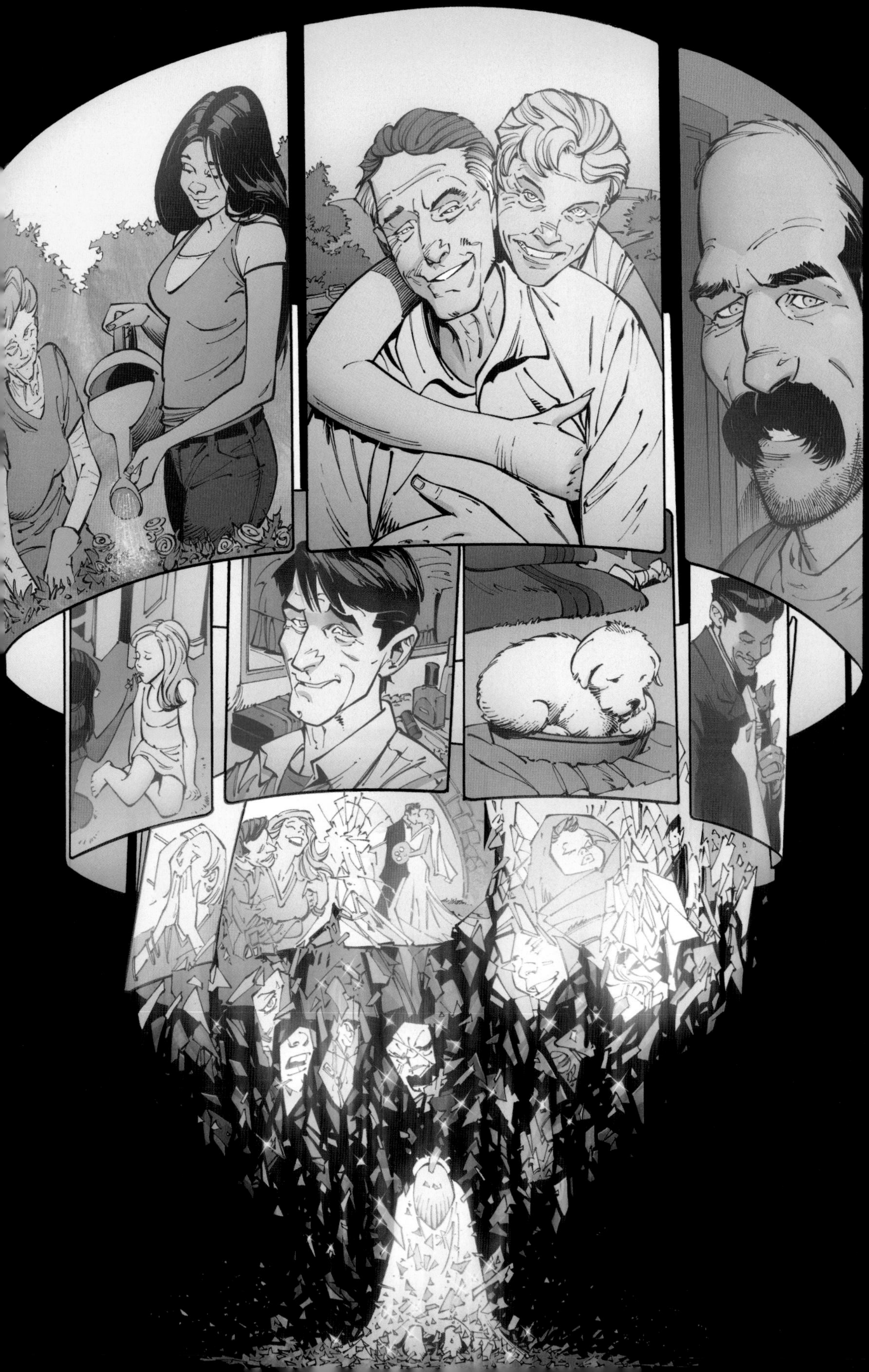

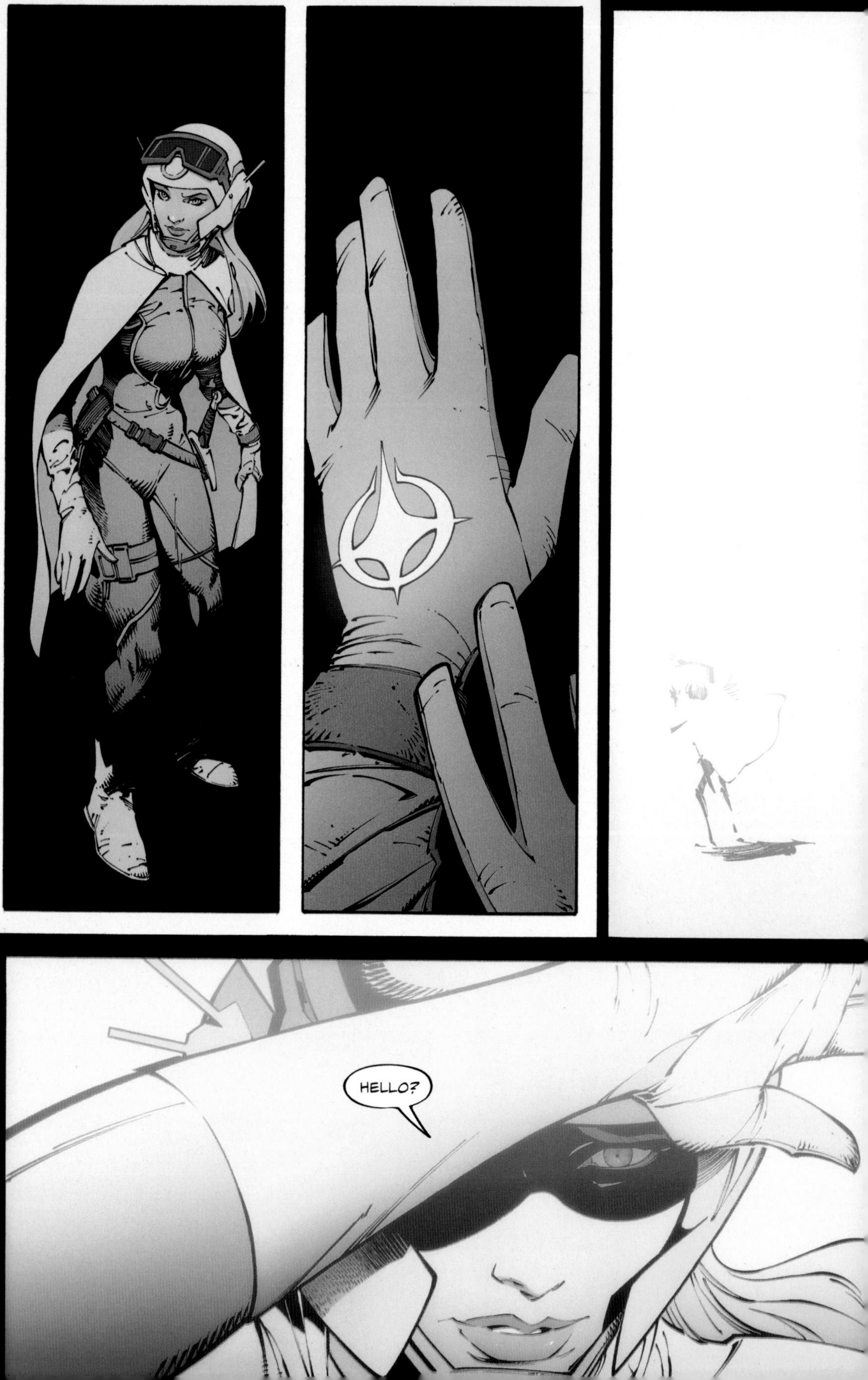
HELLO?

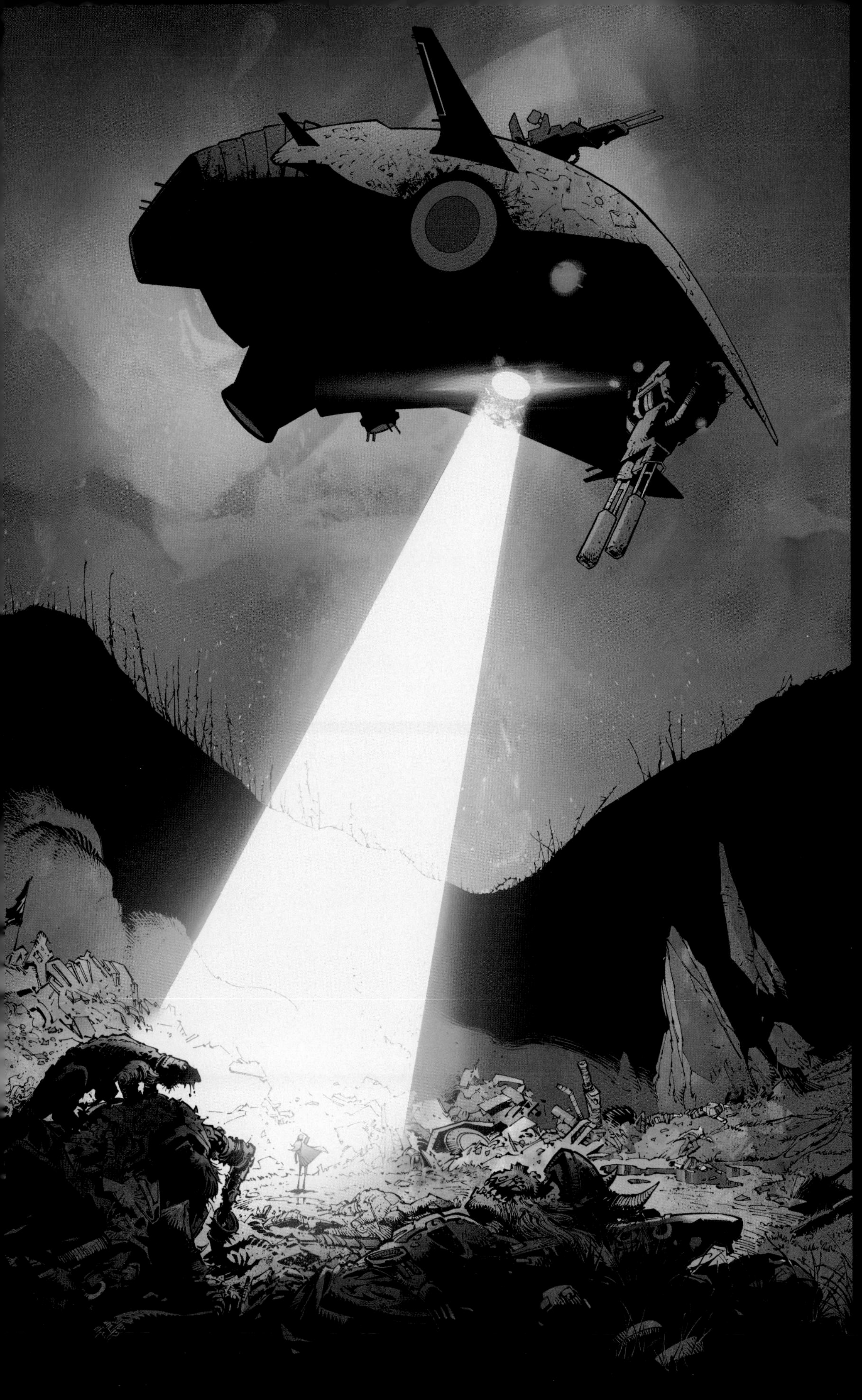

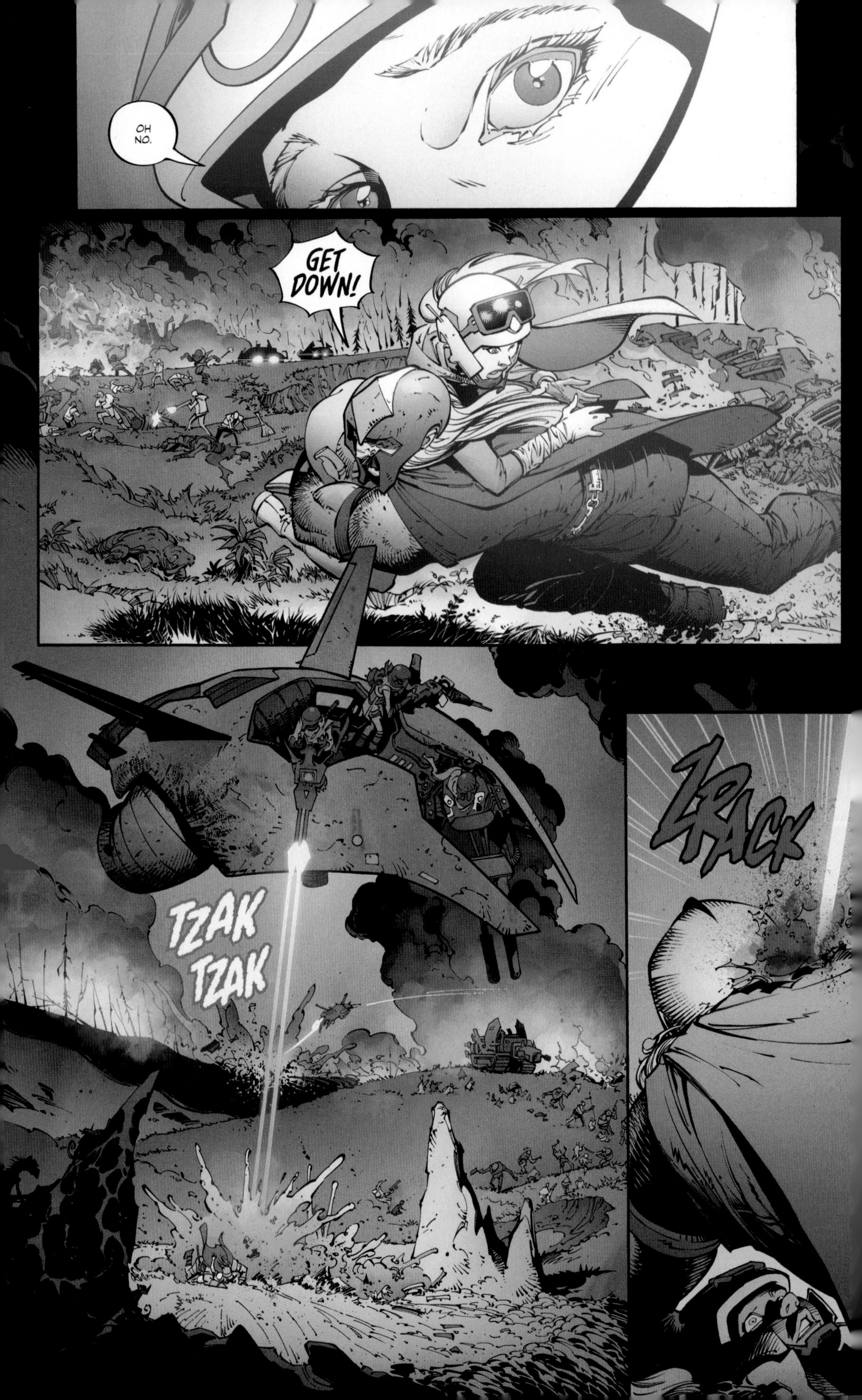
OH NO.
GET DOWN!
TZAK TZAK
ZRACK

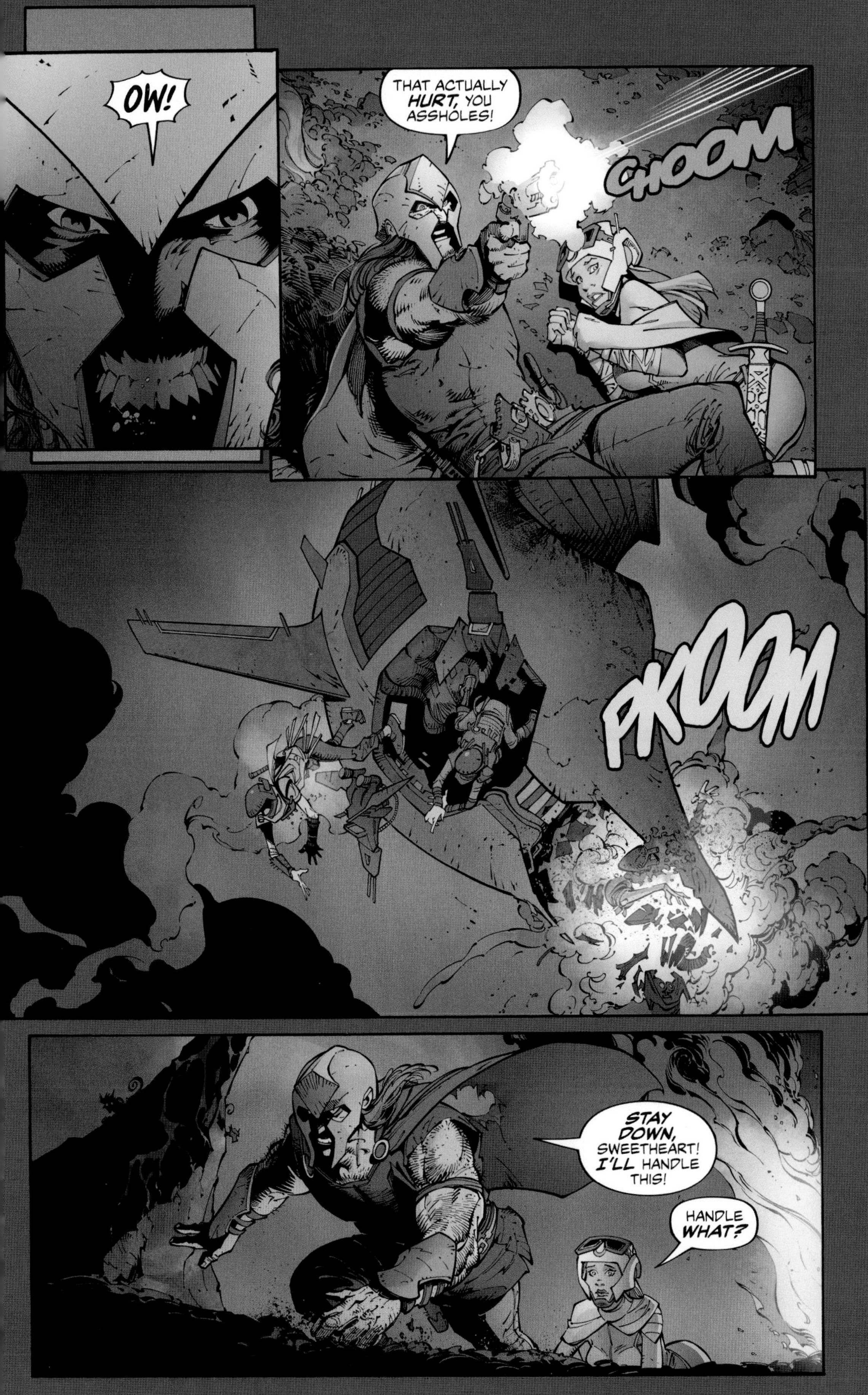
OW!
THAT ACTUALLY HURT, YOU ASSHOLES!
CHOOM
PKOOM
STAY DOWN, SWEETHEART! I'LL HANDLE THIS!
HANDLE WHAT?

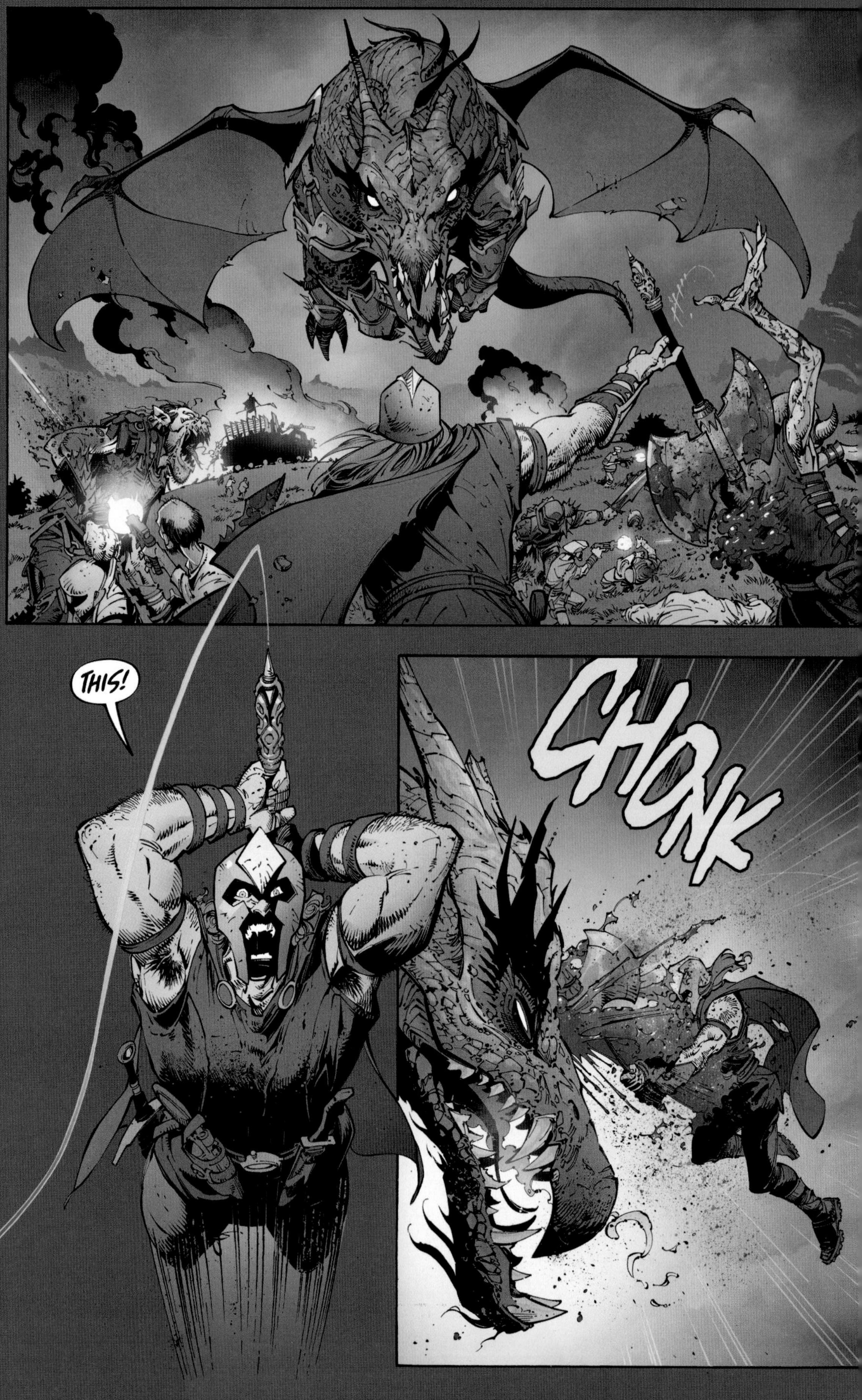
THIS!
CHONK

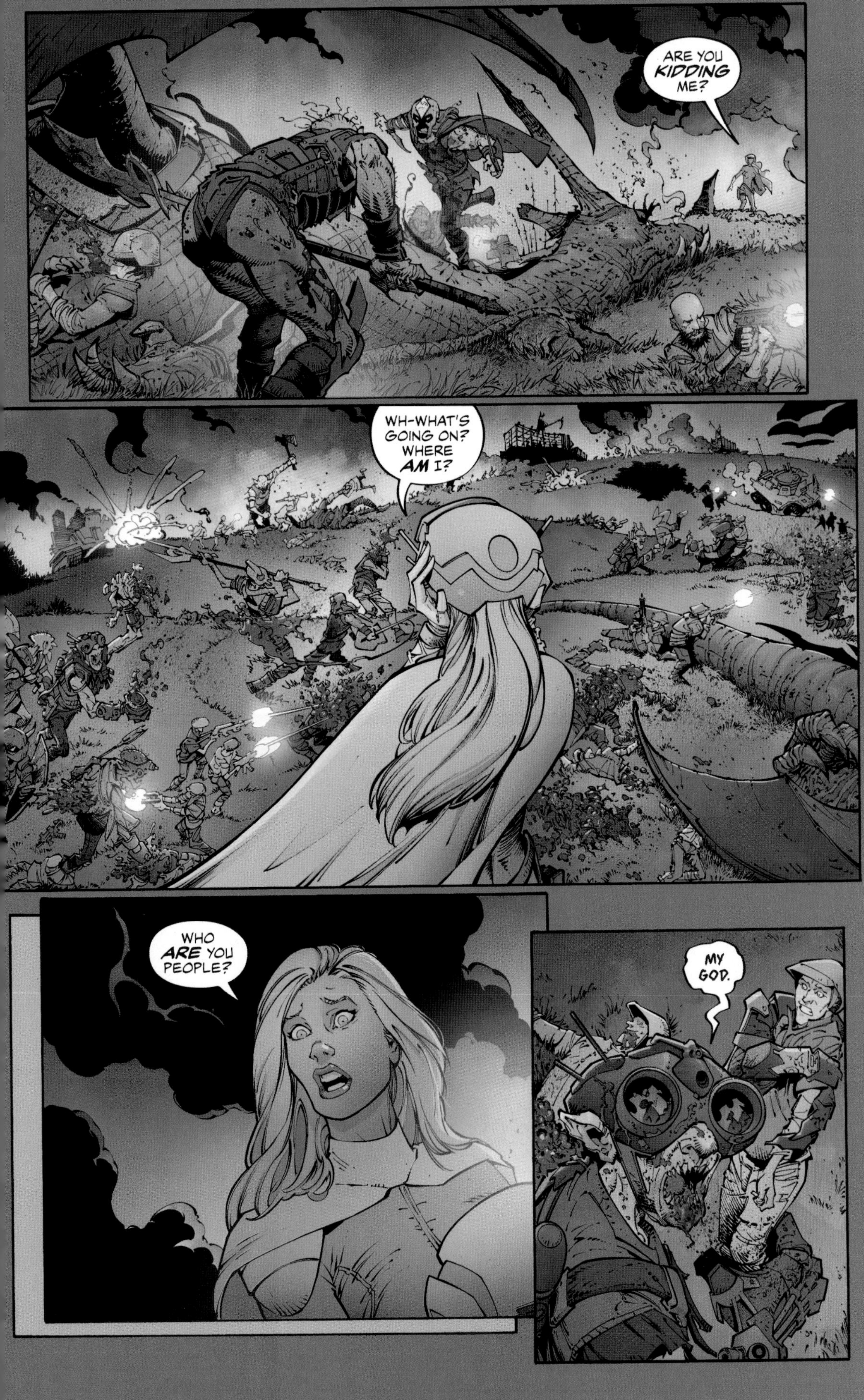
ARE YOU KIDDING ME?
WH-WHAT'S GOING ON? WHERE AM I?
WHO ARE YOU PEOPLE?
MY GOD.

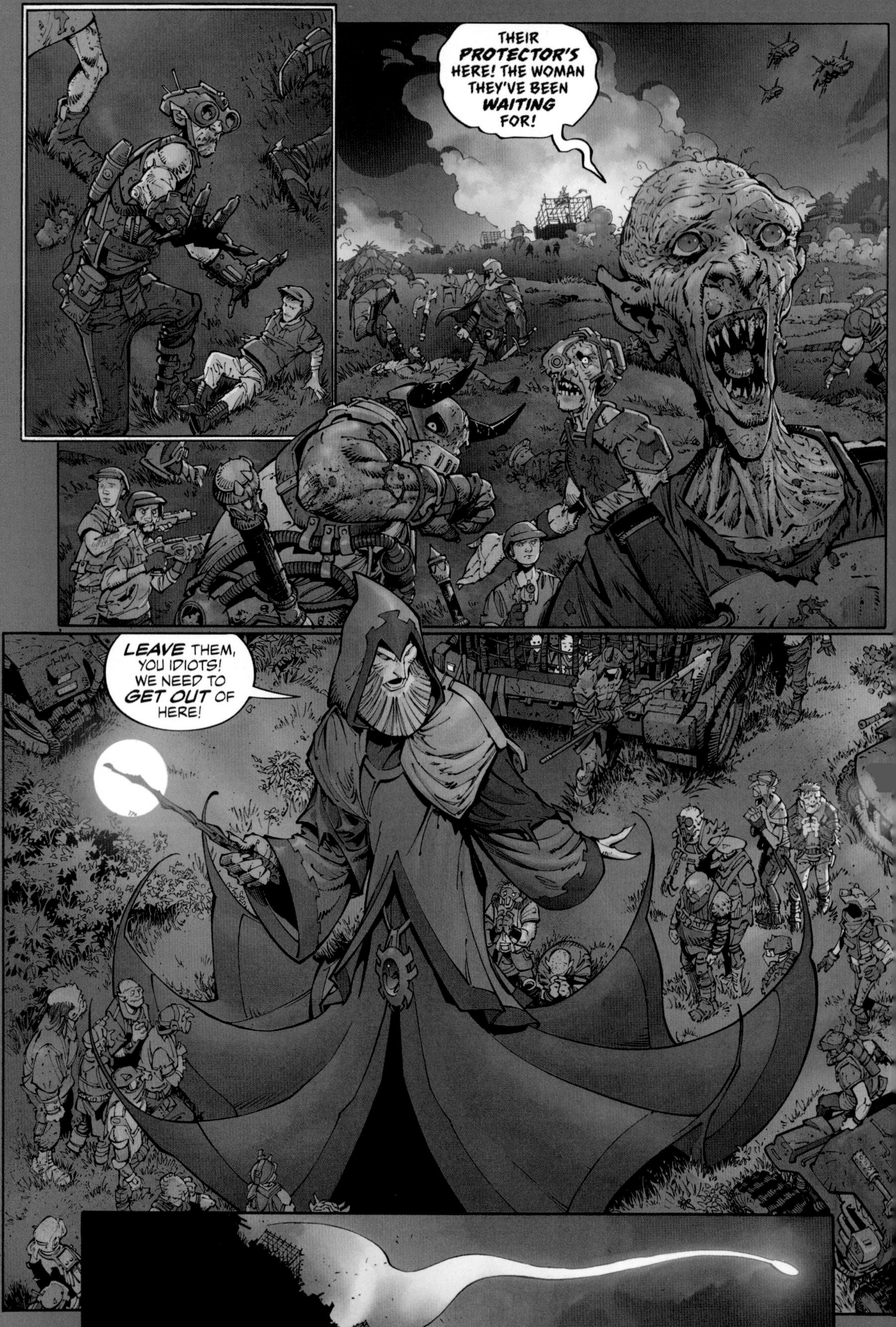
THEIR PROTECTOR'S HERE! THE WOMAN THEY'VE BEEN WAITING FOR!
LEAVE THEM, YOU IDIOTS! WE NEED TO GET OUT OF HERE!

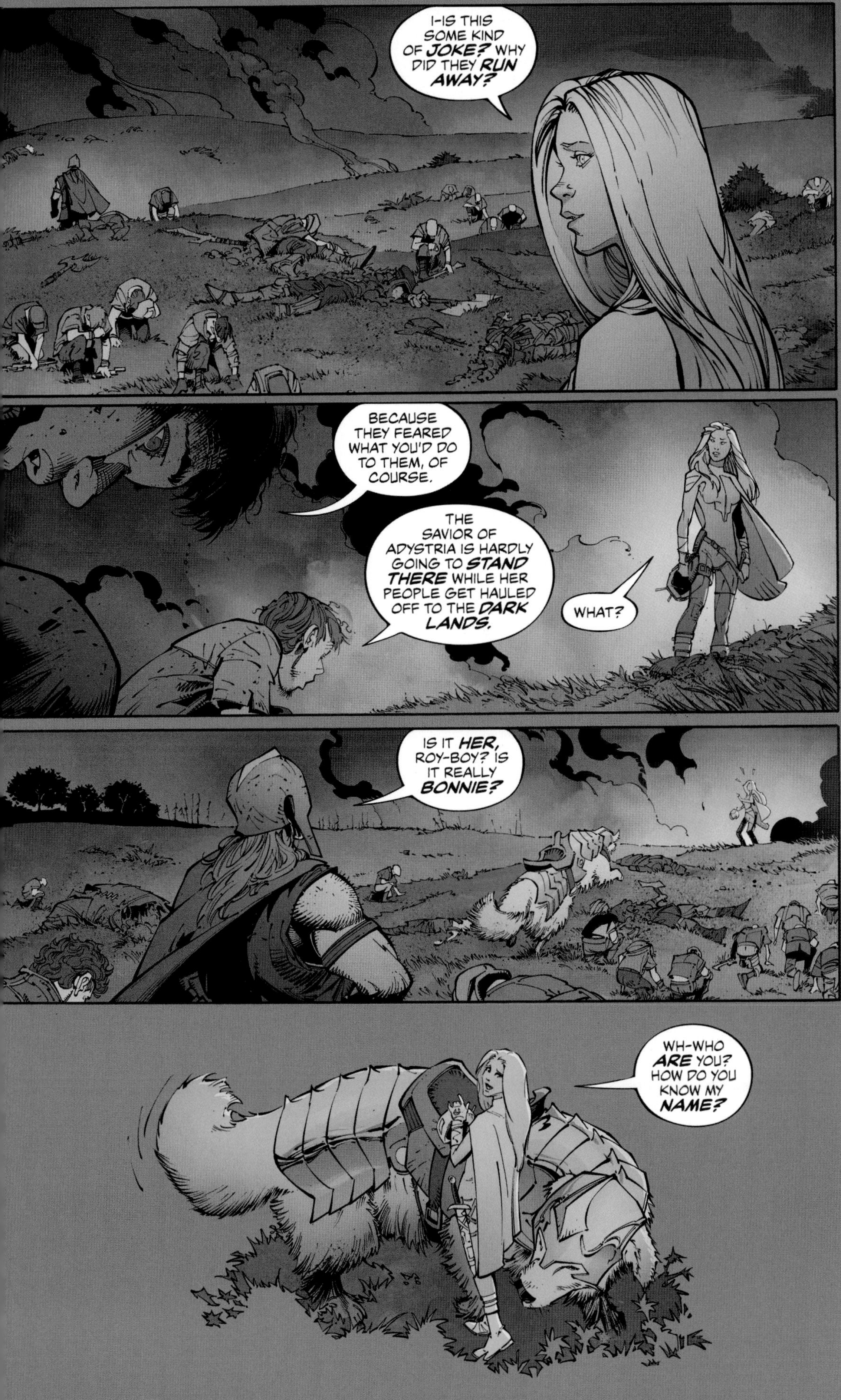

I-IS THIS SOME KIND OF JOKE? WHY DID THEY RUN AWAY?
BECAUSE THEY FEARED WHAT YOU'D DO TO THEM, OF COURSE.
THE SAVIOR OF ADYSTRIA IS HARDLY GOING TO STAND THERE WHILE HER PEOPLE GET HAULED OFF TO THE DARK LANDS.
WHAT?
IS IT HER, ROY-BOY? IS IT REALLY BONNIE?
WH-WHO ARE YOU? HOW DO YOU KNOW MY NAME?

HOW DO YOU *THINK?*

OH, DAD. IS THIS *REAL?*

WE'VE WAITED FOR YOU SUCH A *LONG TIME,* ANGEL.

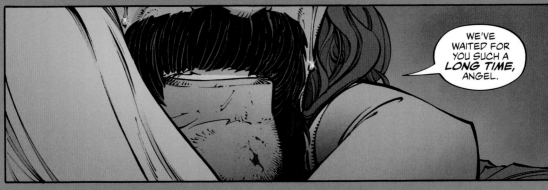

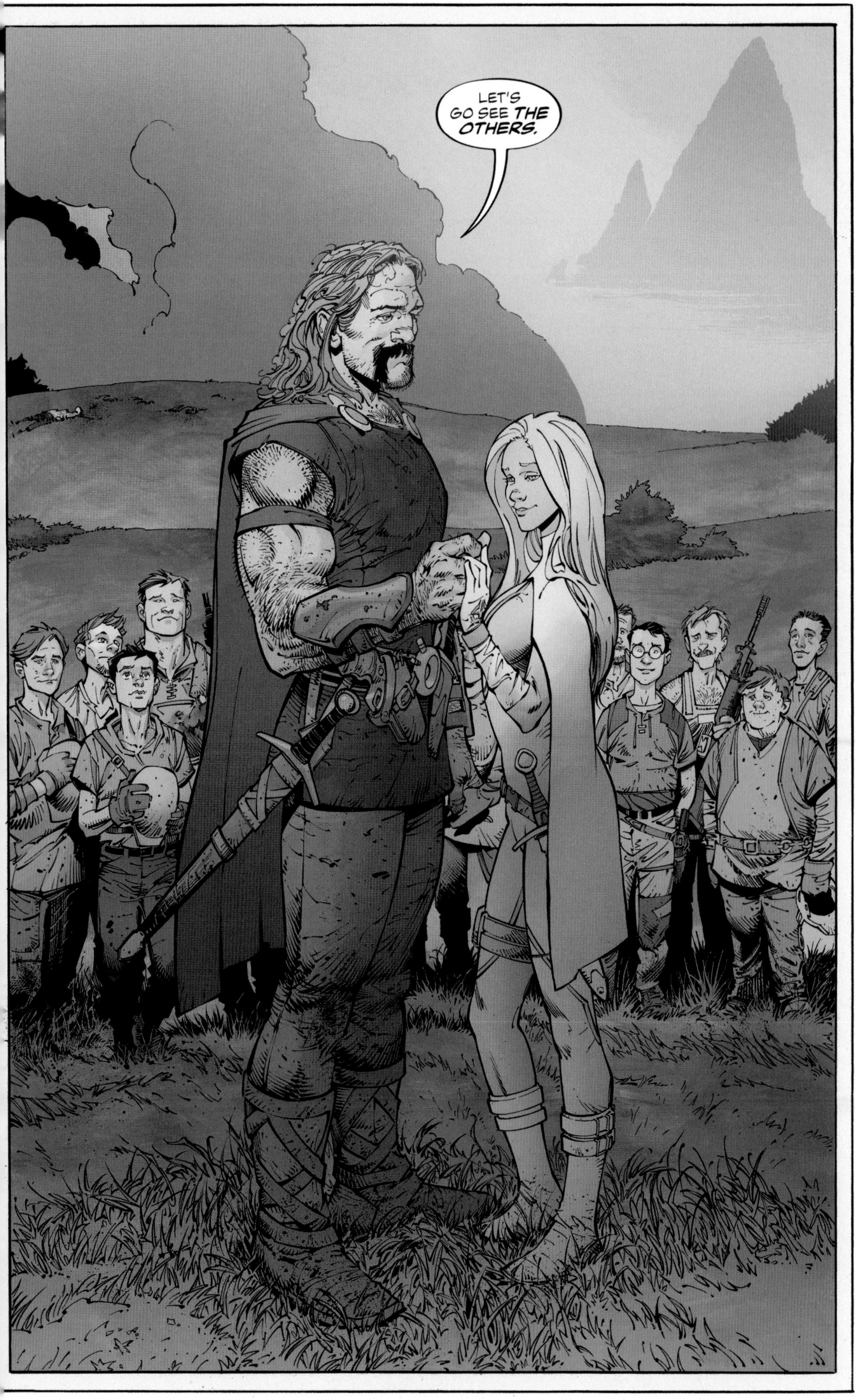
LET'S GO SEE THE OTHERS.

ISSUE ONE, COVER B

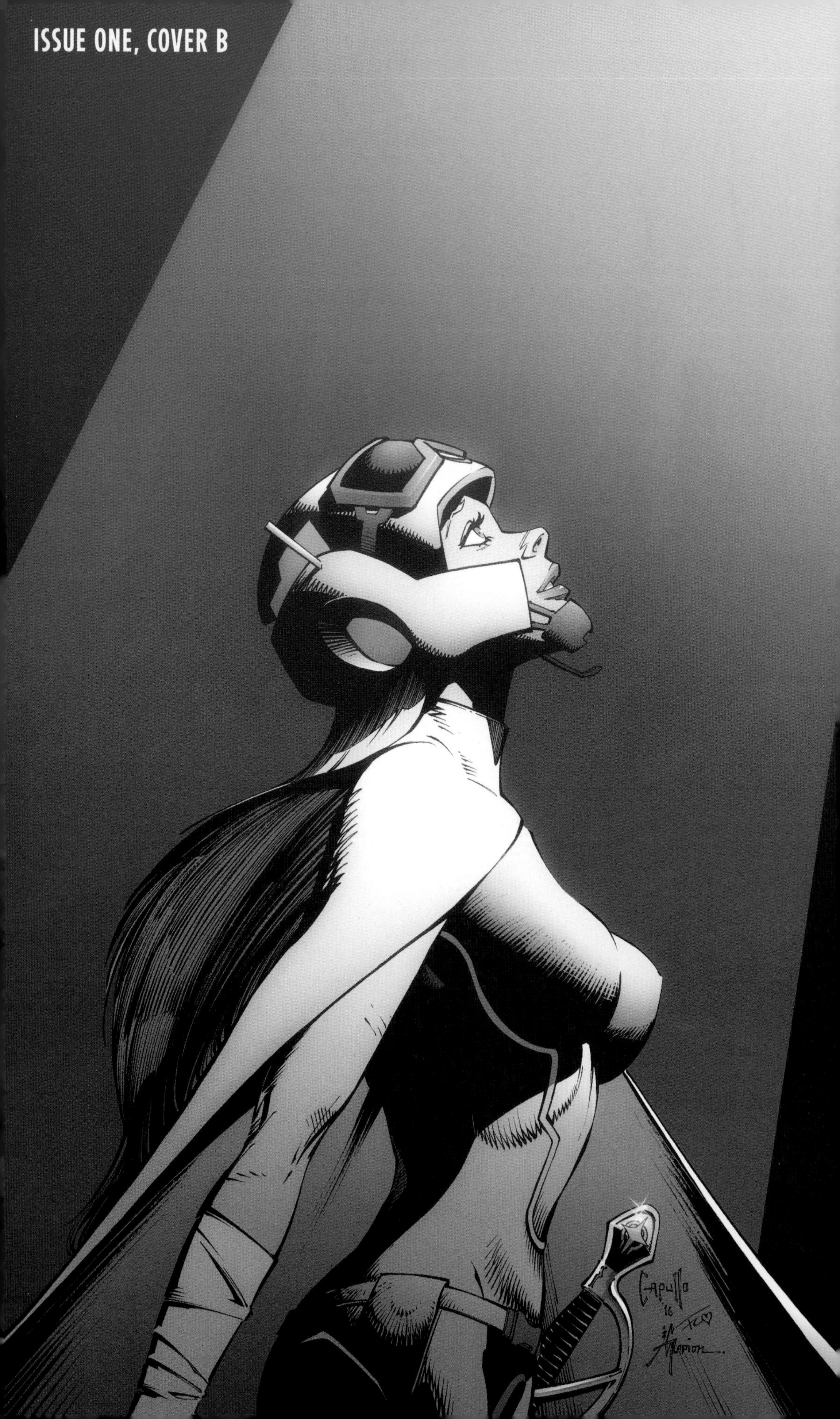

TWO

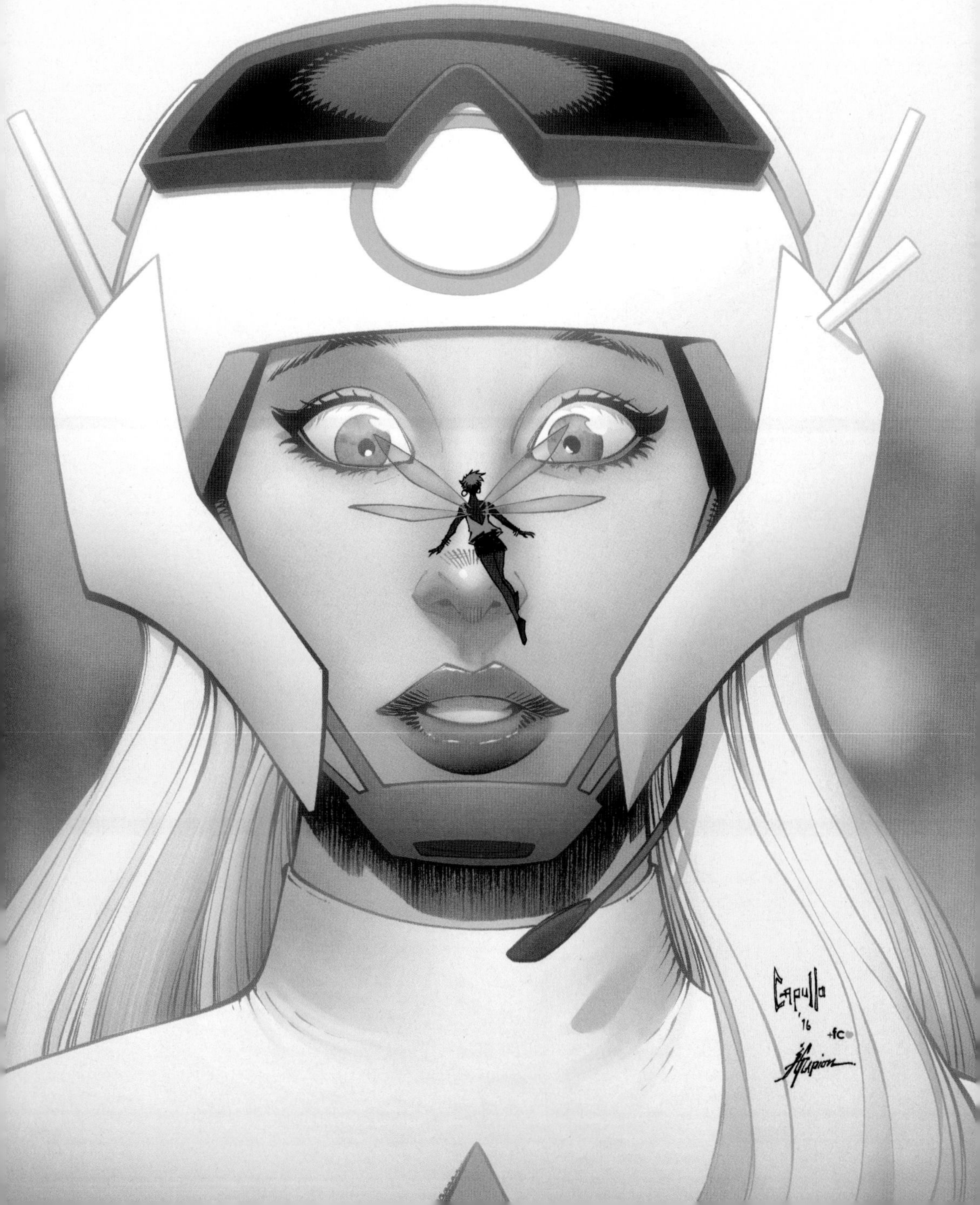

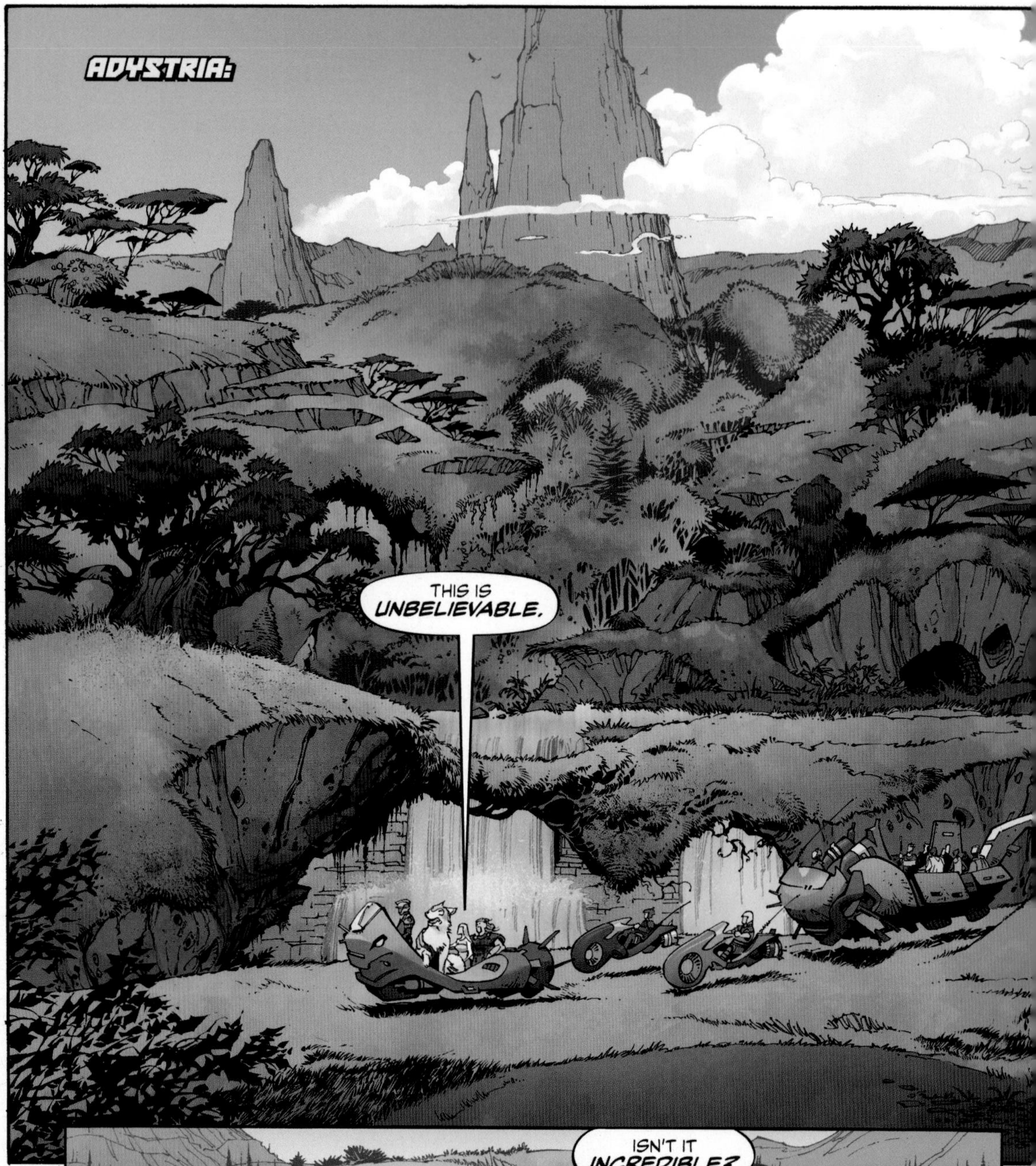
ADYSTRIA:
THIS IS UNBELIEVABLE.

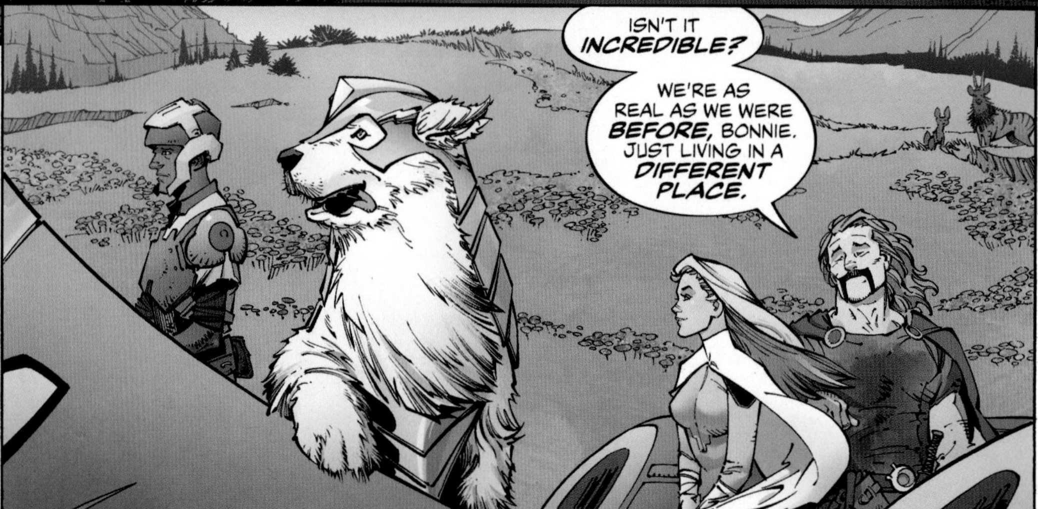
ISN'T IT INCREDIBLE?
WE'RE AS REAL AS WE WERE BEFORE, BONNIE. JUST LIVING IN A DIFFERENT PLACE.

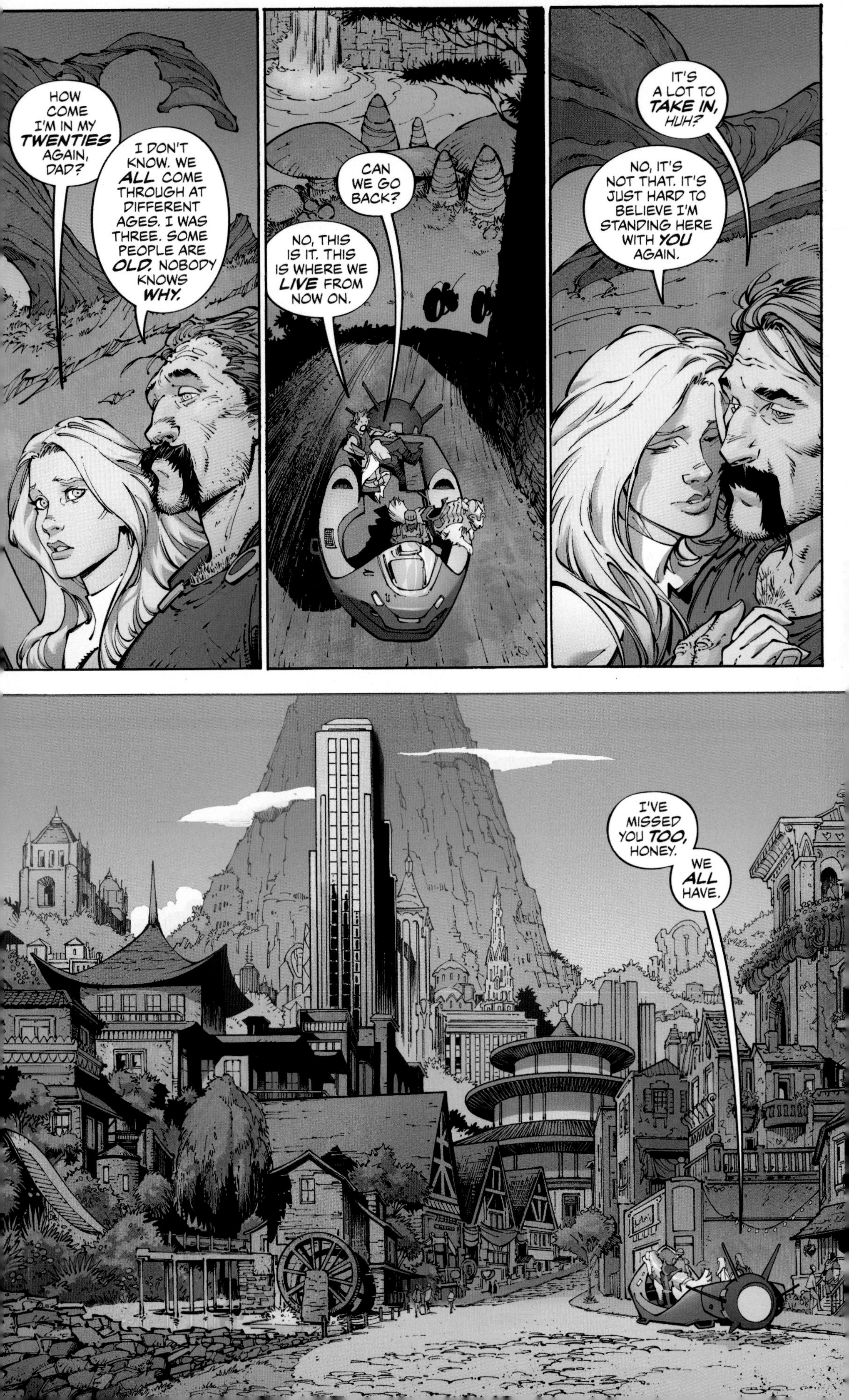
HOW COME I'M IN MY TWENTIES AGAIN, DAD?
I DON'T KNOW. WE ALL COME THROUGH AT DIFFERENT AGES. I WAS THREE. SOME PEOPLE ARE OLD. NOBODY KNOWS WHY.
CAN WE GO BACK?
NO, THIS IS IT. THIS IS WHERE WE LIVE FROM NOW ON.
IT'S A LOT TO TAKE IN, HUH?
NO, IT'S NOT THAT. IT'S JUST HARD TO BELIEVE I'M STANDING HERE WITH YOU AGAIN.
I'VE MISSED YOU TOO, HONEY.
WE ALL HAVE.

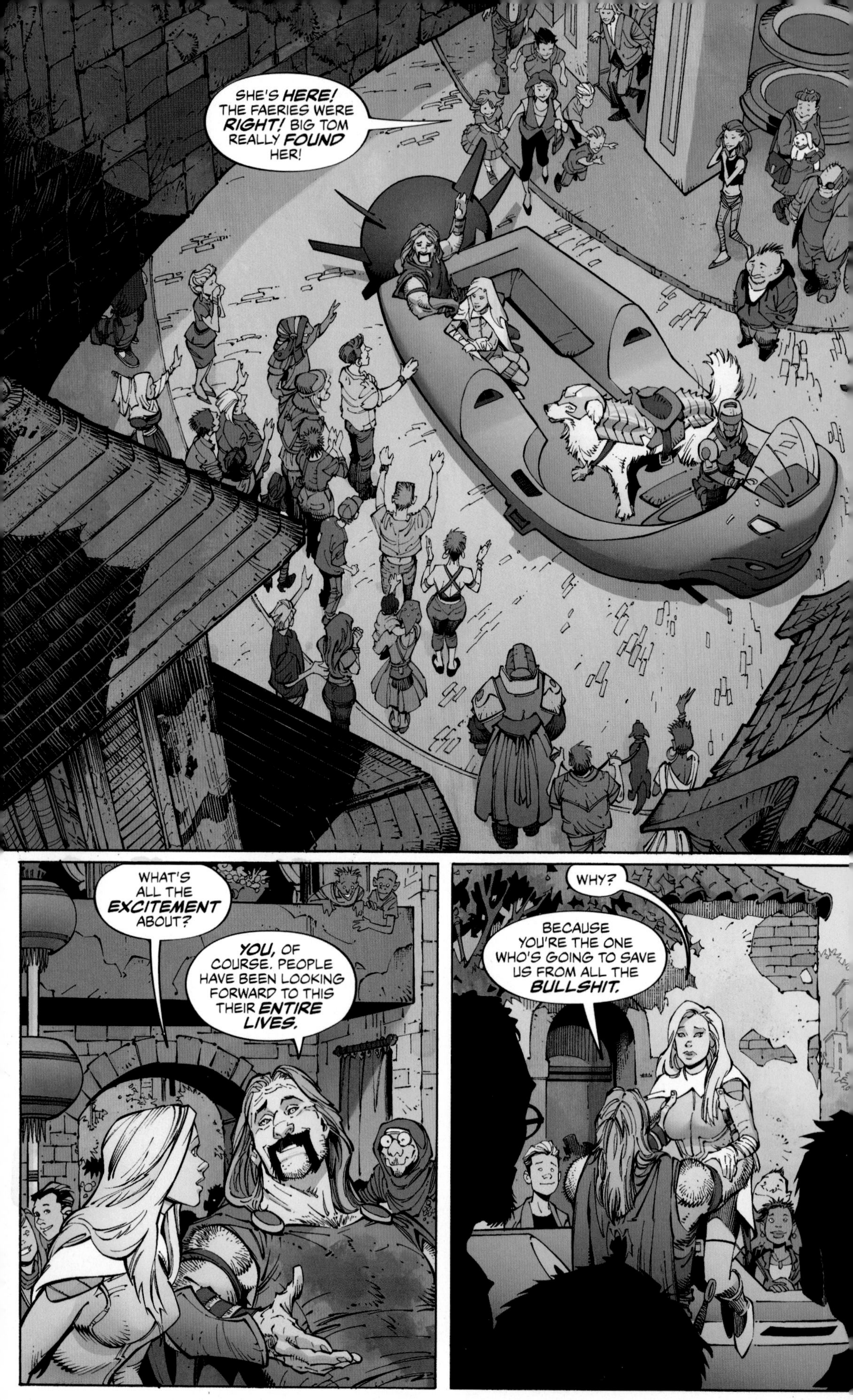
SHE'S **HERE!** THE FAERIES WERE **RIGHT!** BIG TOM REALLY **FOUND** HER!
WHAT'S ALL THE **EXCITEMENT** ABOUT?
YOU, OF COURSE. PEOPLE HAVE BEEN LOOKING FORWARD TO THIS THEIR **ENTIRE LIVES.**
WHY?
BECAUSE YOU'RE THE ONE WHO'S GOING TO SAVE US FROM ALL THE **BULLSHIT.**

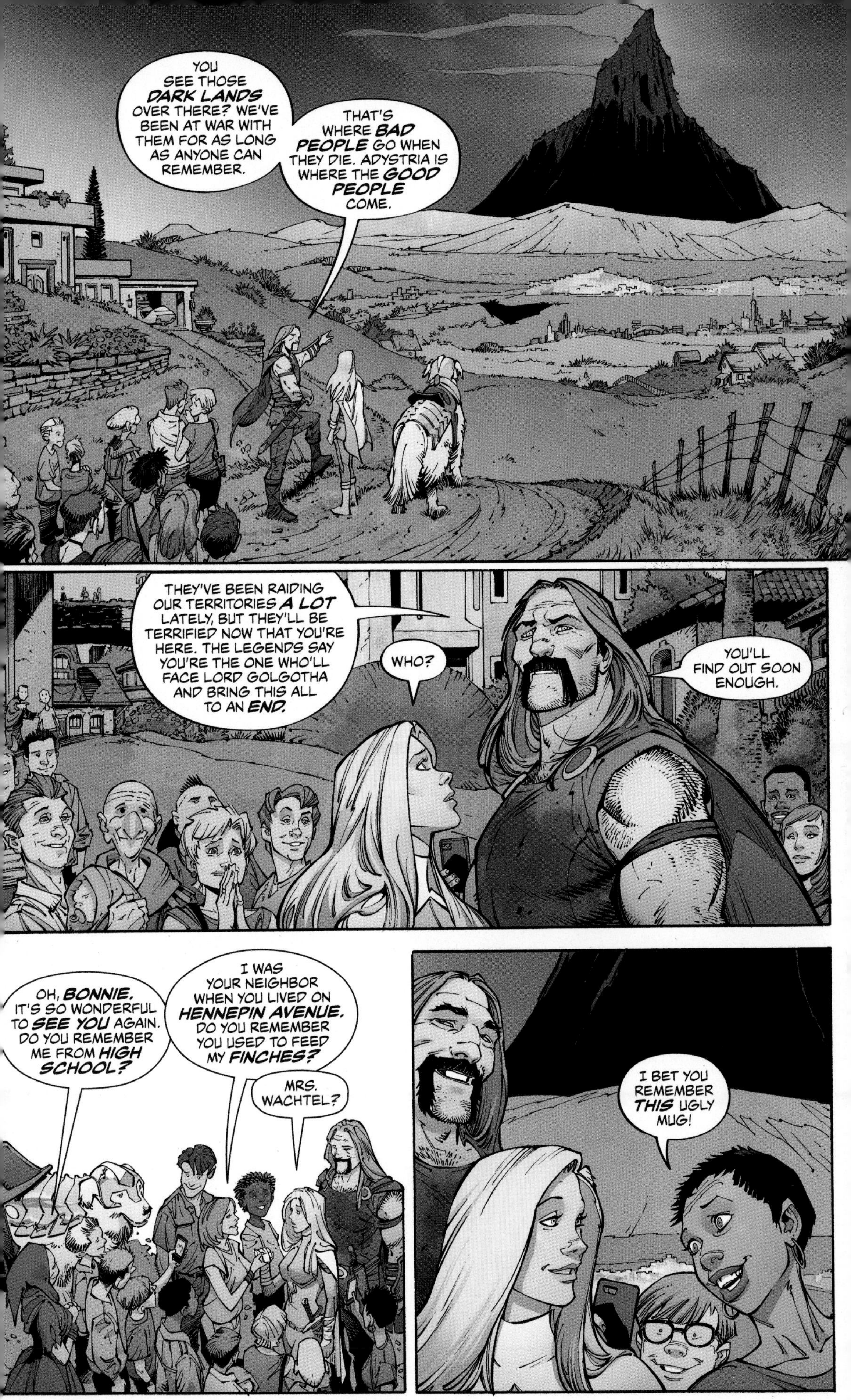
YOU SEE THOSE DARK LANDS OVER THERE? WE'VE BEEN AT WAR WITH THEM FOR AS LONG AS ANYONE CAN REMEMBER.
THAT'S WHERE BAD PEOPLE GO WHEN THEY DIE. ADYSTRIA IS WHERE THE GOOD PEOPLE COME.
THEY'VE BEEN RAIDING OUR TERRITORIES A LOT LATELY, BUT THEY'LL BE TERRIFIED NOW THAT YOU'RE HERE. THE LEGENDS SAY YOU'RE THE ONE WHO'LL FACE LORD GOLGOTHA AND BRING THIS ALL TO AN END.
WHO?
YOU'LL FIND OUT SOON ENOUGH.
OH, BONNIE. IT'S SO WONDERFUL TO SEE YOU AGAIN. DO YOU REMEMBER ME FROM HIGH SCHOOL?
I WAS YOUR NEIGHBOR WHEN YOU LIVED ON HENNEPIN AVENUE. DO YOU REMEMBER YOU USED TO FEED MY FINCHES?
MRS. WACHTEL?
I BET YOU REMEMBER THIS UGLY MUG!

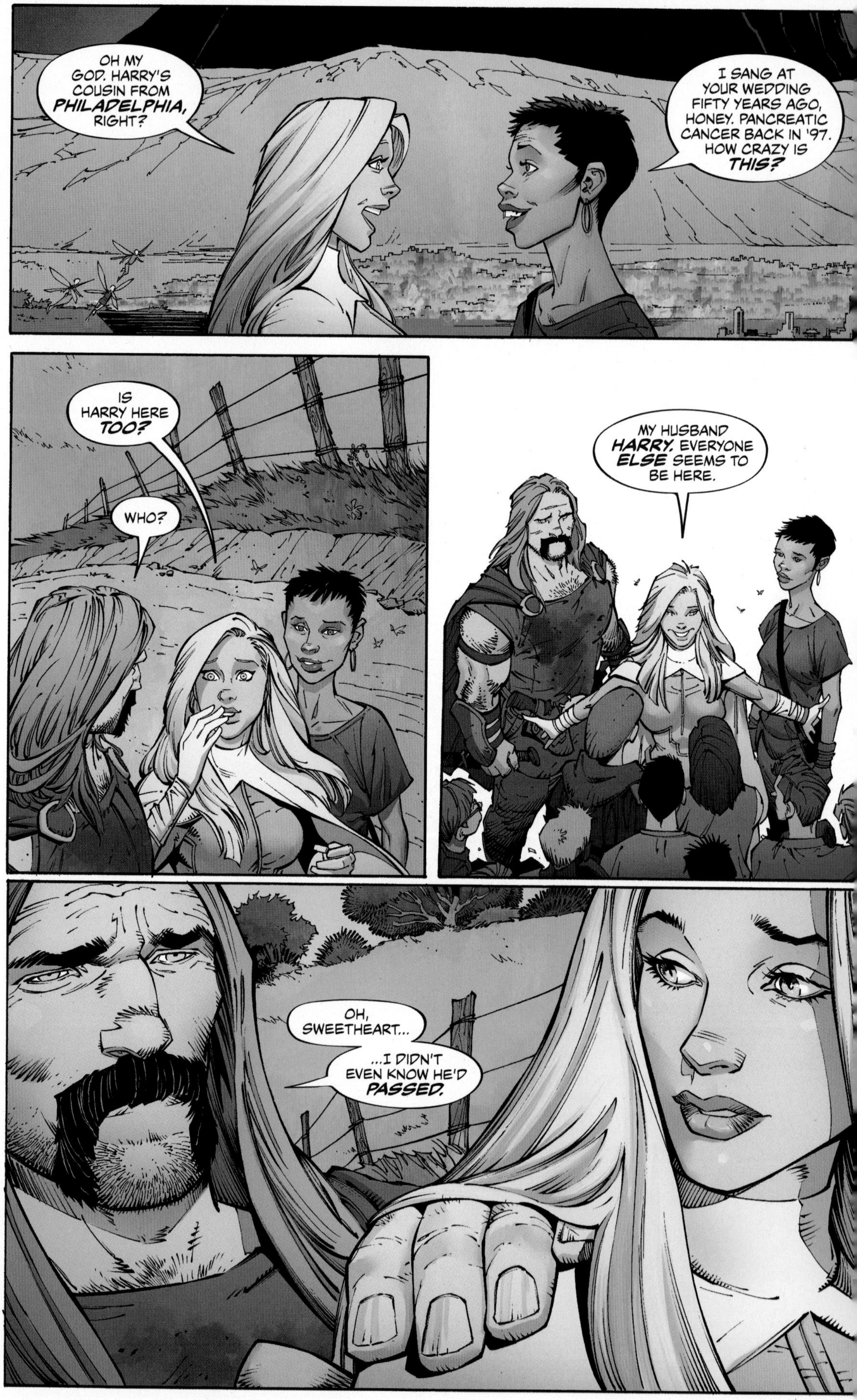
OH MY GOD. HARRY'S COUSIN FROM PHILADELPHIA, RIGHT?
I SANG AT YOUR WEDDING FIFTY YEARS AGO, HONEY. PANCREATIC CANCER BACK IN '97. HOW CRAZY IS THIS?
IS HARRY HERE TOO?
WHO?
MY HUSBAND HARRY. EVERYONE ELSE SEEMS TO BE HERE.
OH, SWEETHEART...
...I DIDN'T EVEN KNOW HE'D PASSED.

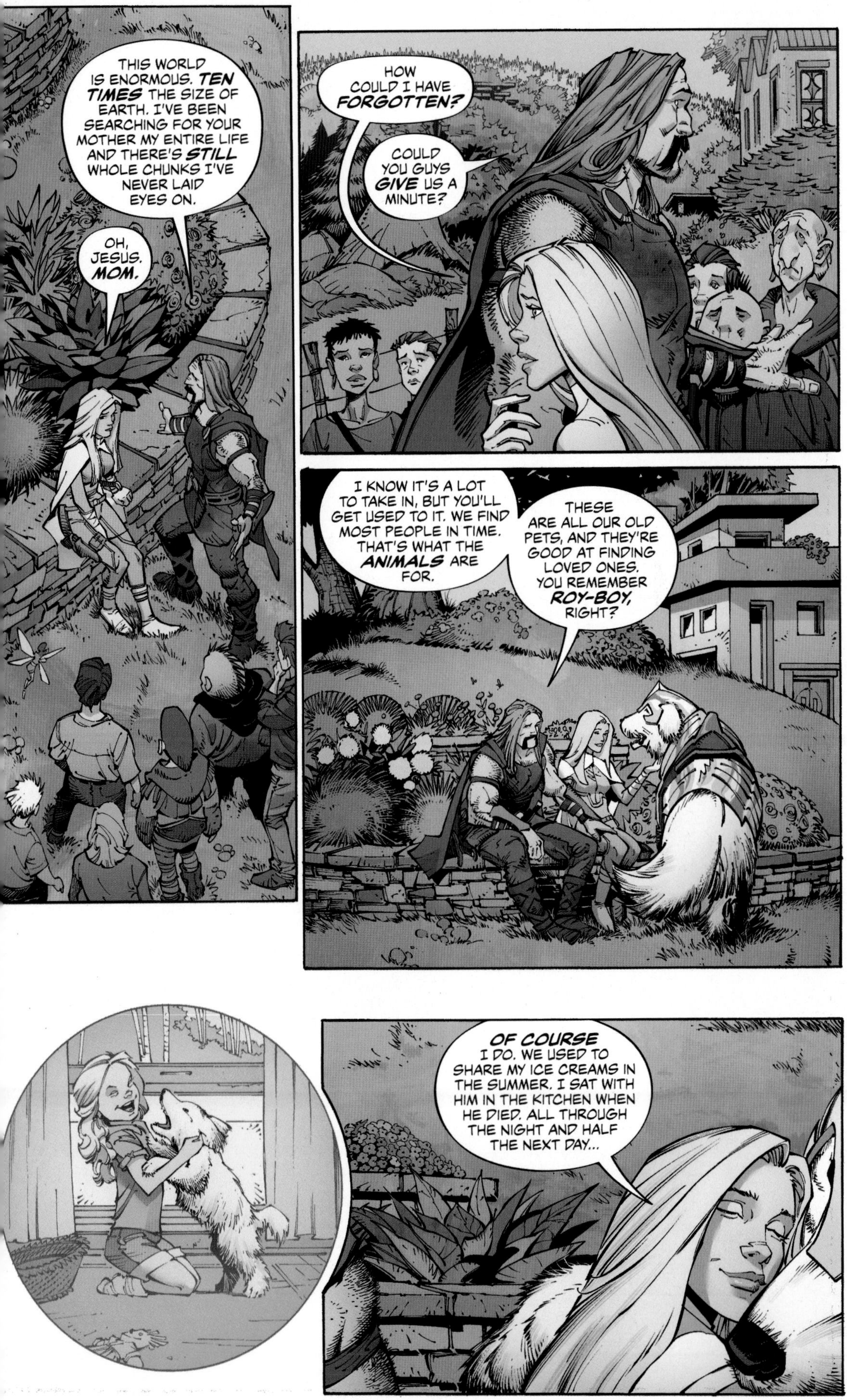
THIS WORLD IS ENORMOUS. TEN TIMES THE SIZE OF EARTH. I'VE BEEN SEARCHING FOR YOUR MOTHER MY ENTIRE LIFE AND THERE'S STILL WHOLE CHUNKS I'VE NEVER LAID EYES ON.
OH, JESUS. MOM.
HOW COULD I HAVE FORGOTTEN?
COULD YOU GUYS GIVE US A MINUTE?
I KNOW IT'S A LOT TO TAKE IN, BUT YOU'LL GET USED TO IT. WE FIND MOST PEOPLE IN TIME. THAT'S WHAT THE ANIMALS ARE FOR.
THESE ARE ALL OUR OLD PETS, AND THEY'RE GOOD AT FINDING LOVED ONES. YOU REMEMBER ROY-BOY, RIGHT?
OF COURSE I DO. WE USED TO SHARE MY ICE CREAMS IN THE SUMMER. I SAT WITH HIM IN THE KITCHEN WHEN HE DIED. ALL THROUGH THE NIGHT AND HALF THE NEXT DAY...

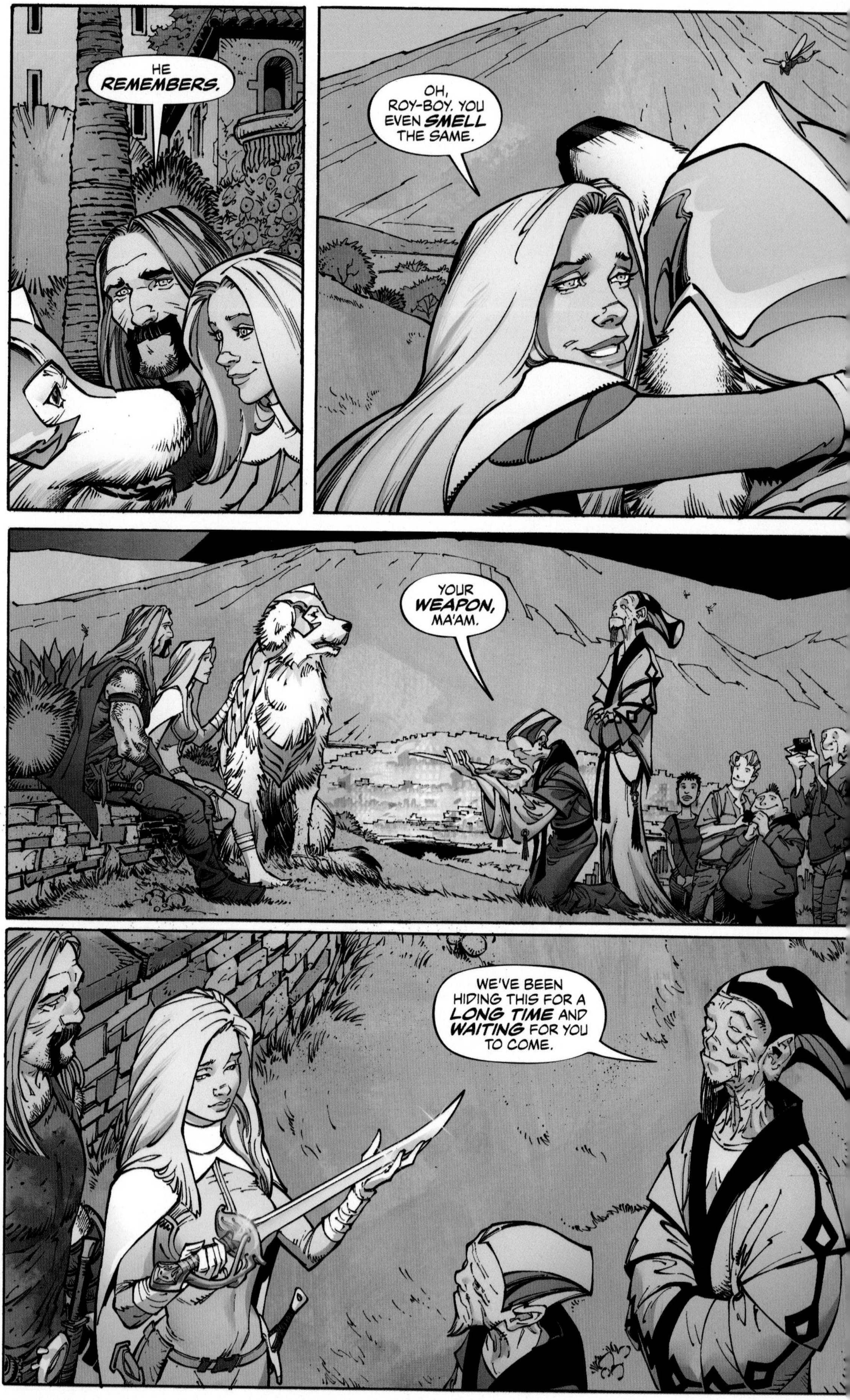
HE REMEMBERS.
OH, ROY-BOY. YOU EVEN SMELL THE SAME.
YOUR WEAPON, MA'AM.
WE'VE BEEN HIDING THIS FOR A LONG TIME AND WAITING FOR YOU TO COME.

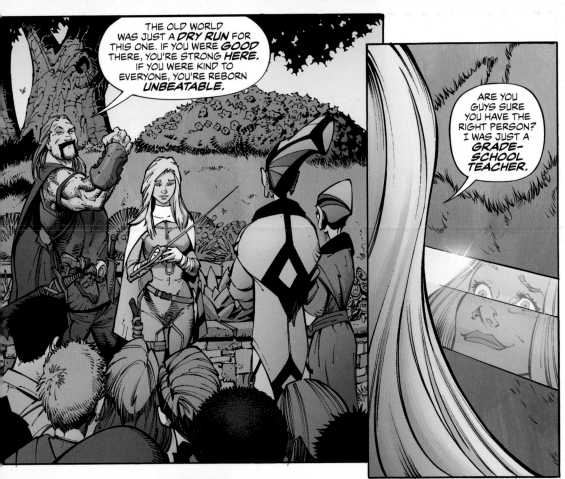

THE OLD WORLD WAS JUST A **DRY RUN** FOR THIS ONE. IF YOU WERE **GOOD** THERE, YOU'RE STRONG **HERE.** IF YOU WERE KIND TO EVERYONE, YOU'RE REBORN **UNBEATABLE.**

ARE YOU GUYS SURE YOU HAVE THE RIGHT PERSON? I WAS JUST A **GRADE-SCHOOL TEACHER.**

ALL YOUR LIFE YOU DID **THE RIGHT THING.** ALWAYS PUTTING OTHERS BEFORE **YOURSELF...**

...THIS IS YOUR **REWARD.**

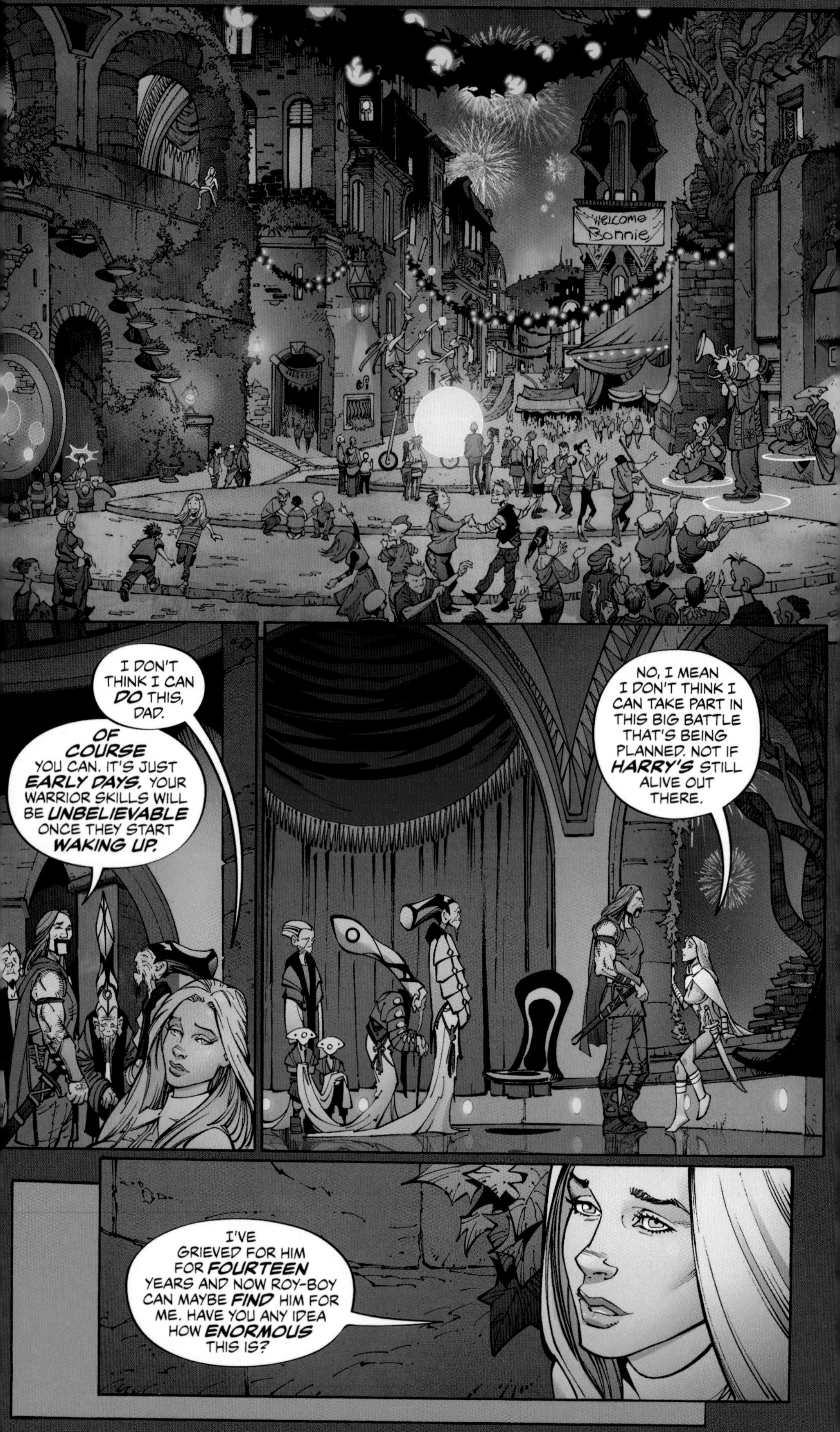
Welcome Bonnie
I DON'T THINK I CAN DO THIS, DAD.
OF COURSE YOU CAN. IT'S JUST EARLY DAYS. YOUR WARRIOR SKILLS WILL BE UNBELIEVABLE ONCE THEY START WAKING UP.
NO, I MEAN I DON'T THINK I CAN TAKE PART IN THIS BIG BATTLE THAT'S BEING PLANNED. NOT IF HARRY'S STILL ALIVE OUT THERE.
I'VE GRIEVED FOR HIM FOR FOURTEEN YEARS AND NOW ROY-BOY CAN MAYBE FIND HIM FOR ME. HAVE YOU ANY IDEA HOW ENORMOUS THIS IS?

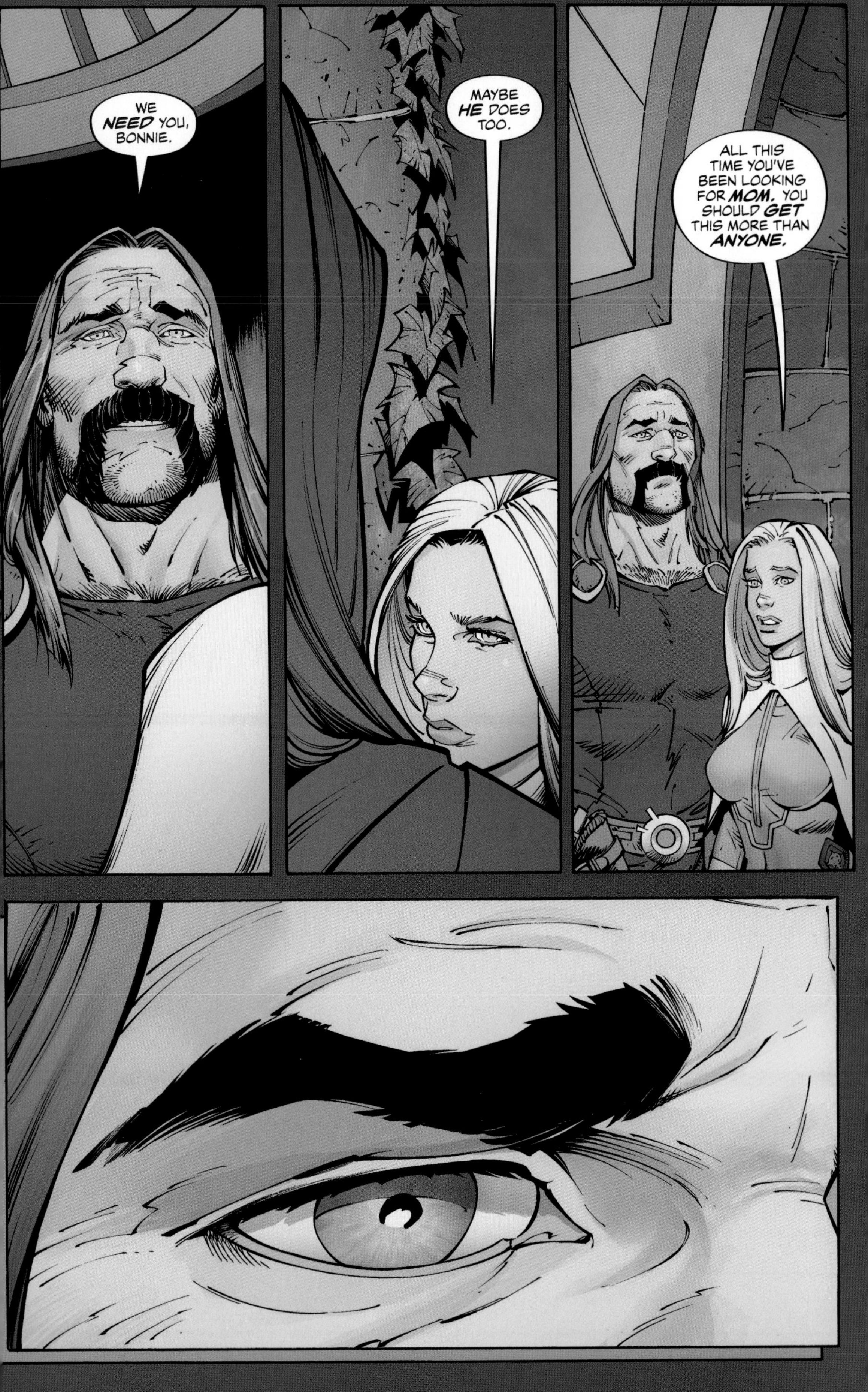

WE NEED YOU, BONNIE.
MAYBE HE DOES TOO.
ALL THIS TIME YOU'VE BEEN LOOKING FOR MOM. YOU SHOULD GET THIS MORE THAN ANYONE.

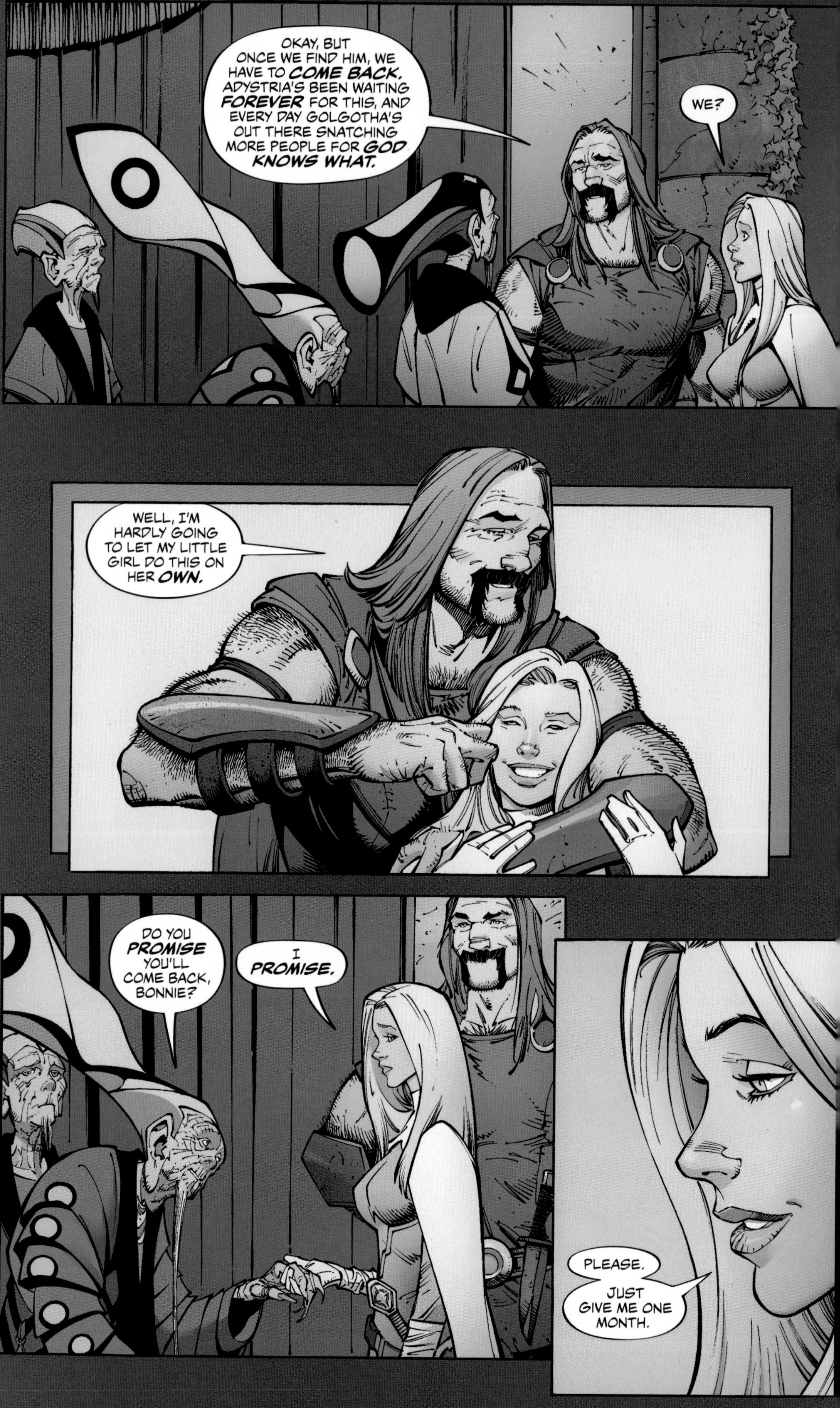
OKAY, BUT ONCE WE FIND HIM, WE HAVE TO COME BACK. ADYSTRIA'S BEEN WAITING FOREVER FOR THIS, AND EVERY DAY GOLGOTHA'S OUT THERE SNATCHING MORE PEOPLE FOR GOD KNOWS WHAT.
WE?
WELL, I'M HARDLY GOING TO LET MY LITTLE GIRL DO THIS ON HER OWN.
DO YOU PROMISE YOU'LL COME BACK, BONNIE?
I PROMISE.
PLEASE. JUST GIVE ME ONE MONTH.

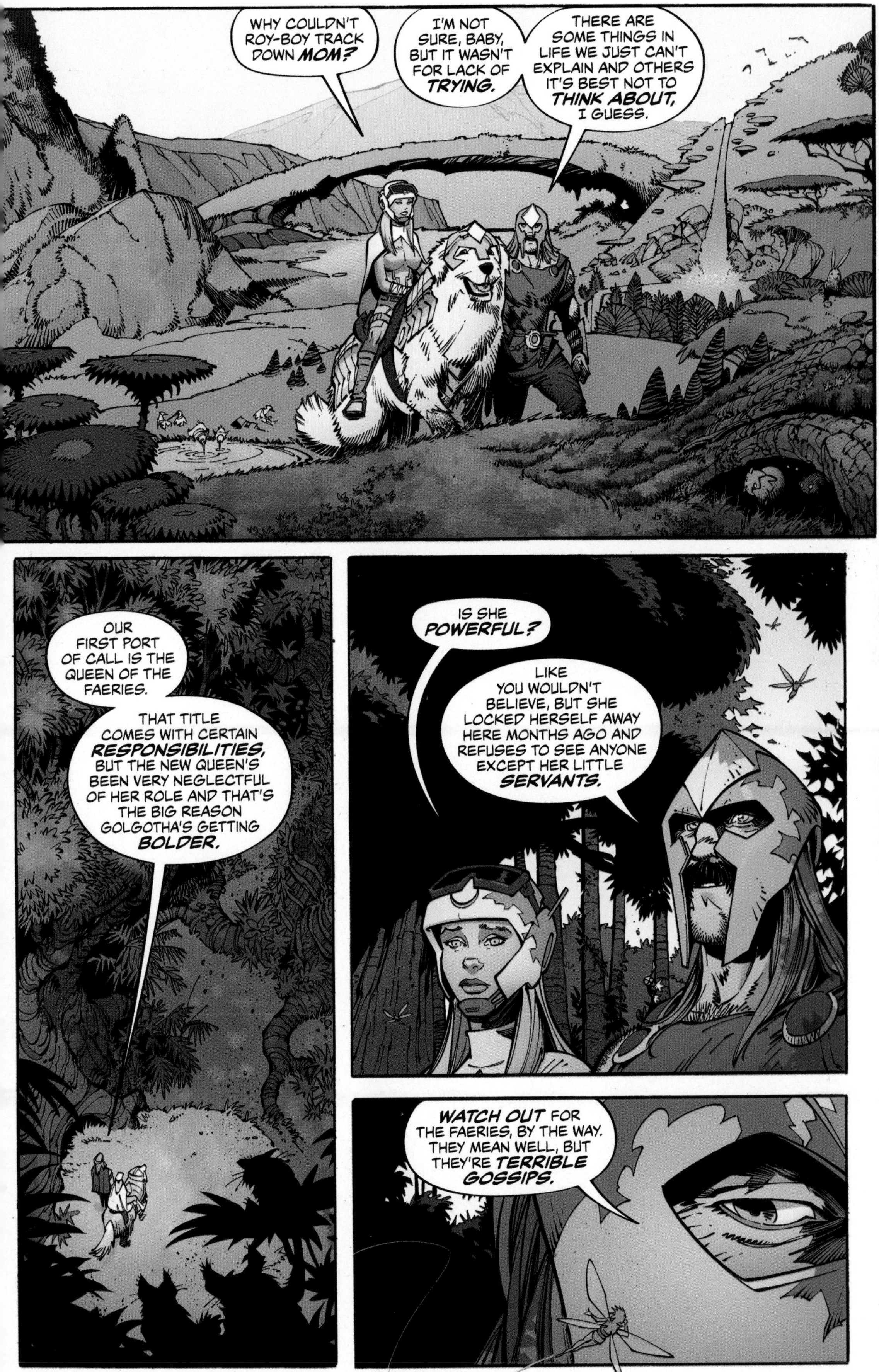
WHY COULDN'T ROY-BOY TRACK DOWN MOM?
I'M NOT SURE, BABY, BUT IT WASN'T FOR LACK OF TRYING.
THERE ARE SOME THINGS IN LIFE WE JUST CAN'T EXPLAIN AND OTHERS IT'S BEST NOT TO THINK ABOUT, I GUESS.
OUR FIRST PORT OF CALL IS THE QUEEN OF THE FAERIES.
THAT TITLE COMES WITH CERTAIN RESPONSIBILITIES, BUT THE NEW QUEEN'S BEEN VERY NEGLECTFUL OF HER ROLE AND THAT'S THE BIG REASON GOLGOTHA'S GETTING BOLDER.
IS SHE POWERFUL?
LIKE YOU WOULDN'T BELIEVE, BUT SHE LOCKED HERSELF AWAY HERE MONTHS AGO AND REFUSES TO SEE ANYONE EXCEPT HER LITTLE SERVANTS.
WATCH OUT FOR THE FAERIES, BY THE WAY. THEY MEAN WELL, BUT THEY'RE TERRIBLE GOSSIPS.

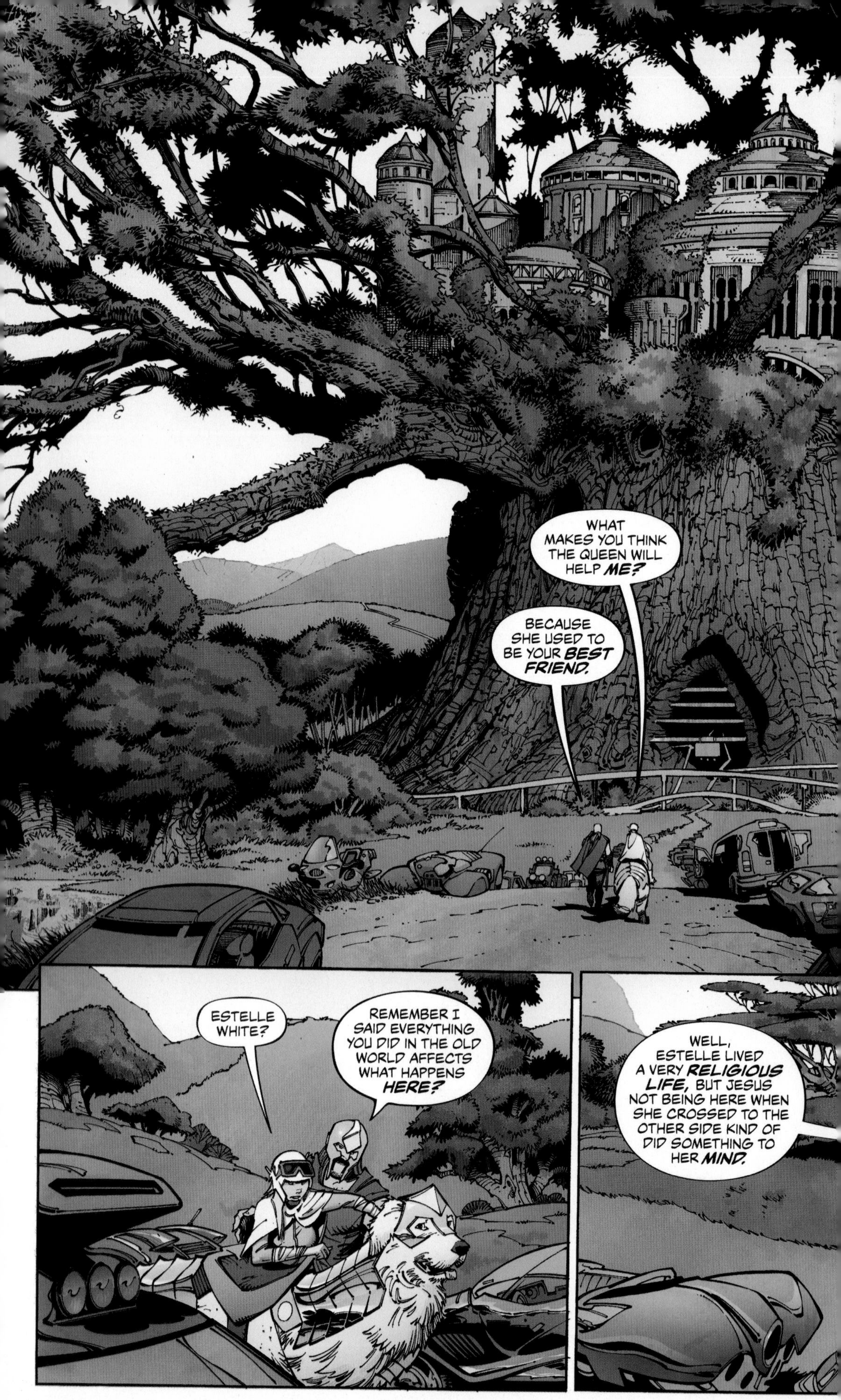
WHAT MAKES YOU THINK THE QUEEN WILL HELP *ME?*
BECAUSE SHE USED TO BE YOUR ***BEST FRIEND.***
ESTELLE WHITE?
REMEMBER I SAID EVERYTHING YOU DID IN THE OLD WORLD AFFECTS WHAT HAPPENS *HERE?*
WELL, ESTELLE LIVED A VERY ***RELIGIOUS LIFE,*** BUT JESUS NOT BEING HERE WHEN SHE CROSSED TO THE OTHER SIDE KIND OF DID SOMETHING TO HER ***MIND.***

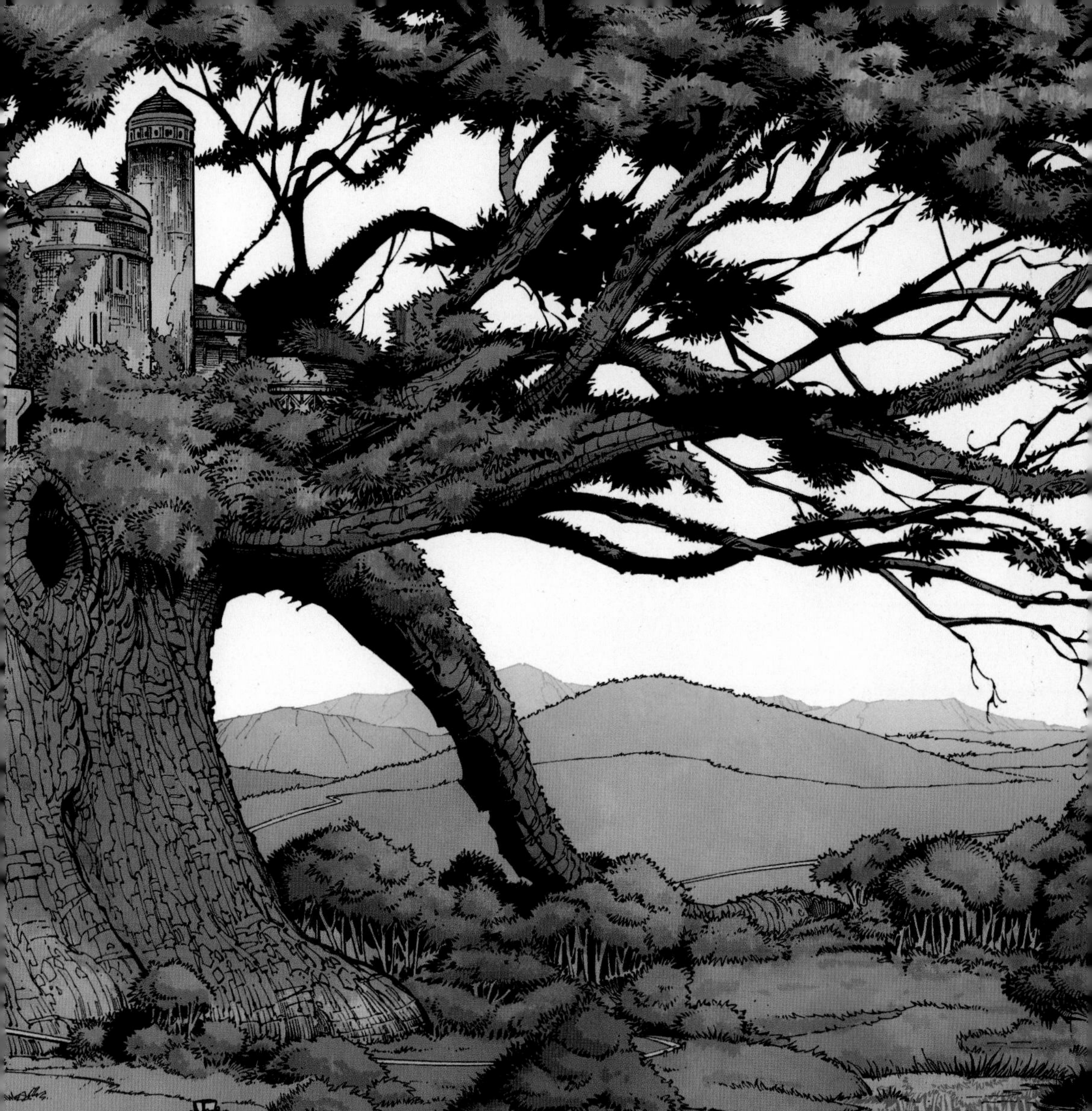

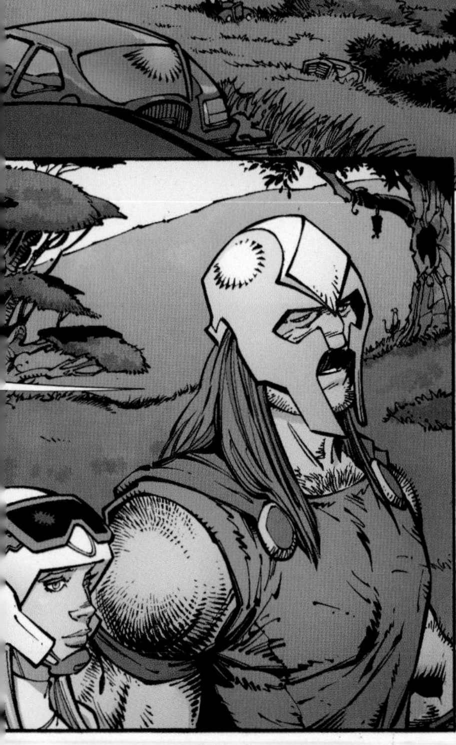

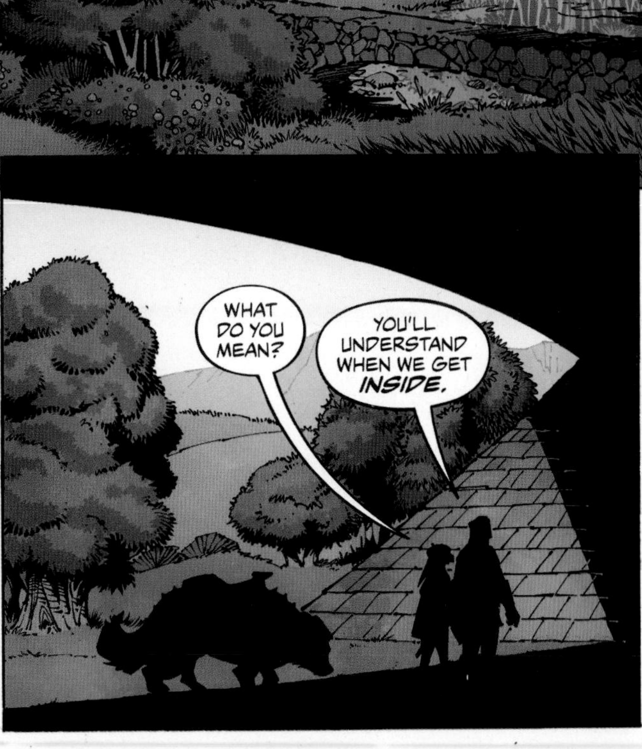
WHAT DO YOU MEAN?
YOU'LL UNDERSTAND WHEN WE GET INSIDE.

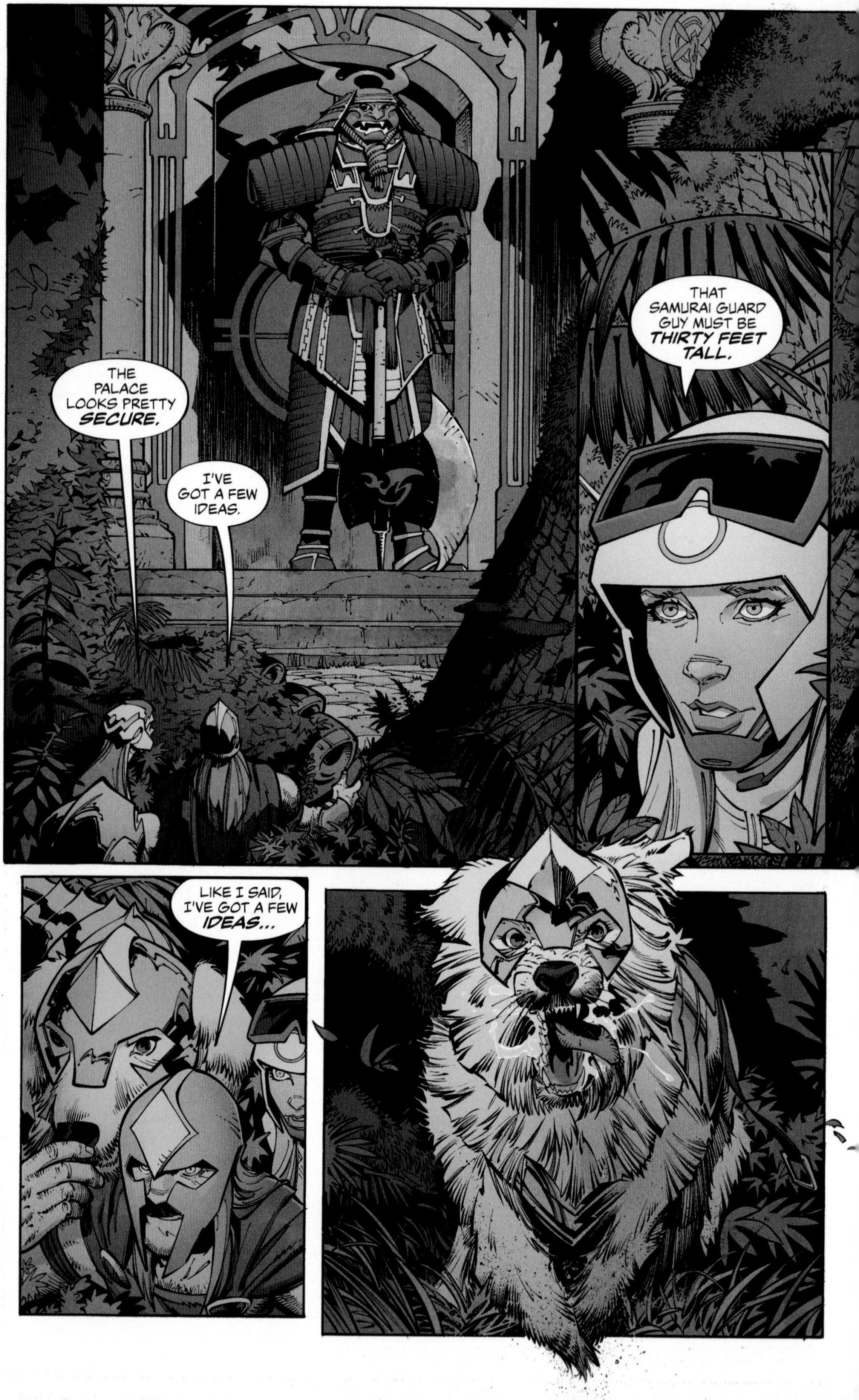
THE PALACE LOOKS PRETTY SECURE.
I'VE GOT A FEW IDEAS.
THAT SAMURAI GUARD GUY MUST BE THIRTY FEET TALL.
LIKE I SAID, I'VE GOT A FEW IDEAS...

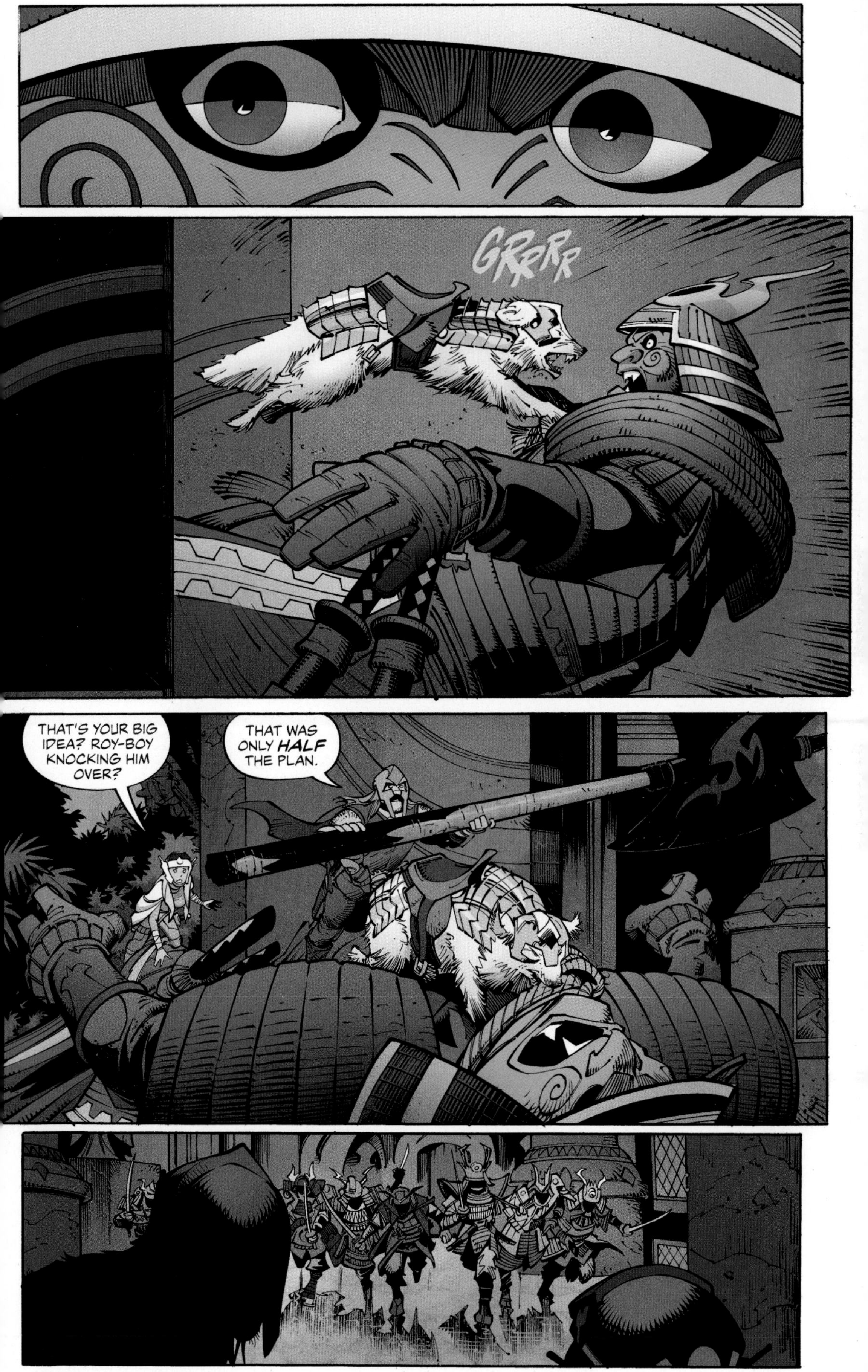
GRRRR
THAT'S YOUR BIG IDEA? ROY-BOY KNOCKING HIM OVER?
THAT WAS ONLY HALF THE PLAN.

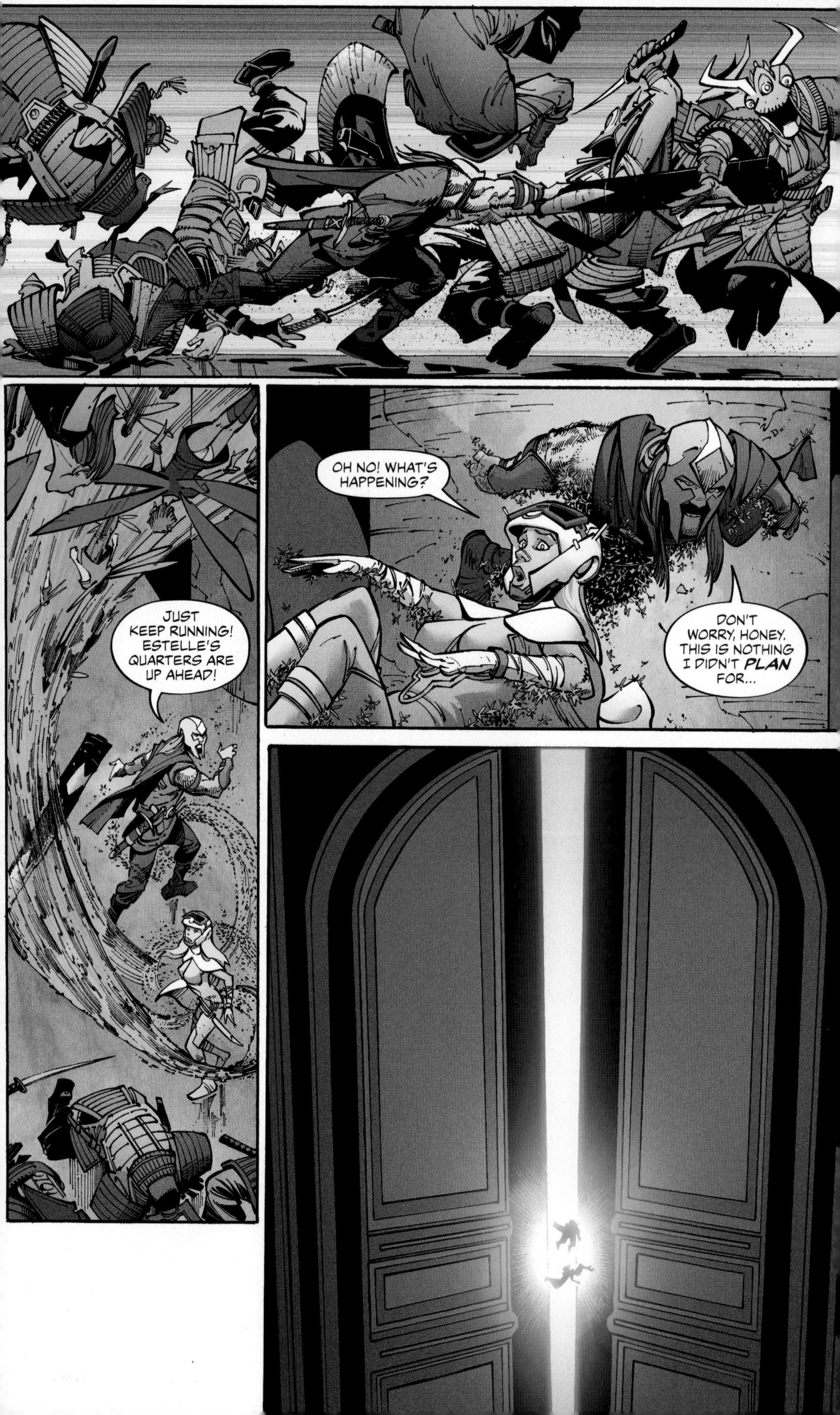
JUST KEEP RUNNING! ESTELLE'S QUARTERS ARE UP AHEAD!
OH NO! WHAT'S HAPPENING?
DON'T WORRY, HONEY. THIS IS NOTHING I DIDN'T **PLAN** FOR...

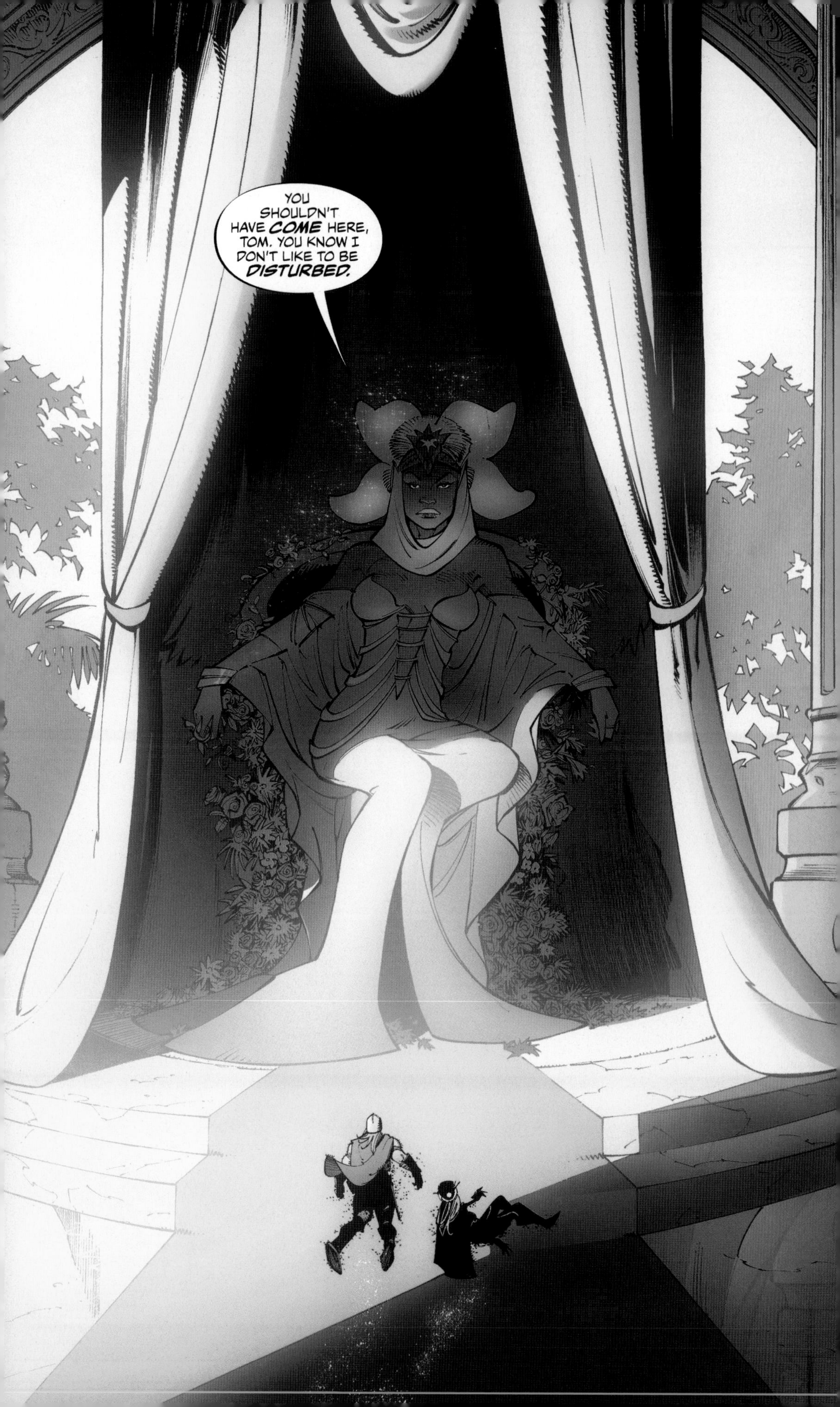
YOU SHOULDN'T HAVE COME HERE, TOM. YOU KNOW I DON'T LIKE TO BE DISTURBED.

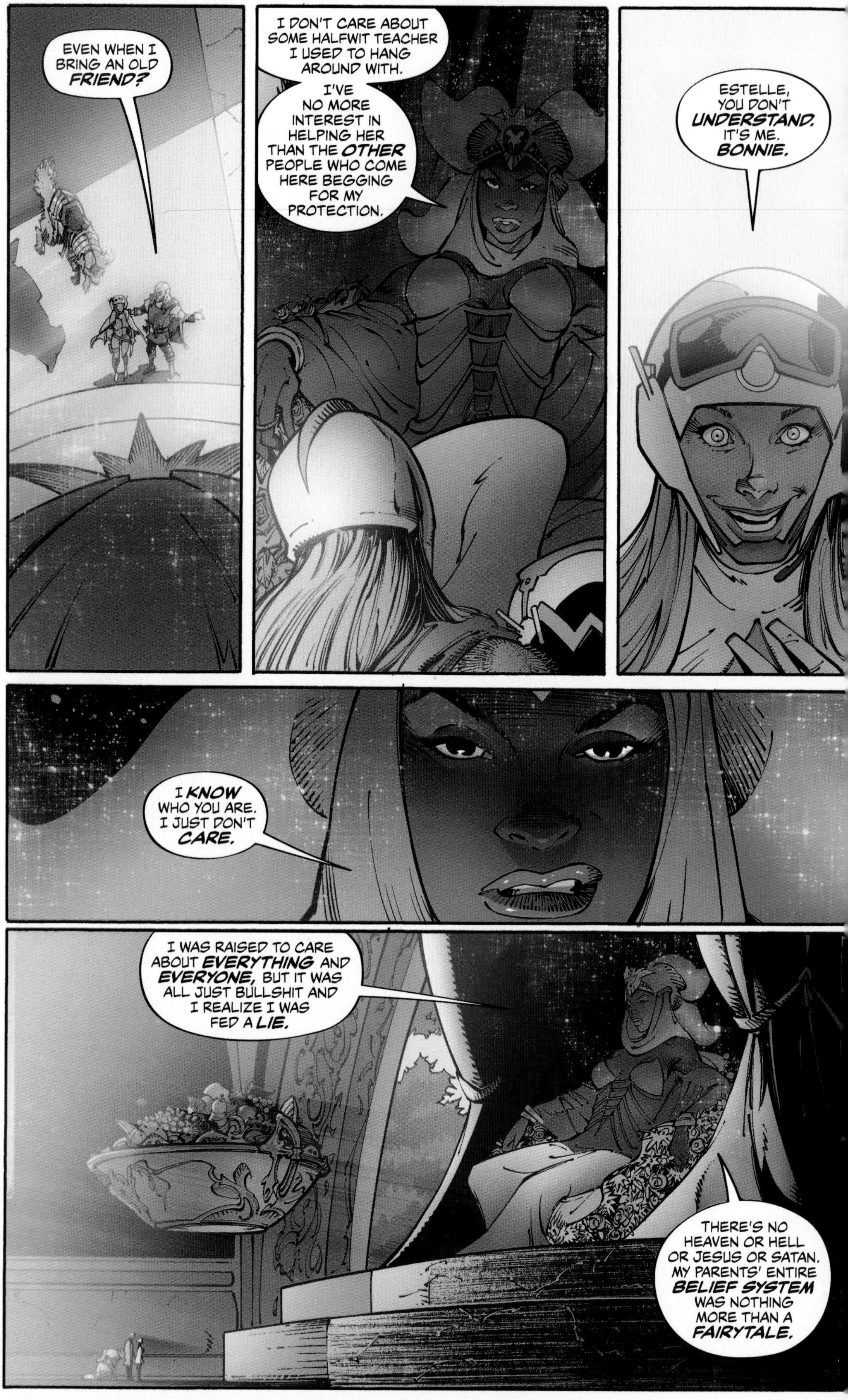
EVEN WHEN I BRING AN OLD FRIEND?
I DON'T CARE ABOUT SOME HALFWIT TEACHER I USED TO HANG AROUND WITH.
I'VE NO MORE INTEREST IN HELPING HER THAN THE OTHER PEOPLE WHO COME HERE BEGGING FOR MY PROTECTION.
ESTELLE, YOU DON'T UNDERSTAND. IT'S ME. BONNIE.
I KNOW WHO YOU ARE. I JUST DON'T CARE.
I WAS RAISED TO CARE ABOUT EVERYTHING AND EVERYONE, BUT IT WAS ALL JUST BULLSHIT AND I REALIZE I WAS FED A LIE.
THERE'S NO HEAVEN OR HELL OR JESUS OR SATAN. MY PARENTS' ENTIRE BELIEF SYSTEM WAS NOTHING MORE THAN A FAIRYTALE.

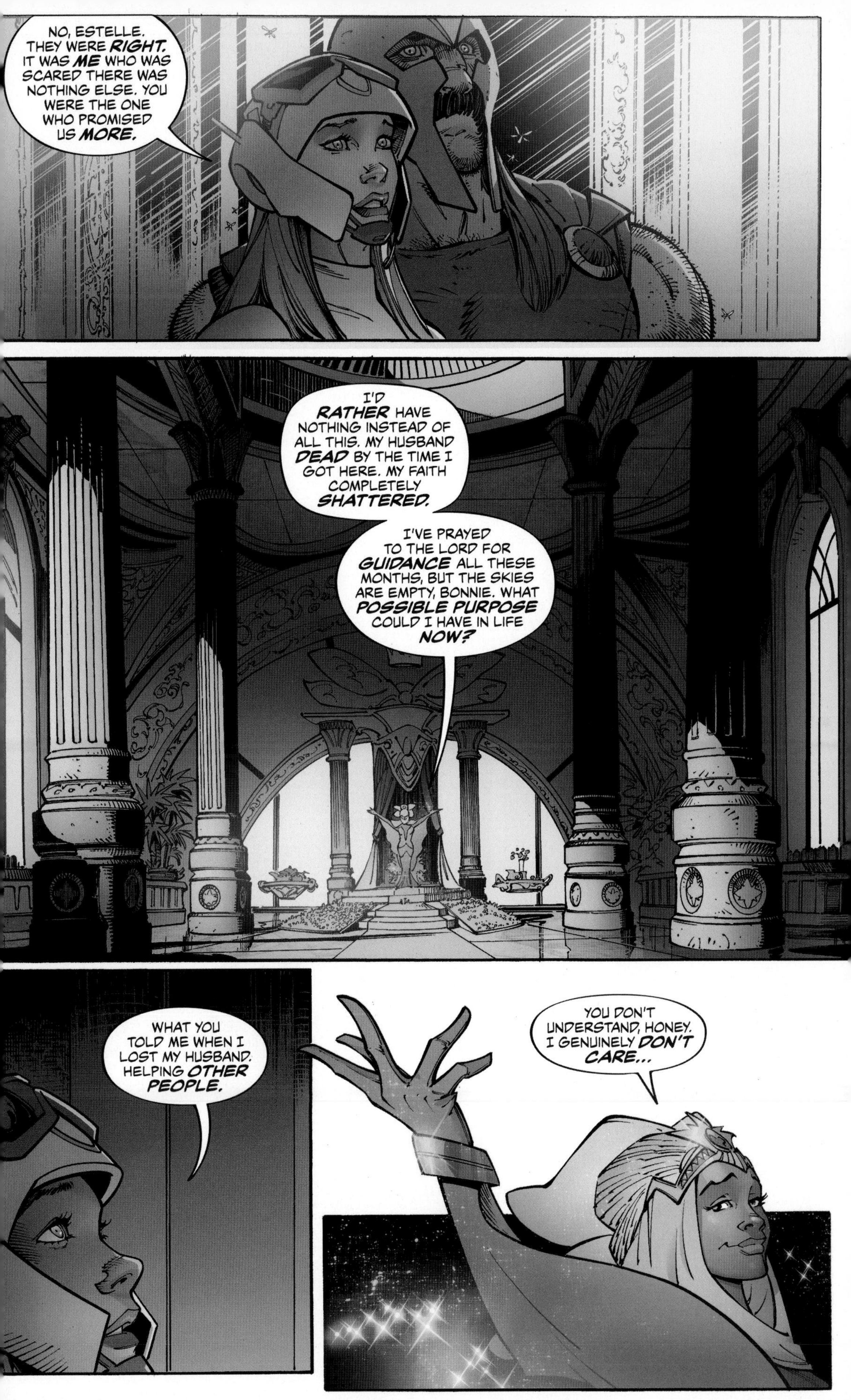
NO, ESTELLE. THEY WERE RIGHT. IT WAS ME WHO WAS SCARED THERE WAS NOTHING ELSE. YOU WERE THE ONE WHO PROMISED US MORE.
I'D RATHER HAVE NOTHING INSTEAD OF ALL THIS. MY HUSBAND DEAD BY THE TIME I GOT HERE. MY FAITH COMPLETELY SHATTERED.
I'VE PRAYED TO THE LORD FOR GUIDANCE ALL THESE MONTHS, BUT THE SKIES ARE EMPTY, BONNIE. WHAT POSSIBLE PURPOSE COULD I HAVE IN LIFE NOW?
WHAT YOU TOLD ME WHEN I LOST MY HUSBAND. HELPING OTHER PEOPLE.
YOU DON'T UNDERSTAND, HONEY. I GENUINELY DON'T CARE...

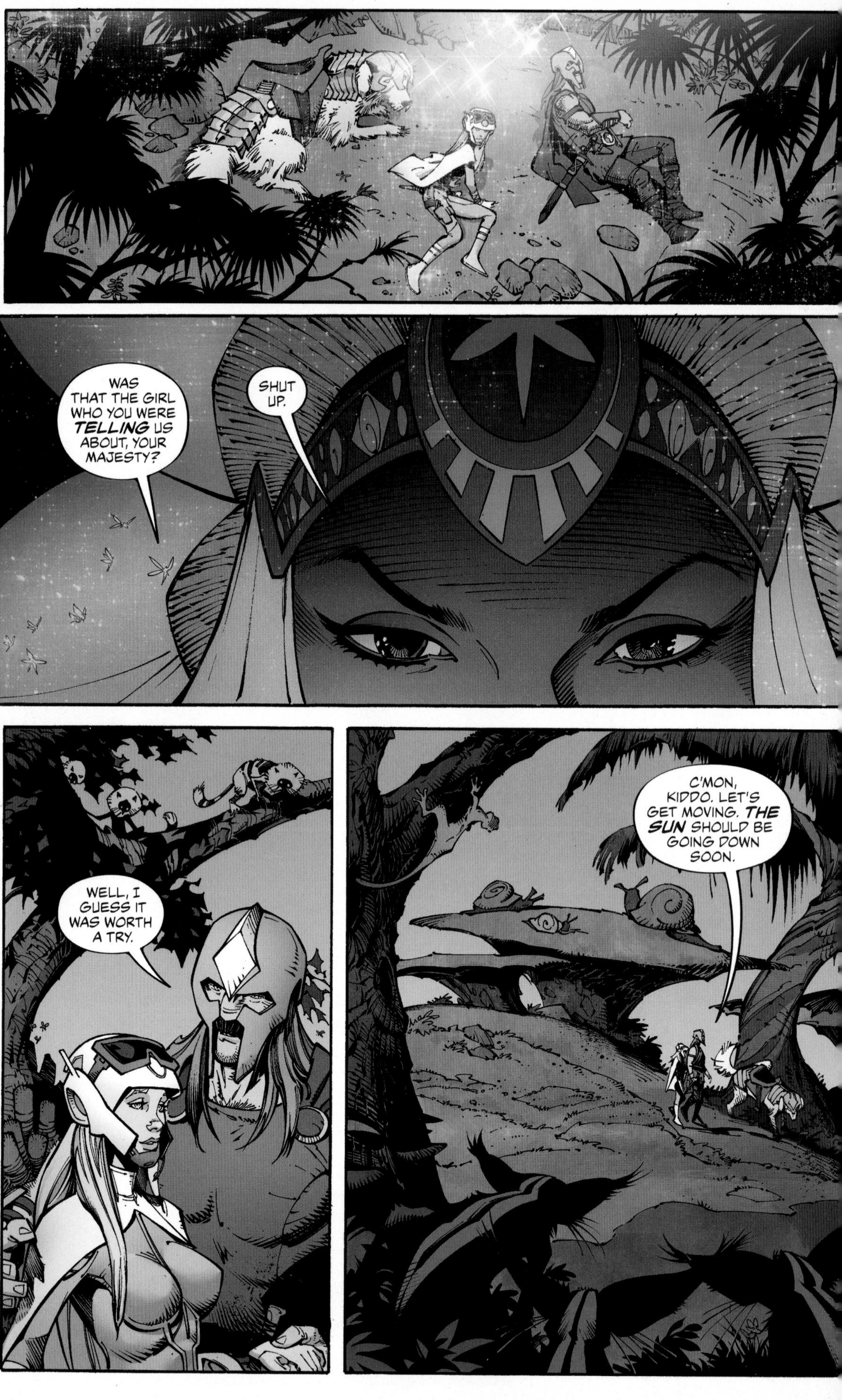

WAS THAT THE GIRL WHO YOU WERE **TELLING** US ABOUT, YOUR MAJESTY?
SHUT UP.
WELL, I GUESS IT WAS WORTH A TRY.
C'MON, KIDDO. LET'S GET MOVING. ***THE SUN*** SHOULD BE GOING DOWN SOON.

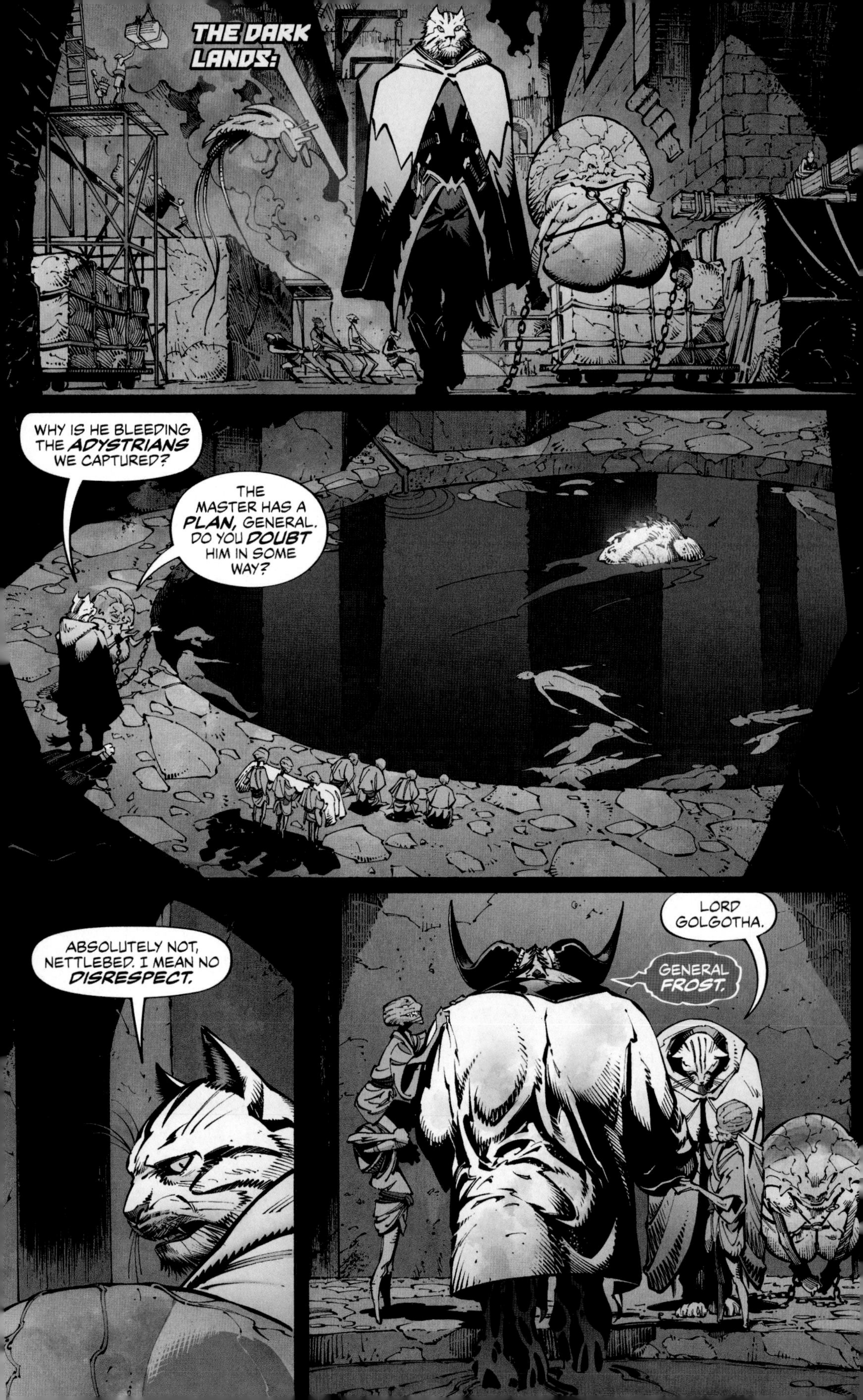
THE DARK LANDS:
WHY IS HE BLEEDING THE ADYSTRIANS WE CAPTURED?
THE MASTER HAS A PLAN, GENERAL. DO YOU DOUBT HIM IN SOME WAY?
ABSOLUTELY NOT, NETTLEBED. I MEAN NO DISRESPECT.
LORD GOLGOTHA.
GENERAL FROST.

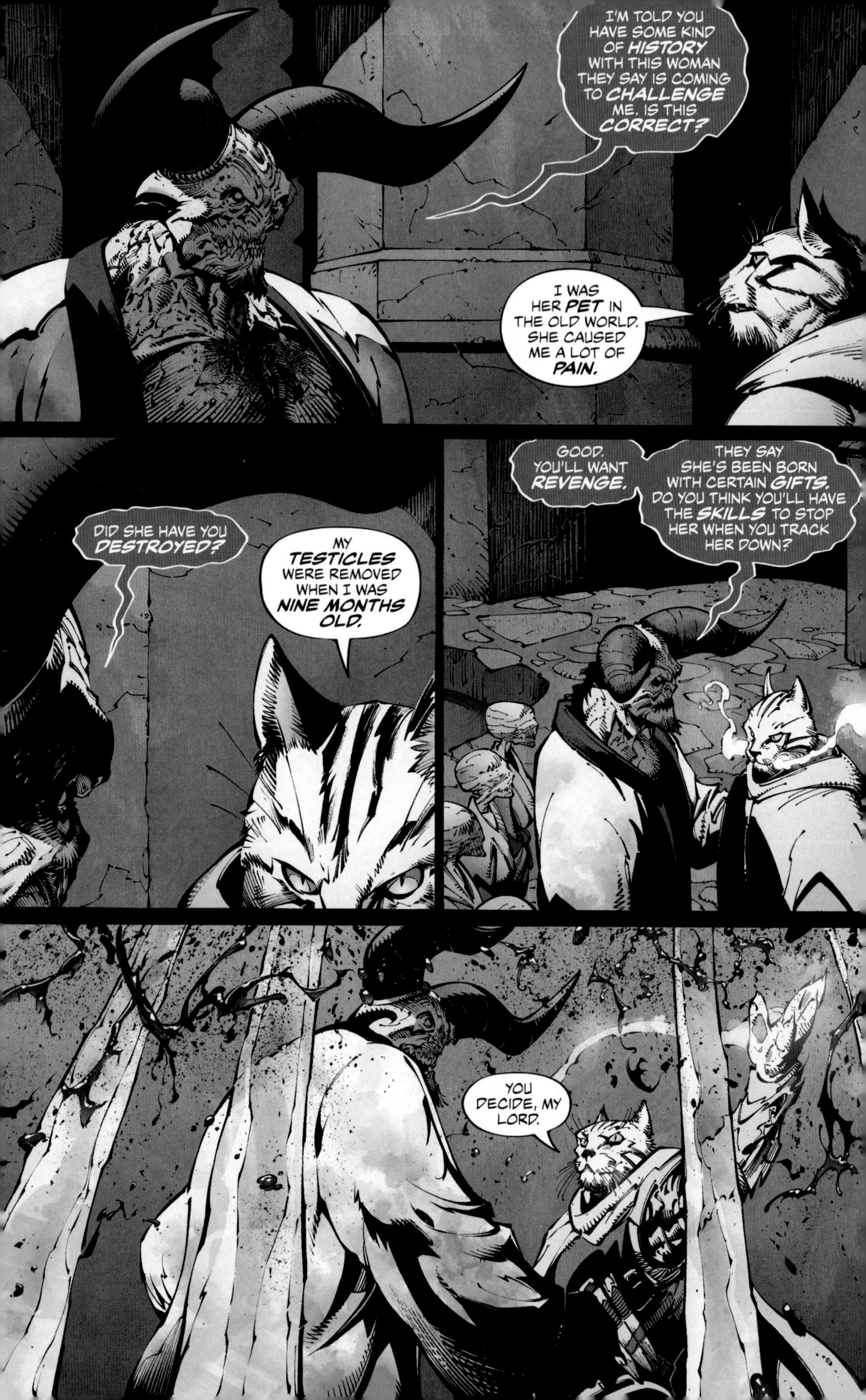

I'M TOLD YOU HAVE SOME KIND OF HISTORY WITH THIS WOMAN THEY SAY IS COMING TO CHALLENGE ME. IS THIS CORRECT?
I WAS HER PET IN THE OLD WORLD. SHE CAUSED ME A LOT OF PAIN.
DID SHE HAVE YOU DESTROYED?
MY TESTICLES WERE REMOVED WHEN I WAS NINE MONTHS OLD.
GOOD. YOU'LL WANT REVENGE.
THEY SAY SHE'S BEEN BORN WITH CERTAIN GIFTS. DO YOU THINK YOU'LL HAVE THE SKILLS TO STOP HER WHEN YOU TRACK HER DOWN?
YOU DECIDE, MY LORD.

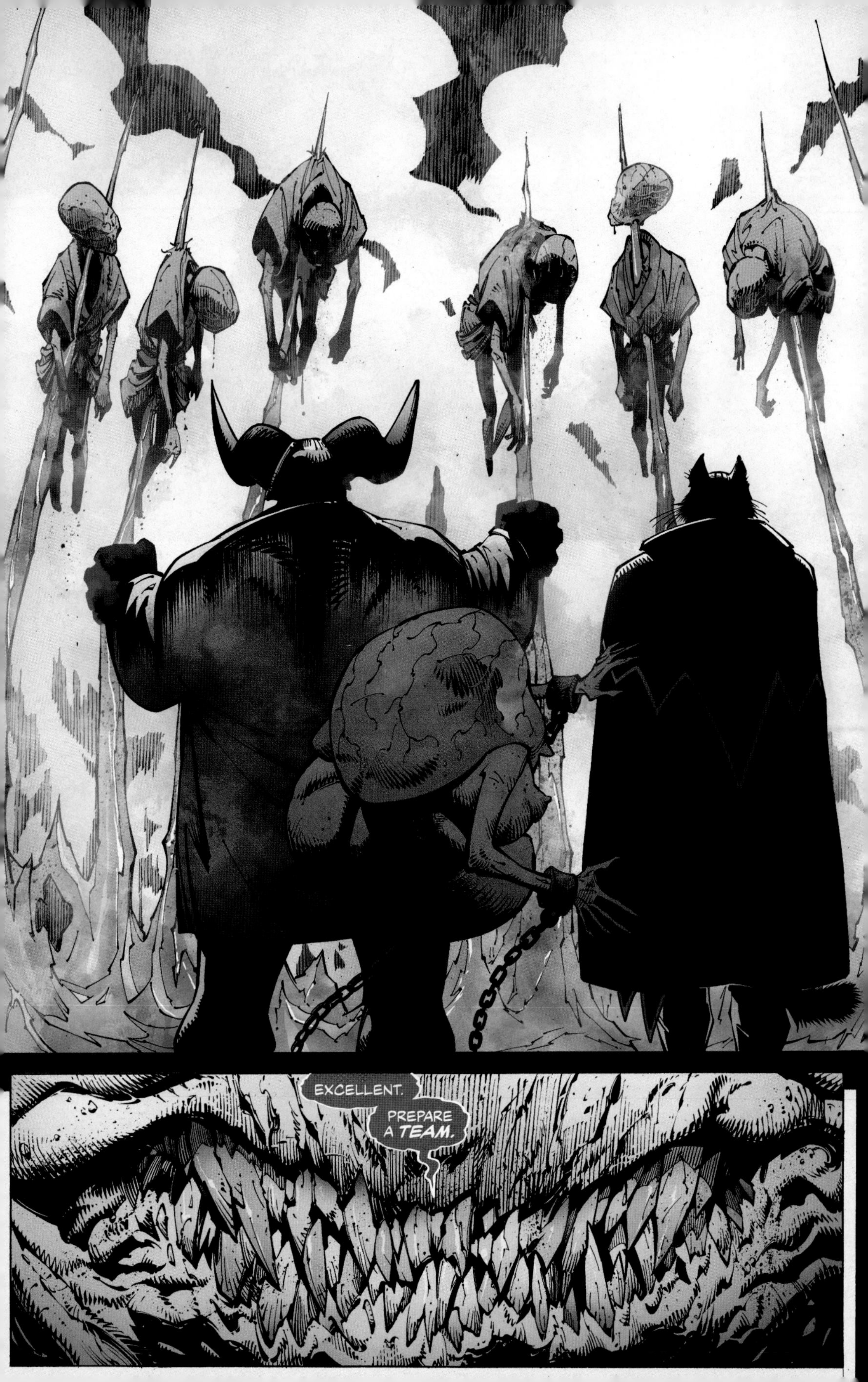
EXCELLENT.
PREPARE A TEAM.

THREE

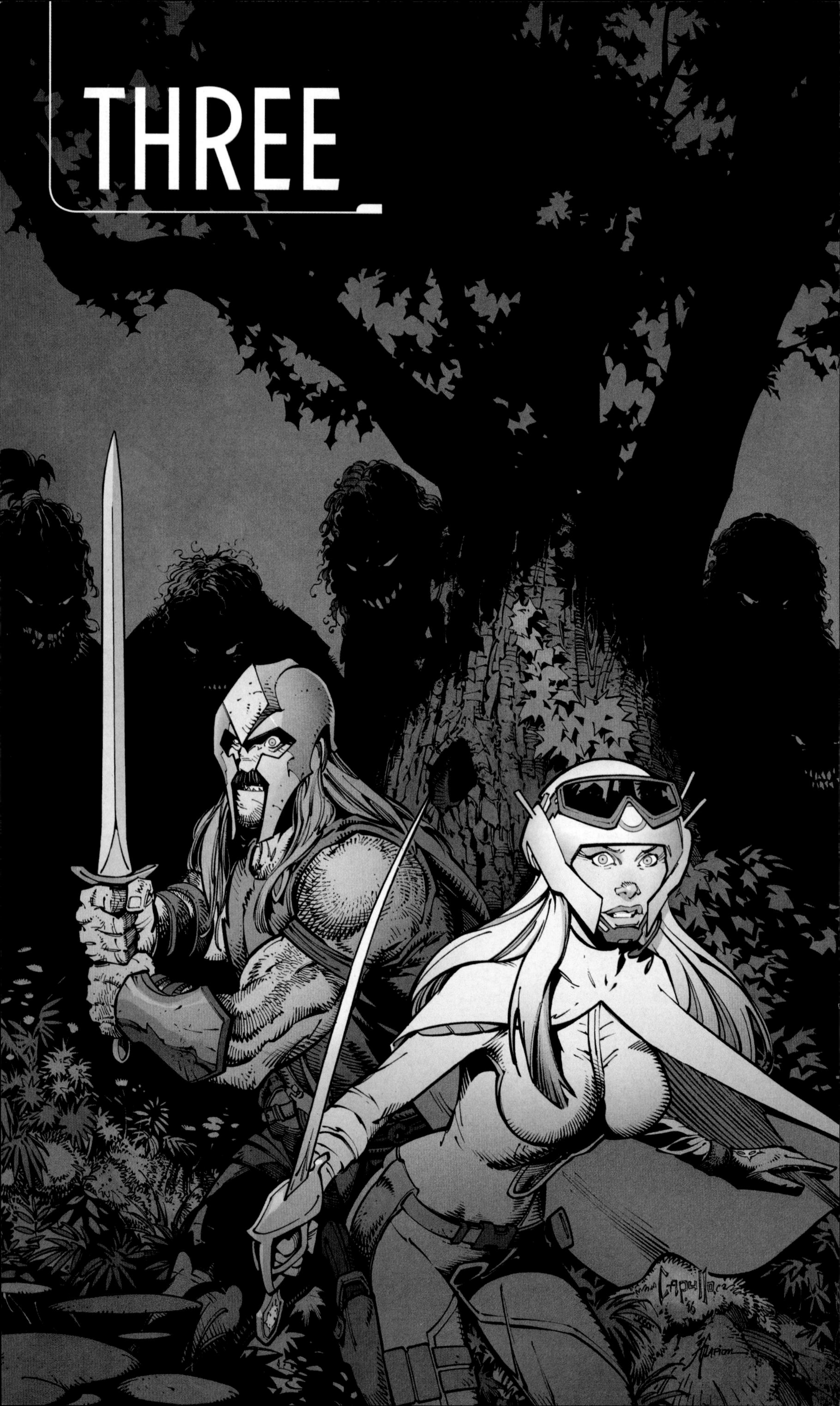

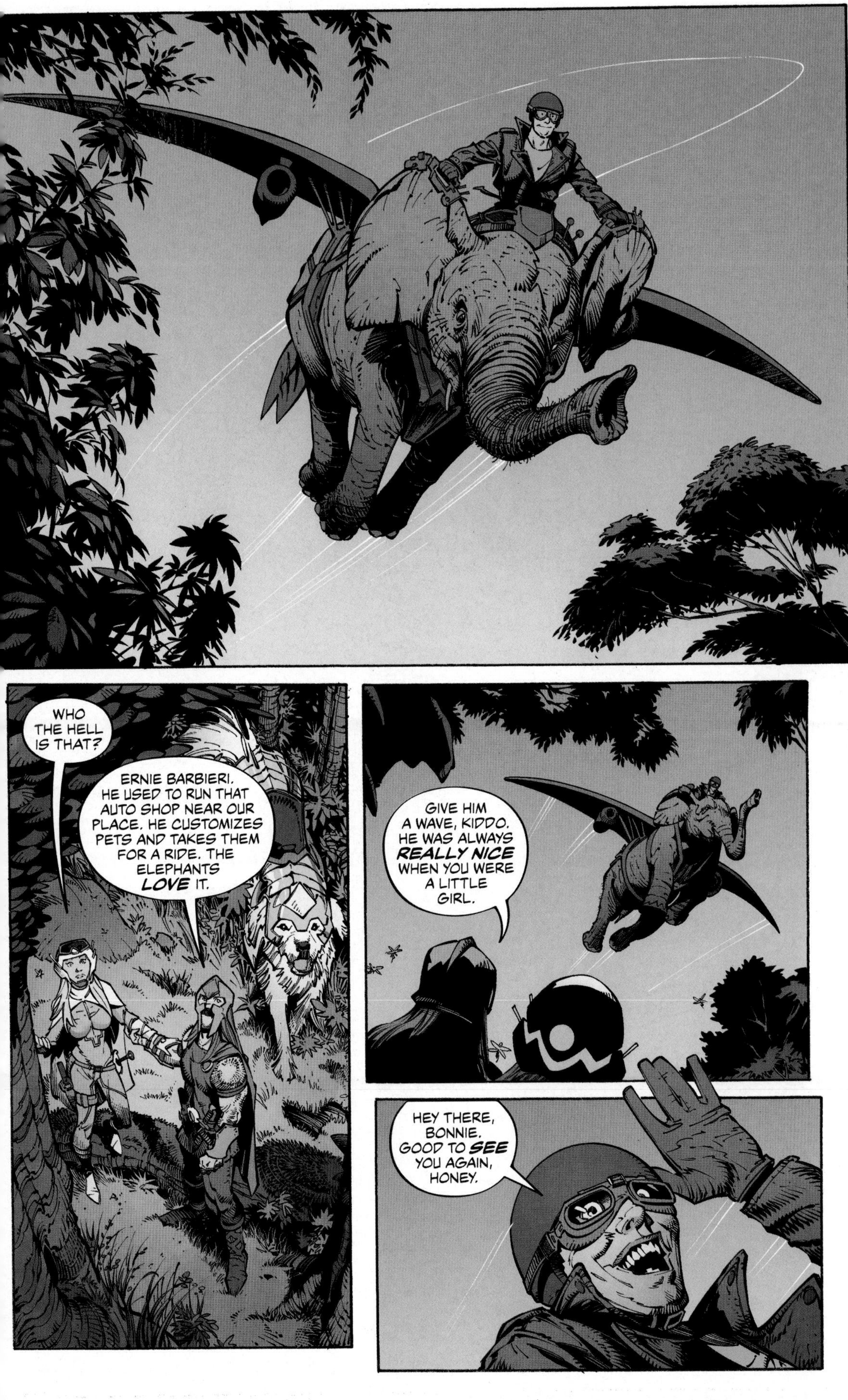
WHO THE HELL IS THAT?
ERNIE BARBIERI. HE USED TO RUN THAT AUTO SHOP NEAR OUR PLACE. HE CUSTOMIZES PETS AND TAKES THEM FOR A RIDE. THE ELEPHANTS LOVE IT.
GIVE HIM A WAVE, KIDDO. HE WAS ALWAYS REALLY NICE WHEN YOU WERE A LITTLE GIRL.
HEY THERE, BONNIE. GOOD TO SEE YOU AGAIN, HONEY.

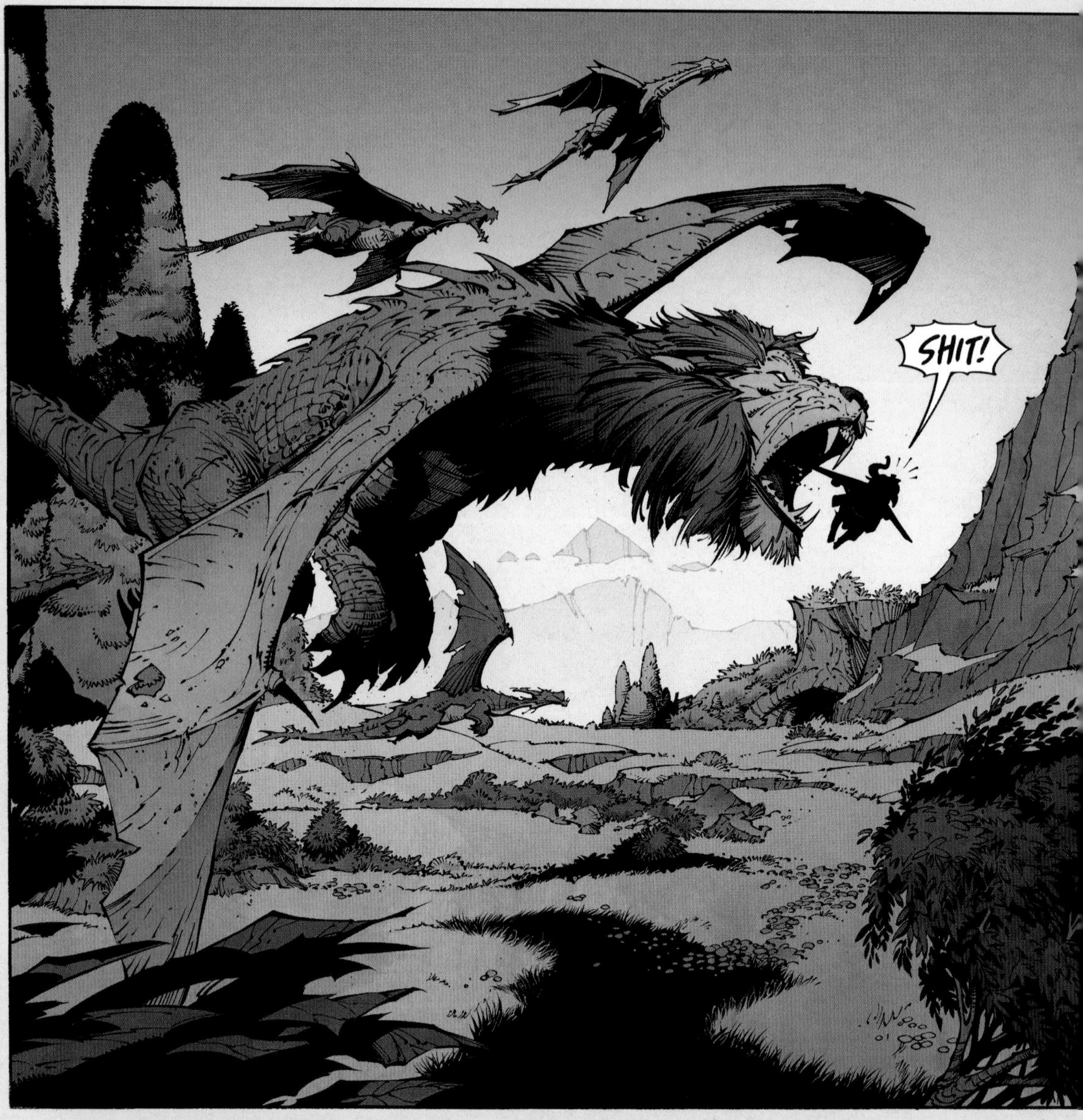
SHIT!

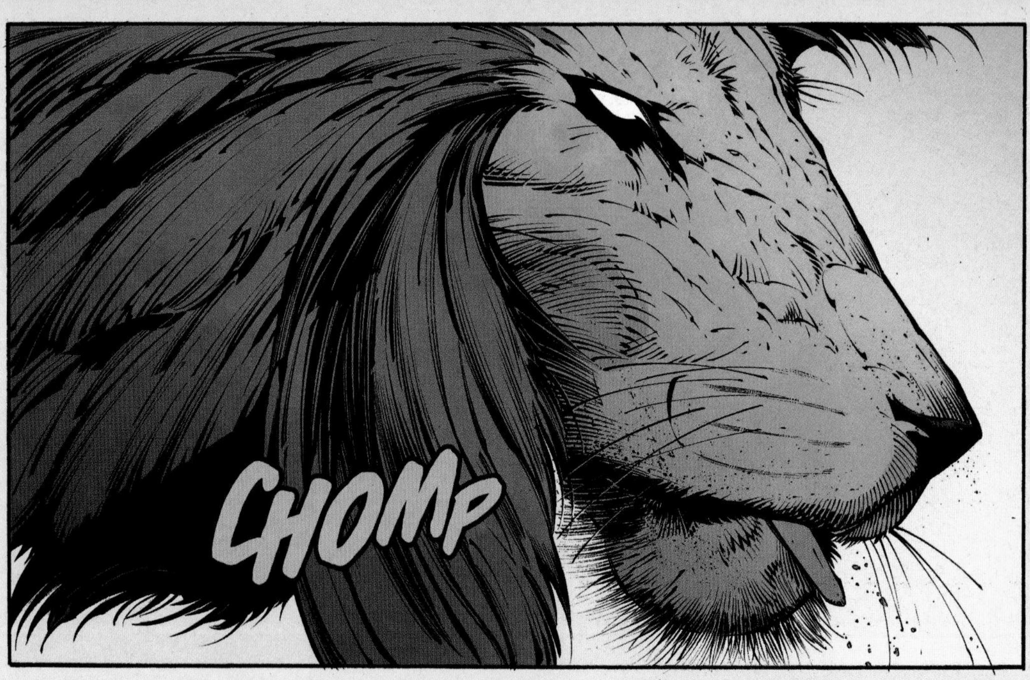
CHOMP

GET UNDER *THE TREES!*

SNAKT

WHAT'S *GOING ON?*

FLOCK OF DRAGONS HEADING FOR THE DARK LANDS. THEY AREN'T SUPPOSED TO CROSS THE LINE, BUT I TOLD YOU... THEY'RE GETTING *BOLDER.*

WHY DOES ONE OF THEM HAVE A LION'S HEAD?

THAT'S THEIR KING, *ARIMATHEA*. HE'S ONE OF LORD GOLGOTHA'S LOVERS AND THE MOST DANGEROUS SON OF A BITCH YOU EVER *MET.*

COME ON. LET'S GET DEEPER INTO THE WOODS. THE LAST THING WE NEED IS *THOSE* GUYS SEEING US.

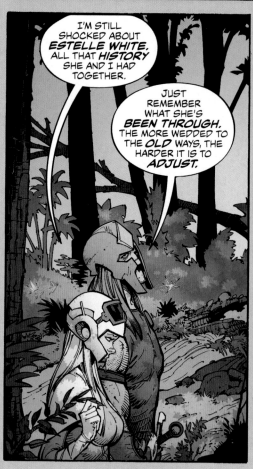

I'M STILL SHOCKED ABOUT *ESTELLE WHITE,* ALL THAT *HISTORY* SHE AND I HAD TOGETHER.

JUST REMEMBER WHAT SHE'S *BEEN THROUGH.* THE MORE WEDDED TO THE *OLD* WAYS, THE HARDER IT IS TO *ADJUST.*

THIS IS WHERE HER *HUSBAND'S* BURIED. *THE FAERIE KING.*

HE CAME THROUGH YEARS AGO, BUT HE WAS OLD WHEN HE ARRIVED AND DIED BEFORE SHE GOT HERE. THAT ALWAYS MAKES IT HARDER *TOO.*

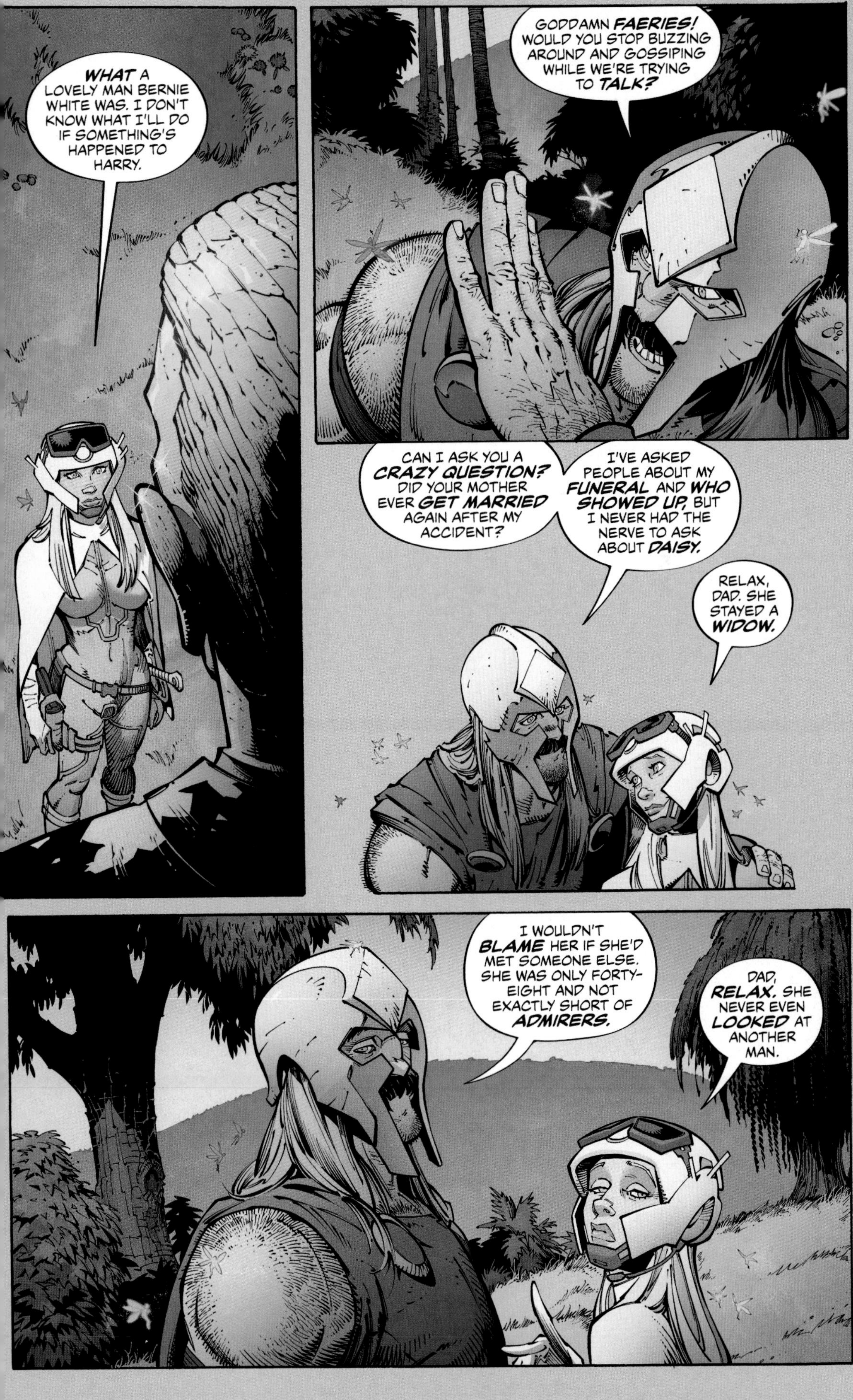

WHAT A LOVELY MAN BERNIE WHITE WAS. I DON'T KNOW WHAT I'LL DO IF SOMETHING'S HAPPENED TO HARRY.
GODDAMN FAERIES! WOULD YOU STOP BUZZING AROUND AND GOSSIPING WHILE WE'RE TRYING TO TALK?
CAN I ASK YOU A CRAZY QUESTION? DID YOUR MOTHER EVER GET MARRIED AGAIN AFTER MY ACCIDENT?
I'VE ASKED PEOPLE ABOUT MY FUNERAL AND WHO SHOWED UP, BUT I NEVER HAD THE NERVE TO ASK ABOUT DAISY.
RELAX, DAD. SHE STAYED A WIDOW.
I WOULDN'T BLAME HER IF SHE'D MET SOMEONE ELSE. SHE WAS ONLY FORTY-EIGHT AND NOT EXACTLY SHORT OF ADMIRERS.
DAD, RELAX. SHE NEVER EVEN LOOKED AT ANOTHER MAN.

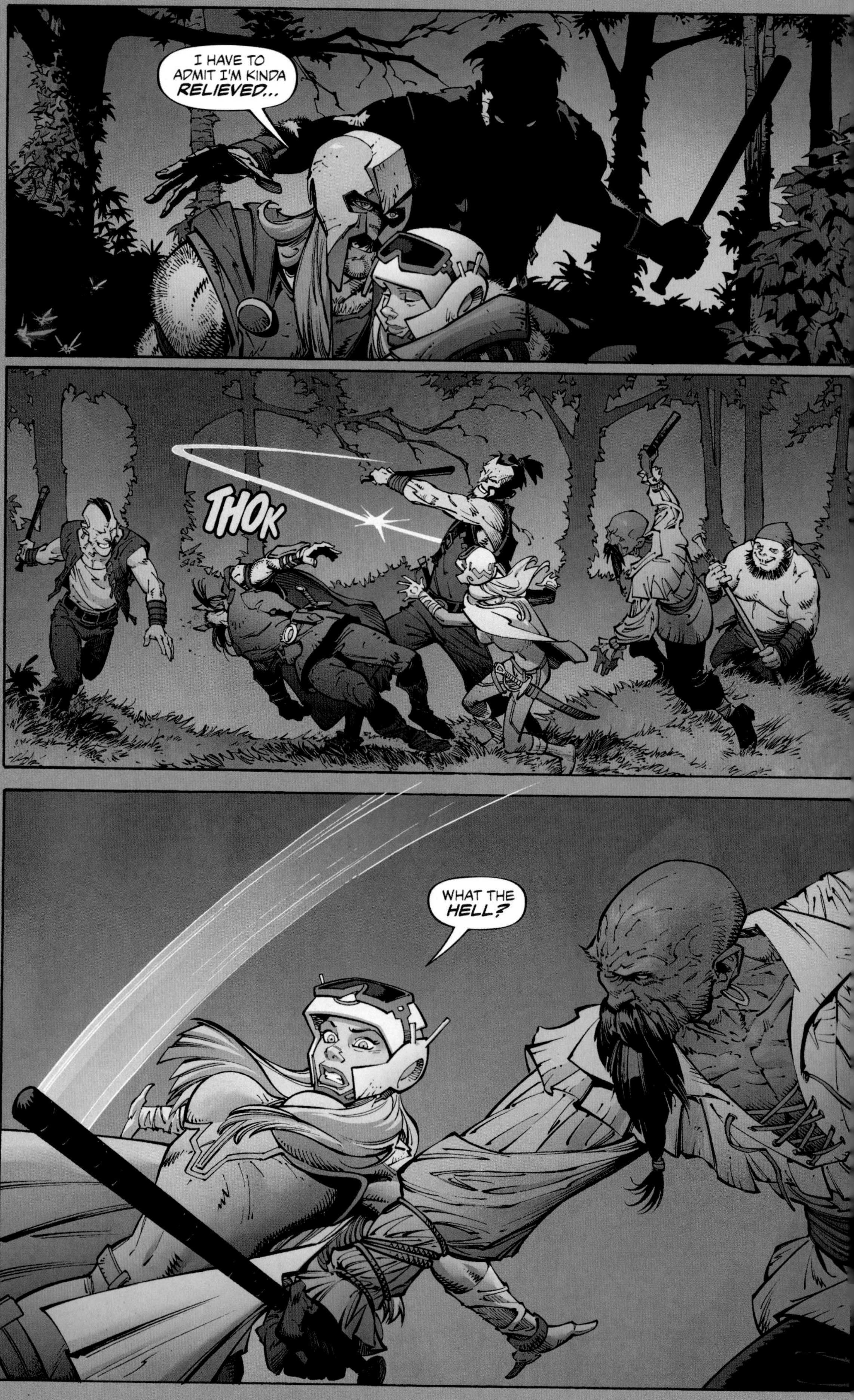
I HAVE TO ADMIT I'M KINDA RELIEVED...
THOK
WHAT THE HELL?

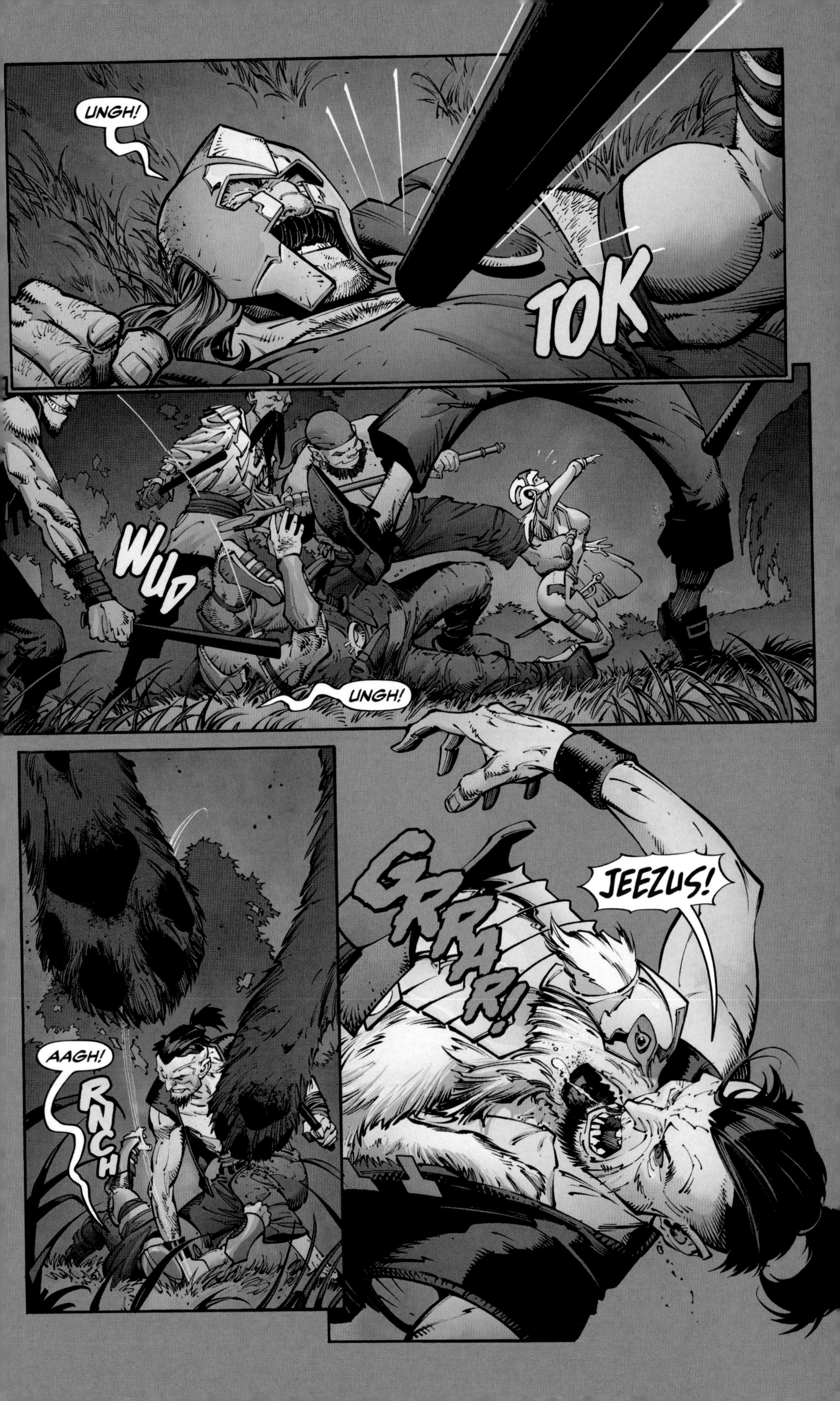
UNGH!
TOK
WUD
UNGH!
GRRAR!
JEEZUS!
AAGH!
RNCH

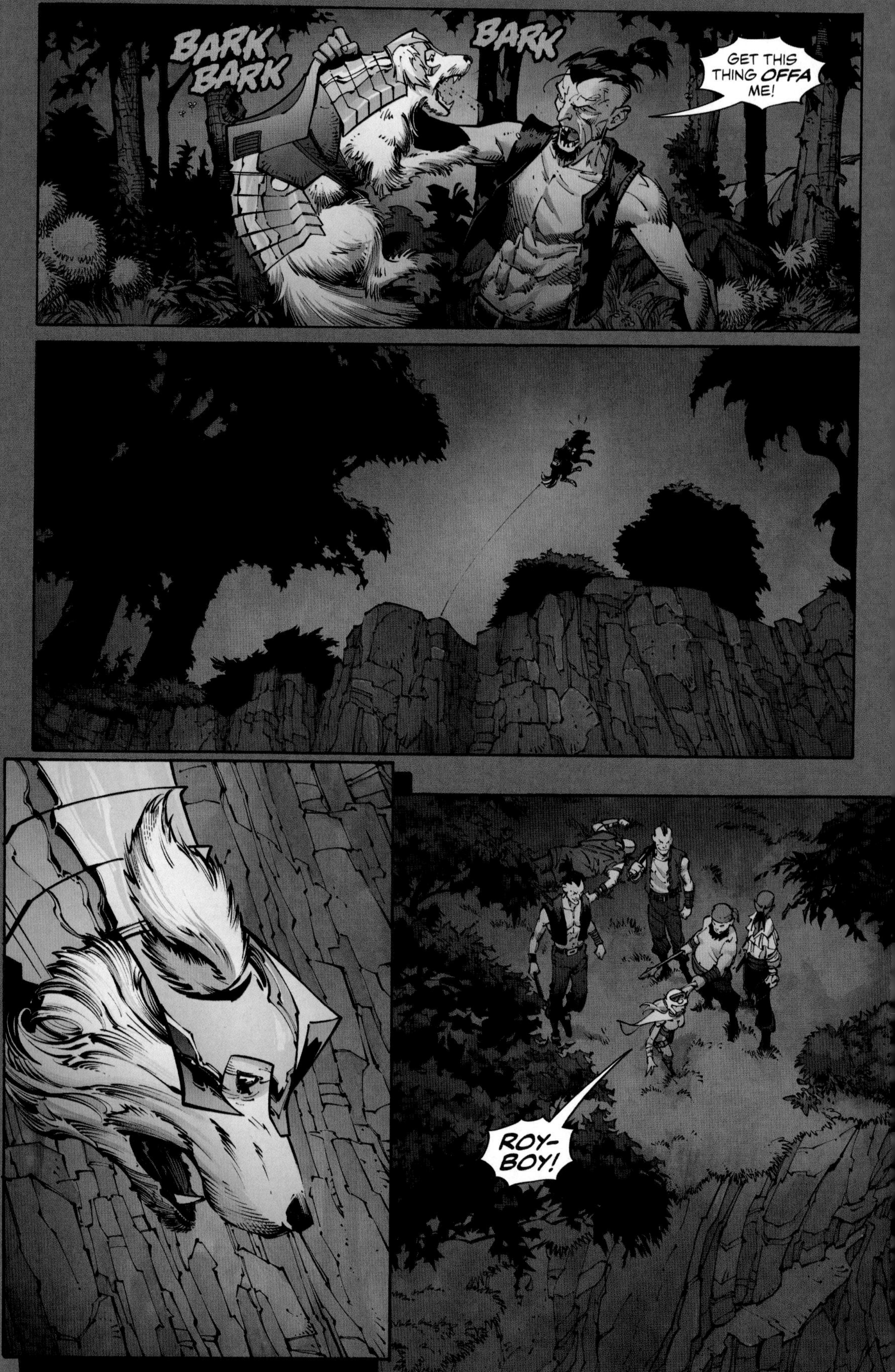
BARK BARK
BARK
GET THIS THING OFFA ME!
ROY-BOY!

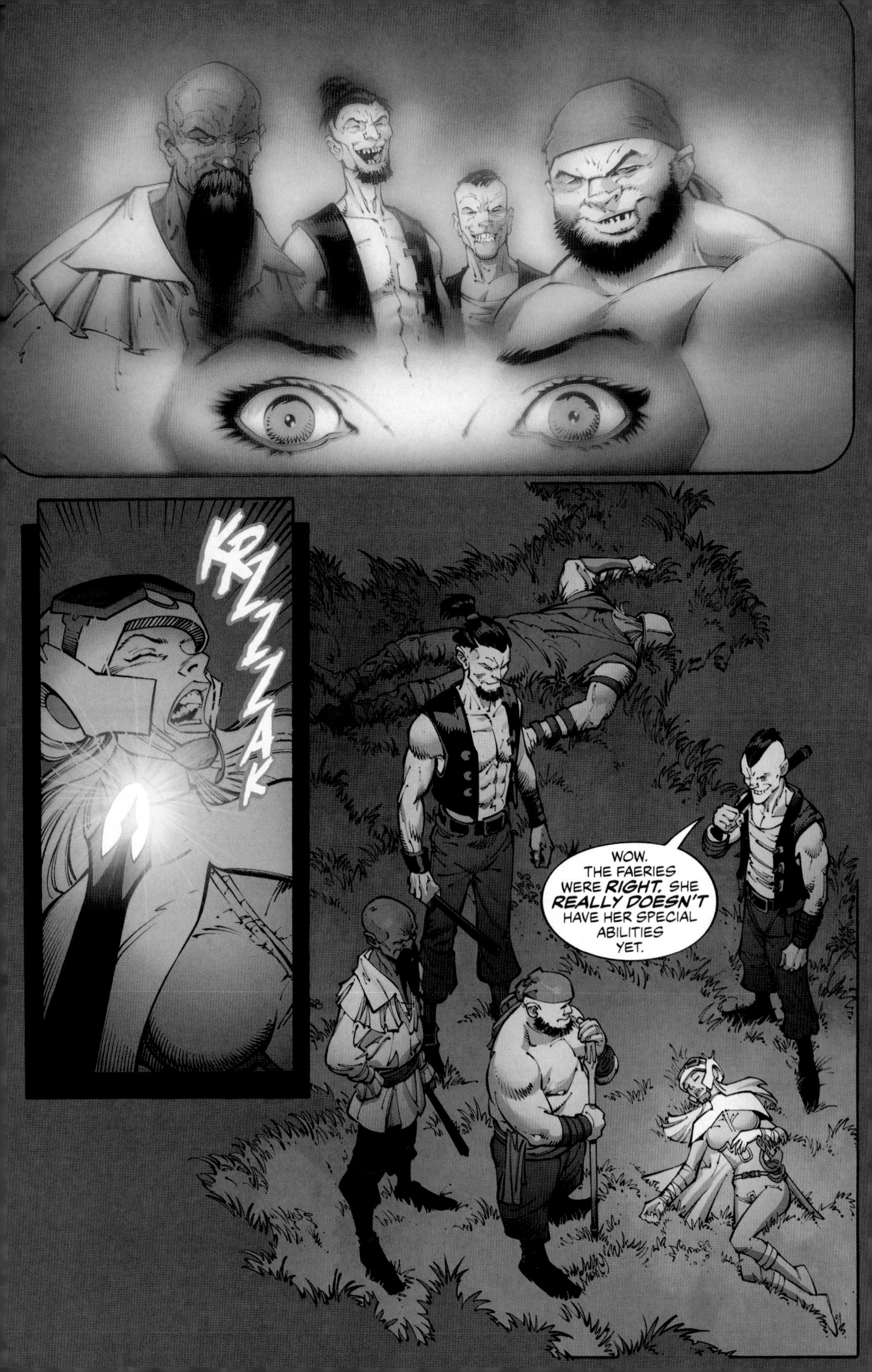
KRZZZZAK
WOW. THE FAERIES WERE RIGHT. SHE REALLY DOESN'T HAVE HER SPECIAL ABILITIES YET.

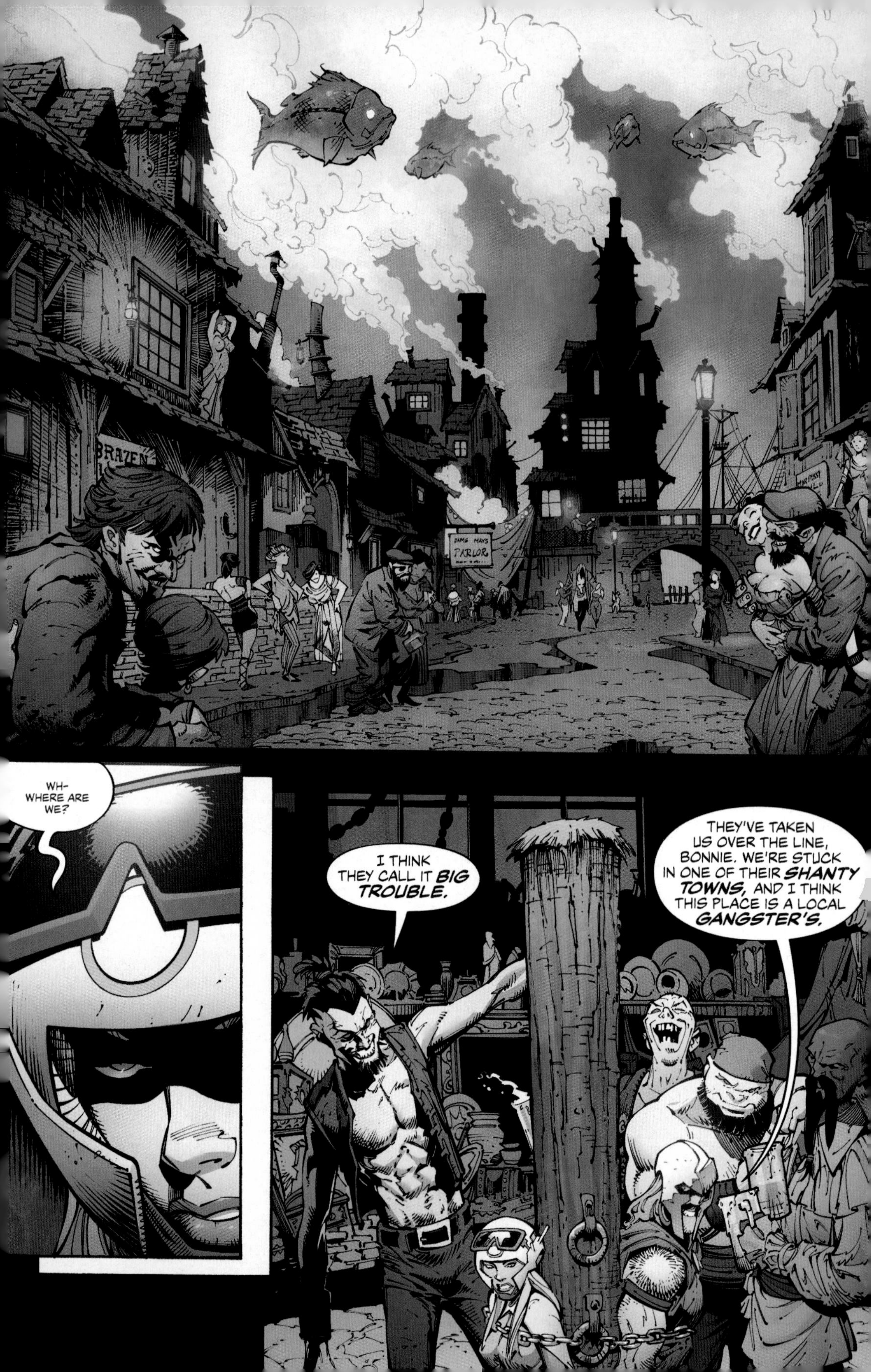
BRAZEN
WH- WHERE ARE WE?
I THINK THEY CALL IT BIG TROUBLE.
THEY'VE TAKEN US OVER THE LINE, BONNIE. WE'RE STUCK IN ONE OF THEIR SHANTY TOWNS, AND I THINK THIS PLACE IS A LOCAL GANGSTER'S.

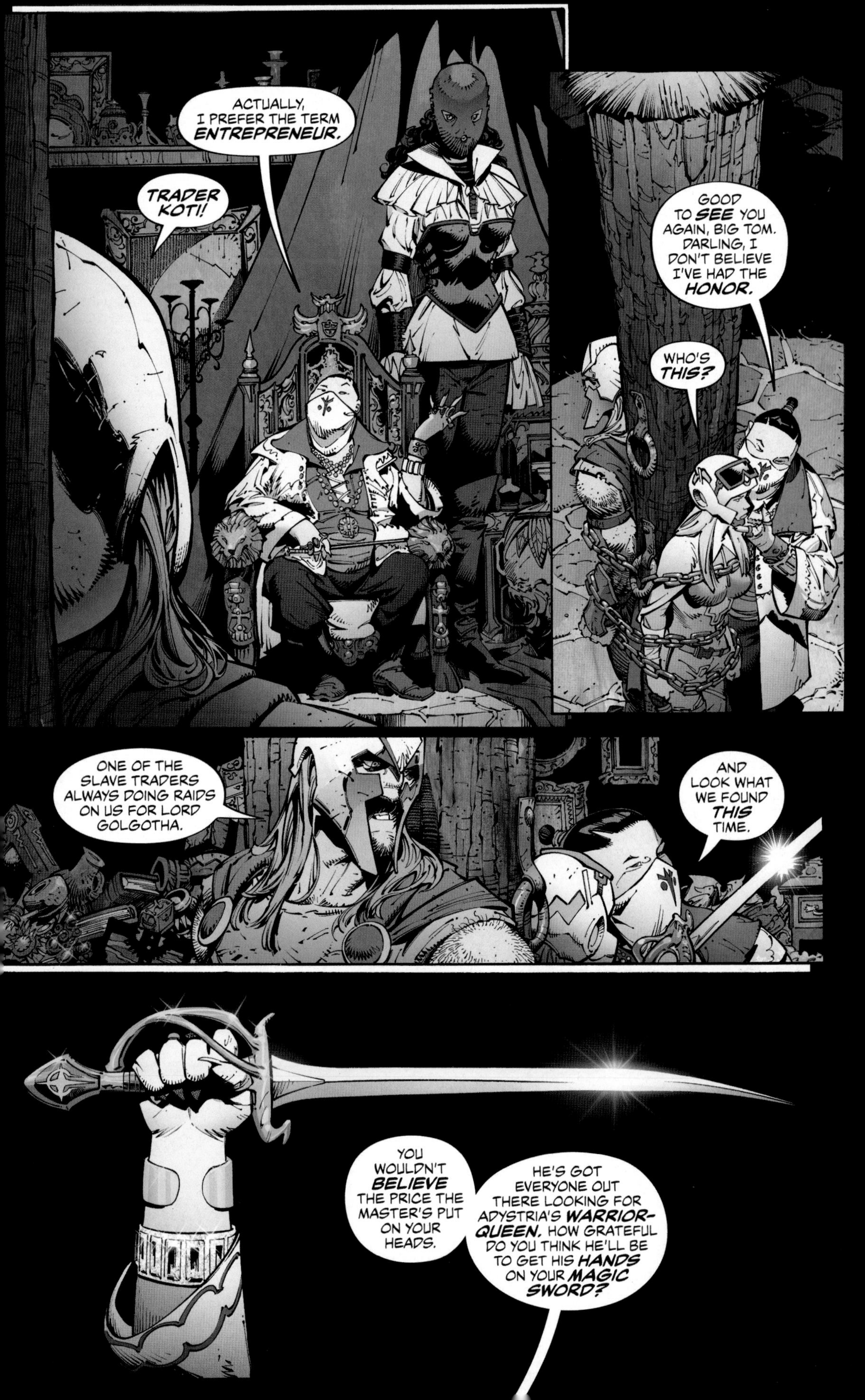
TRADER KOTI!
ACTUALLY, I PREFER THE TERM ENTREPRENEUR.
GOOD TO SEE YOU AGAIN, BIG TOM. DARLING, I DON'T BELIEVE I'VE HAD THE HONOR.
WHO'S THIS?
ONE OF THE SLAVE TRADERS ALWAYS DOING RAIDS ON US FOR LORD GOLGOTHA.
AND LOOK WHAT WE FOUND THIS TIME.
YOU WOULDN'T BELIEVE THE PRICE THE MASTER'S PUT ON YOUR HEADS.
HE'S GOT EVERYONE OUT THERE LOOKING FOR ADYSTRIA'S WARRIOR-QUEEN. HOW GRATEFUL DO YOU THINK HE'LL BE TO GET HIS HANDS ON YOUR MAGIC SWORD?

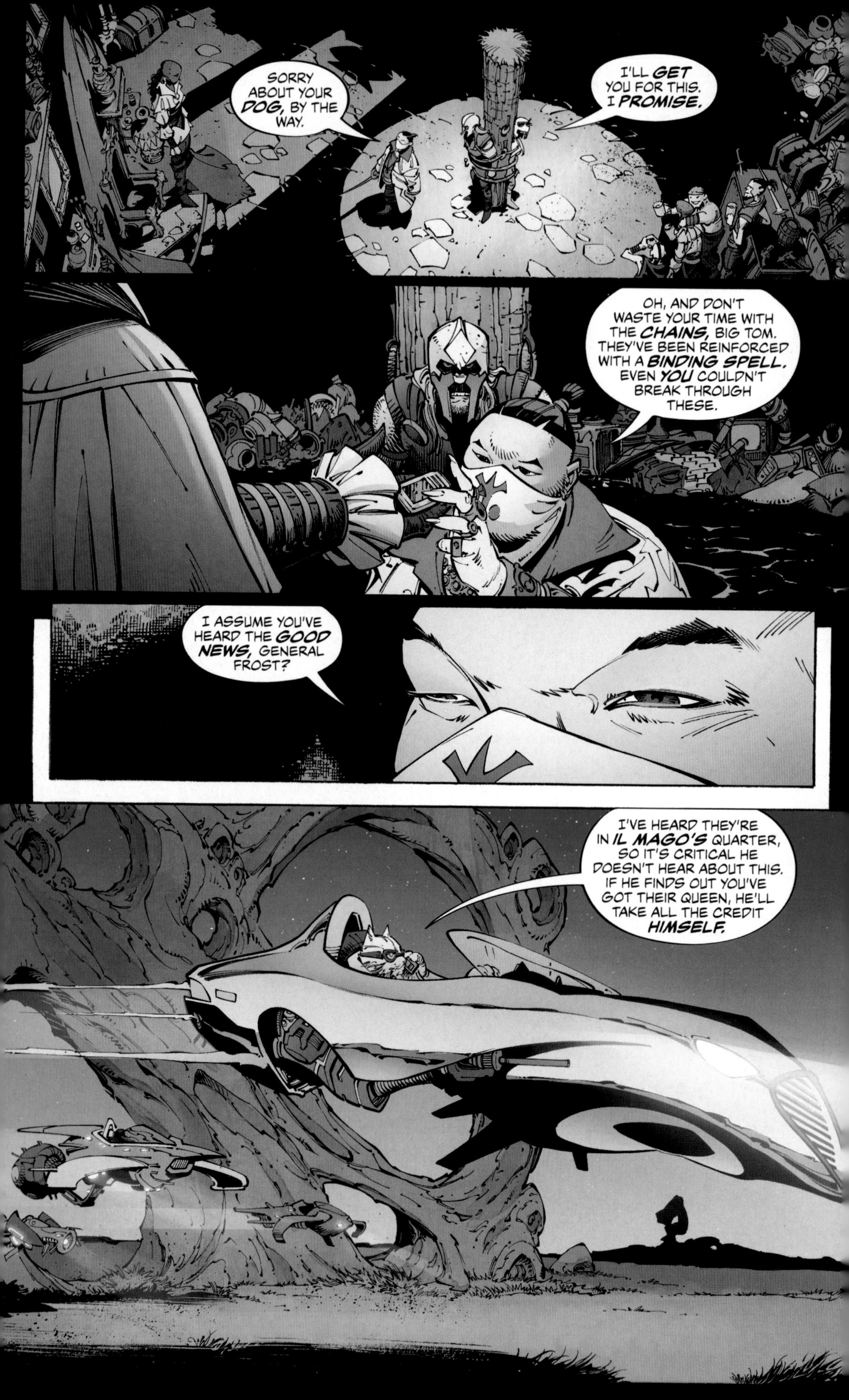
SORRY ABOUT YOUR DOG, BY THE WAY.
I'LL GET YOU FOR THIS. I PROMISE.
OH, AND DON'T WASTE YOUR TIME WITH THE CHAINS, BIG TOM. THEY'VE BEEN REINFORCED WITH A BINDING SPELL. EVEN YOU COULDN'T BREAK THROUGH THESE.
I ASSUME YOU'VE HEARD THE GOOD NEWS, GENERAL FROST?
I'VE HEARD THEY'RE IN IL MAGO'S QUARTER, SO IT'S CRITICAL HE DOESN'T HEAR ABOUT THIS. IF HE FINDS OUT YOU'VE GOT THEIR QUEEN, HE'LL TAKE ALL THE CREDIT HIMSELF.

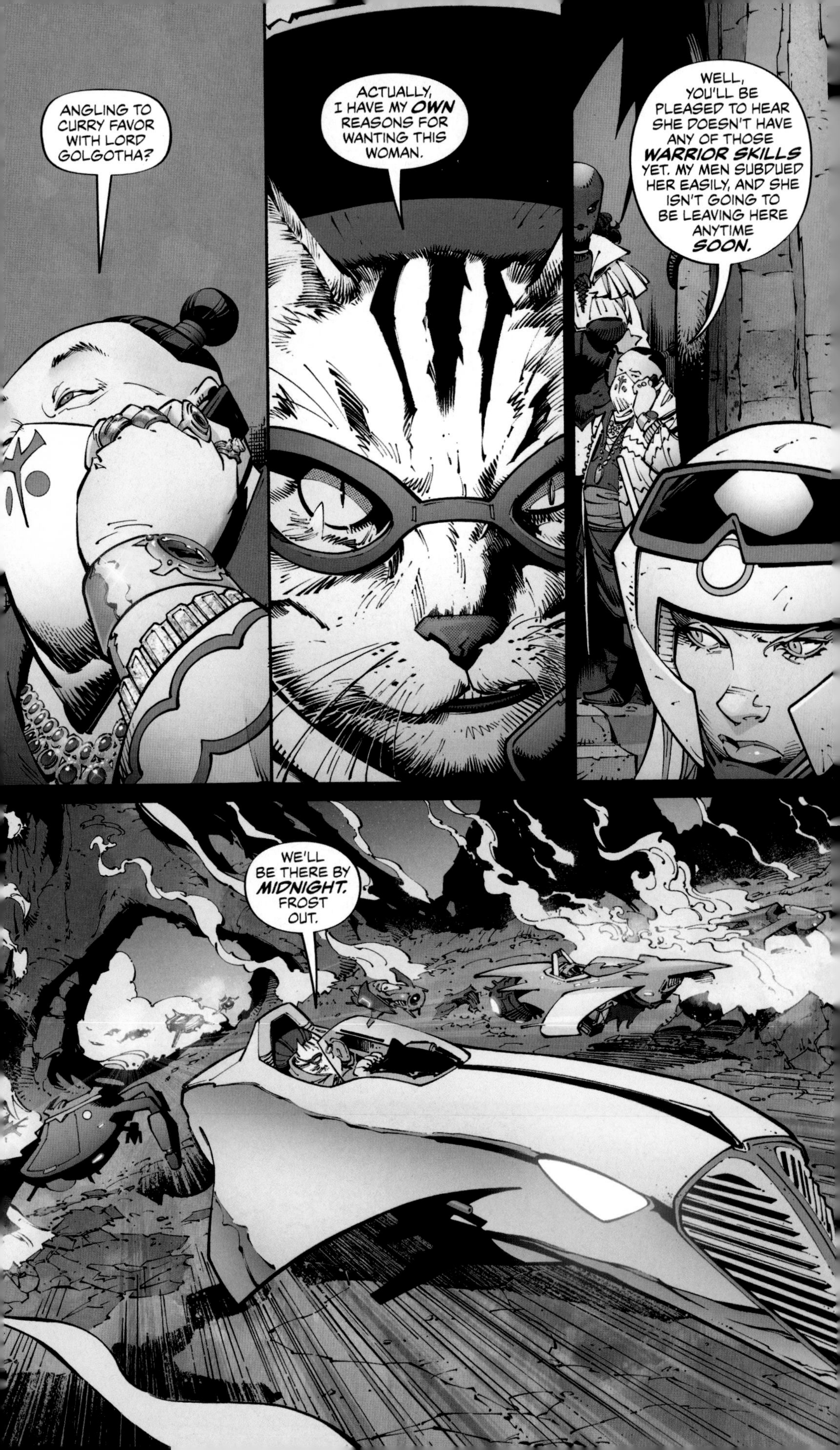
ANGLING TO CURRY FAVOR WITH LORD GOLGOTHA?
ACTUALLY, I HAVE MY **OWN** REASONS FOR WANTING THIS WOMAN.
WELL, YOU'LL BE PLEASED TO HEAR SHE DOESN'T HAVE ANY OF THOSE **WARRIOR SKILLS** YET. MY MEN SUBDUED HER EASILY, AND SHE ISN'T GOING TO BE LEAVING HERE ANYTIME **SOON.**
WE'LL BE THERE BY **MIDNIGHT.** FROST OUT.

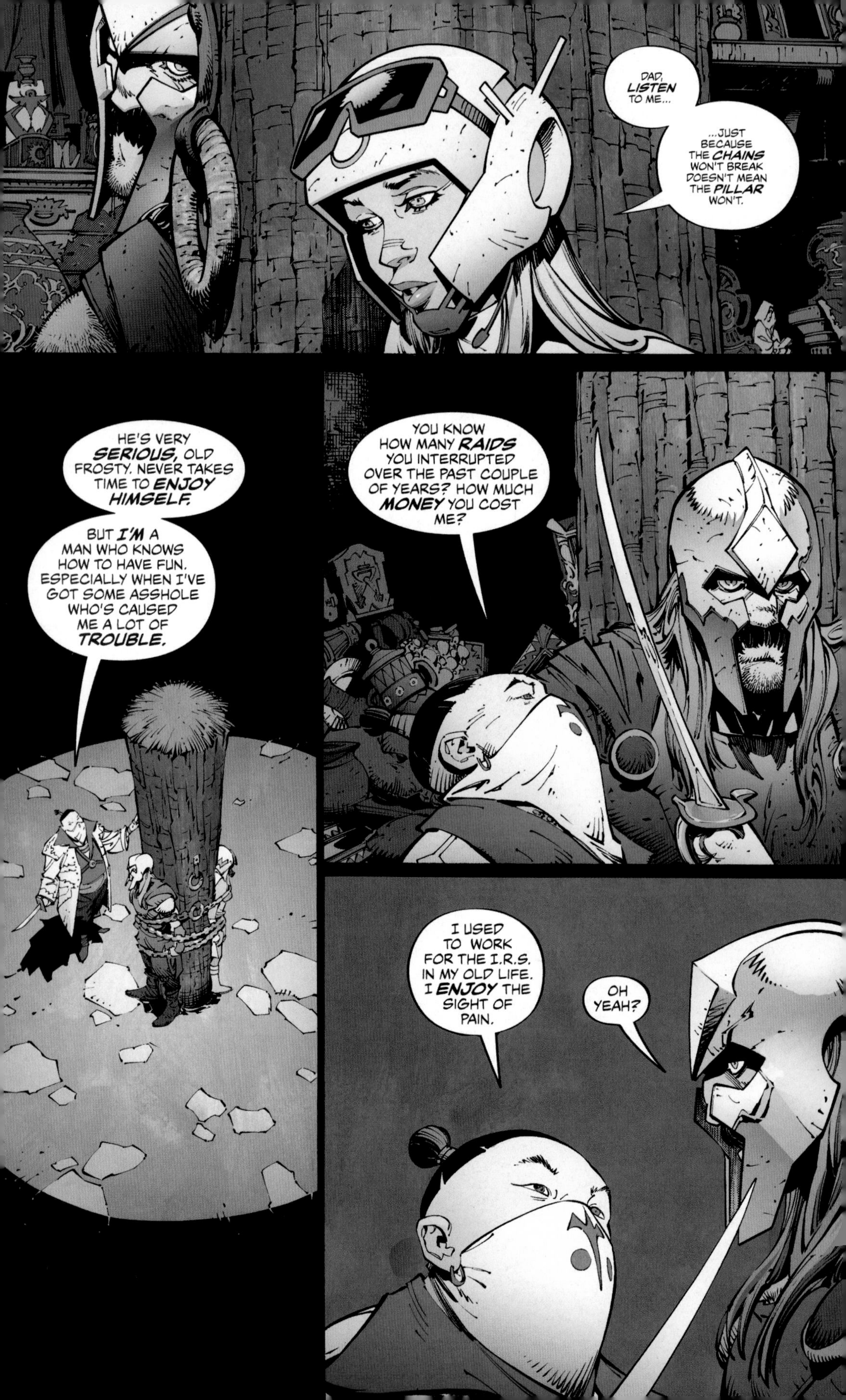
DAD, LISTEN TO ME...
...JUST BECAUSE THE CHAINS WON'T BREAK DOESN'T MEAN THE PILLAR WON'T.
HE'S VERY SERIOUS, OLD FROSTY. NEVER TAKES TIME TO ENJOY HIMSELF.
BUT I'M A MAN WHO KNOWS HOW TO HAVE FUN. ESPECIALLY WHEN I'VE GOT SOME ASSHOLE WHO'S CAUSED ME A LOT OF TROUBLE.
YOU KNOW HOW MANY RAIDS YOU INTERRUPTED OVER THE PAST COUPLE OF YEARS? HOW MUCH MONEY YOU COST ME?
I USED TO WORK FOR THE I.R.S. IN MY OLD LIFE. I ENJOY THE SIGHT OF PAIN.
OH YEAH?

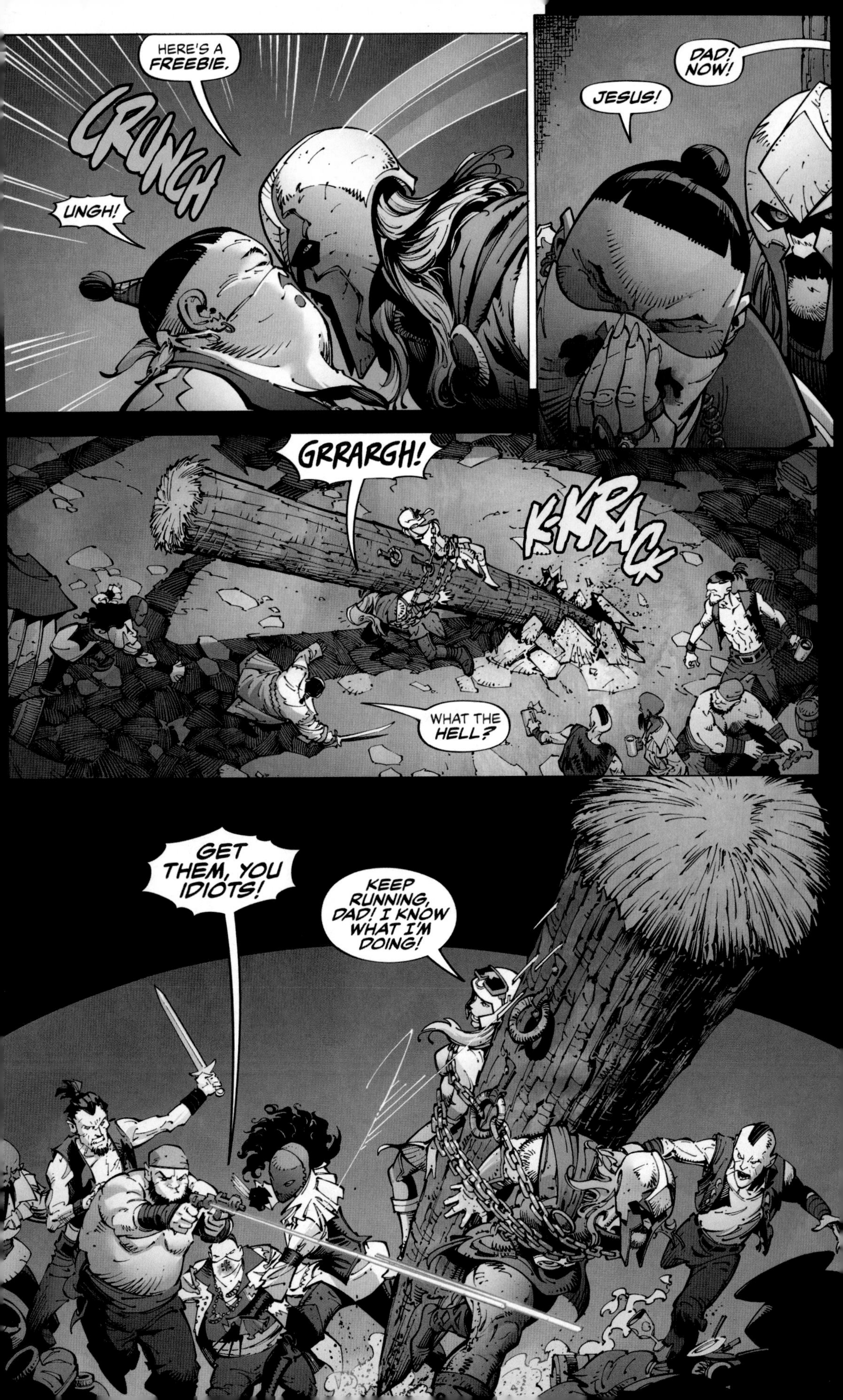
HERE'S A FREEBIE.
CRUNCH
UNGH!
DAD! NOW!
JESUS!
GRRARGH!
K-KRACK
WHAT THE HELL?
GET THEM, YOU IDIOTS!
KEEP RUNNING, DAD! I KNOW WHAT I'M DOING!

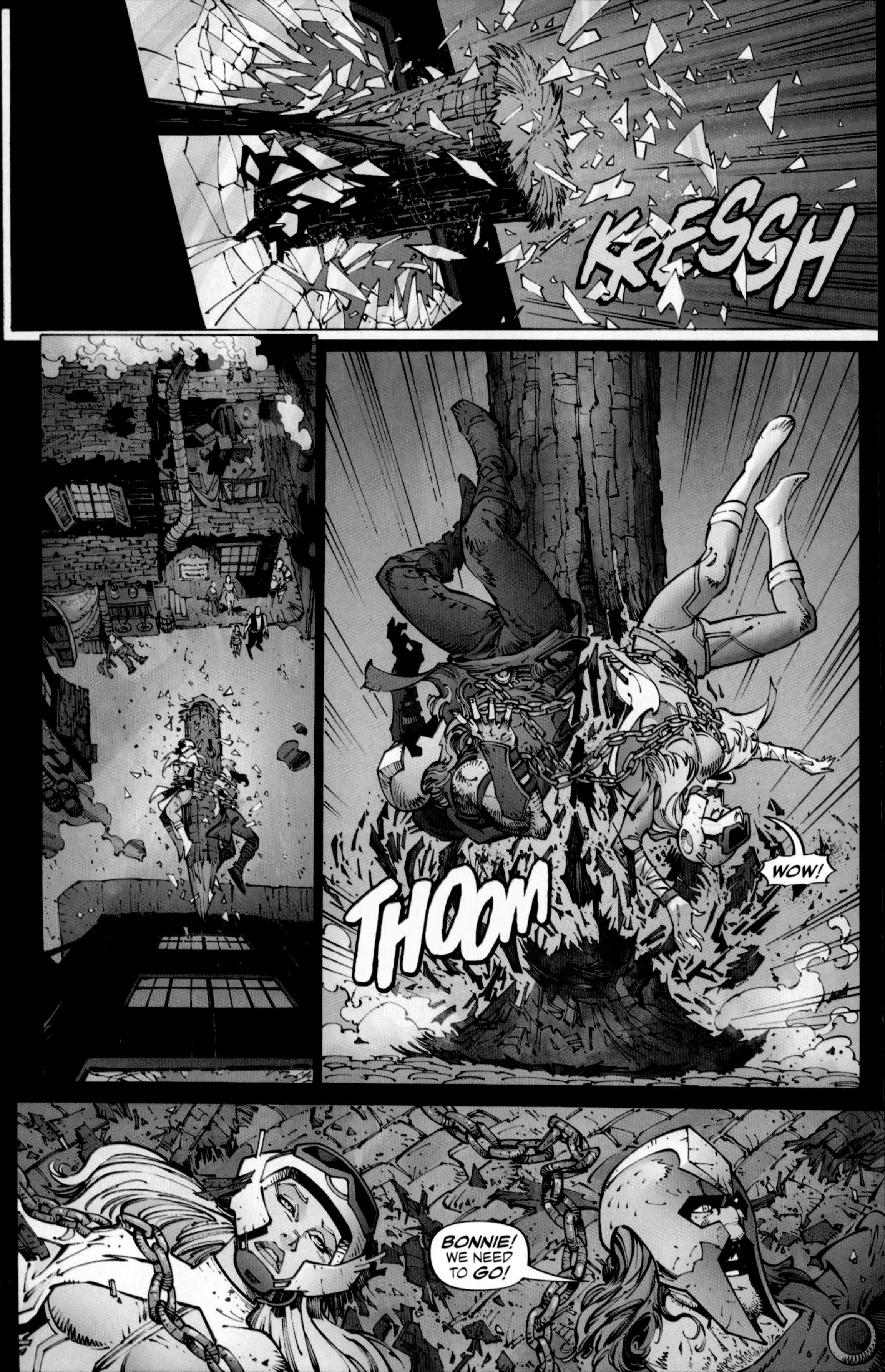
KRESSH
THOOM
WOW!
BONNIE! WE NEED TO GO!

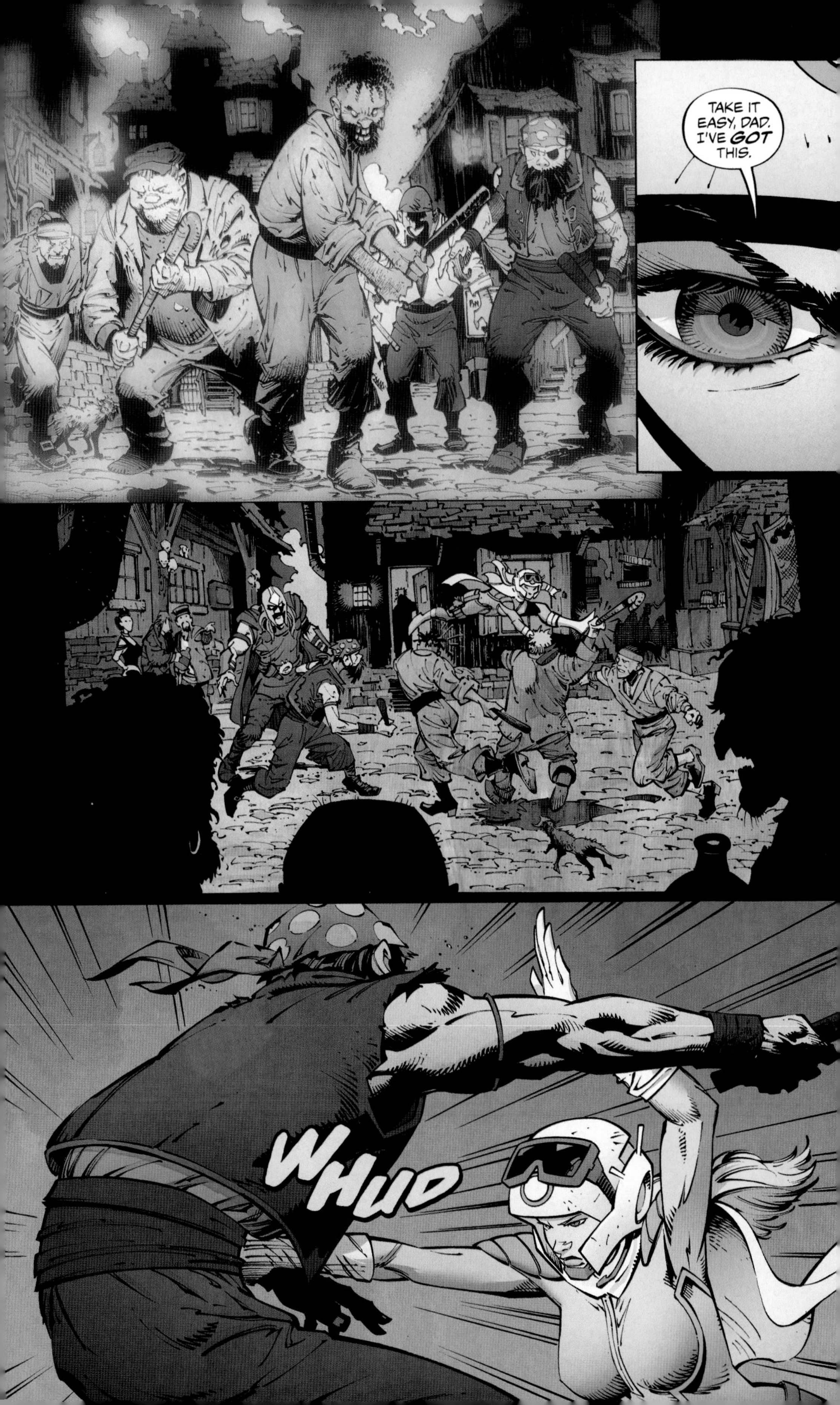
TAKE IT EASY, DAD. I'VE GOT THIS.
WHUD

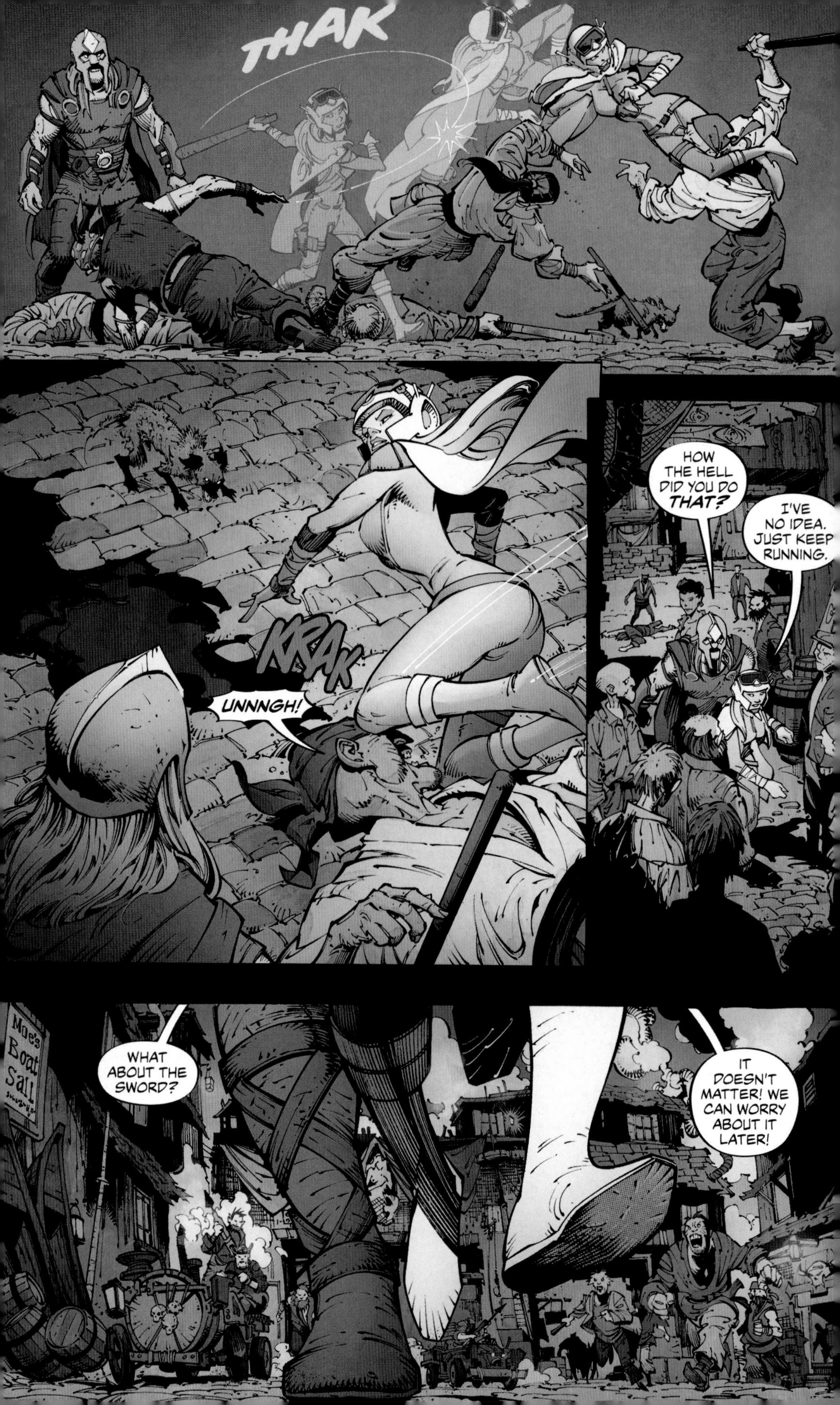
THAK
KRAK
UNNNGH!
HOW THE HELL DID YOU DO THAT?
I'VE NO IDEA. JUST KEEP RUNNING.
Moe's Boat Sail
WHAT ABOUT THE SWORD?
IT DOESN'T MATTER! WE CAN WORRY ABOUT IT LATER!

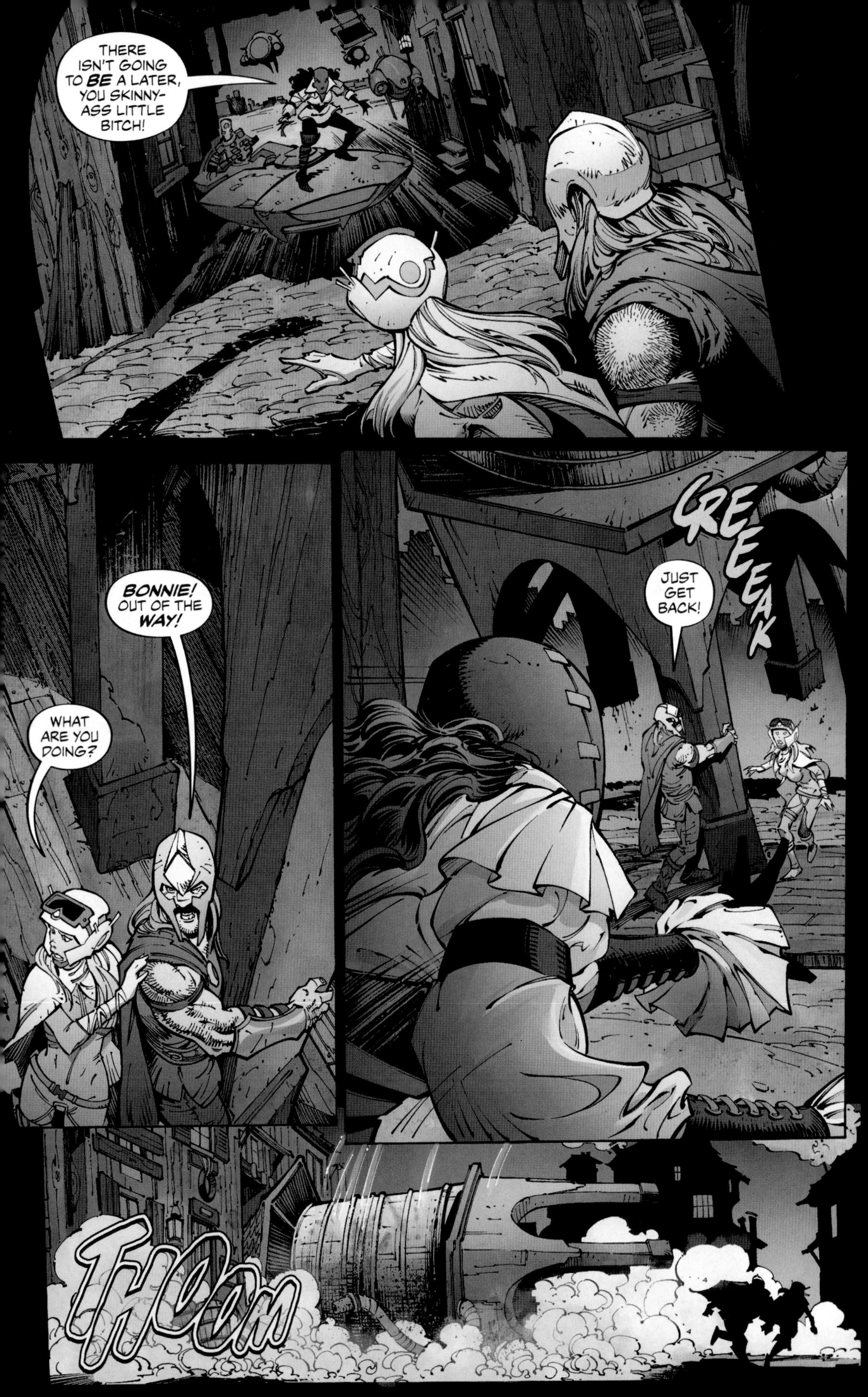
THERE ISN'T GOING TO BE A LATER, YOU SKINNY-ASS LITTLE BITCH!
BONNIE! OUT OF THE WAY!
WHAT ARE YOU DOING?
CREEEEAK
JUST GET BACK!

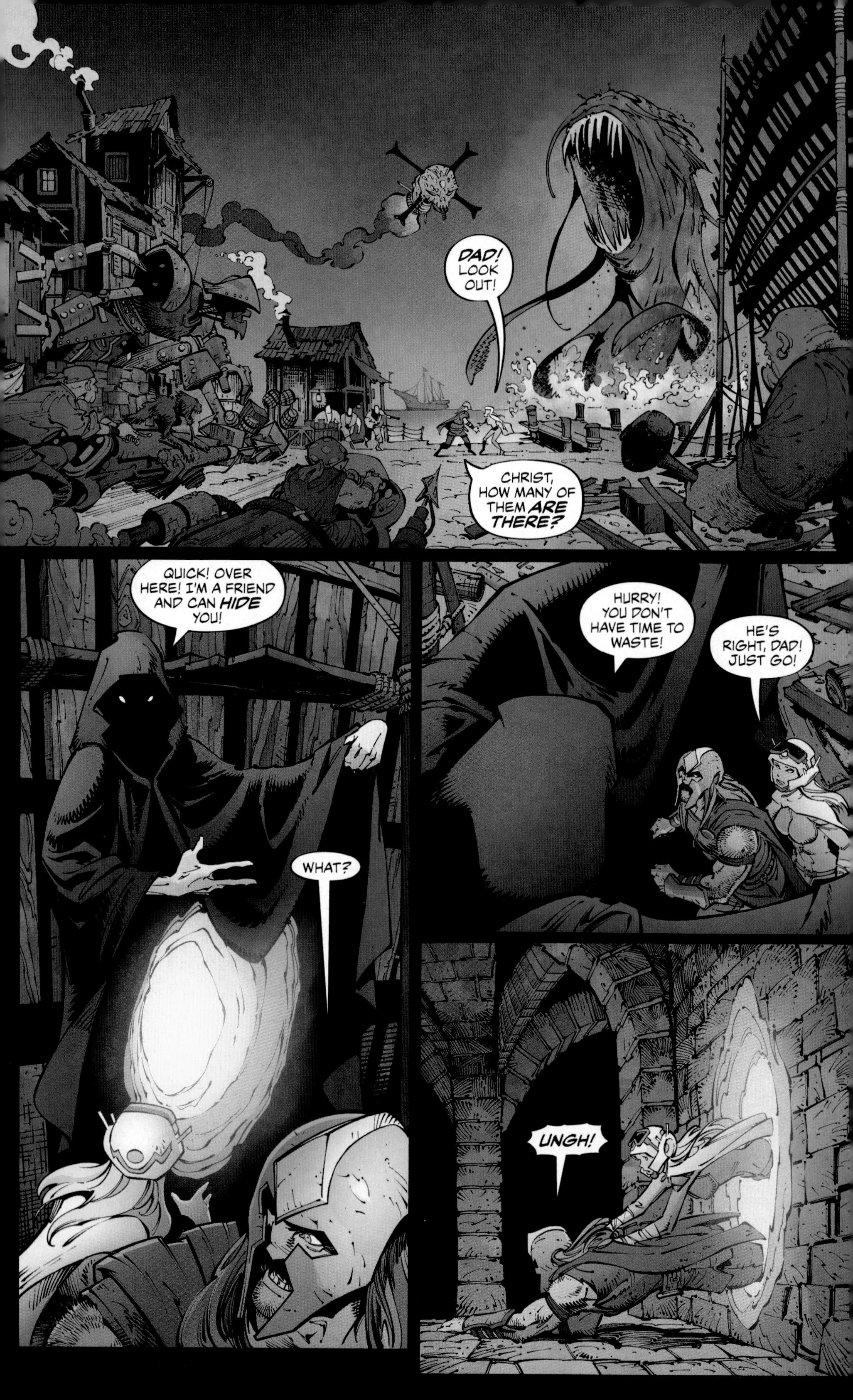
DAD! LOOK OUT!
CHRIST, HOW MANY OF THEM ARE THERE?
QUICK! OVER HERE! I'M A FRIEND AND CAN HIDE YOU!
WHAT?
HURRY! YOU DON'T HAVE TIME TO WASTE!
HE'S RIGHT, DAD! JUST GO!
UNGH!

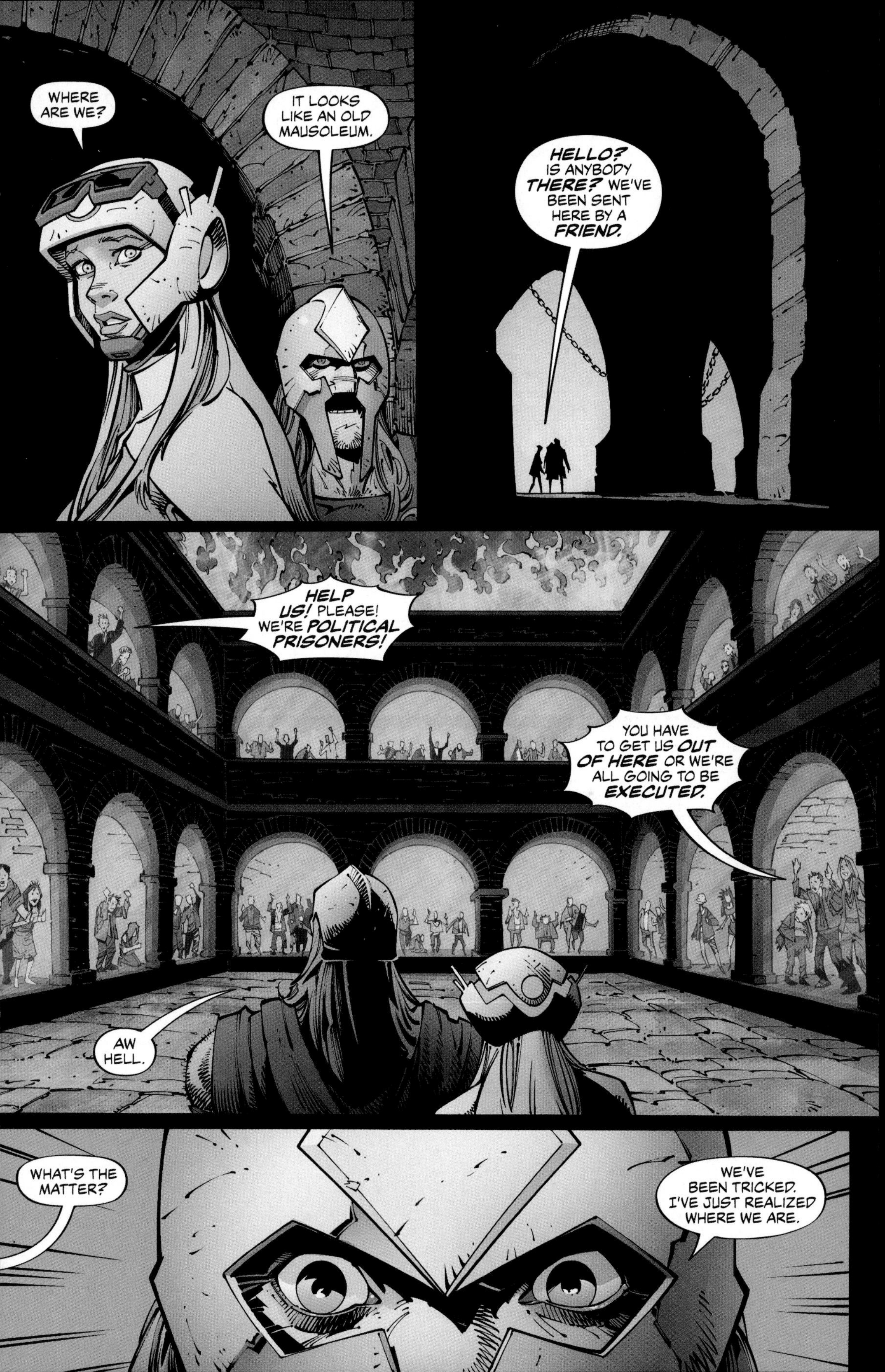
WHERE ARE WE?
IT LOOKS LIKE AN OLD MAUSOLEUM.
HELLO? IS ANYBODY THERE? WE'VE BEEN SENT HERE BY A FRIEND.
HELP US! PLEASE! WE'RE POLITICAL PRISONERS!
YOU HAVE TO GET US OUT OF HERE OR WE'RE ALL GOING TO BE EXECUTED.
AW HELL.
WHAT'S THE MATTER?
WE'VE BEEN TRICKED. I'VE JUST REALIZED WHERE WE ARE.

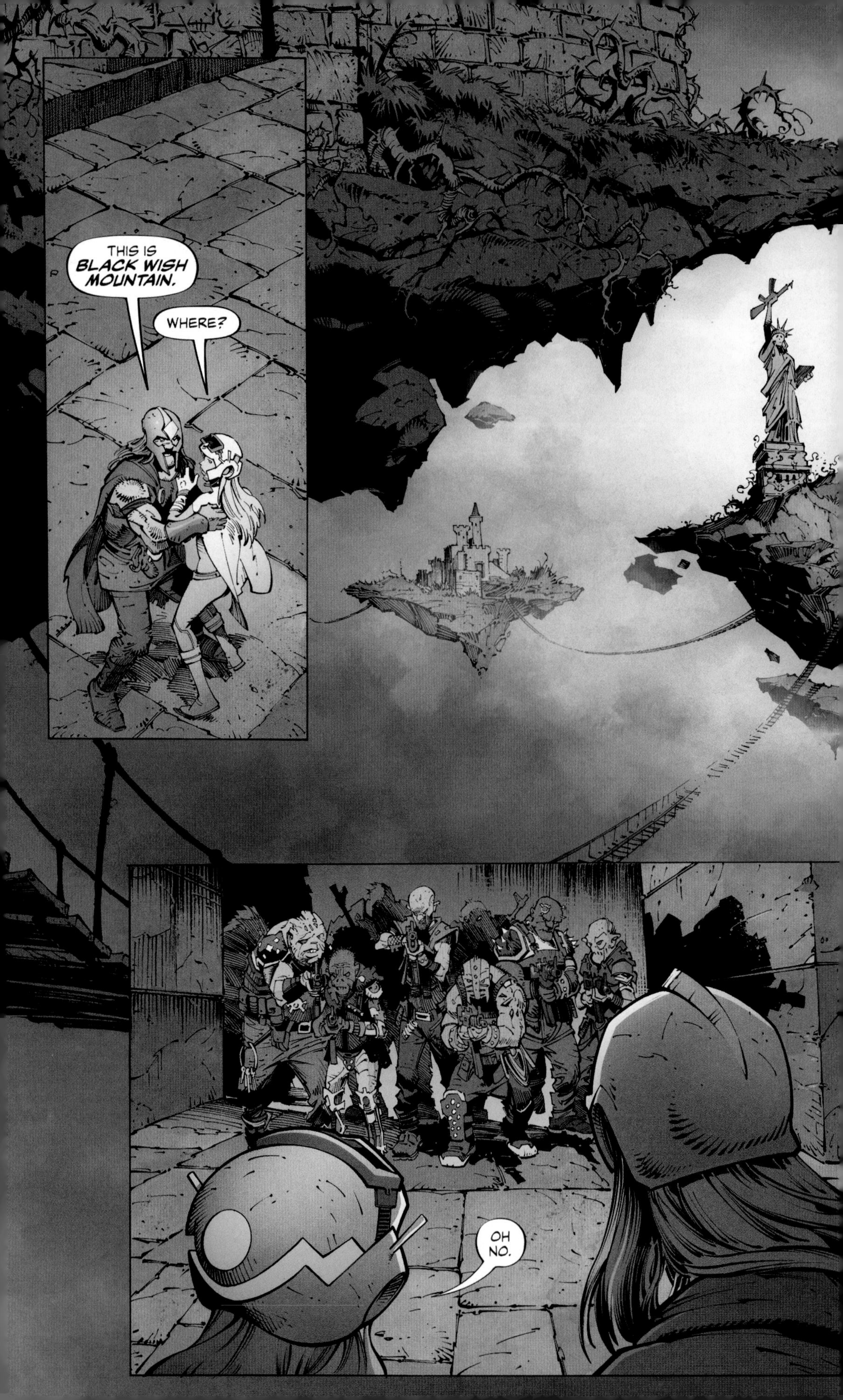
THIS IS BLACK WISH MOUNTAIN.
WHERE?
OH NO.

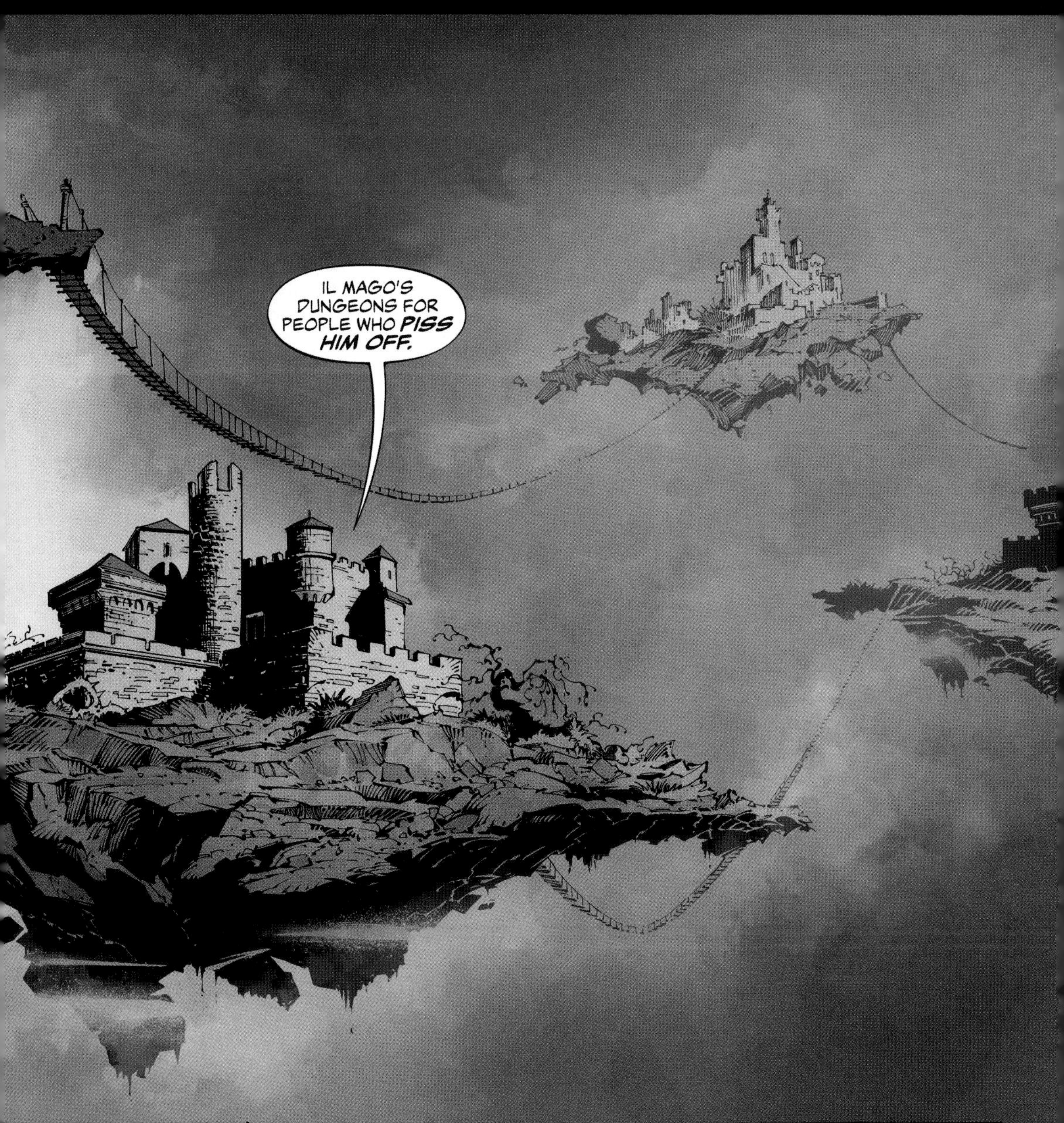
IL MAGO'S DUNGEONS FOR PEOPLE WHO PISS HIM OFF.

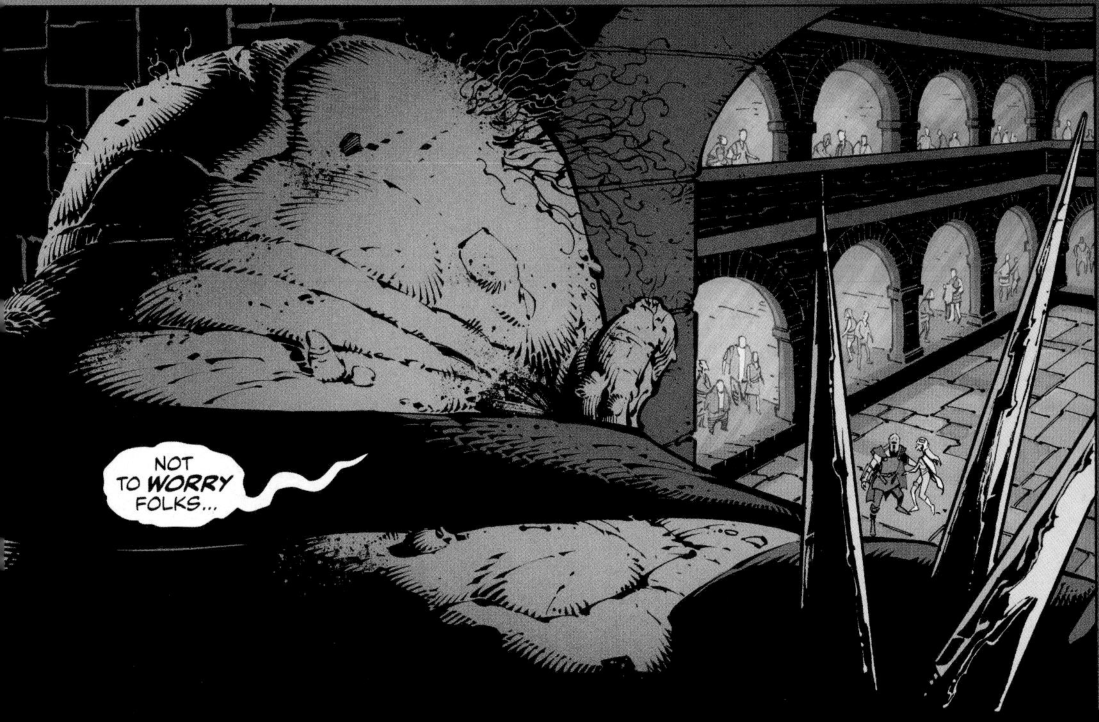
NOT TO WORRY FOLKS...

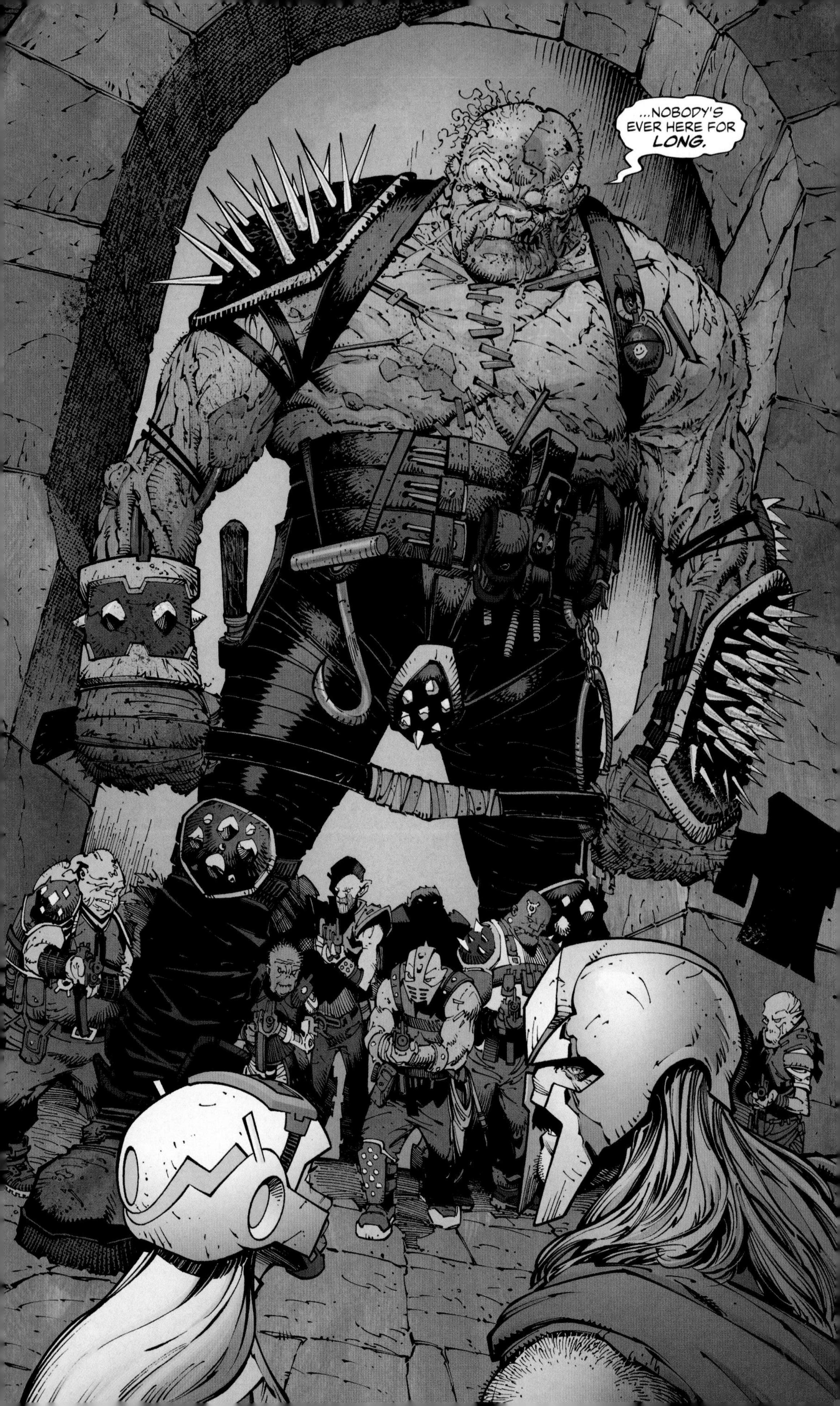
...NOBODY'S EVER HERE FOR LONG.

ISSUE THREE, COVER B

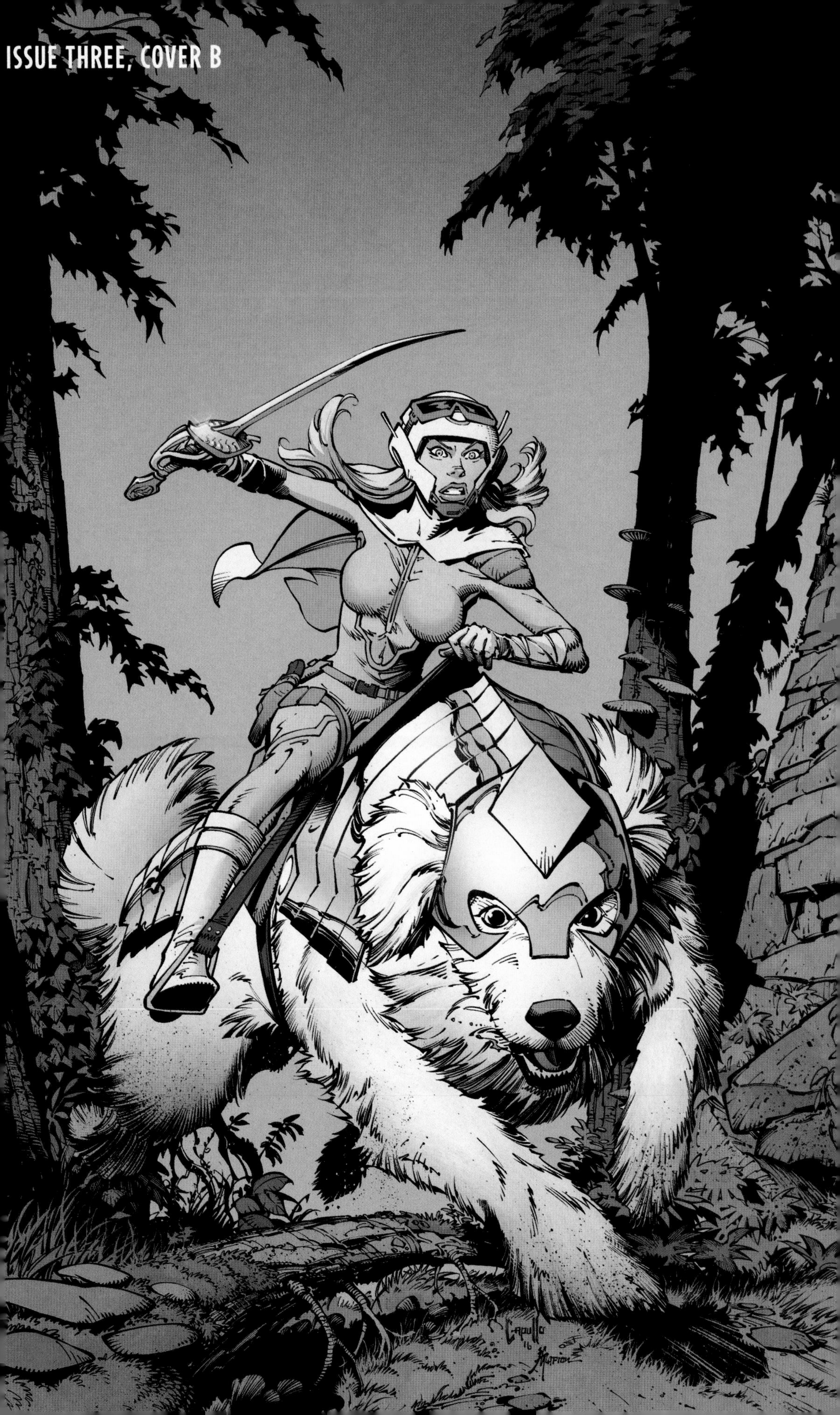

FOUR

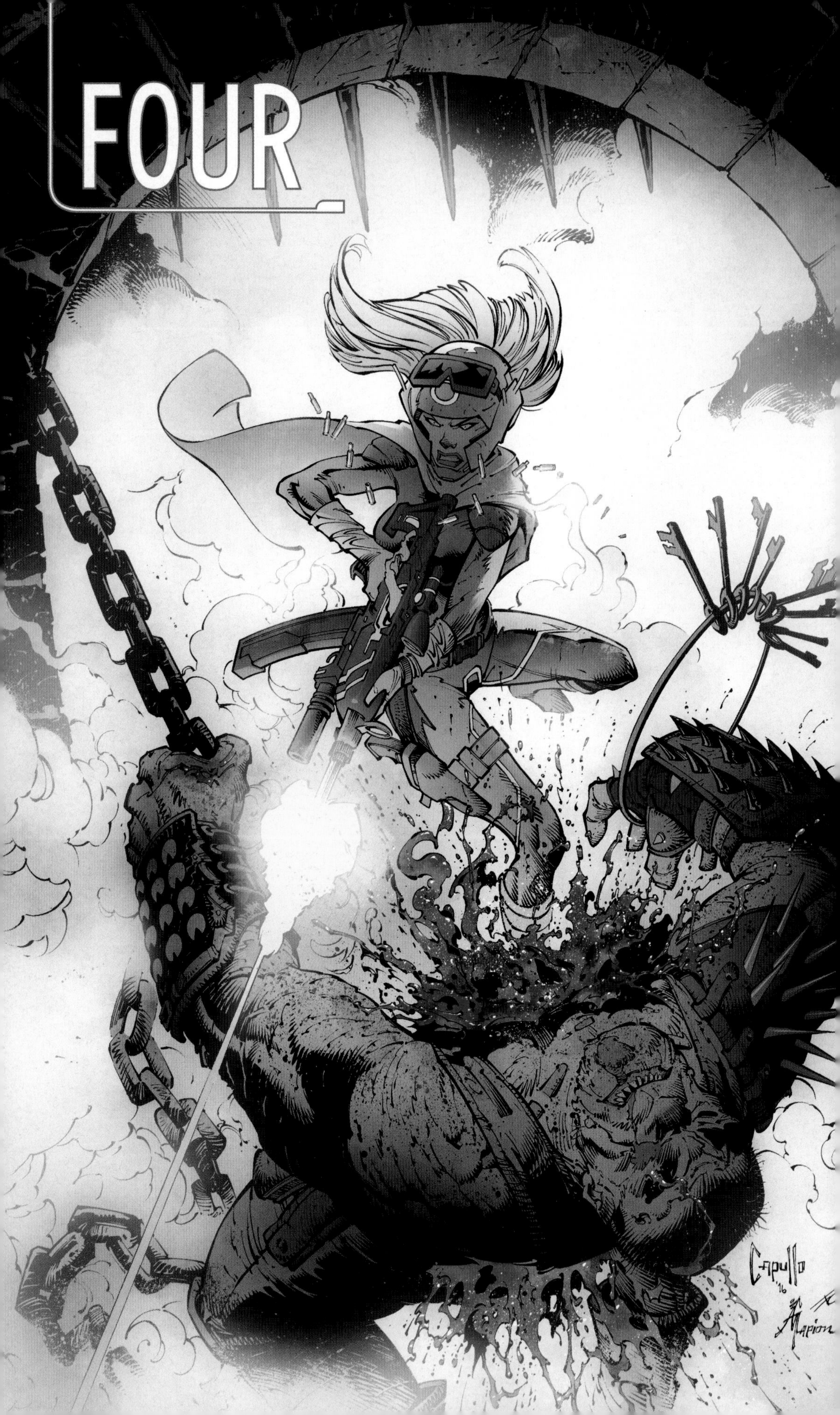

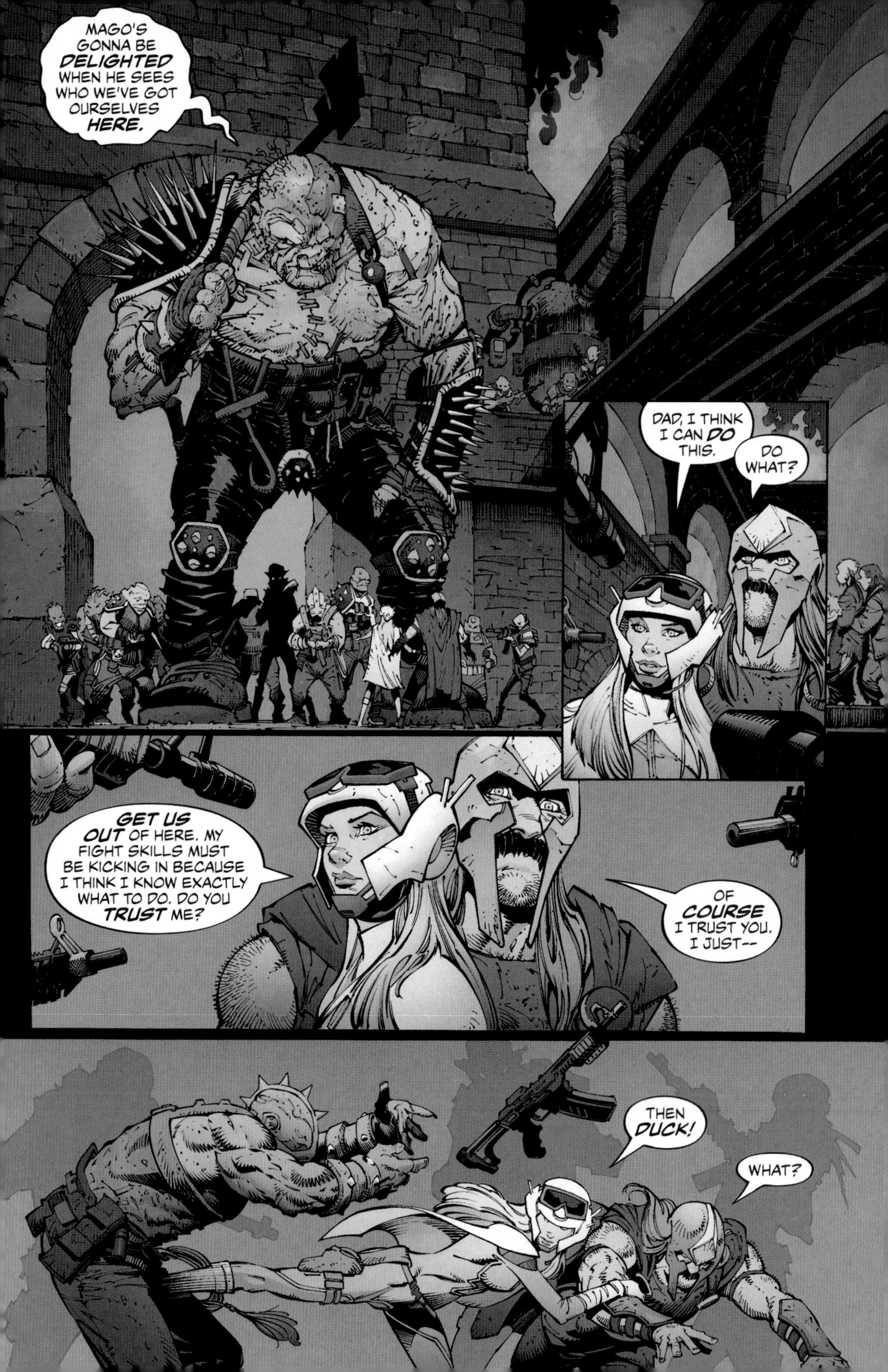
MAGO'S GONNA BE DELIGHTED WHEN HE SEES WHO WE'VE GOT OURSELVES HERE.
DAD, I THINK I CAN DO THIS.
DO WHAT?
GET US OUT OF HERE. MY FIGHT SKILLS MUST BE KICKING IN BECAUSE I THINK I KNOW EXACTLY WHAT TO DO. DO YOU TRUST ME?
OF COURSE I TRUST YOU. I JUST--
THEN DUCK!
WHAT?

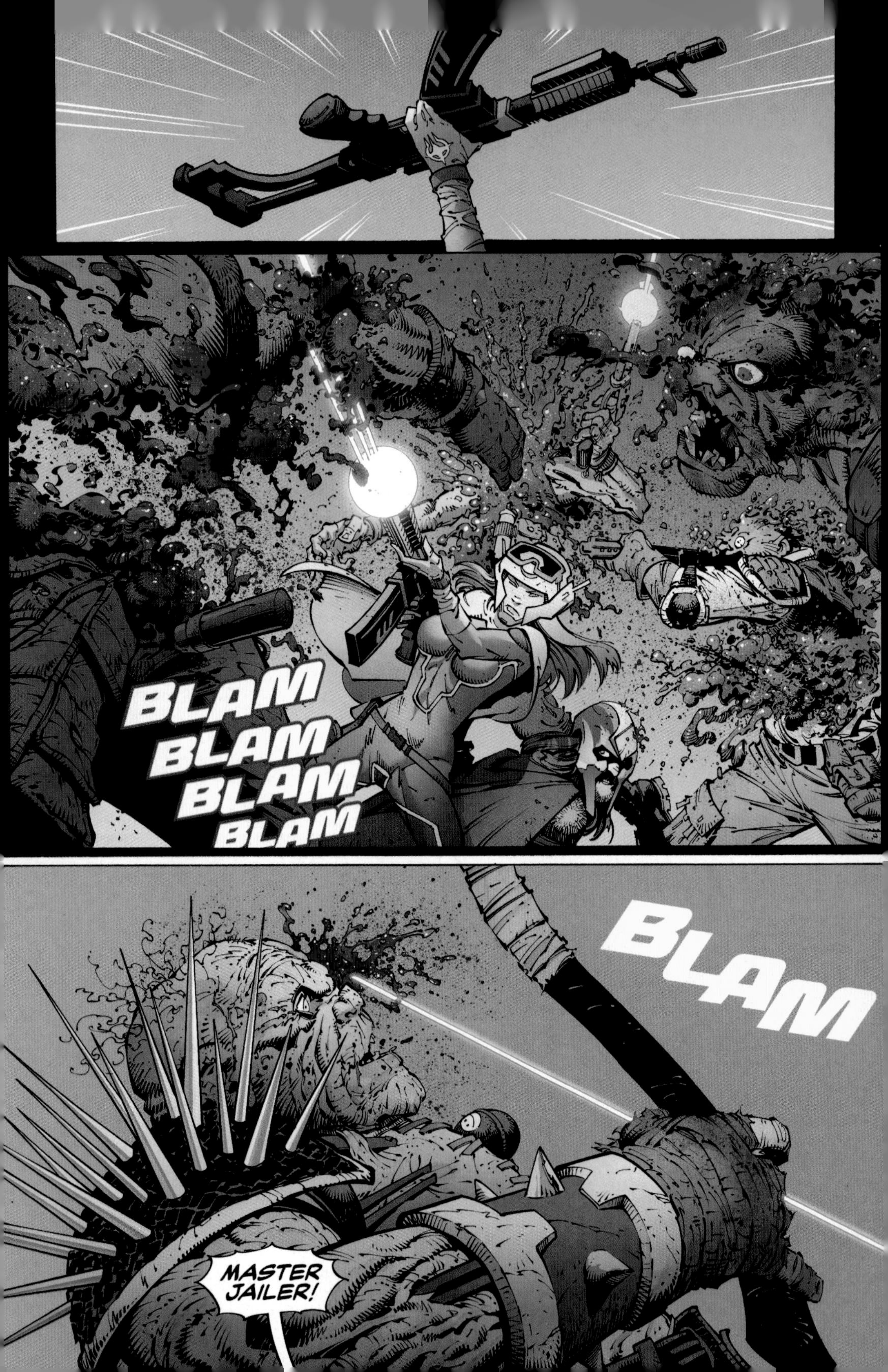
BLAM
BLAM
BLAM
BLAM
BLAM
MASTER JAILER!

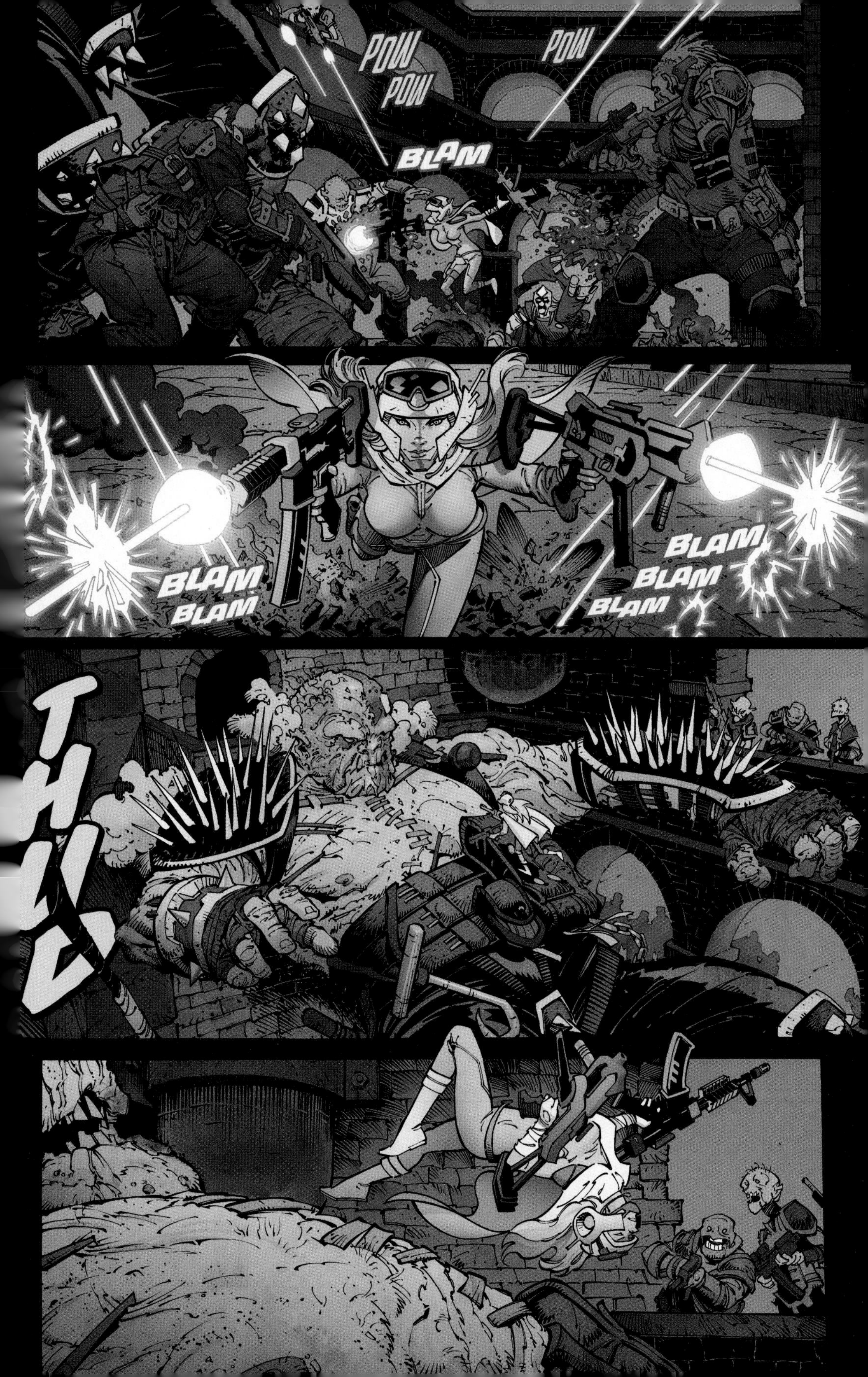
POW
POW
POW
BLAM
BLAM
BLAM
BLAM
BLAM
BLAM
THUD

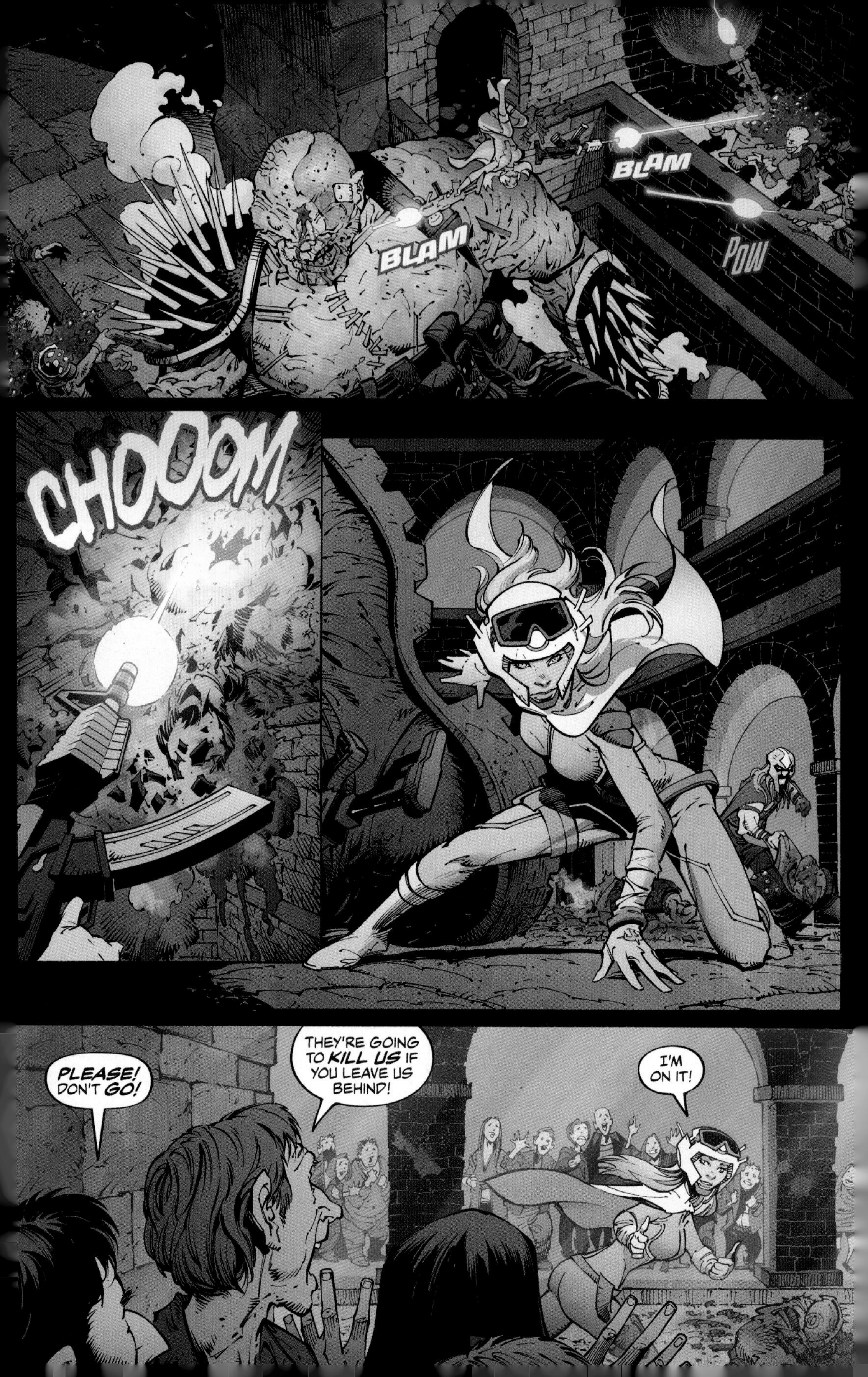

BLAM
BLAM
POW
CHOOOM
PLEASE! DON'T GO!
THEY'RE GOING TO KILL US IF YOU LEAVE US BEHIND!
I'M ON IT!

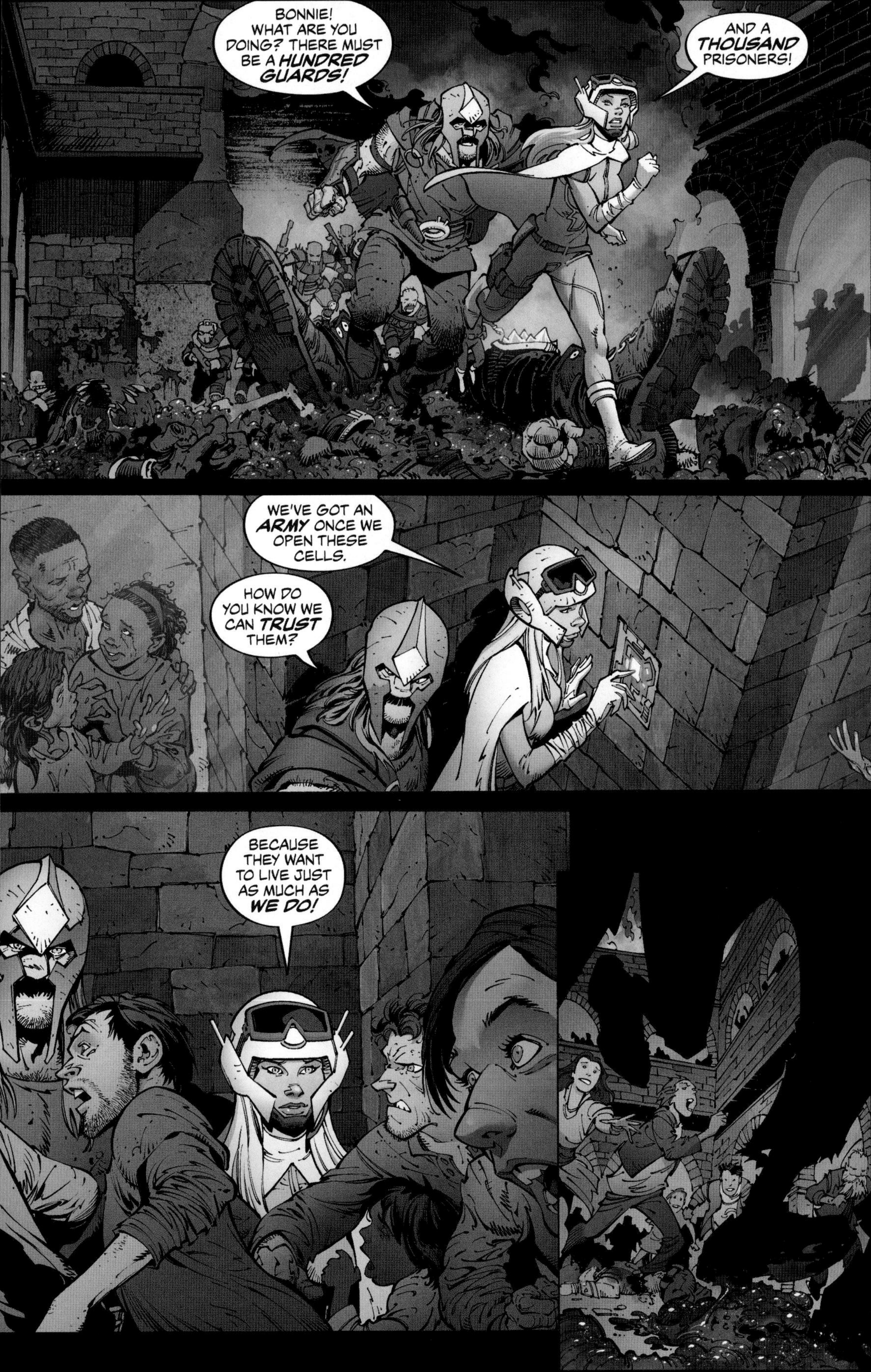
BONNIE! WHAT ARE YOU DOING? THERE MUST BE A HUNDRED GUARDS!
AND A THOUSAND PRISONERS!
WE'VE GOT AN ARMY ONCE WE OPEN THESE CELLS.
HOW DO YOU KNOW WE CAN TRUST THEM?
BECAUSE THEY WANT TO LIVE JUST AS MUCH AS WE DO!

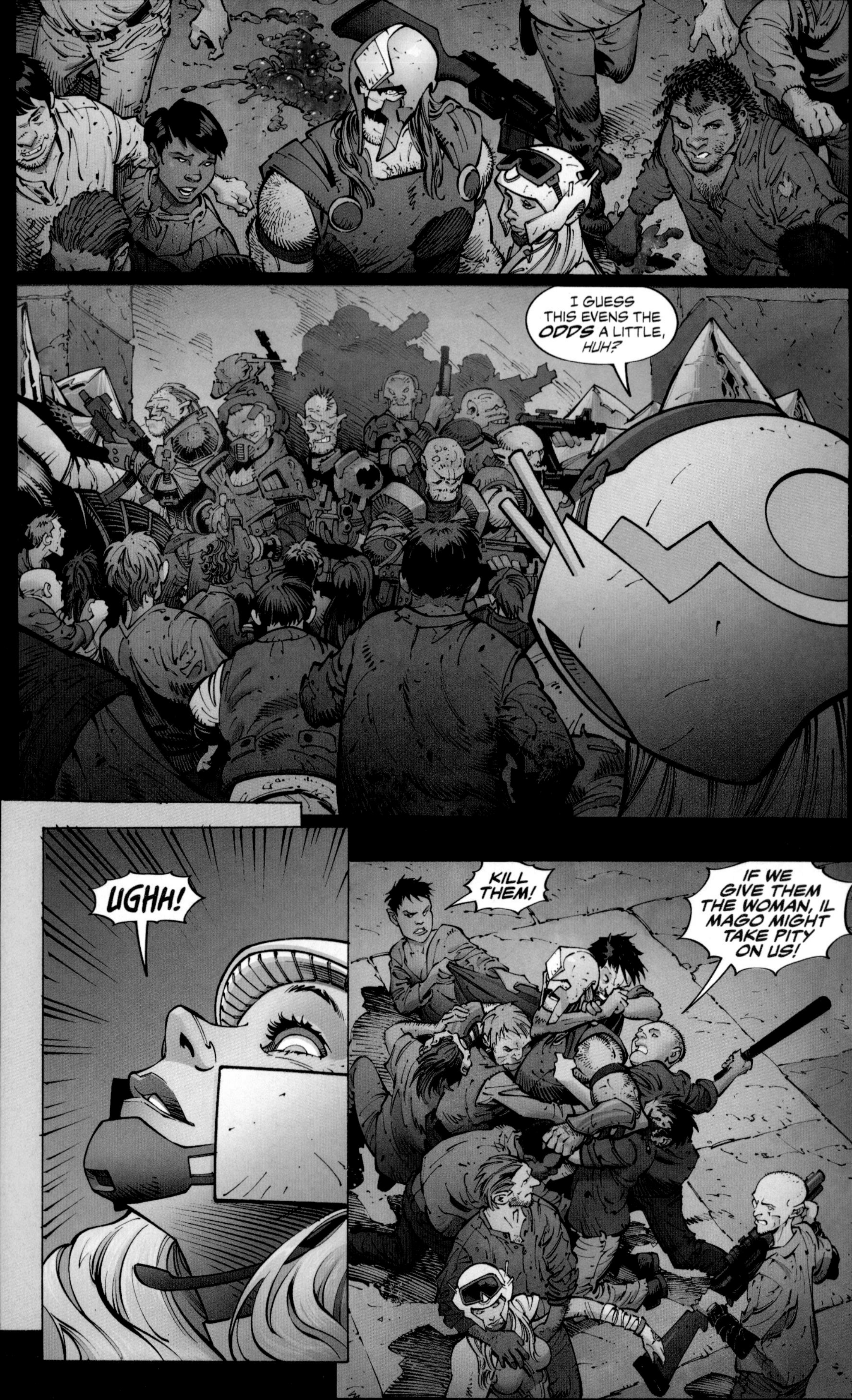
I GUESS THIS EVENS THE ODDS A LITTLE, HUH?
UGHH!
KILL THEM!
IF WE GIVE THEM THE WOMAN, IL MAGO MIGHT TAKE PITY ON US!

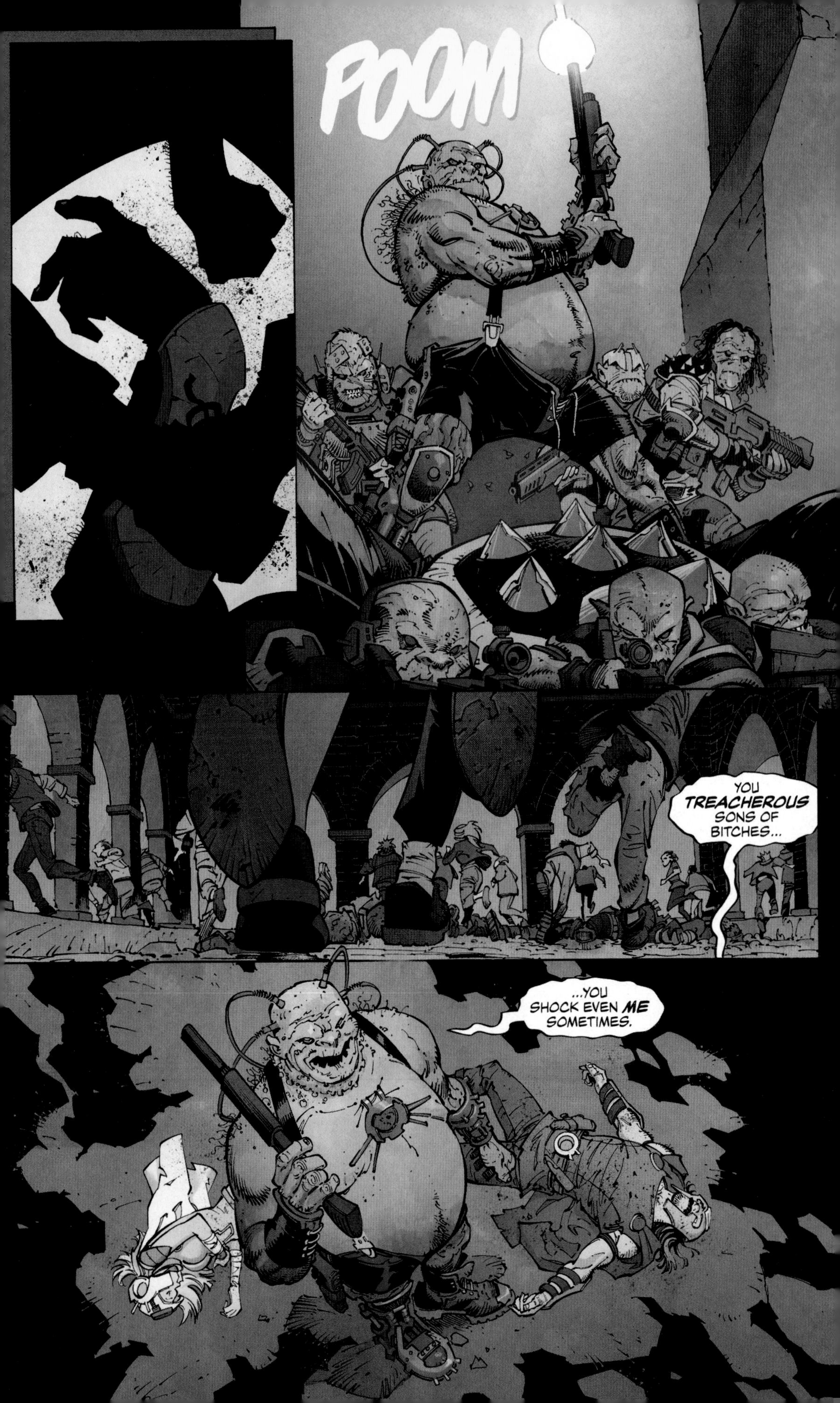
POOM
YOU TREACHEROUS SONS OF BITCHES...
...YOU SHOCK EVEN ME SOMETIMES.

WHY DID THEY ATTACK US WHEN WE WERE THEIR ONLY CHANCE?

I ALREADY *TOLD* YOU. THIS IS WHERE *BAD PEOPLE* COME. EVEN IF YOU'RE TRYING TO HELP, THEY'RE ALWAYS GOING TO DO THE *WRONG THING.*

WHAT ARE THEY GOING TO *DO* WITH US?

KILL US ON THE MOUNTAIN AND MAKE IL MAGO A LITTLE STRONGER. THERE'S A *POWER* IN HUMAN SACRIFICE, AND BLACK WISH MOUNTAIN IS THE ROOT OF THE *MAGIC* IN THESE PARTS.

EVERYONE THEY KILL HERE CREATES ANOTHER *WISH,* BUT IT ONLY WORKS IF IT'S SOMETHING *NEGATIVE.* YOU CAN NEVER WISH FOR ANYTHING *GOOD.*

IS THIS IL MAGO GUY AN *ENEMY* OF GOLGOTHA?

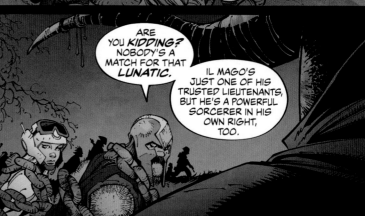

ARE YOU *KIDDING?* NOBODY'S A MATCH FOR THAT *LUNATIC.*

IL MAGO'S JUST ONE OF HIS TRUSTED LIEUTENANTS, BUT HE'S A POWERFUL SORCERER IN HIS OWN RIGHT, TOO.

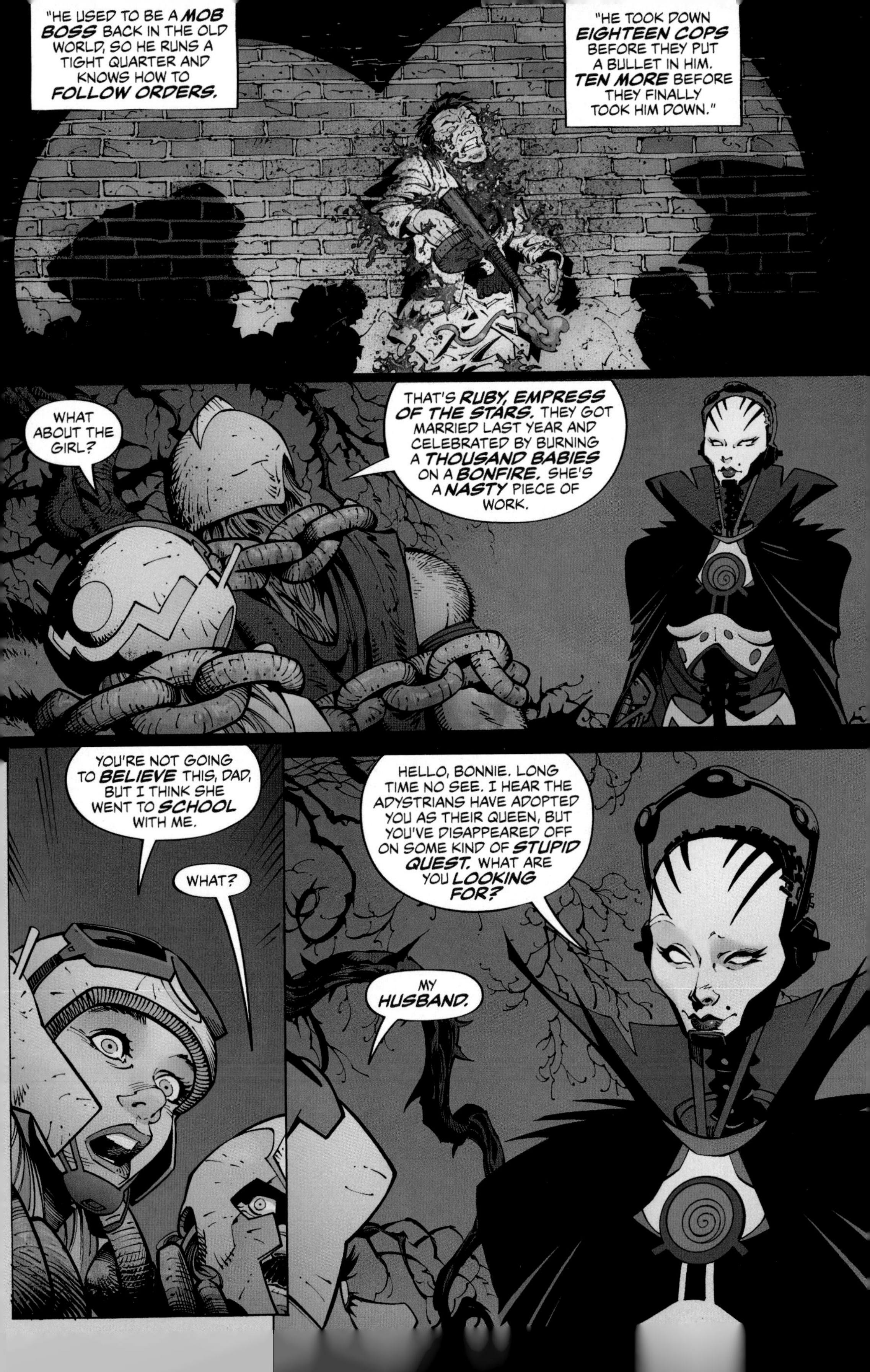
"HE USED TO BE A MOB BOSS BACK IN THE OLD WORLD, SO HE RUNS A TIGHT QUARTER AND KNOWS HOW TO FOLLOW ORDERS.
"HE TOOK DOWN EIGHTEEN COPS BEFORE THEY PUT A BULLET IN HIM. TEN MORE BEFORE THEY FINALLY TOOK HIM DOWN."
WHAT ABOUT THE GIRL?
THAT'S RUBY, EMPRESS OF THE STARS. THEY GOT MARRIED LAST YEAR AND CELEBRATED BY BURNING A THOUSAND BABIES ON A BONFIRE. SHE'S A NASTY PIECE OF WORK.
YOU'RE NOT GOING TO BELIEVE THIS, DAD, BUT I THINK SHE WENT TO SCHOOL WITH ME.
WHAT?
HELLO, BONNIE. LONG TIME NO SEE. I HEAR THE ADYSTRIANS HAVE ADOPTED YOU AS THEIR QUEEN, BUT YOU'VE DISAPPEARED OFF ON SOME KIND OF STUPID QUEST. WHAT ARE YOU LOOKING FOR?
MY HUSBAND.

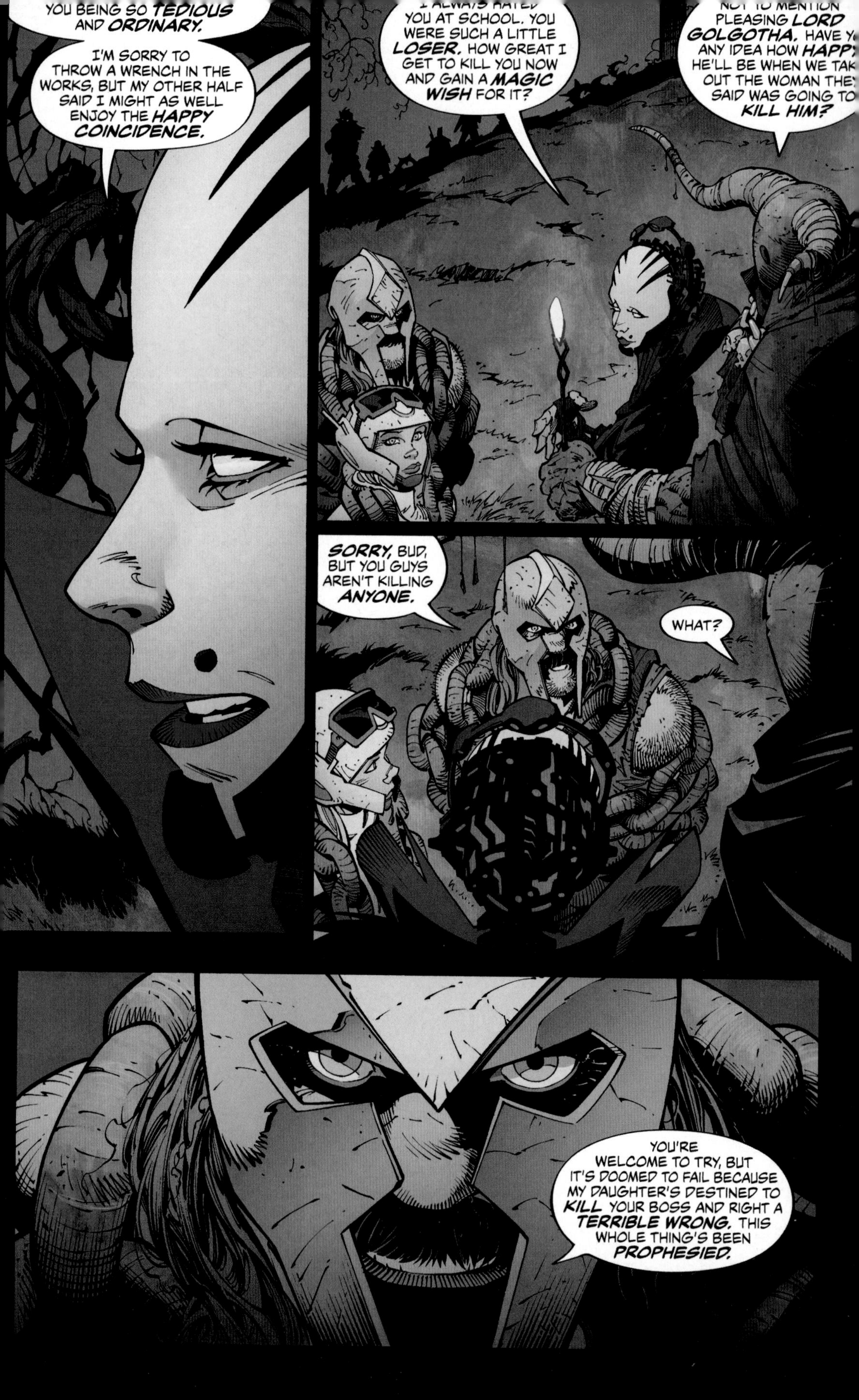
YOU BEING SO TEDIOUS AND ORDINARY.
I'M SORRY TO THROW A WRENCH IN THE WORKS, BUT MY OTHER HALF SAID I MIGHT AS WELL ENJOY THE HAPPY COINCIDENCE.
YOU AT SCHOOL. YOU WERE SUCH A LITTLE LOSER. HOW GREAT I GET TO KILL YOU NOW AND GAIN A MAGIC WISH FOR IT?
PLEASING LORD GOLGOTHA.
SAID WAS GOING TO KILL HIM?
SORRY, BUD, BUT YOU GUYS AREN'T KILLING ANYONE.
WHAT?
YOU'RE WELCOME TO TRY, BUT IT'S DOOMED TO FAIL BECAUSE MY DAUGHTER'S DESTINED TO KILL YOUR BOSS AND RIGHT A TERRIBLE WRONG. THIS WHOLE THING'S BEEN PROPHESIED.

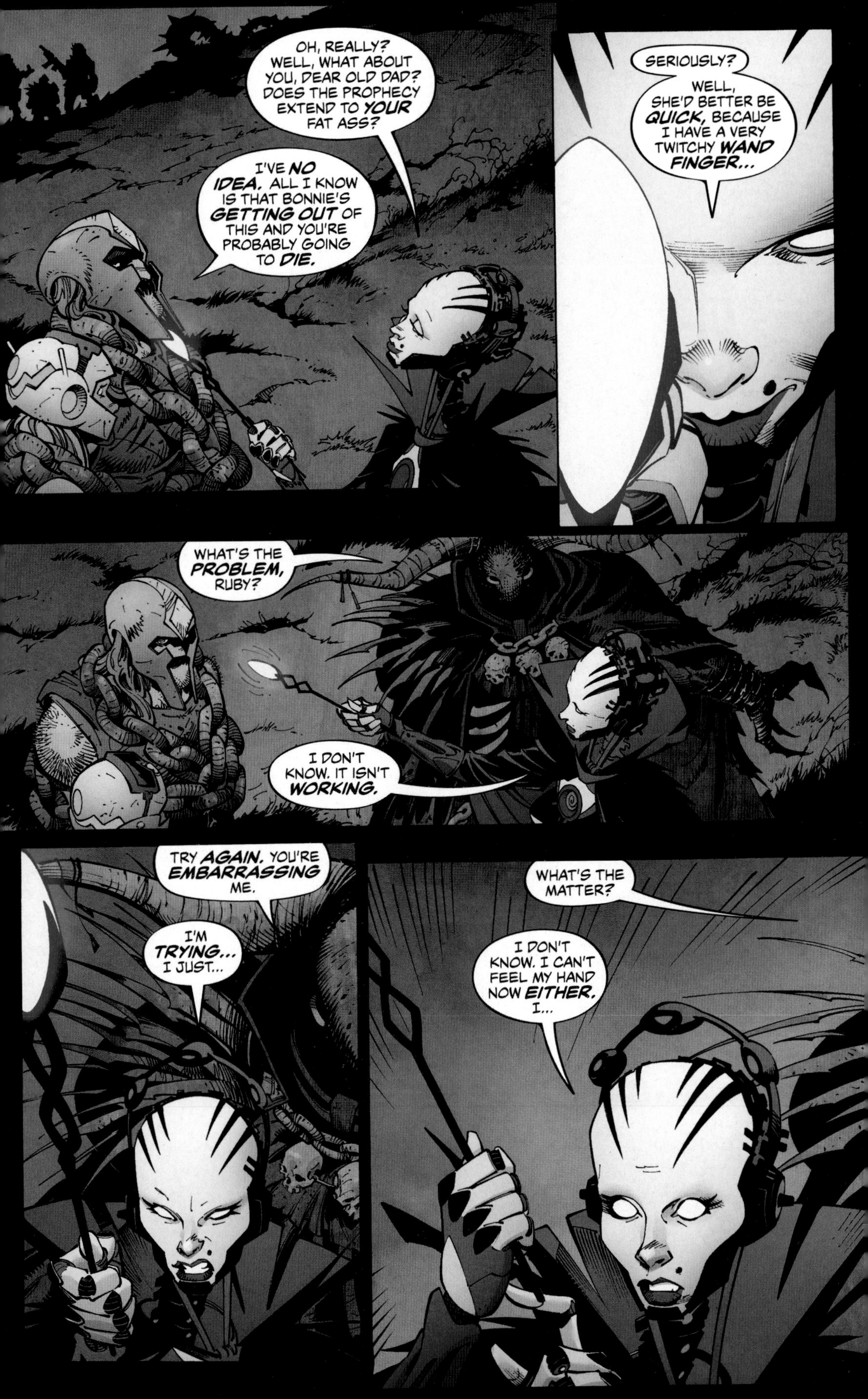
OH, REALLY? WELL, WHAT ABOUT YOU, DEAR OLD DAD? DOES THE PROPHECY EXTEND TO YOUR FAT ASS?
I'VE NO IDEA. ALL I KNOW IS THAT BONNIE'S GETTING OUT OF THIS AND YOU'RE PROBABLY GOING TO DIE.
SERIOUSLY?
WELL, SHE'D BETTER BE QUICK, BECAUSE I HAVE A VERY TWITCHY WAND FINGER...
WHAT'S THE PROBLEM, RUBY?
I DON'T KNOW. IT ISN'T WORKING.
TRY AGAIN. YOU'RE EMBARRASSING ME.
I'M TRYING... I JUST...
WHAT'S THE MATTER?
I DON'T KNOW. I CAN'T FEEL MY HAND NOW EITHER. I...

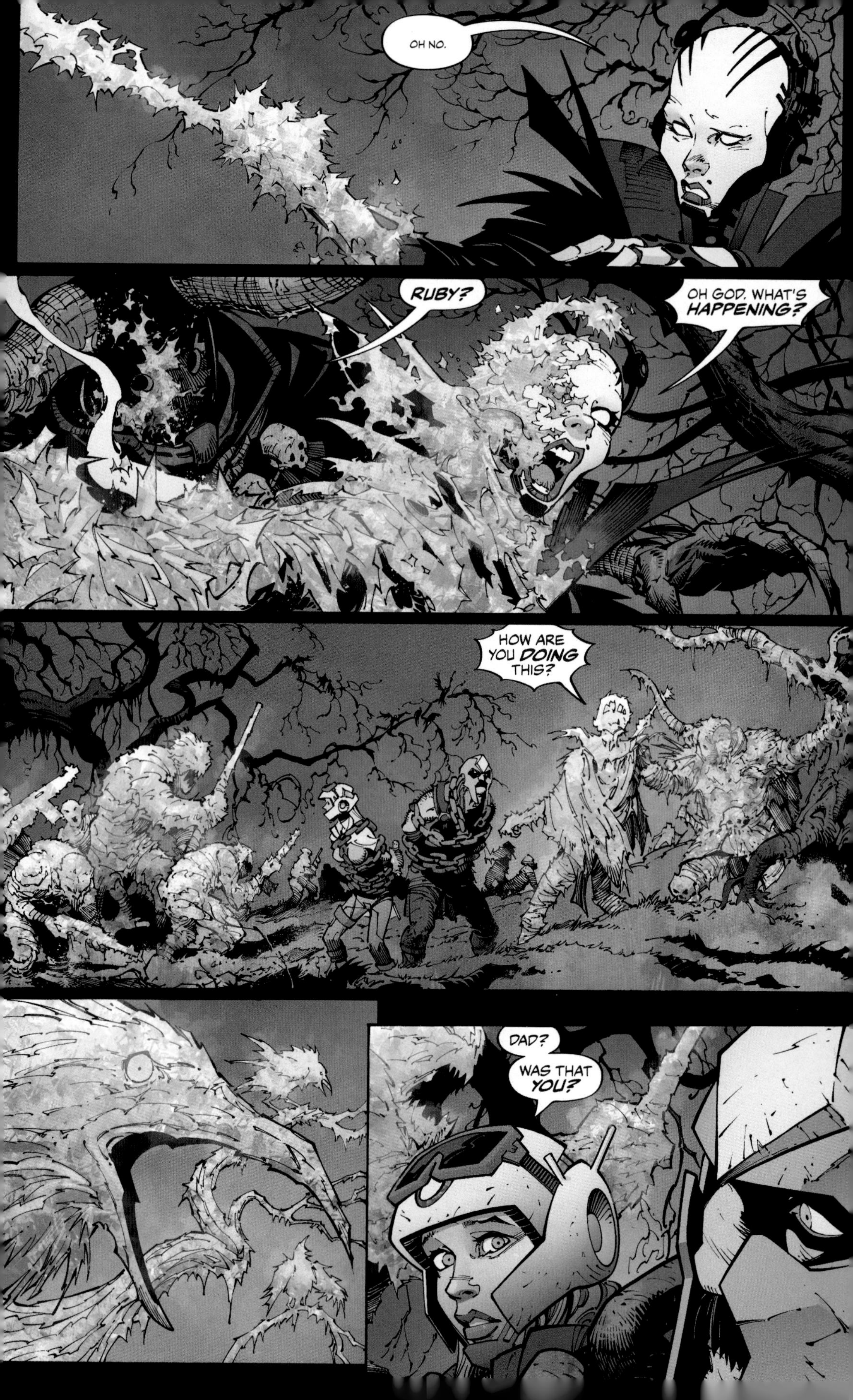
OH NO.
RUBY?
OH GOD. WHAT'S HAPPENING?
HOW ARE YOU DOING THIS?
DAD?
WAS THAT YOU?

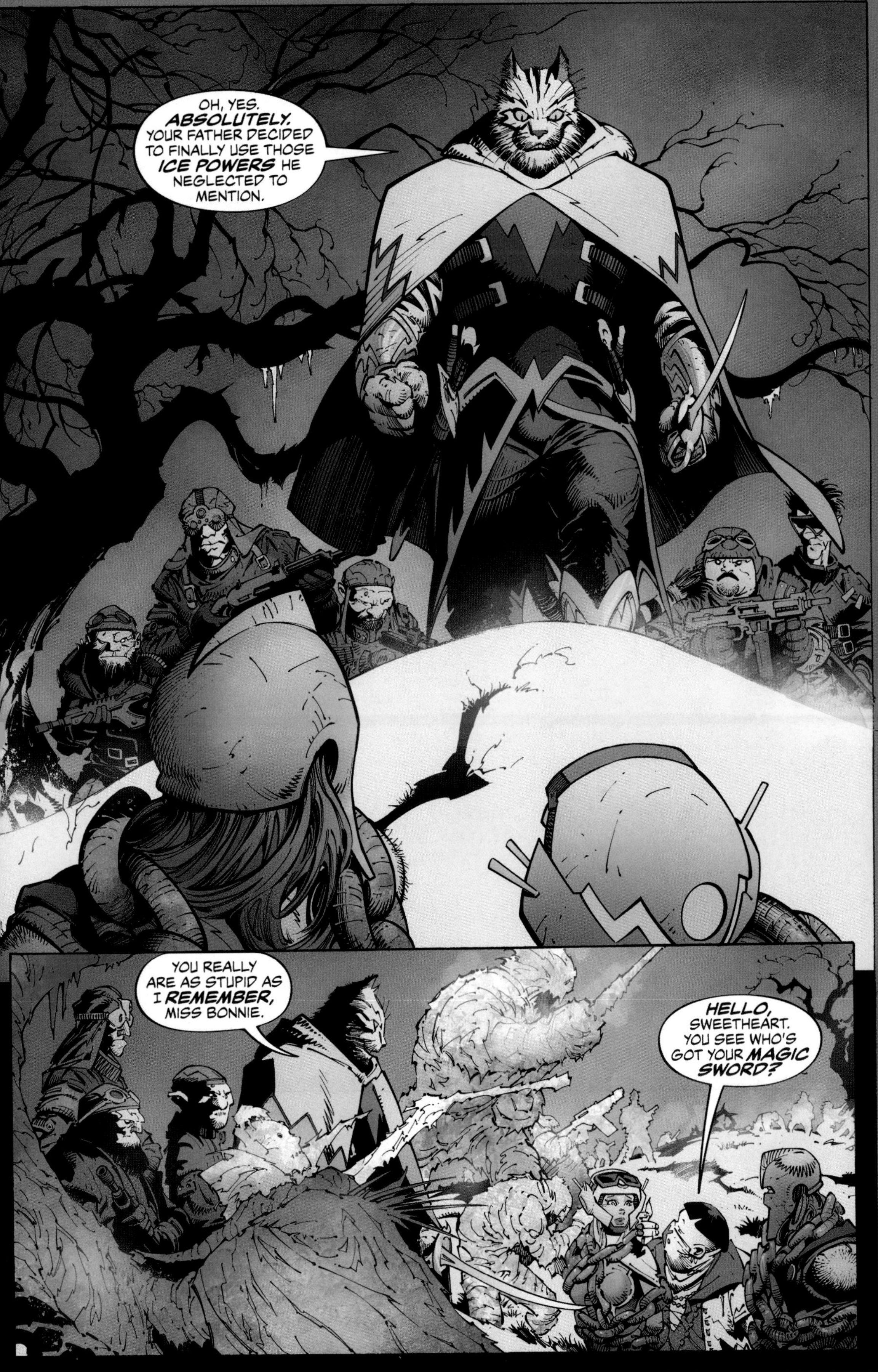
OH, YES. ABSOLUTELY. YOUR FATHER DECIDED TO FINALLY USE THOSE ICE POWERS HE NEGLECTED TO MENTION.
YOU REALLY ARE AS STUPID AS I REMEMBER, MISS BONNIE.
HELLO, SWEETHEART. YOU SEE WHO'S GOT YOUR MAGIC SWORD?

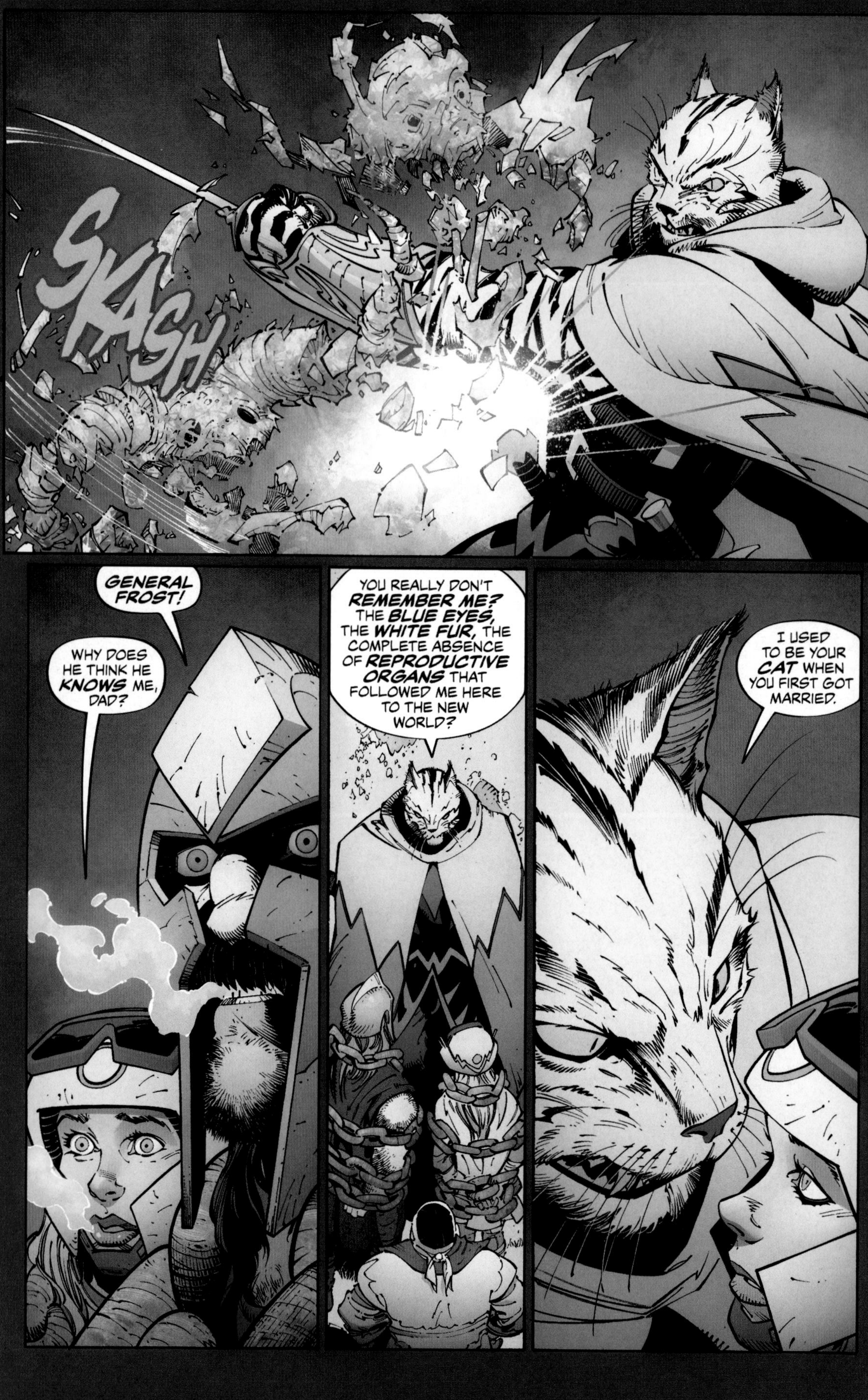

SKASH
GENERAL FROST!
WHY DOES HE THINK HE KNOWS ME, DAD?
YOU REALLY DON'T REMEMBER ME? THE BLUE EYES, THE WHITE FUR, THE COMPLETE ABSENCE OF REPRODUCTIVE ORGANS THAT FOLLOWED ME HERE TO THE NEW WORLD?
I USED TO BE YOUR CAT WHEN YOU FIRST GOT MARRIED.

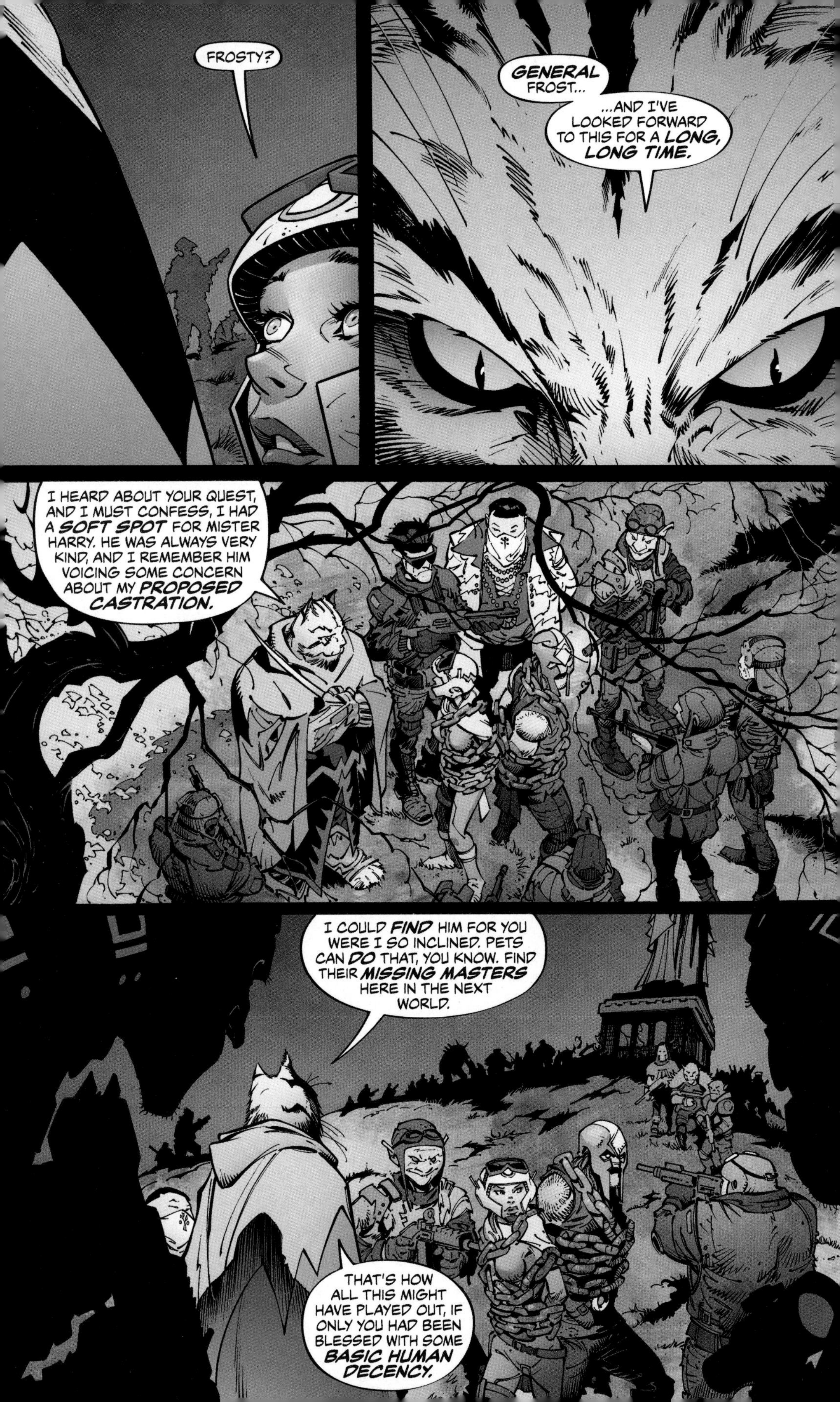

FROSTY?
GENERAL FROST...
...AND I'VE LOOKED FORWARD TO THIS FOR A LONG, LONG TIME.
I HEARD ABOUT YOUR QUEST, AND I MUST CONFESS, I HAD A SOFT SPOT FOR MISTER HARRY. HE WAS ALWAYS VERY KIND, AND I REMEMBER HIM VOICING SOME CONCERN ABOUT MY PROPOSED CASTRATION.
I COULD FIND HIM FOR YOU WERE I SO INCLINED. PETS CAN DO THAT, YOU KNOW. FIND THEIR MISSING MASTERS HERE IN THE NEXT WORLD.
THAT'S HOW ALL THIS MIGHT HAVE PLAYED OUT, IF ONLY YOU HAD BEEN BLESSED WITH SOME BASIC HUMAN DECENCY.

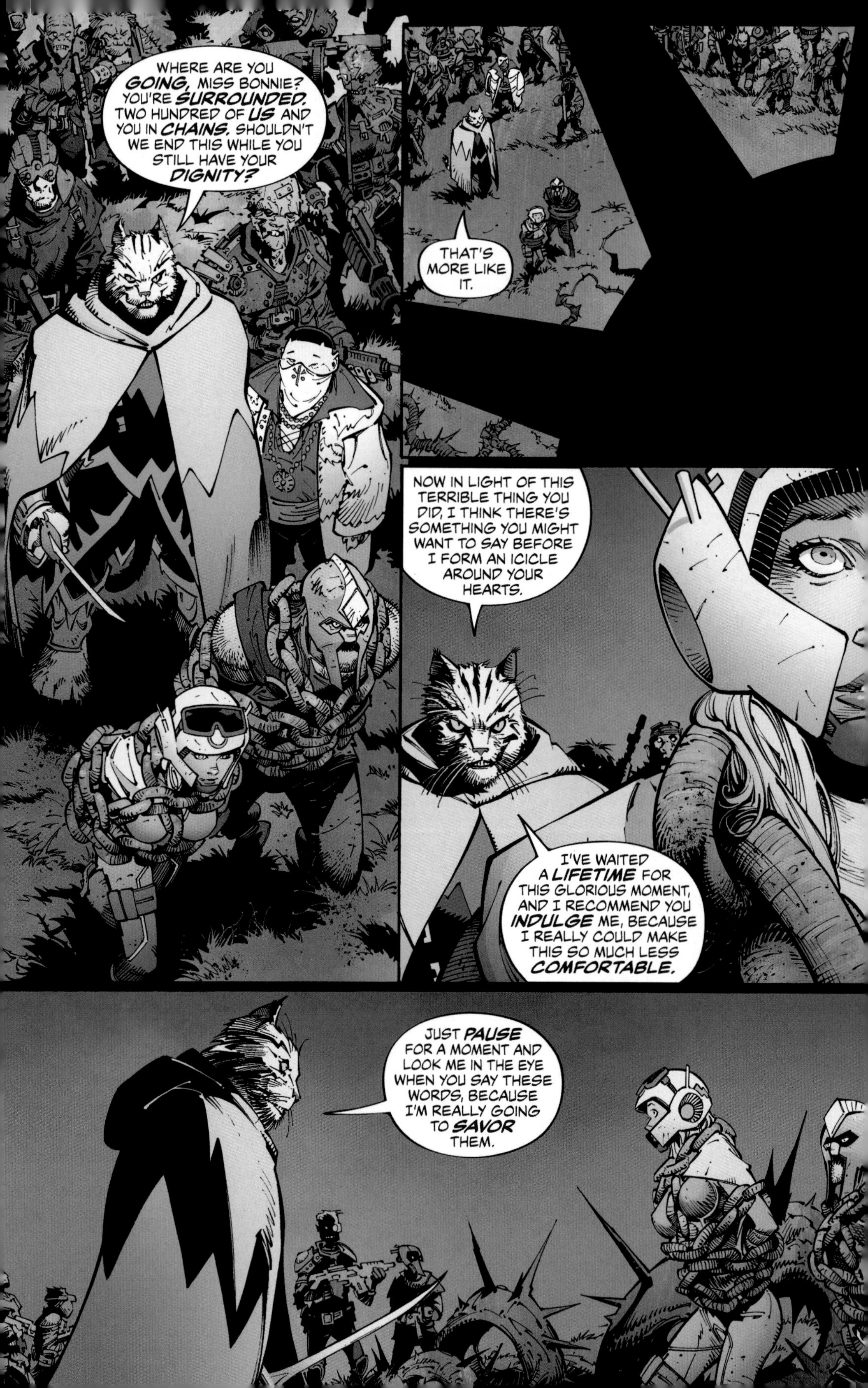
WHERE ARE YOU GOING, MISS BONNIE? YOU'RE SURROUNDED. TWO HUNDRED OF US AND YOU IN CHAINS. SHOULDN'T WE END THIS WHILE YOU STILL HAVE YOUR DIGNITY?
THAT'S MORE LIKE IT.
NOW IN LIGHT OF THIS TERRIBLE THING YOU DID, I THINK THERE'S SOMETHING YOU MIGHT WANT TO SAY BEFORE I FORM AN ICICLE AROUND YOUR HEARTS.
I'VE WAITED A LIFETIME FOR THIS GLORIOUS MOMENT, AND I RECOMMEND YOU INDULGE ME, BECAUSE I REALLY COULD MAKE THIS SO MUCH LESS COMFORTABLE.
JUST PAUSE FOR A MOMENT AND LOOK ME IN THE EYE WHEN YOU SAY THESE WORDS, BECAUSE I'M REALLY GOING TO SAVOR THEM.

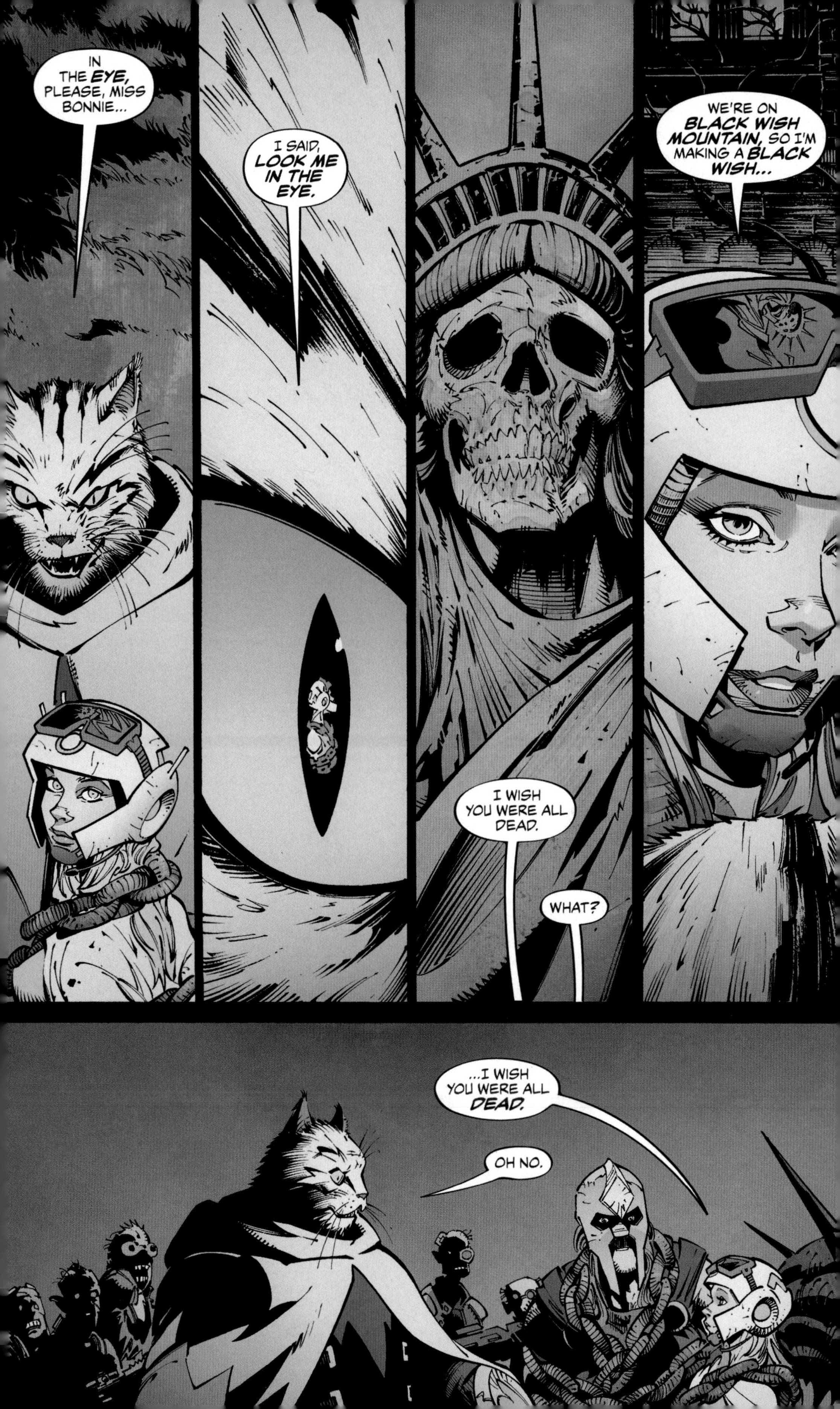

IN THE EYE, PLEASE, MISS BONNIE...
I SAID, LOOK ME IN THE EYE.
WE'RE ON BLACK WISH MOUNTAIN, SO I'M MAKING A BLACK WISH...
I WISH YOU WERE ALL DEAD.
WHAT?
...I WISH YOU WERE ALL DEAD.
OH NO.

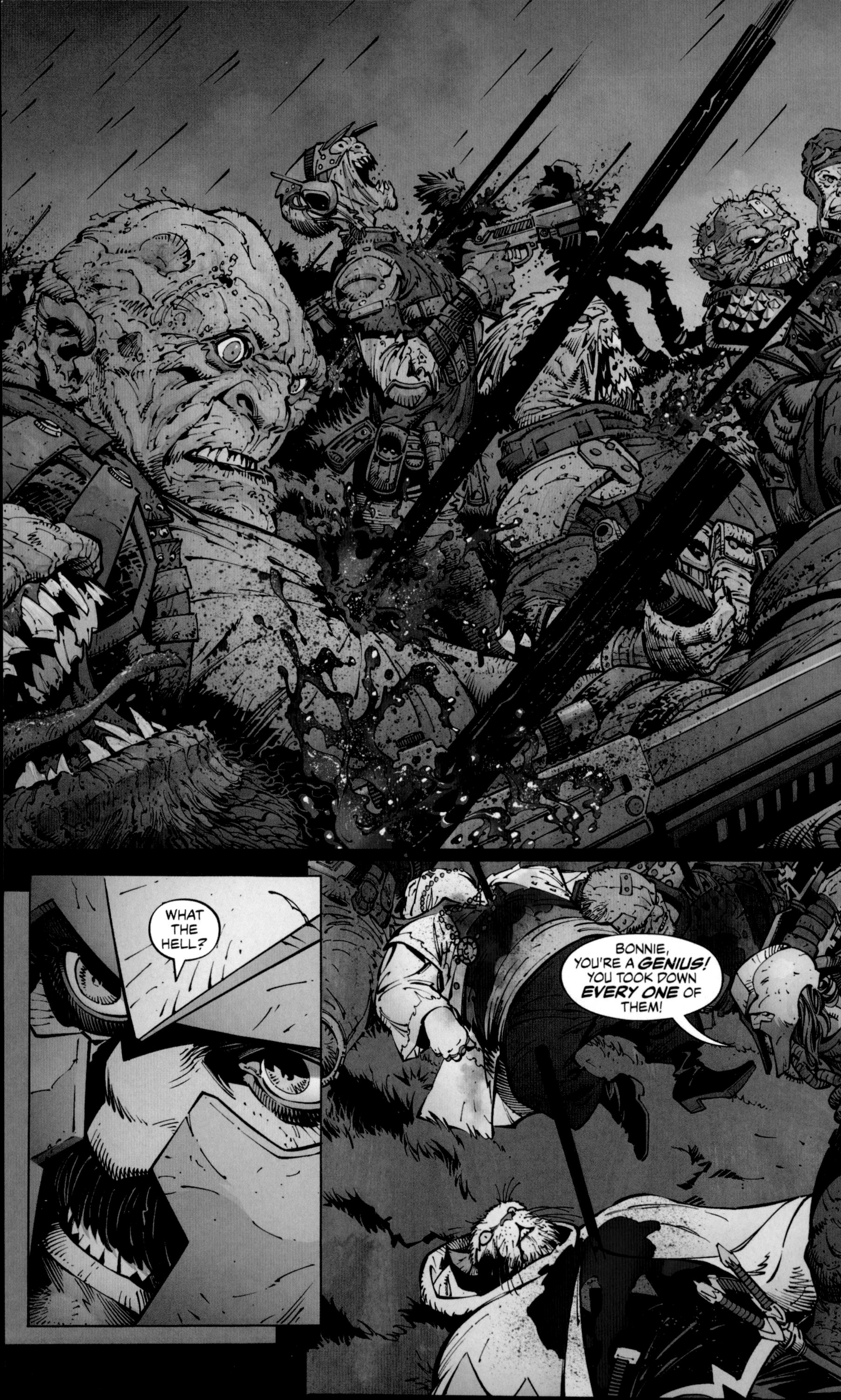
WHAT THE HELL?
BONNIE, YOU'RE A GENIUS! YOU TOOK DOWN EVERY ONE OF THEM!

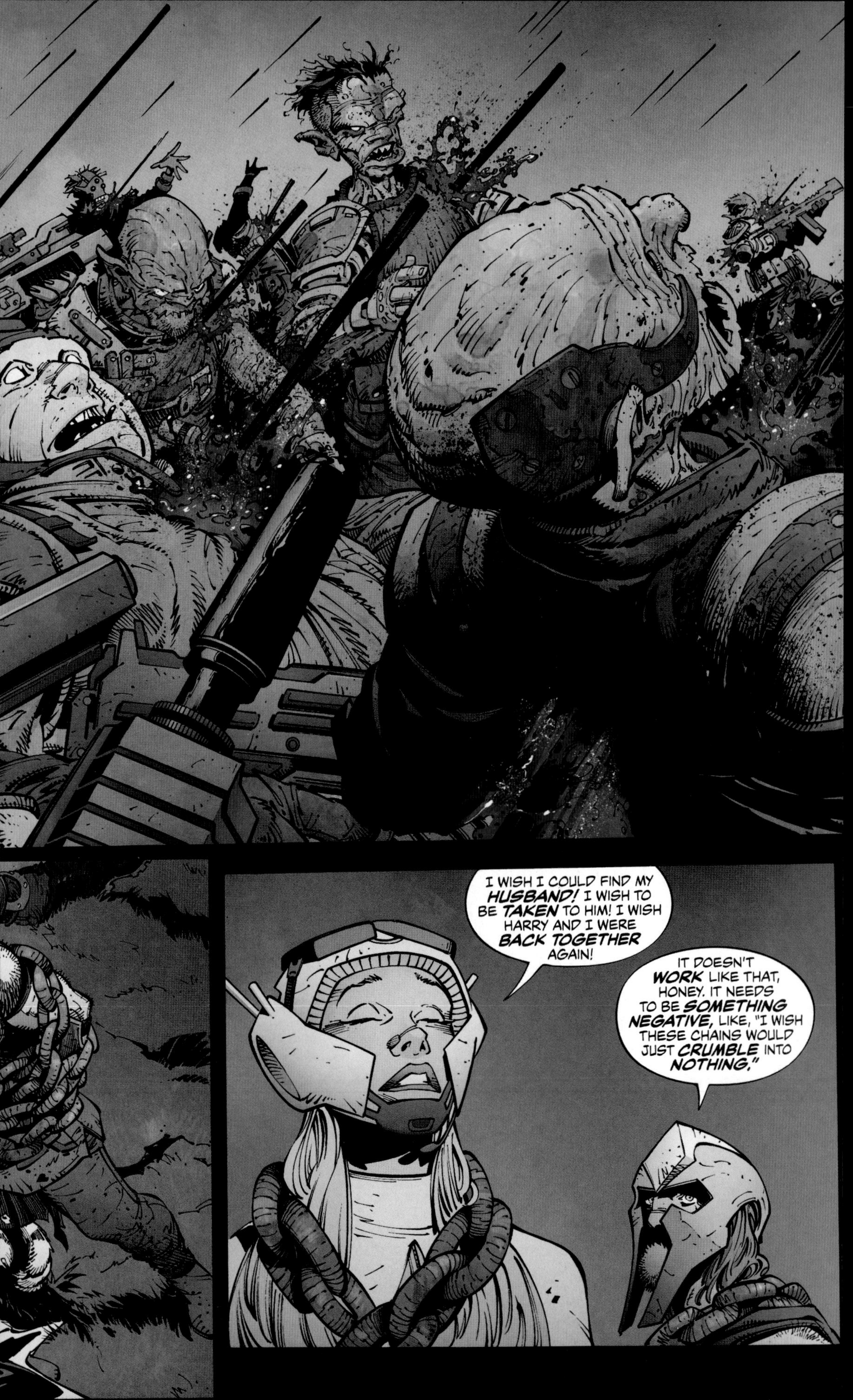
I WISH I COULD FIND MY HUSBAND! I WISH TO BE TAKEN TO HIM! I WISH HARRY AND I WERE BACK TOGETHER AGAIN!
IT DOESN'T WORK LIKE THAT, HONEY. IT NEEDS TO BE SOMETHING NEGATIVE, LIKE, "I WISH THESE CHAINS WOULD JUST CRUMBLE INTO NOTHING."

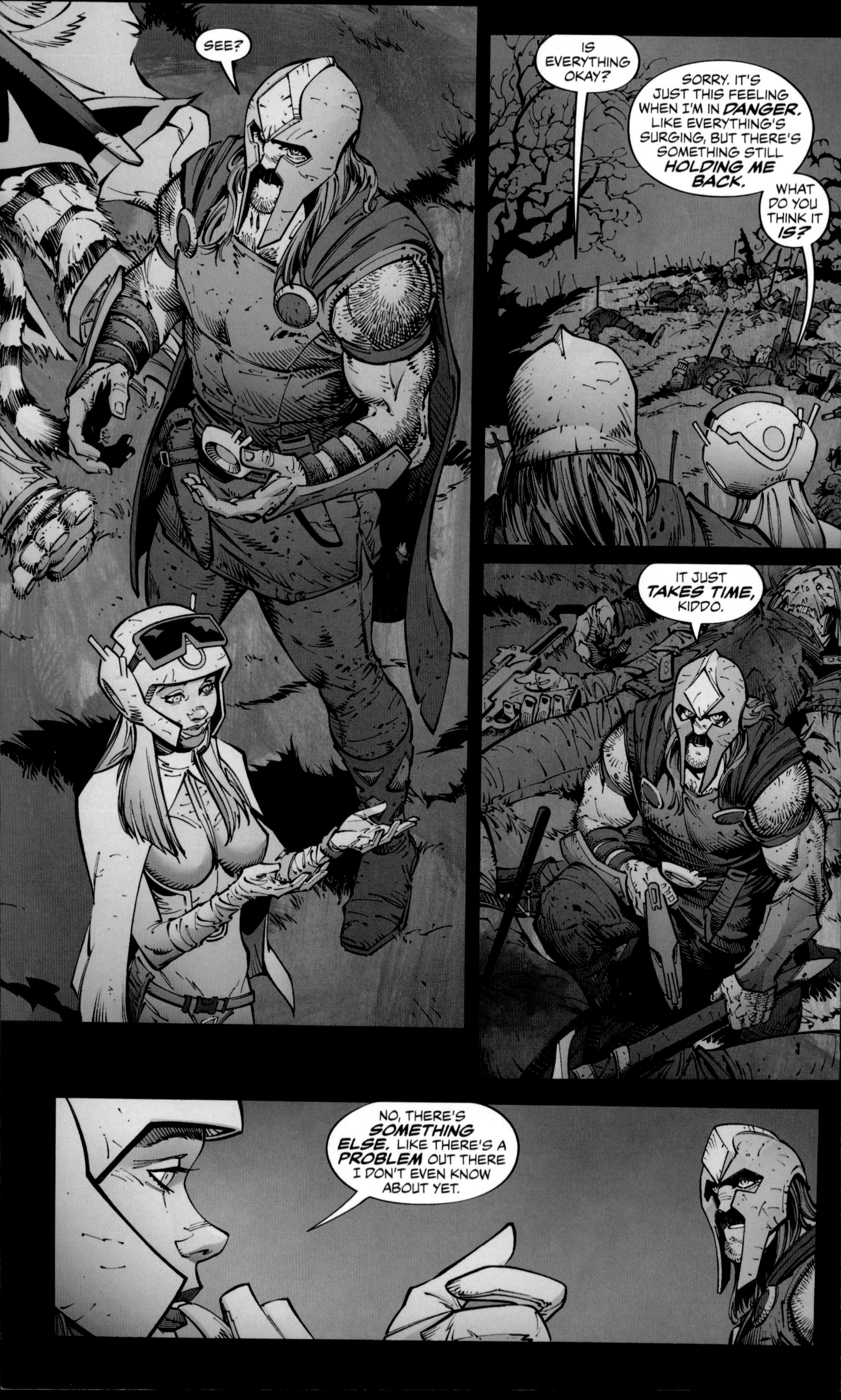
SEE?
IS EVERYTHING OKAY?
SORRY. IT'S JUST THIS FEELING WHEN I'M IN *DANGER.* LIKE EVERYTHING'S SURGING, BUT THERE'S SOMETHING STILL *HOLDING ME BACK.*
WHAT DO YOU THINK IT *IS?*
IT JUST *TAKES TIME,* KIDDO.
NO, THERE'S *SOMETHING ELSE.* LIKE THERE'S A *PROBLEM* OUT THERE I DON'T EVEN KNOW ABOUT YET.

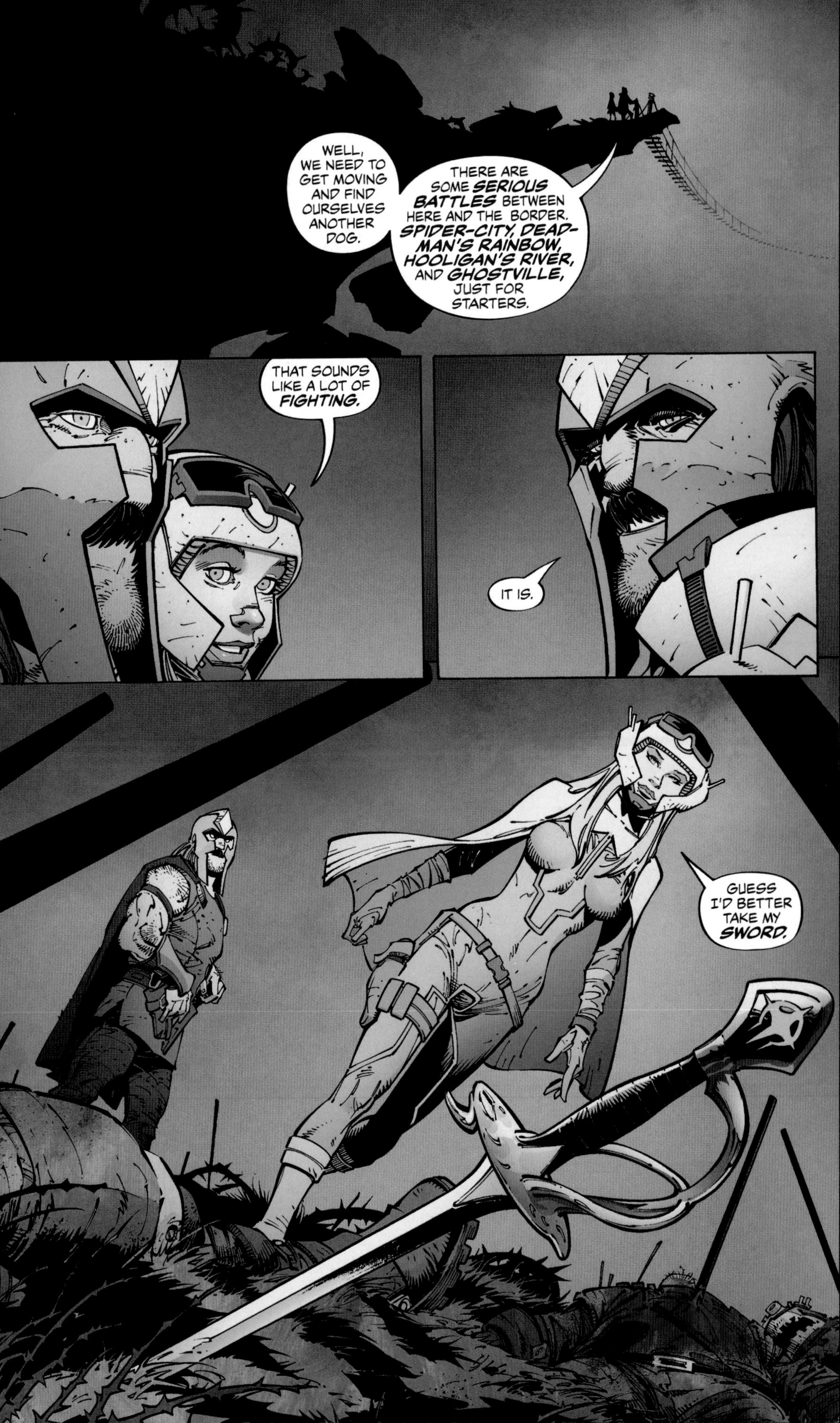
WELL, WE NEED TO GET MOVING AND FIND OURSELVES ANOTHER DOG.
THERE ARE SOME SERIOUS BATTLES BETWEEN HERE AND THE BORDER. SPIDER-CITY, DEAD-MAN'S RAINBOW, HOOLIGAN'S RIVER, AND GHOSTVILLE, JUST FOR STARTERS.
THAT SOUNDS LIKE A LOT OF FIGHTING.
IT IS.
GUESS I'D BETTER TAKE MY SWORD.

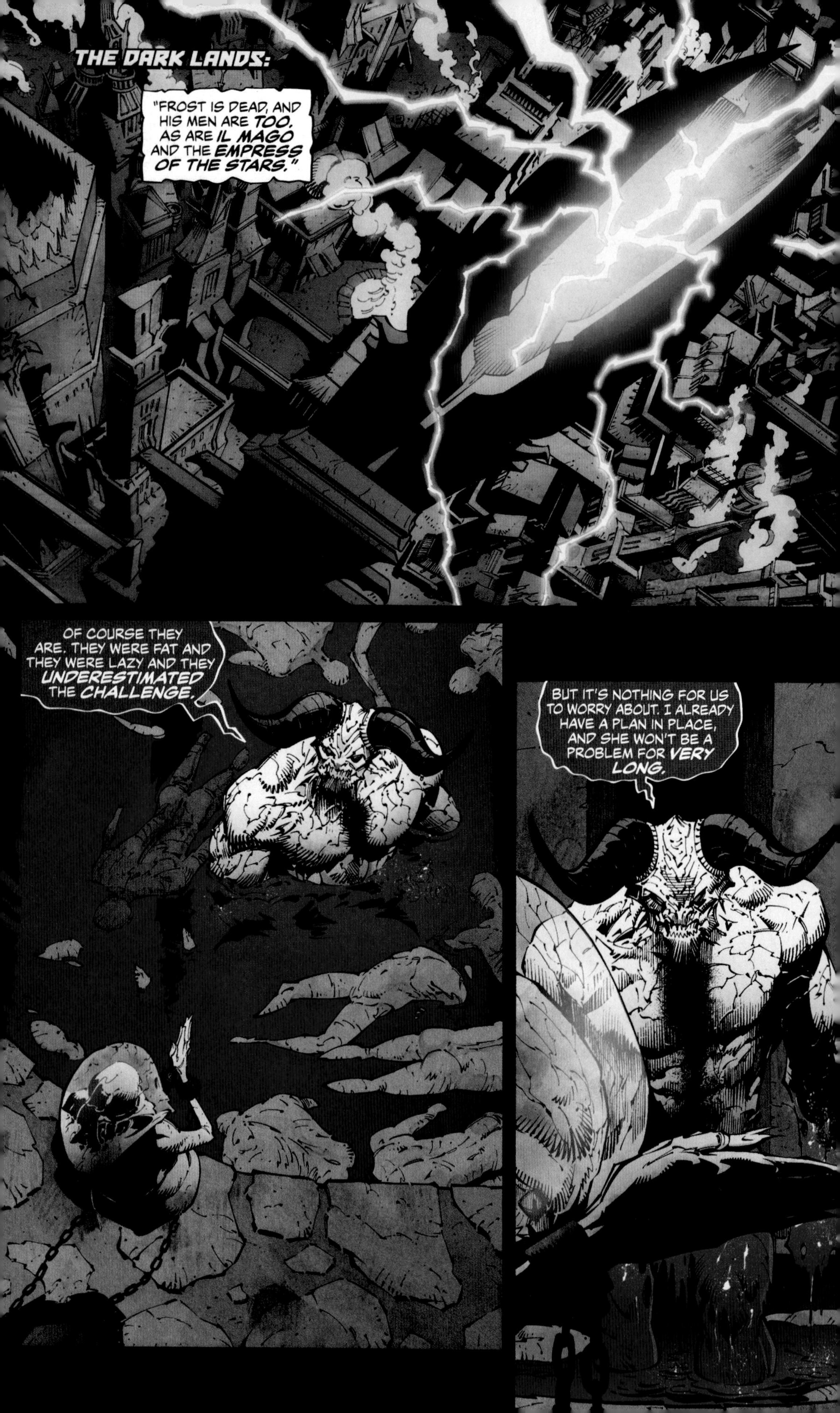
THE DARK LANDS:
"FROST IS DEAD, AND HIS MEN ARE TOO. AS ARE IL MAGO AND THE EMPRESS OF THE STARS."
OF COURSE THEY ARE. THEY WERE FAT AND THEY WERE LAZY AND THEY UNDERESTIMATED THE CHALLENGE.
BUT IT'S NOTHING FOR US TO WORRY ABOUT. I ALREADY HAVE A PLAN IN PLACE, AND SHE WON'T BE A PROBLEM FOR VERY LONG.

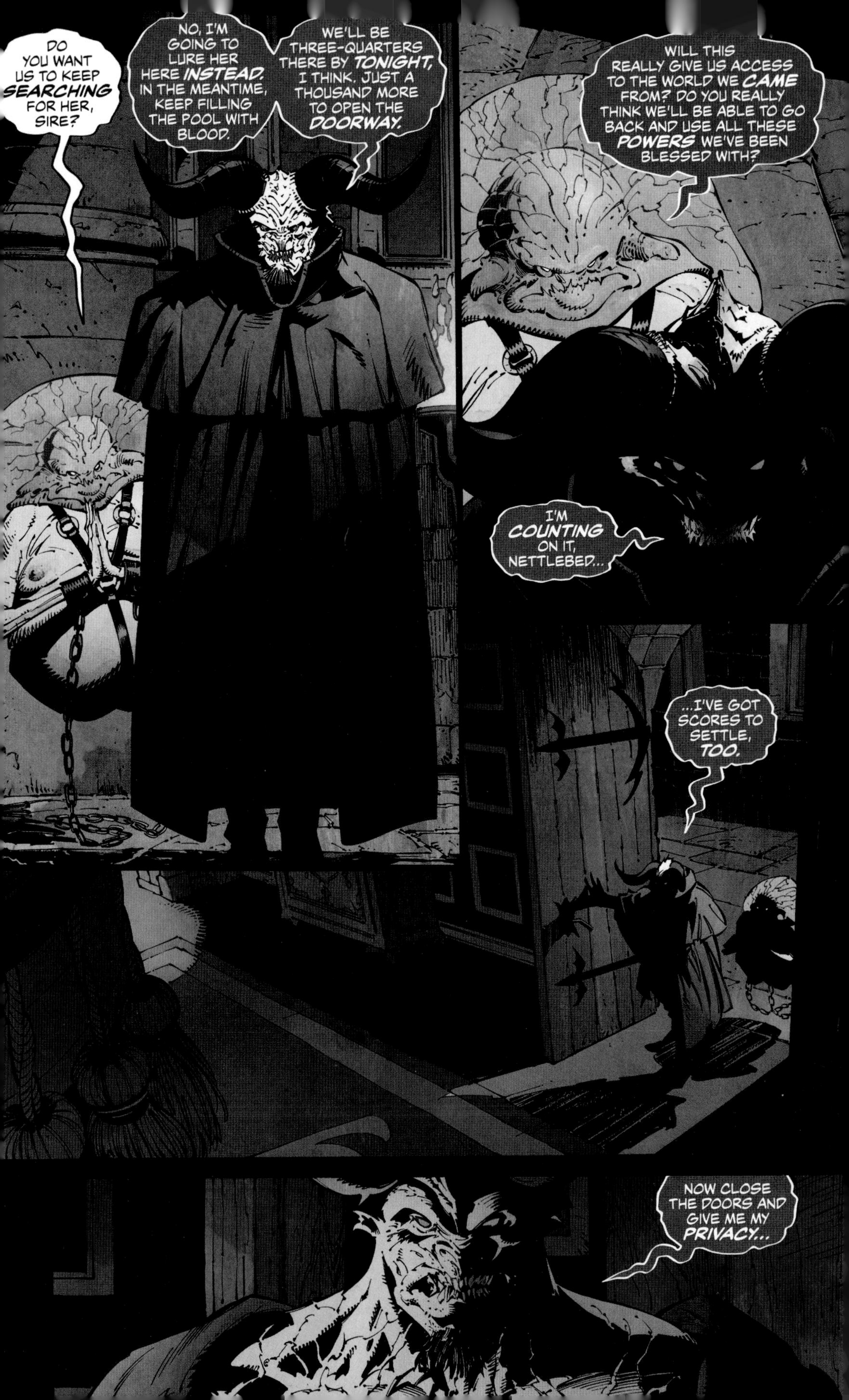
DO YOU WANT US TO KEEP SEARCHING FOR HER, SIRE?
NO, I'M GOING TO LURE HER HERE INSTEAD. IN THE MEANTIME, KEEP FILLING THE POOL WITH BLOOD.
WE'LL BE THREE-QUARTERS THERE BY TONIGHT, I THINK. JUST A THOUSAND MORE TO OPEN THE DOORWAY.
WILL THIS REALLY GIVE US ACCESS TO THE WORLD WE CAME FROM? DO YOU REALLY THINK WE'LL BE ABLE TO GO BACK AND USE ALL THESE POWERS WE'VE BEEN BLESSED WITH?
I'M COUNTING ON IT, NETTLEBED...
...I'VE GOT SCORES TO SETTLE, TOO.
NOW CLOSE THE DOORS AND GIVE ME MY PRIVACY...

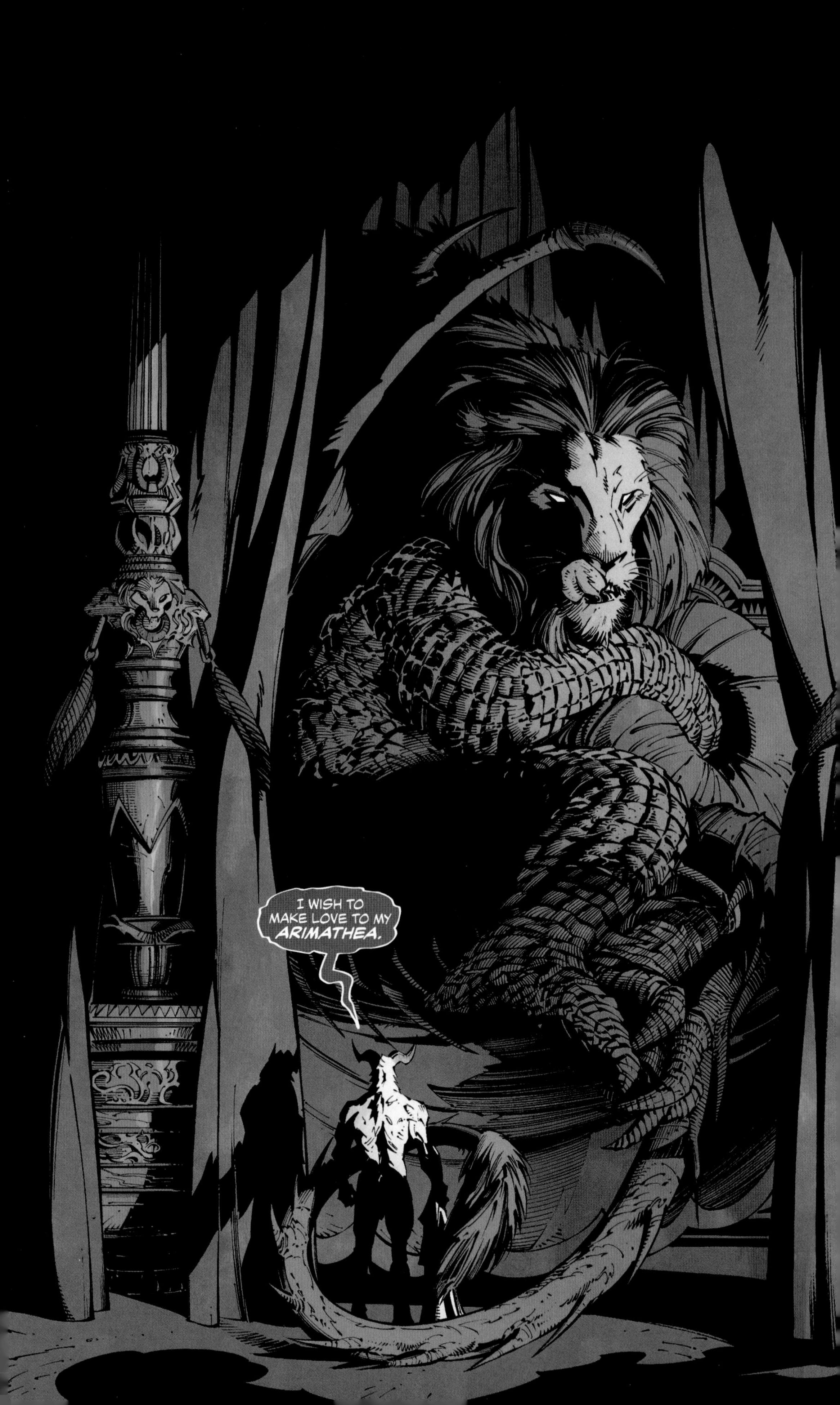
I WISH TO MAKE LOVE TO MY *ARIMATHEA.*

ISSUE FOUR, COVER B

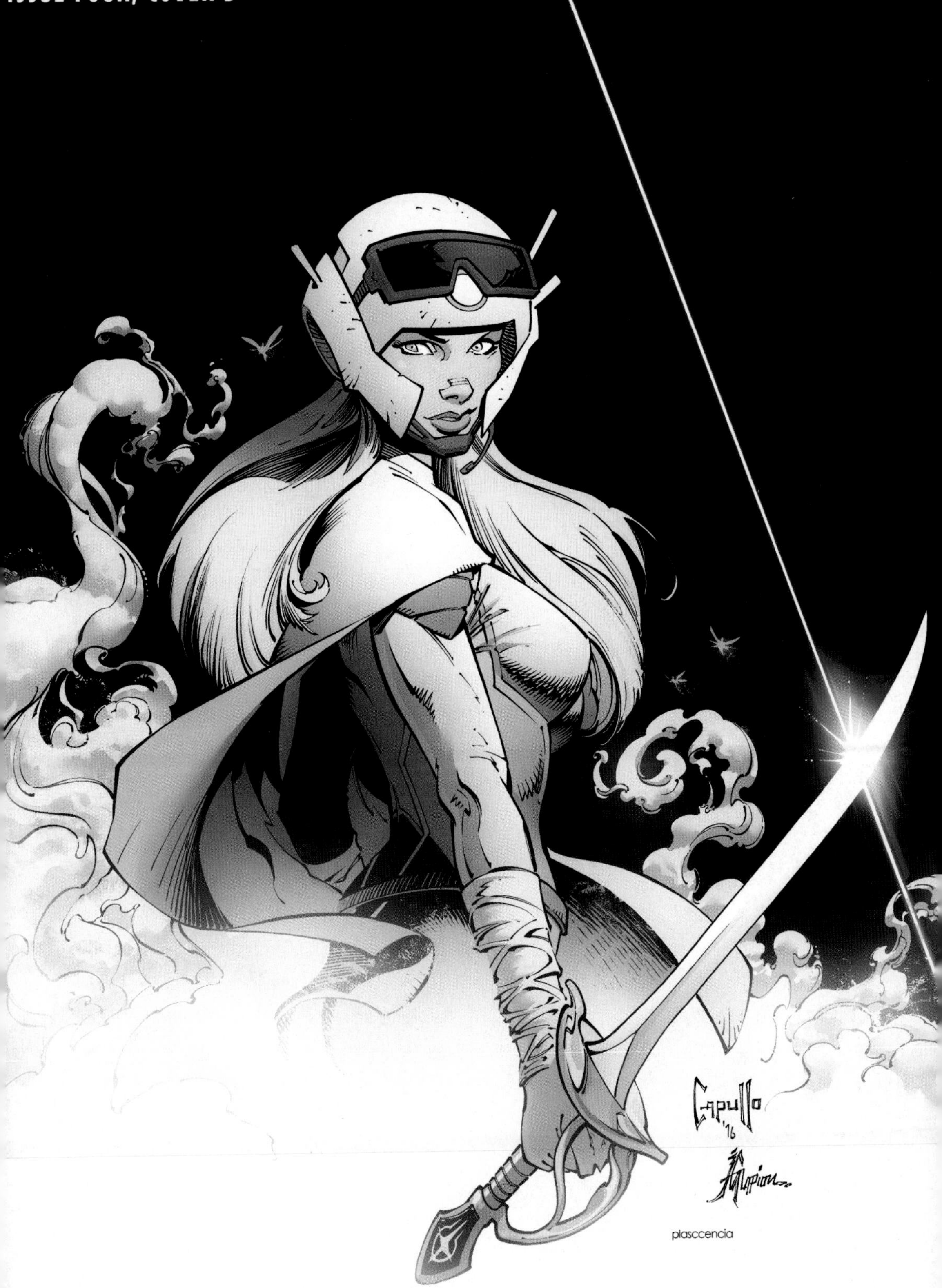
Capullo '16
plascencia

FIVE

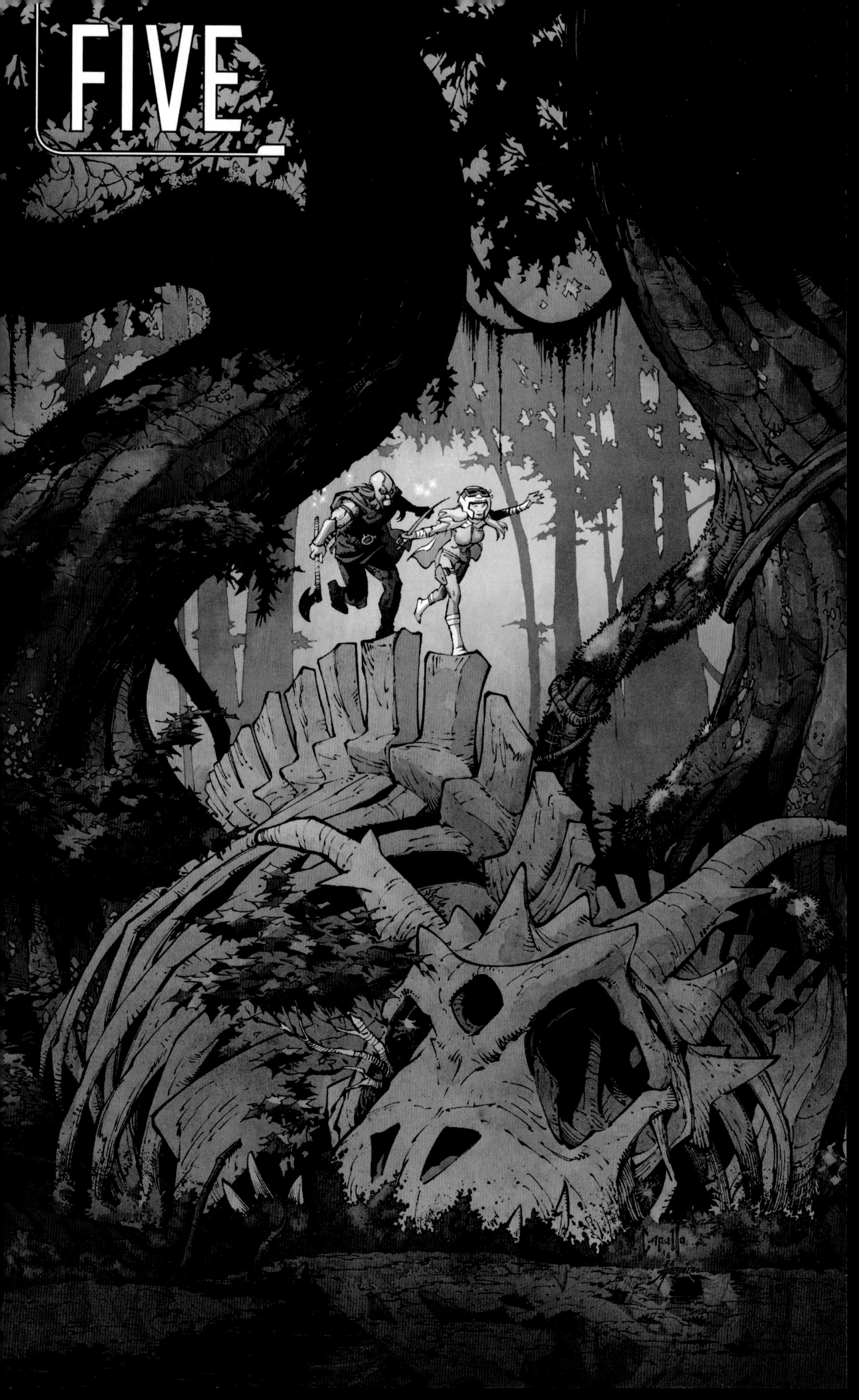

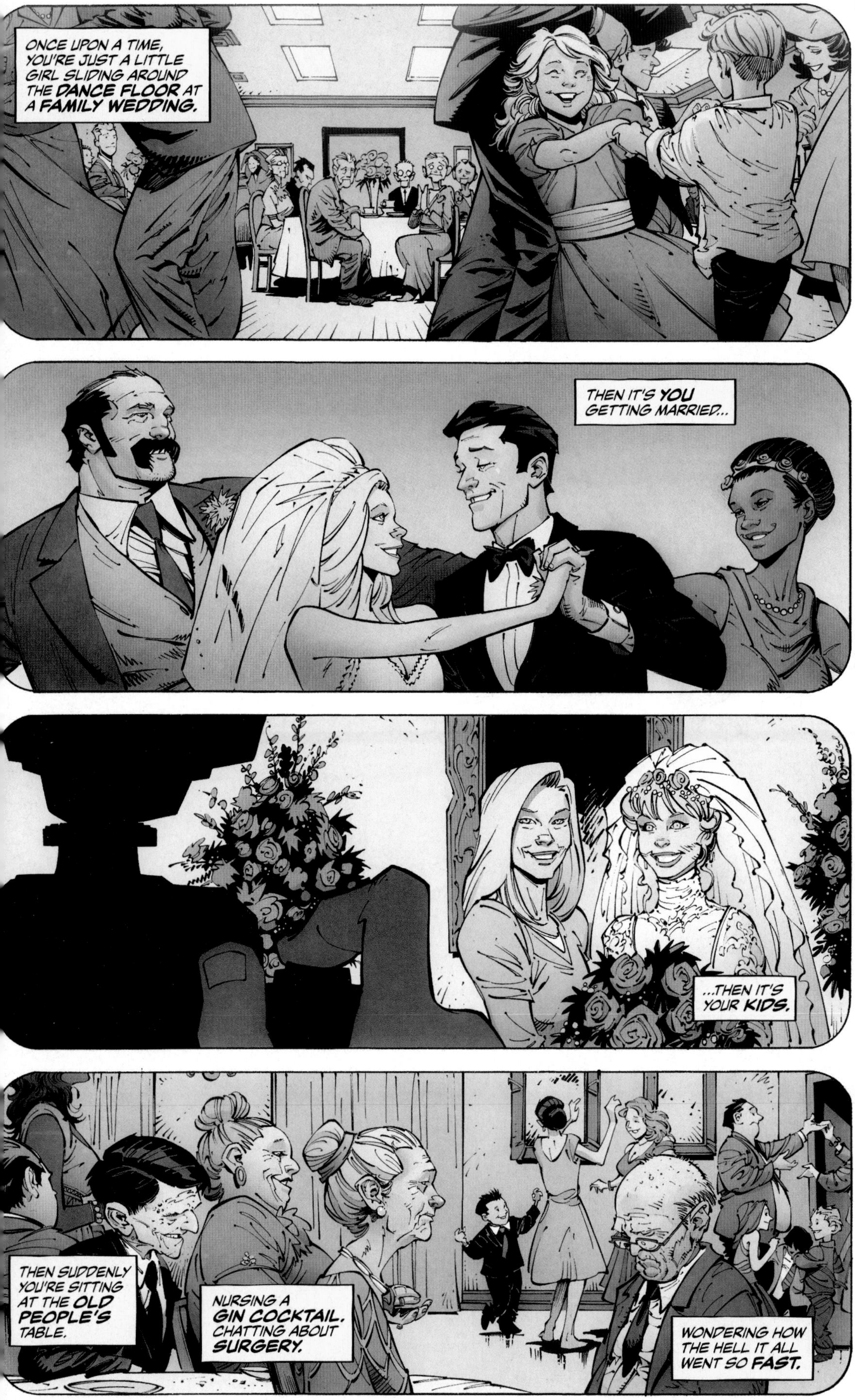
ONCE UPON A TIME, YOU'RE JUST A LITTLE GIRL SLIDING AROUND THE DANCE FLOOR AT A FAMILY WEDDING.
THEN IT'S YOU GETTING MARRIED...
...THEN IT'S YOUR KIDS.
THEN SUDDENLY YOU'RE SITTING AT THE OLD PEOPLE'S TABLE.
NURSING A GIN COCKTAIL. CHATTING ABOUT SURGERY.
WONDERING HOW THE HELL IT ALL WENT SO FAST.

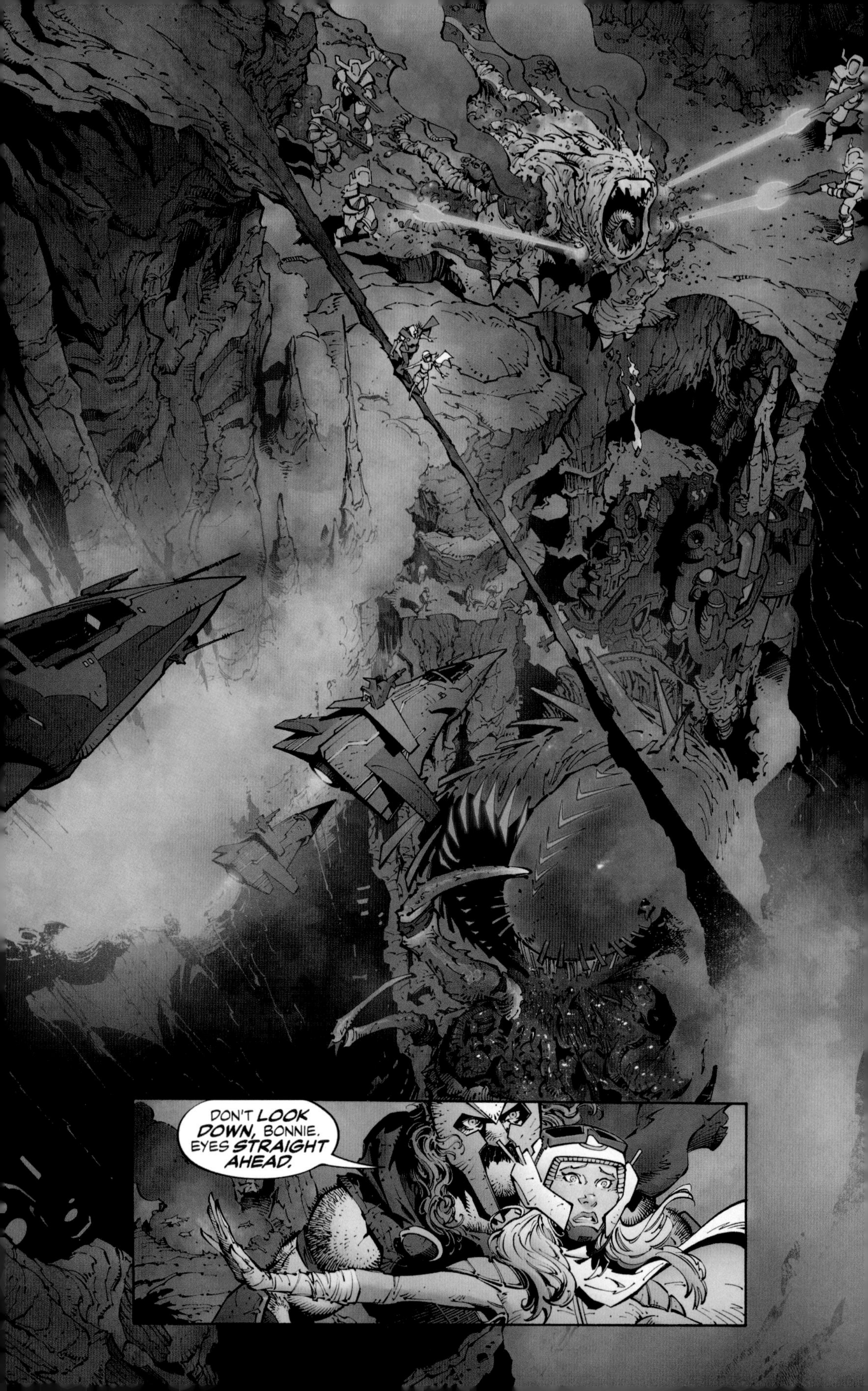
DON'T LOOK DOWN, BONNIE. EYES STRAIGHT AHEAD.

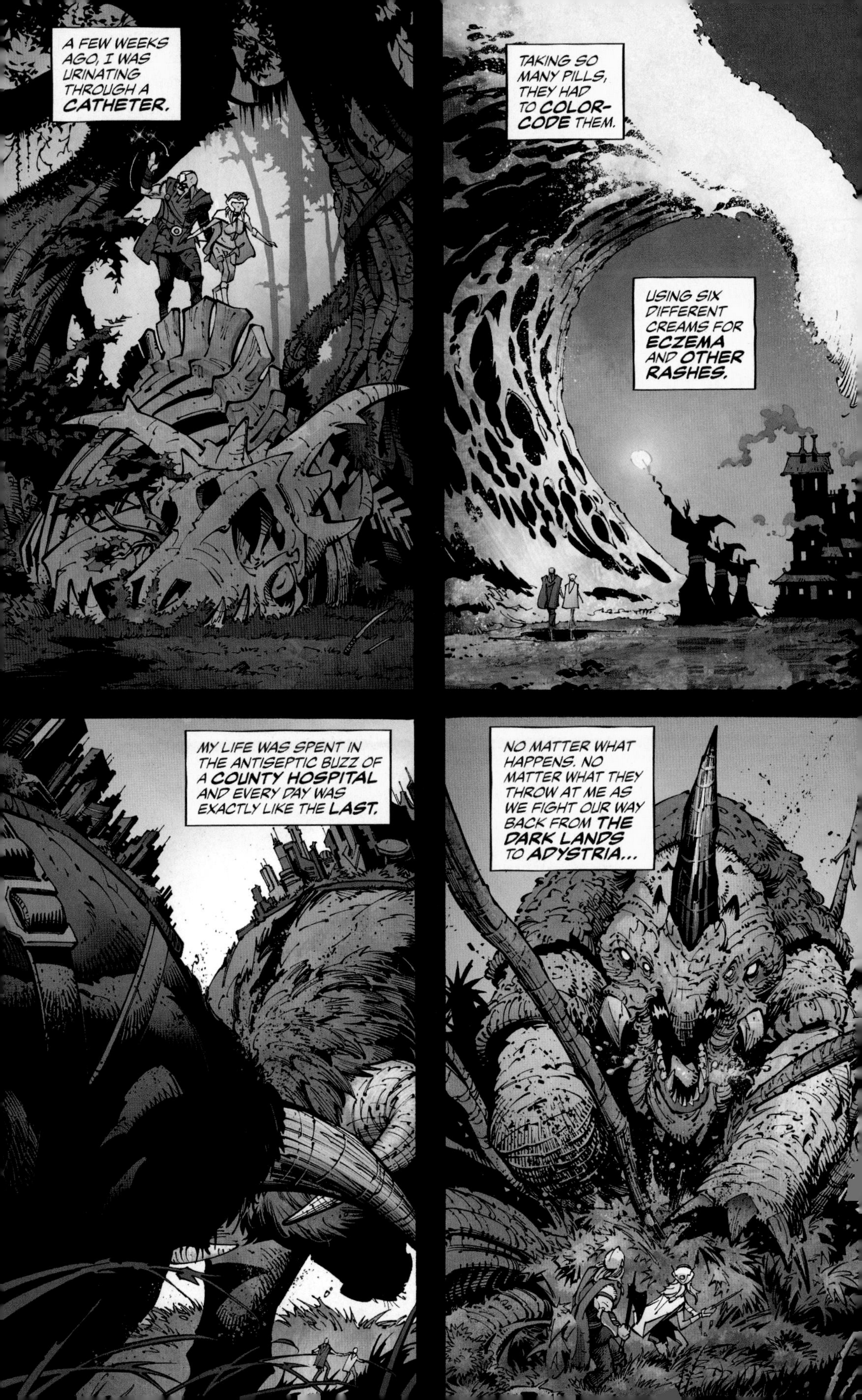
A FEW WEEKS AGO, I WAS URINATING THROUGH A CATHETER.
TAKING SO MANY PILLS, THEY HAD TO COLOR-CODE THEM.
USING SIX DIFFERENT CREAMS FOR ECZEMA AND OTHER RASHES.
MY LIFE WAS SPENT IN THE ANTISEPTIC BUZZ OF A COUNTY HOSPITAL AND EVERY DAY WAS EXACTLY LIKE THE LAST.
NO MATTER WHAT HAPPENS. NO MATTER WHAT THEY THROW AT ME AS WE FIGHT OUR WAY BACK FROM THE DARK LANDS TO ADYSTRIA...

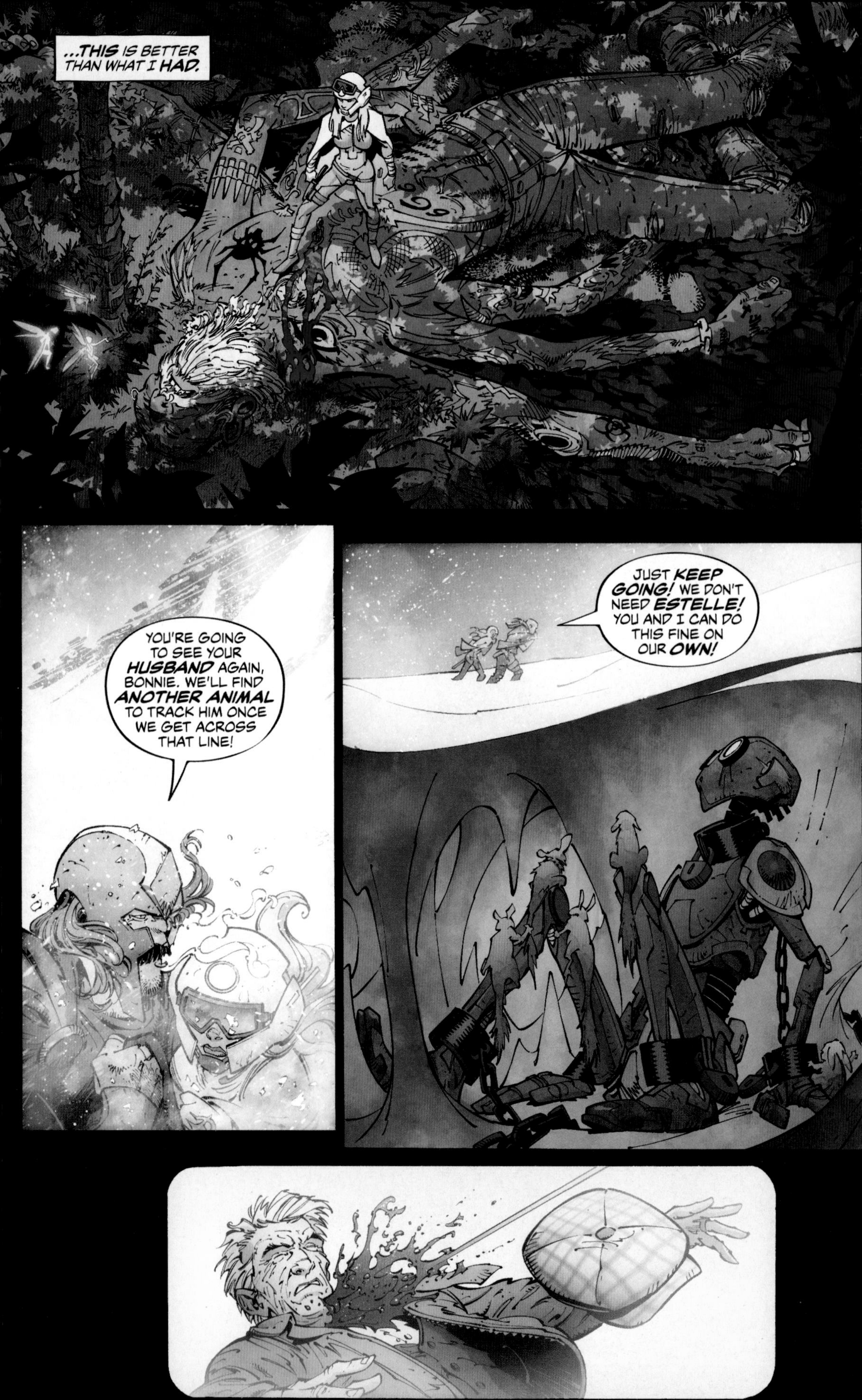

...THIS IS BETTER THAN WHAT I HAD.
YOU'RE GOING TO SEE YOUR HUSBAND AGAIN, BONNIE. WE'LL FIND ANOTHER ANIMAL TO TRACK HIM ONCE WE GET ACROSS THAT LINE!
JUST KEEP GOING! WE DON'T NEED ESTELLE! YOU AND I CAN DO THIS FINE ON OUR OWN!

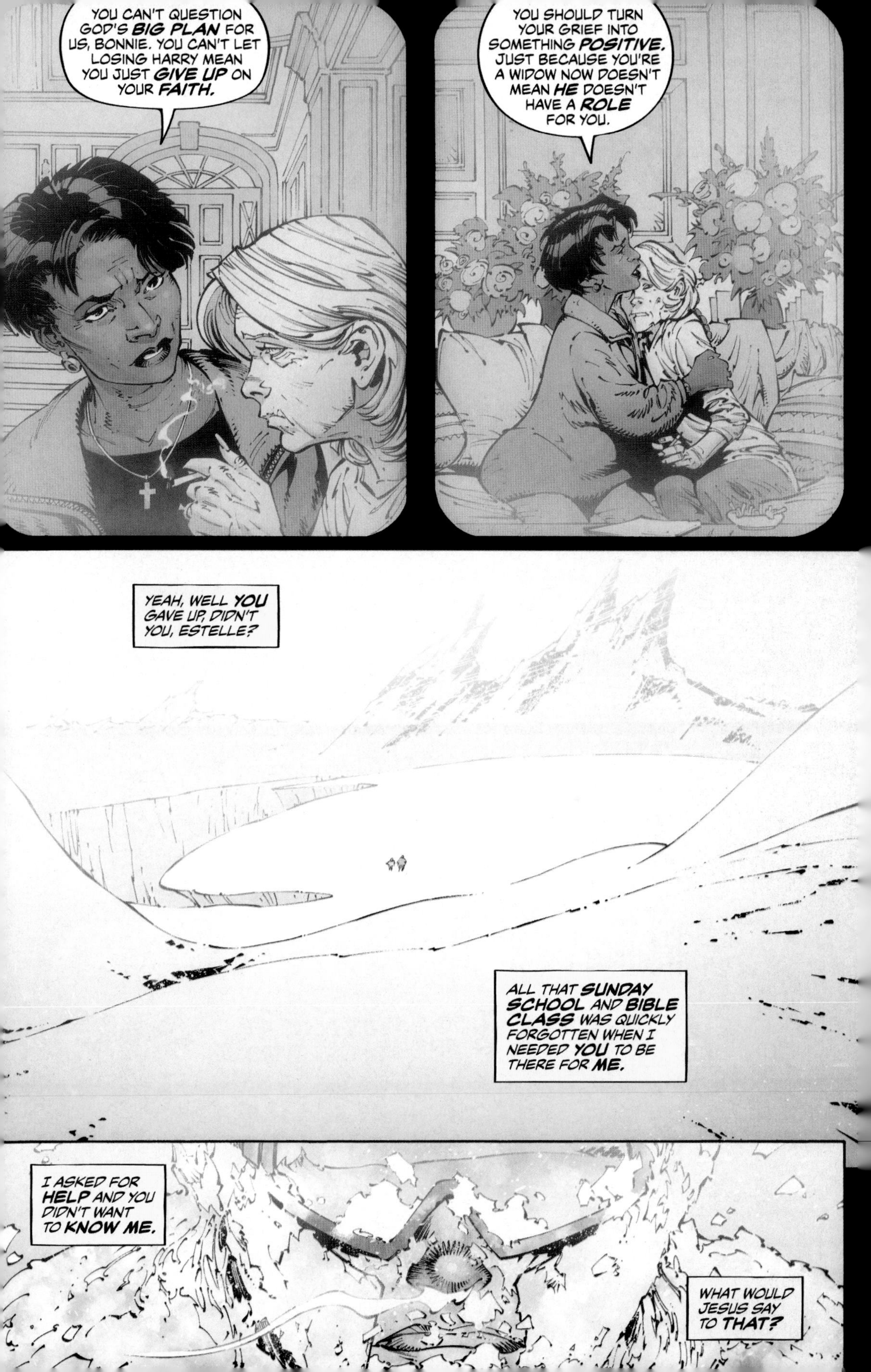
YOU CAN'T QUESTION GOD'S BIG PLAN FOR US, BONNIE. YOU CAN'T LET LOSING HARRY MEAN YOU JUST GIVE UP ON YOUR FAITH.
YOU SHOULD TURN YOUR GRIEF INTO SOMETHING POSITIVE. JUST BECAUSE YOU'RE A WIDOW NOW DOESN'T MEAN HE DOESN'T HAVE A ROLE FOR YOU.
YEAH, WELL YOU GAVE UP, DIDN'T YOU, ESTELLE?
ALL THAT SUNDAY SCHOOL AND BIBLE CLASS WAS QUICKLY FORGOTTEN WHEN I NEEDED YOU TO BE THERE FOR ME.
I ASKED FOR HELP AND YOU DIDN'T WANT TO KNOW ME.
WHAT WOULD JESUS SAY TO THAT?

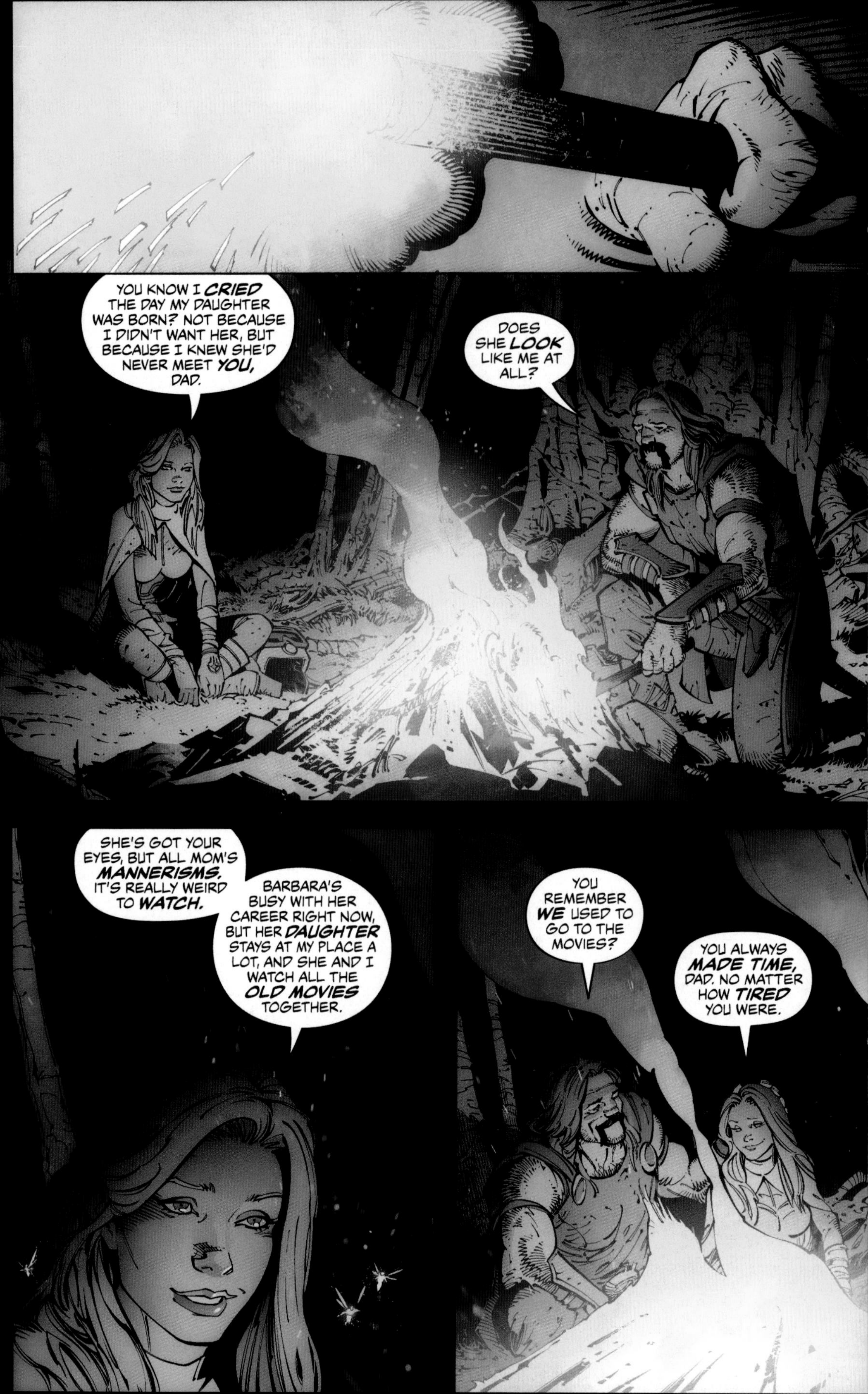

YOU KNOW I CRIED THE DAY MY DAUGHTER WAS BORN? NOT BECAUSE I DIDN'T WANT HER, BUT BECAUSE I KNEW SHE'D NEVER MEET YOU, DAD.
DOES SHE LOOK LIKE ME AT ALL?
SHE'S GOT YOUR EYES, BUT ALL MOM'S MANNERISMS. IT'S REALLY WEIRD TO WATCH.
BARBARA'S BUSY WITH HER CAREER RIGHT NOW, BUT HER DAUGHTER STAYS AT MY PLACE A LOT, AND SHE AND I WATCH ALL THE OLD MOVIES TOGETHER.
YOU REMEMBER WE USED TO GO TO THE MOVIES?
YOU ALWAYS MADE TIME, DAD. NO MATTER HOW TIRED YOU WERE.

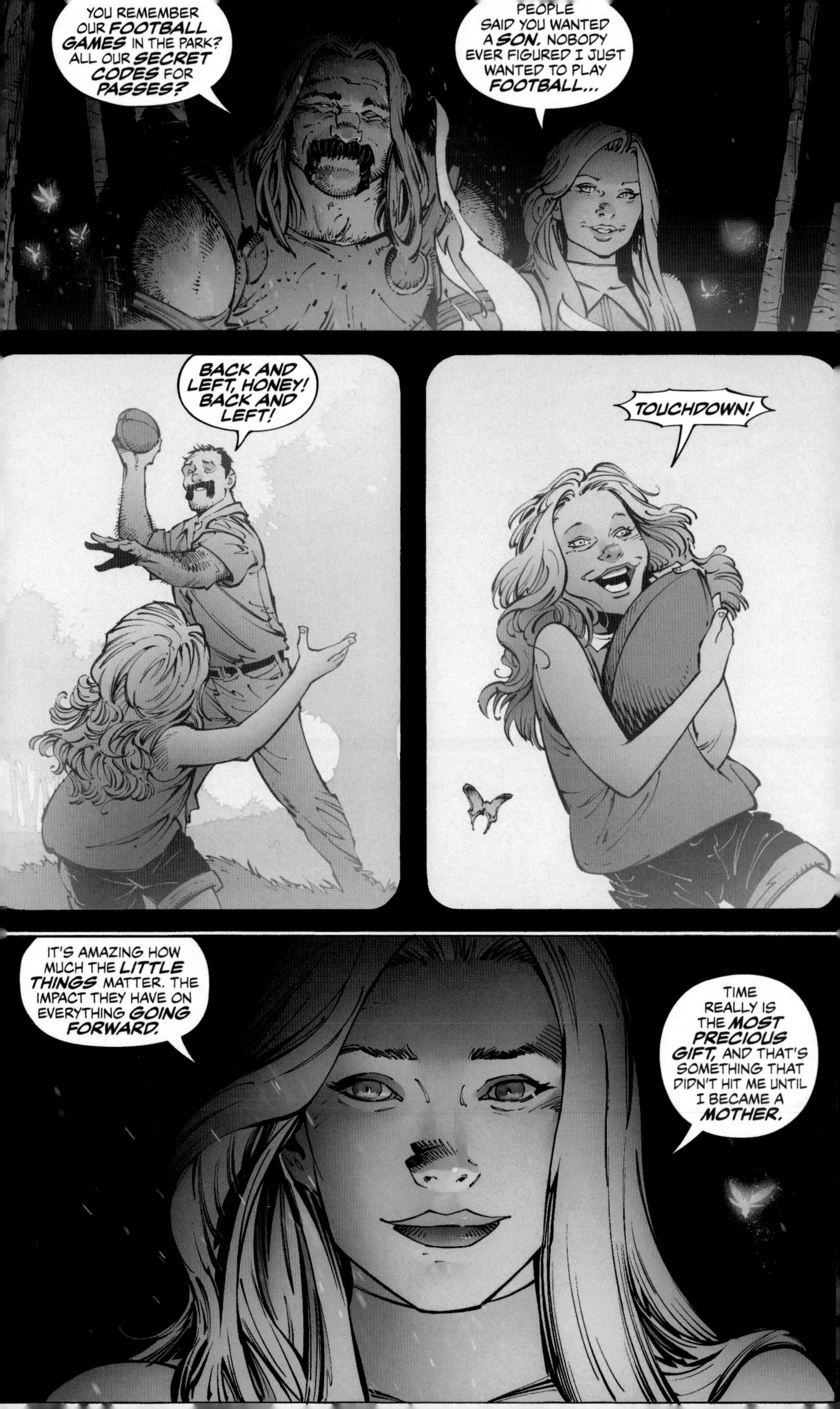

YOU REMEMBER OUR FOOTBALL GAMES IN THE PARK? ALL OUR SECRET CODES FOR PASSES?
PEOPLE SAID YOU WANTED A SON. NOBODY EVER FIGURED I JUST WANTED TO PLAY FOOTBALL...
BACK AND LEFT, HONEY! BACK AND LEFT!
TOUCHDOWN!
IT'S AMAZING HOW MUCH THE LITTLE THINGS MATTER. THE IMPACT THEY HAVE ON EVERYTHING GOING FORWARD.
TIME REALLY IS THE MOST PRECIOUS GIFT, AND THAT'S SOMETHING THAT DIDN'T HIT ME UNTIL I BECAME A MOTHER.

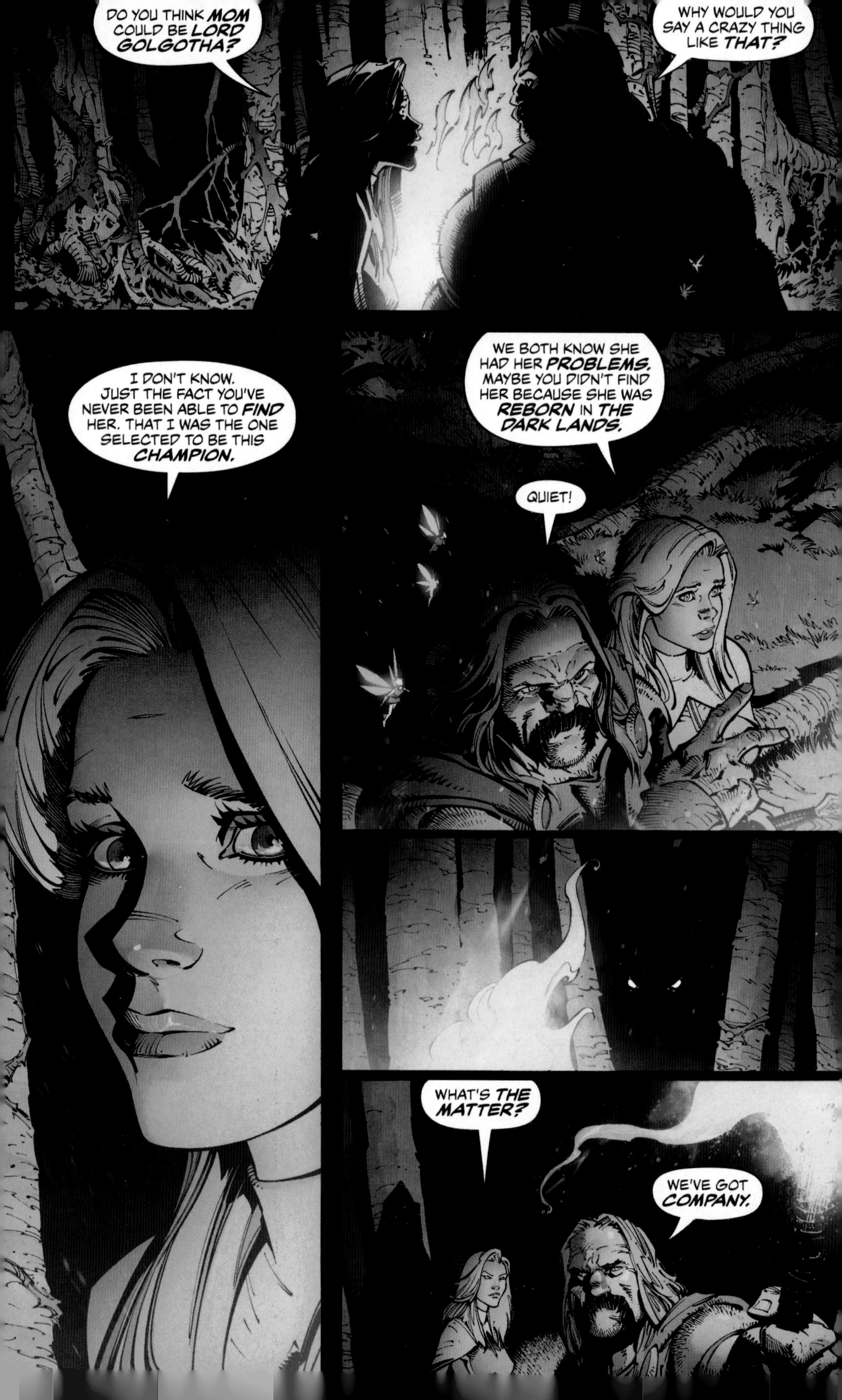

DO YOU THINK MOM COULD BE LORD GOLGOTHA?
WHY WOULD YOU SAY A CRAZY THING LIKE THAT?
I DON'T KNOW. JUST THE FACT YOU'VE NEVER BEEN ABLE TO FIND HER. THAT I WAS THE ONE SELECTED TO BE THIS CHAMPION.
WE BOTH KNOW SHE HAD HER PROBLEMS. MAYBE YOU DIDN'T FIND HER BECAUSE SHE WAS REBORN IN THE DARK LANDS.
QUIET!
WHAT'S THE MATTER?
WE'VE GOT COMPANY.

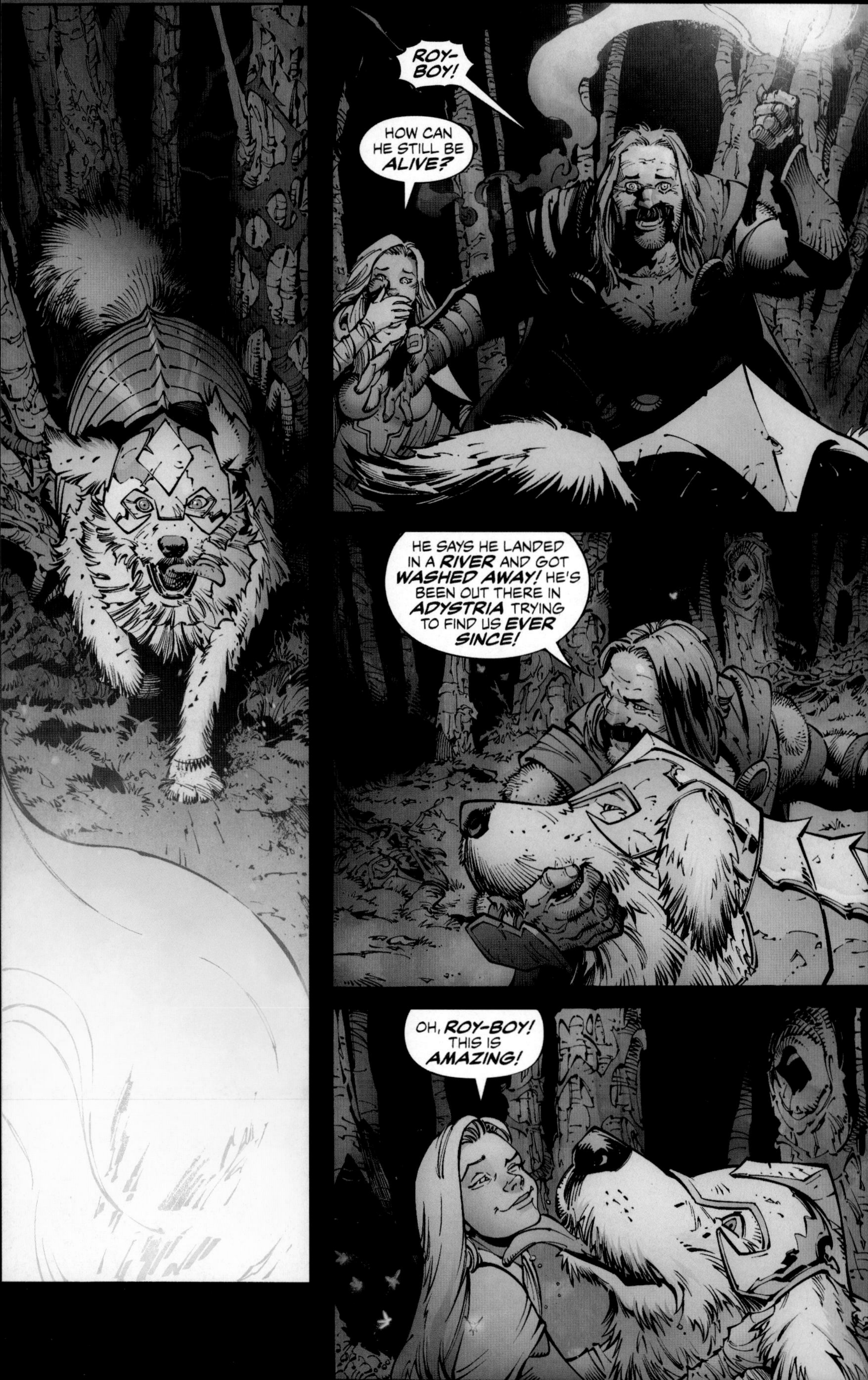
ROY-BOY!
HOW CAN HE STILL BE ALIVE?
HE SAYS HE LANDED IN A RIVER AND GOT WASHED AWAY! HE'S BEEN OUT THERE IN ADYSTRIA TRYING TO FIND US EVER SINCE!
OH, ROY-BOY! THIS IS AMAZING!

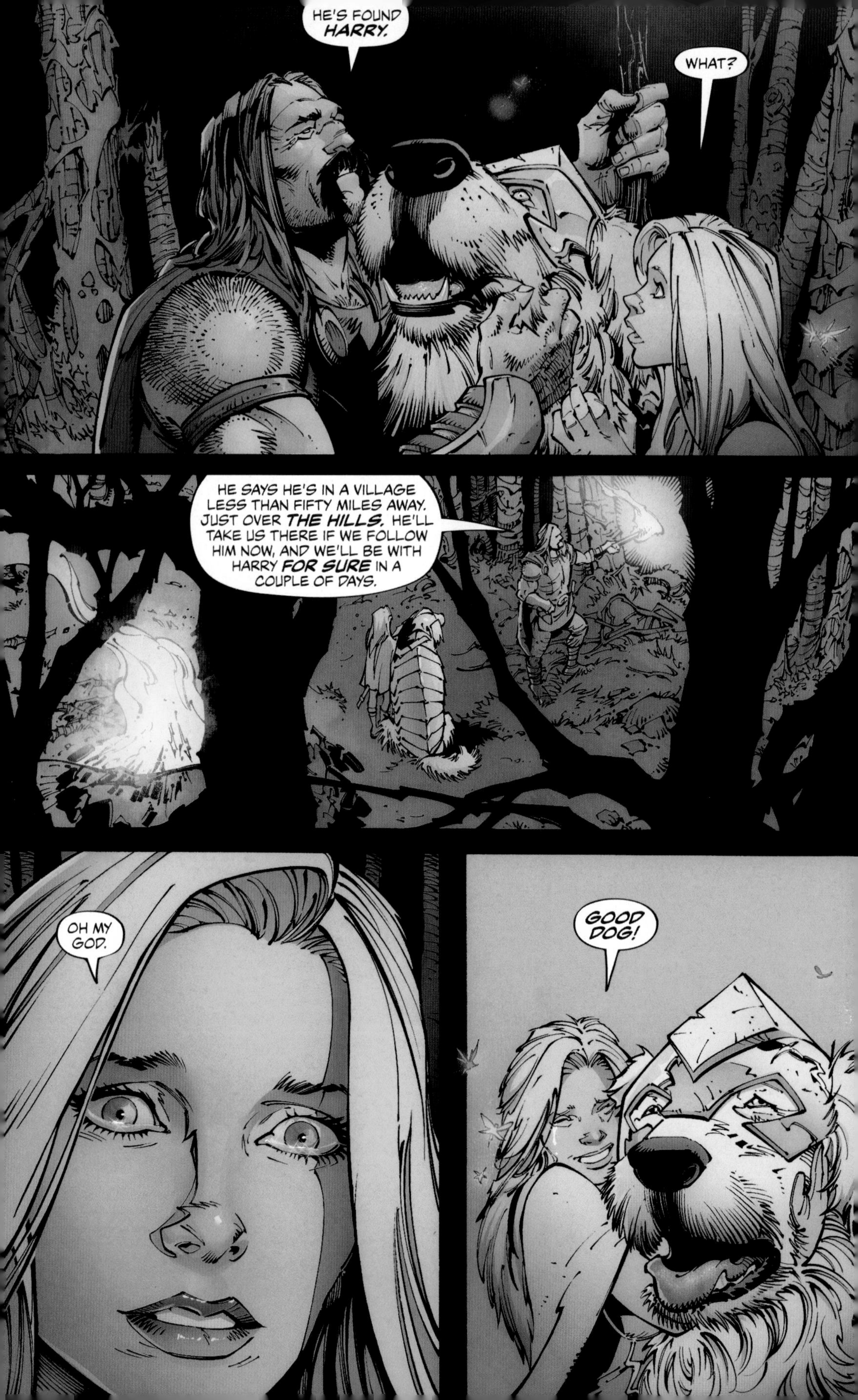
HE'S FOUND HARRY.
WHAT?
HE SAYS HE'S IN A VILLAGE LESS THAN FIFTY MILES AWAY. JUST OVER THE HILLS. HE'LL TAKE US THERE IF WE FOLLOW HIM NOW, AND WE'LL BE WITH HARRY FOR SURE IN A COUPLE OF DAYS.
OH MY GOD.
GOOD DOG!

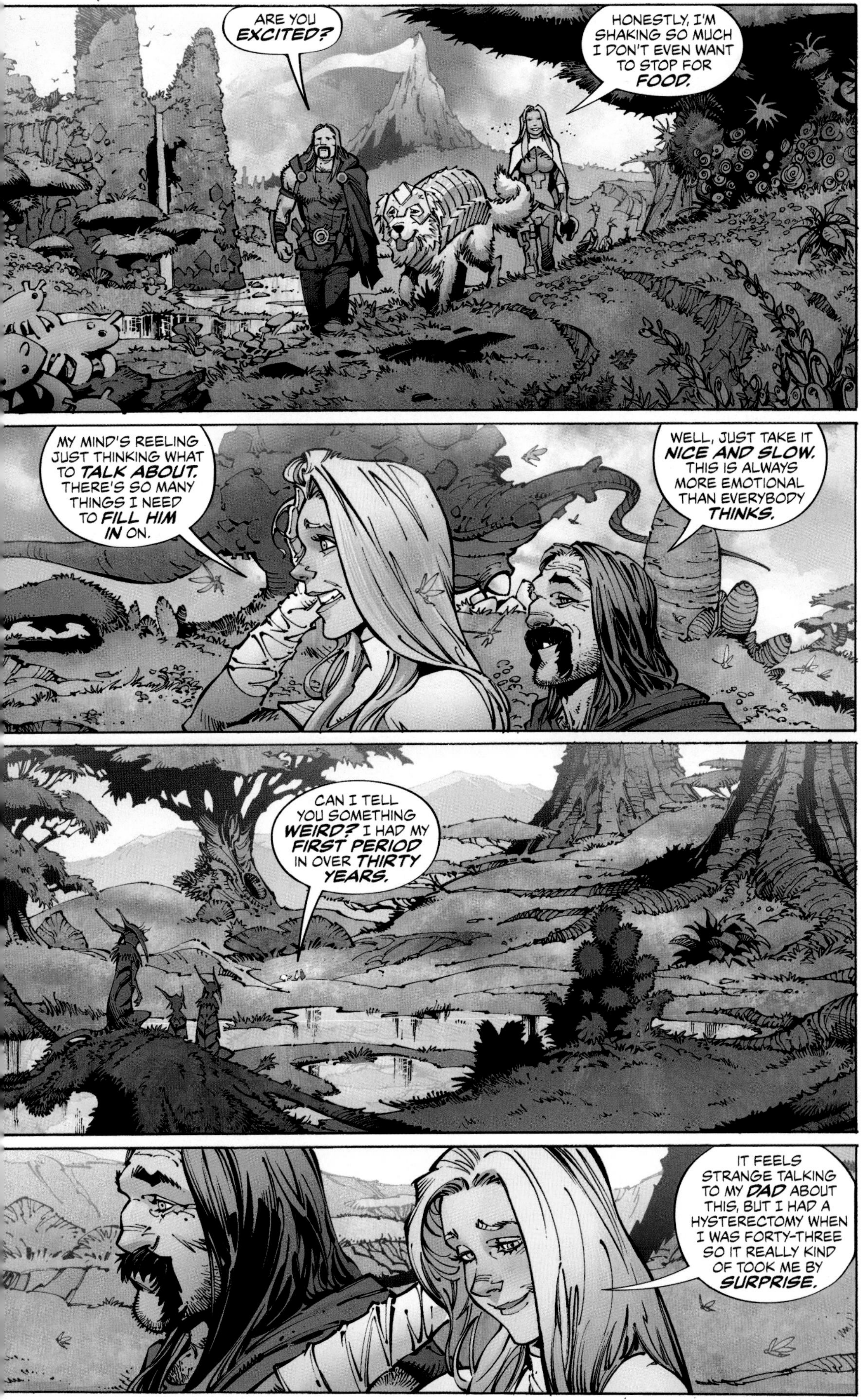
ARE YOU EXCITED?
HONESTLY, I'M SHAKING SO MUCH I DON'T EVEN WANT TO STOP FOR FOOD.
MY MIND'S REELING JUST THINKING WHAT TO TALK ABOUT. THERE'S SO MANY THINGS I NEED TO FILL HIM IN ON.
WELL, JUST TAKE IT NICE AND SLOW. THIS IS ALWAYS MORE EMOTIONAL THAN EVERYBODY THINKS.
CAN I TELL YOU SOMETHING WEIRD? I HAD MY FIRST PERIOD IN OVER THIRTY YEARS.
IT FEELS STRANGE TALKING TO MY DAD ABOUT THIS, BUT I HAD A HYSTERECTOMY WHEN I WAS FORTY-THREE SO IT REALLY KIND OF TOOK ME BY SURPRISE.

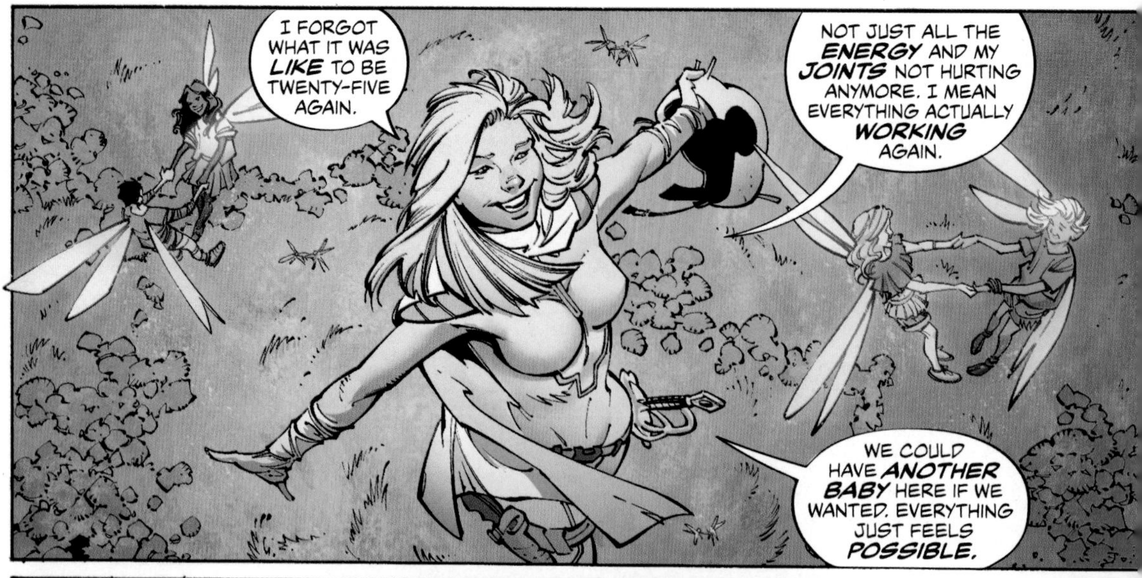
I FORGOT WHAT IT WAS LIKE TO BE TWENTY-FIVE AGAIN.
NOT JUST ALL THE ENERGY AND MY JOINTS NOT HURTING ANYMORE. I MEAN EVERYTHING ACTUALLY WORKING AGAIN.
WE COULD HAVE ANOTHER BABY HERE IF WE WANTED. EVERYTHING JUST FEELS POSSIBLE.

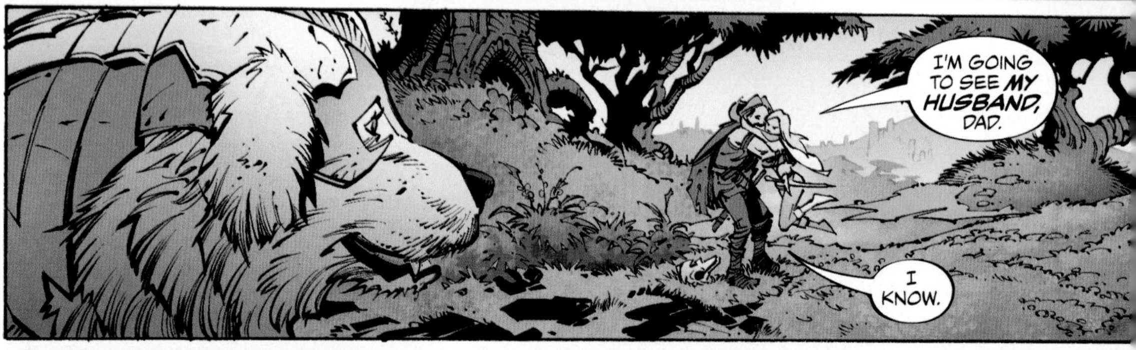
I'M GOING TO SEE MY HUSBAND, DAD.
I KNOW.

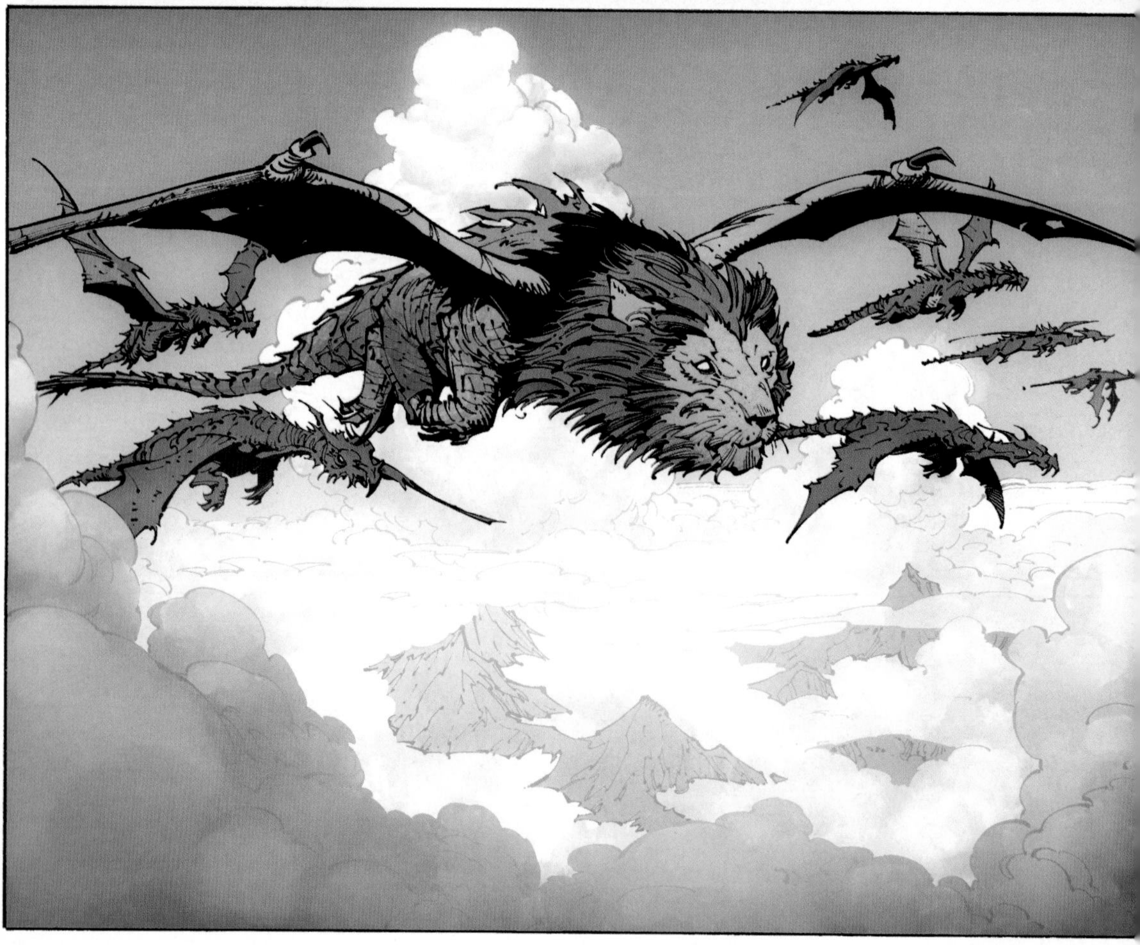

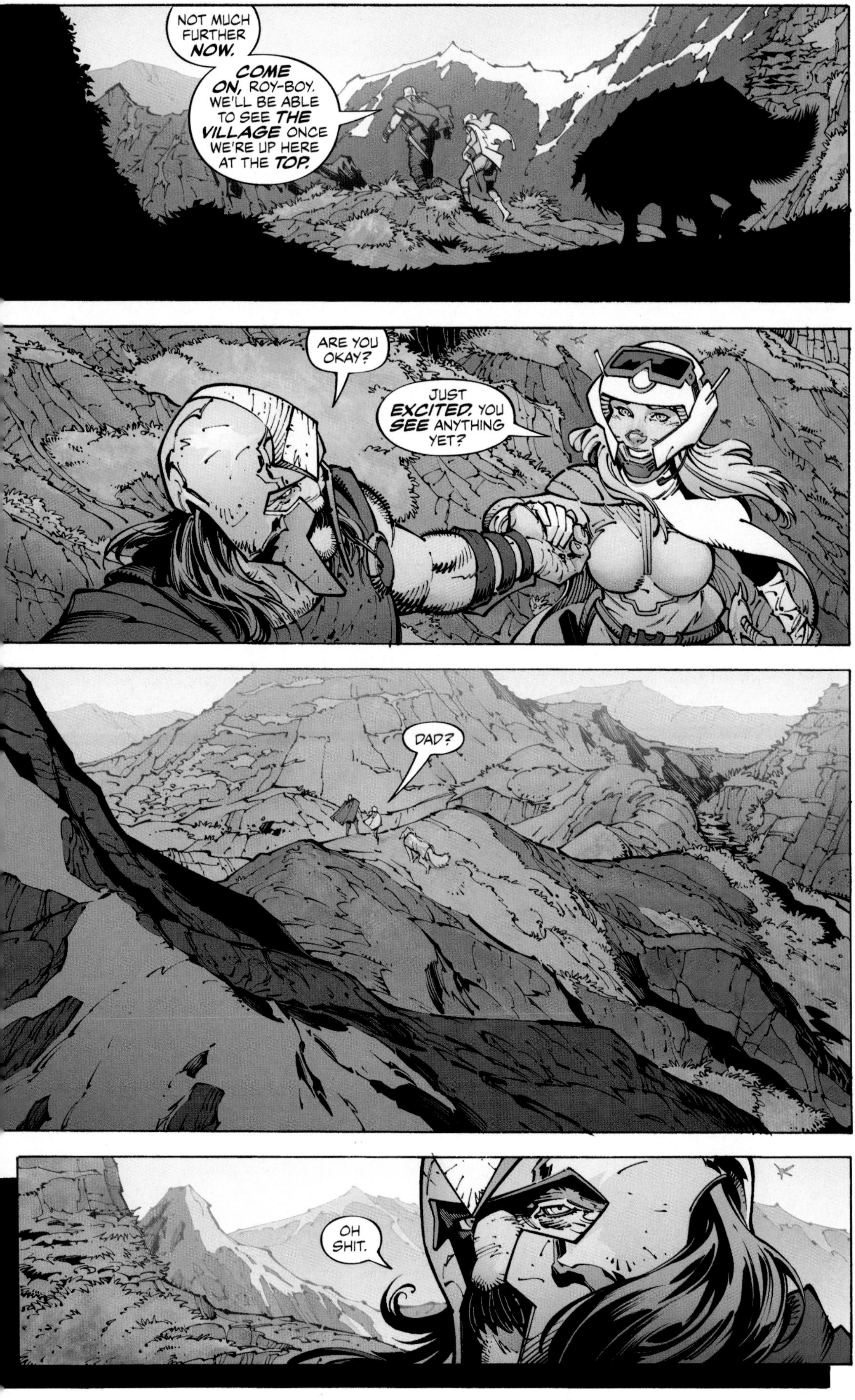
NOT MUCH FURTHER NOW.
COME ON, ROY-BOY. WE'LL BE ABLE TO SEE THE VILLAGE ONCE WE'RE UP HERE AT THE TOP.
ARE YOU OKAY?
JUST EXCITED. YOU SEE ANYTHING YET?
DAD?
OH SHIT.

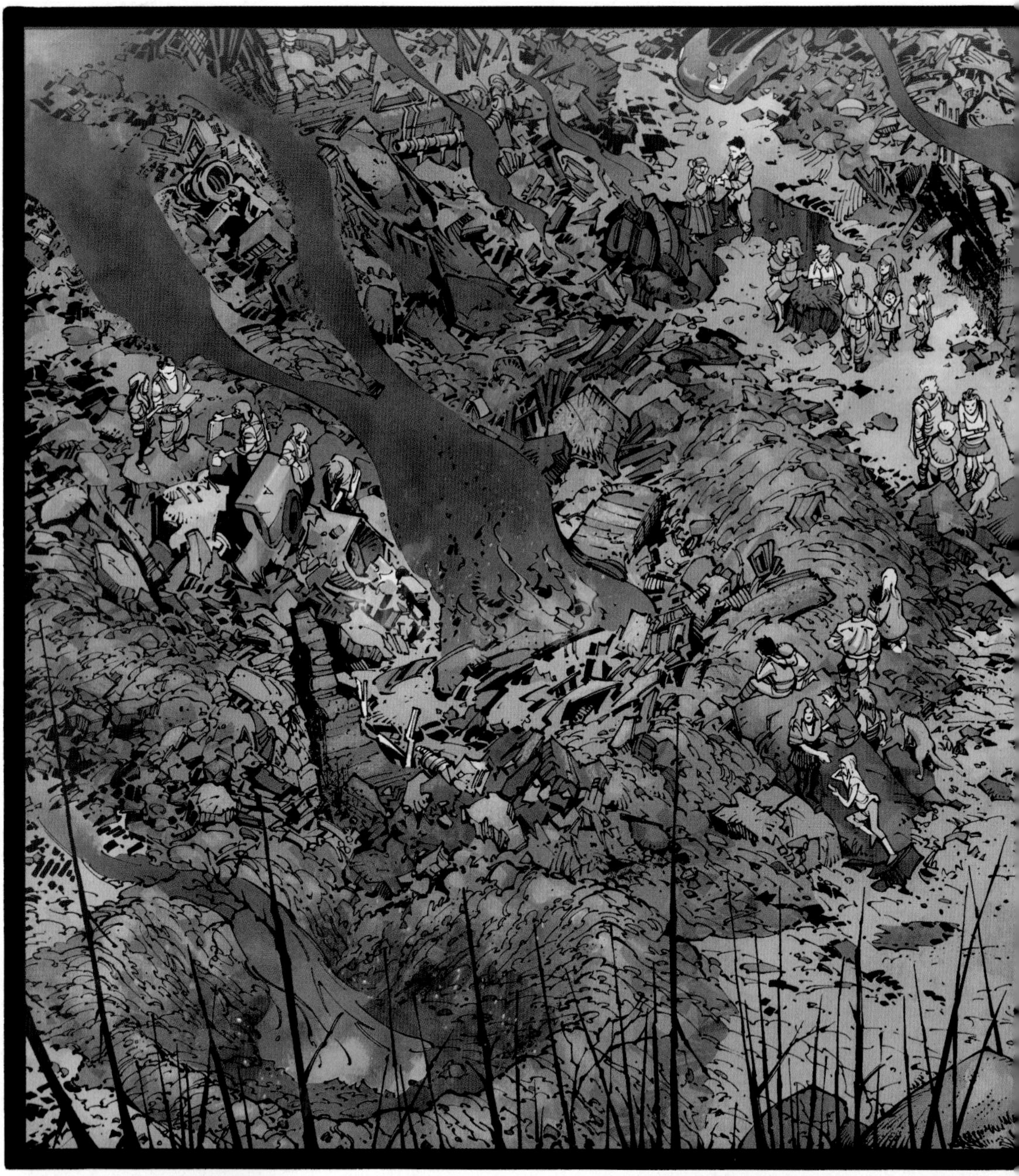
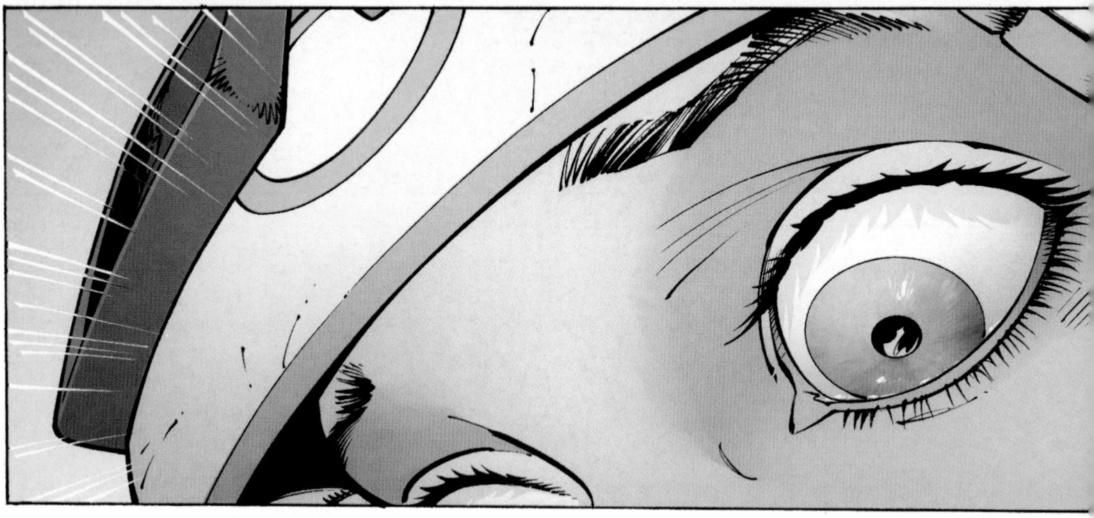

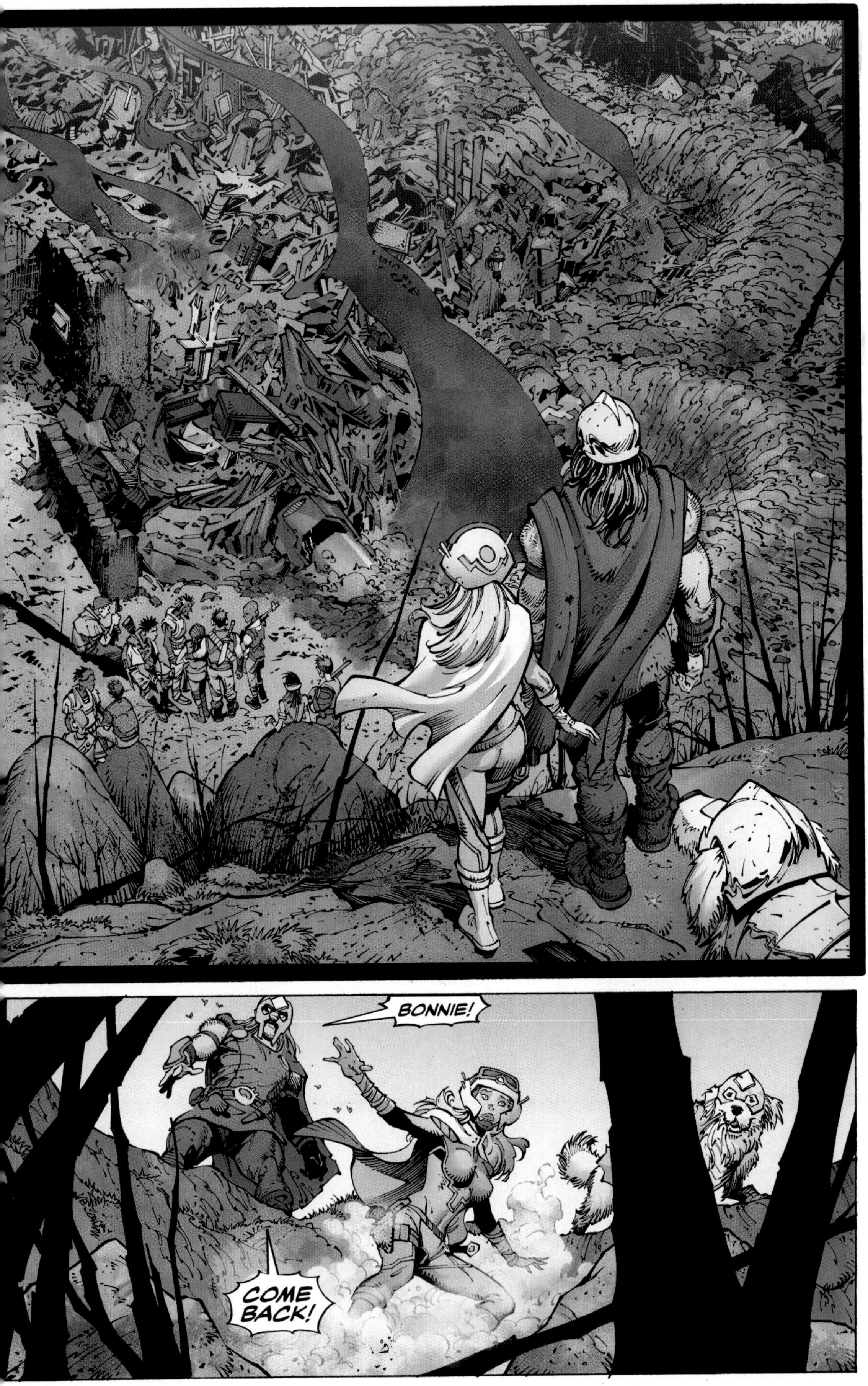
BONNIE!
COME BACK!

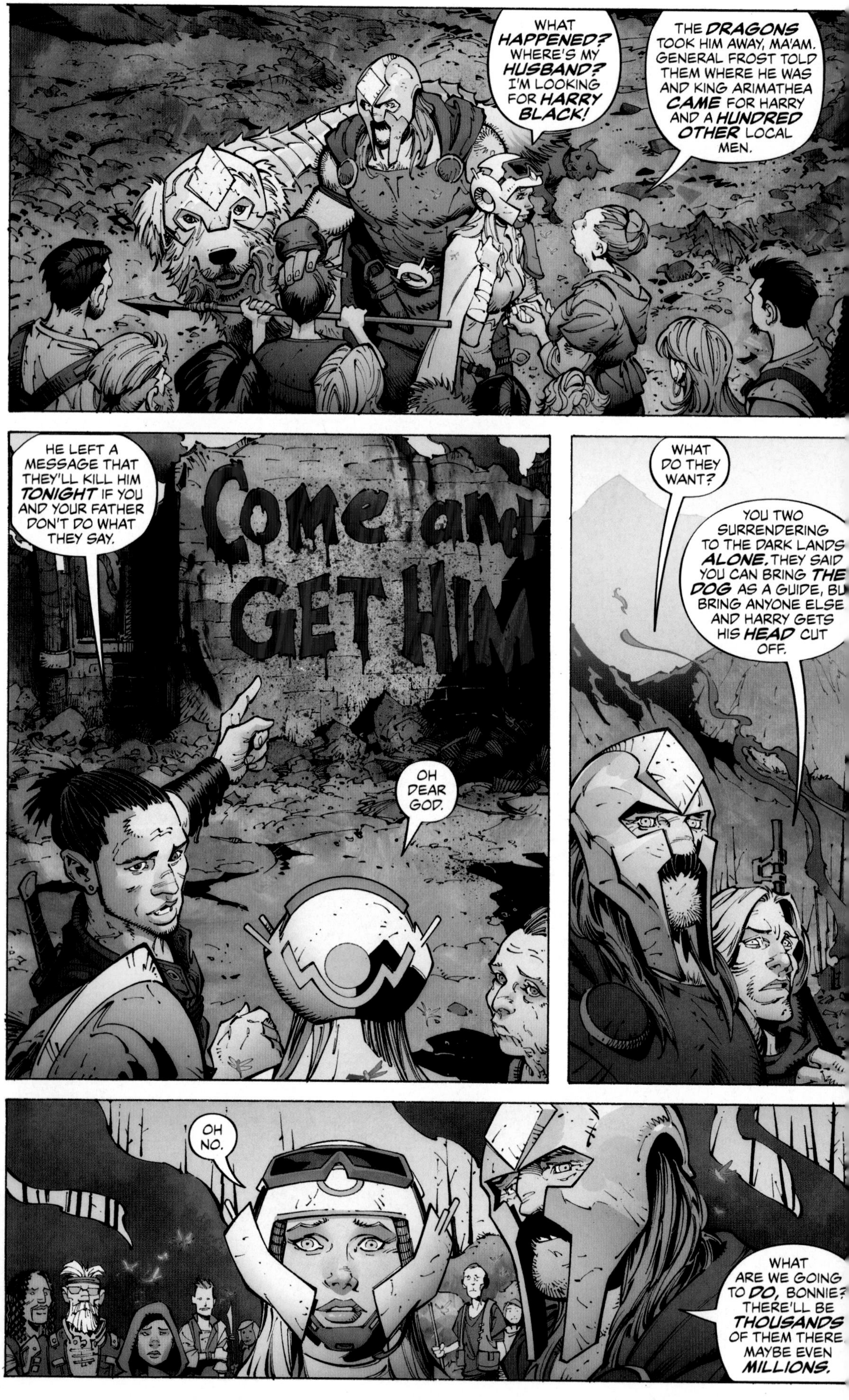

WHAT HAPPENED? WHERE'S MY HUSBAND? I'M LOOKING FOR HARRY BLACK!
THE DRAGONS TOOK HIM AWAY, MA'AM. GENERAL FROST TOLD THEM WHERE HE WAS AND KING ARIMATHEA CAME FOR HARRY AND A HUNDRED OTHER LOCAL MEN.
HE LEFT A MESSAGE THAT THEY'LL KILL HIM TONIGHT IF YOU AND YOUR FATHER DON'T DO WHAT THEY SAY.
Come and GET HIM
OH DEAR GOD.
WHAT DO THEY WANT?
YOU TWO SURRENDERING TO THE DARK LANDS ALONE. THEY SAID YOU CAN BRING THE DOG AS A GUIDE, BU BRING ANYONE ELSE AND HARRY GETS HIS HEAD CUT OFF.
OH NO.
WHAT ARE WE GOING TO DO, BONNIE? THERE'LL BE THOUSANDS OF THEM THERE MAYBE EVEN MILLIONS.

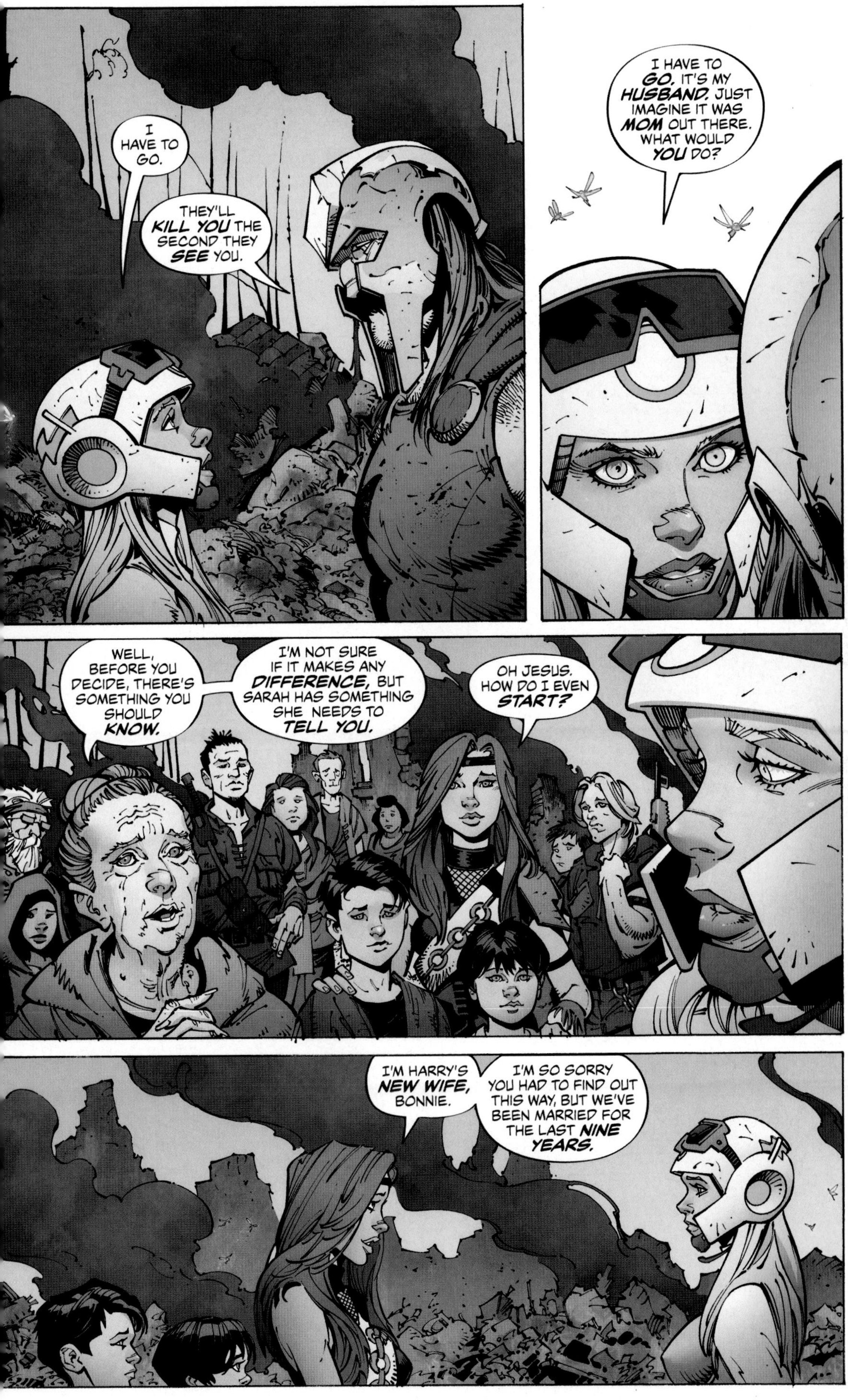
I HAVE TO GO.
THEY'LL KILL YOU THE SECOND THEY SEE YOU.
I HAVE TO GO, IT'S MY HUSBAND. JUST IMAGINE IT WAS MOM OUT THERE. WHAT WOULD YOU DO?
WELL, BEFORE YOU DECIDE, THERE'S SOMETHING YOU SHOULD KNOW.
I'M NOT SURE IF IT MAKES ANY DIFFERENCE, BUT SARAH HAS SOMETHING SHE NEEDS TO TELL YOU.
OH JESUS. HOW DO I EVEN START?
I'M HARRY'S NEW WIFE, BONNIE.
I'M SO SORRY YOU HAD TO FIND OUT THIS WAY, BUT WE'VE BEEN MARRIED FOR THE LAST NINE YEARS.

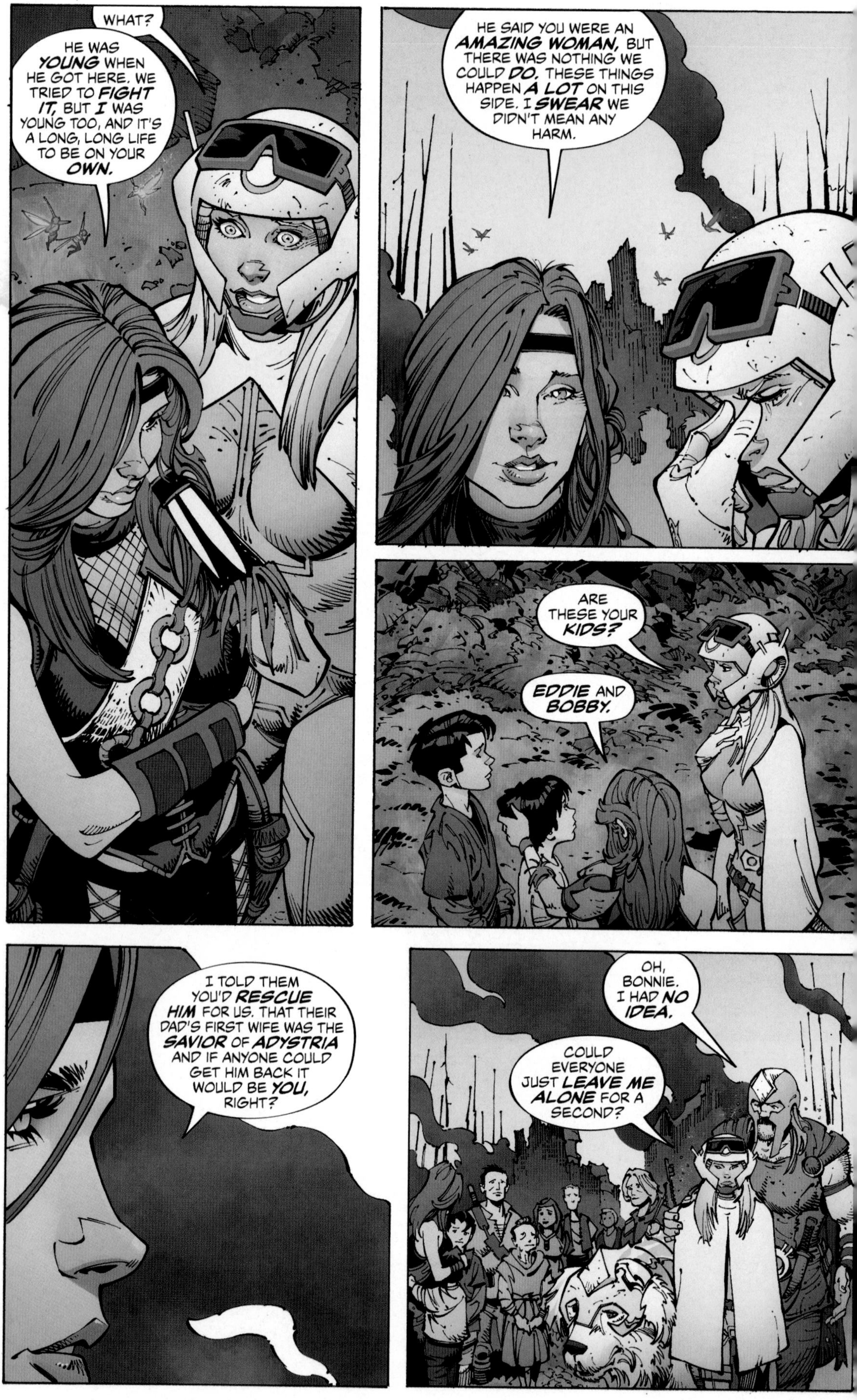
WHAT?
HE WAS YOUNG WHEN HE GOT HERE. WE TRIED TO FIGHT IT, BUT I WAS YOUNG TOO, AND IT'S A LONG, LONG LIFE TO BE ON YOUR OWN.
HE SAID YOU WERE AN AMAZING WOMAN, BUT THERE WAS NOTHING WE COULD DO. THESE THINGS HAPPEN A LOT ON THIS SIDE. I SWEAR WE DIDN'T MEAN ANY HARM.
ARE THESE YOUR KIDS?
EDDIE AND BOBBY.
I TOLD THEM YOU'D RESCUE HIM FOR US. THAT THEIR DAD'S FIRST WIFE WAS THE SAVIOR OF ADYSTRIA AND IF ANYONE COULD GET HIM BACK IT WOULD BE YOU, RIGHT?
OH, BONNIE. I HAD NO IDEA.
COULD EVERYONE JUST LEAVE ME ALONE FOR A SECOND?

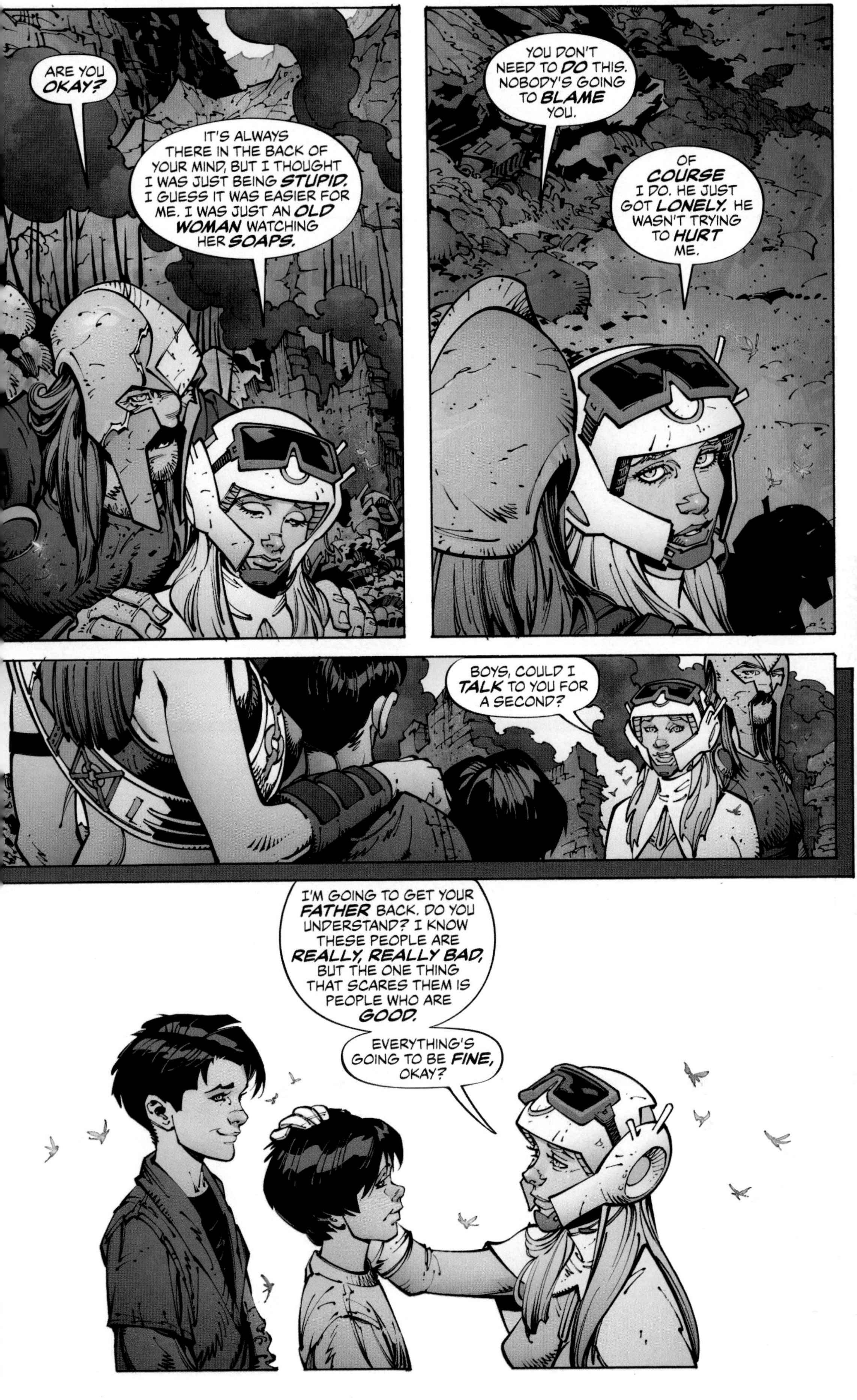
ARE YOU OKAY?
IT'S ALWAYS THERE IN THE BACK OF YOUR MIND, BUT I THOUGHT I WAS JUST BEING STUPID. I GUESS IT WAS EASIER FOR ME. I WAS JUST AN OLD WOMAN WATCHING HER SOAPS.
YOU DON'T NEED TO DO THIS. NOBODY'S GOING TO BLAME YOU.
OF COURSE I DO. HE JUST GOT LONELY. HE WASN'T TRYING TO HURT ME.
BOYS, COULD I TALK TO YOU FOR A SECOND?
I'M GOING TO GET YOUR FATHER BACK. DO YOU UNDERSTAND? I KNOW THESE PEOPLE ARE REALLY, REALLY BAD, BUT THE ONE THING THAT SCARES THEM IS PEOPLE WHO ARE GOOD.
EVERYTHING'S GOING TO BE FINE, OKAY?

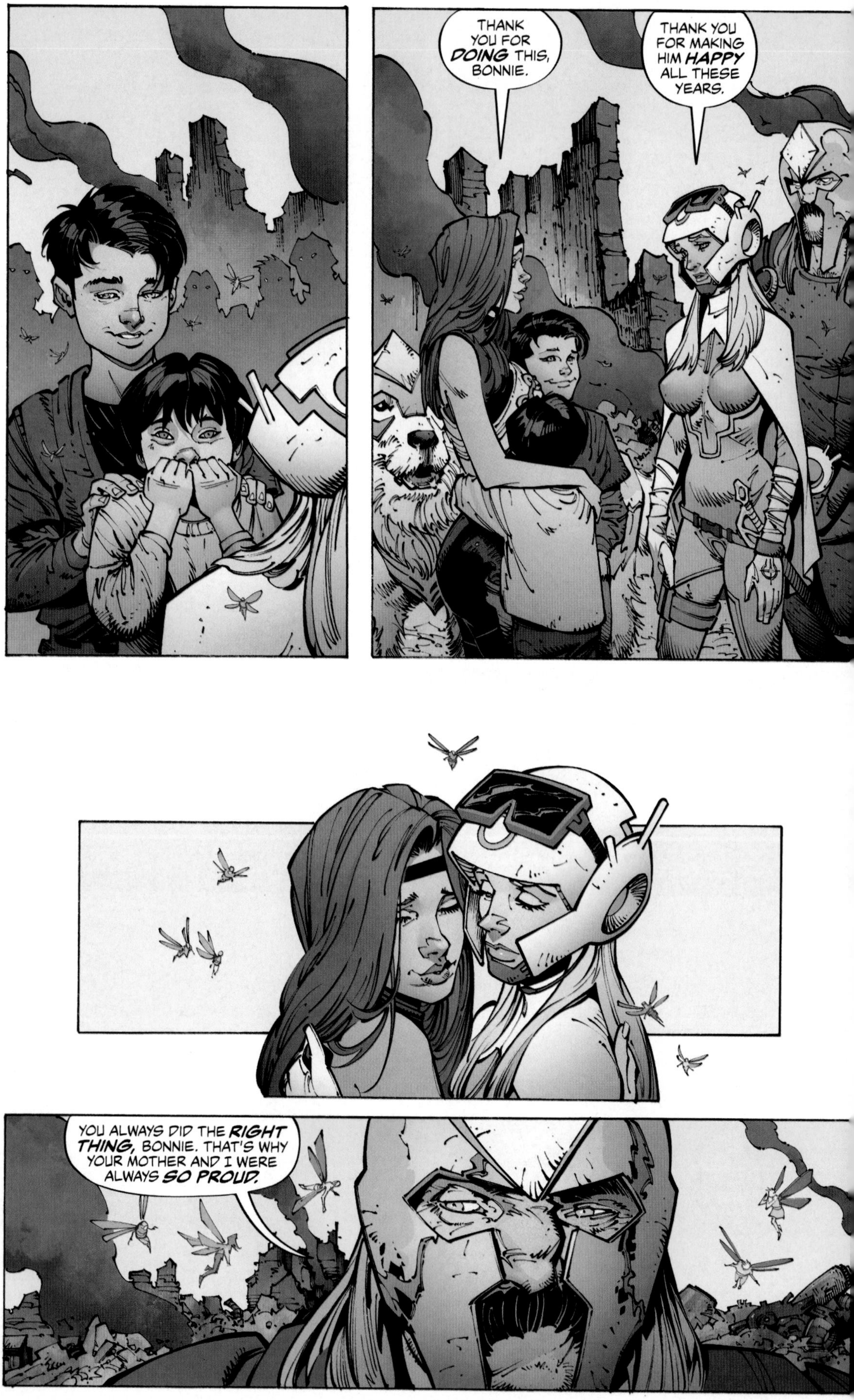
THANK YOU FOR DOING THIS, BONNIE.
THANK YOU FOR MAKING HIM HAPPY ALL THESE YEARS.
YOU ALWAYS DID THE RIGHT THING, BONNIE. THAT'S WHY YOUR MOTHER AND I WERE ALWAYS SO PROUD.

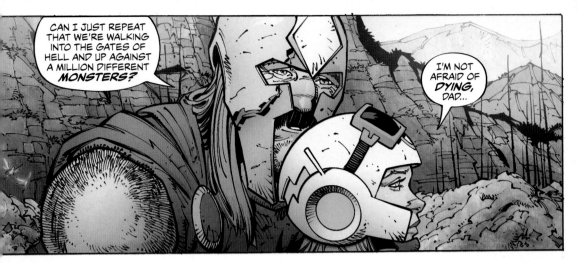

CAN I JUST REPEAT THAT WE'RE WALKING INTO THE GATES OF HELL AND UP AGAINST A MILLION DIFFERENT *MONSTERS?*

I'M NOT AFRAID OF *DYING,* DAD...

...NOT *ANYMORE.*

BESIDES, IF THE PROPHECY IS *TRUE* AND I'M THE ONE WHO'S GOING TO *KILL* THIS GUY...

...HE'S THE ONE WHO SHOULD BE *NERVOUS.*

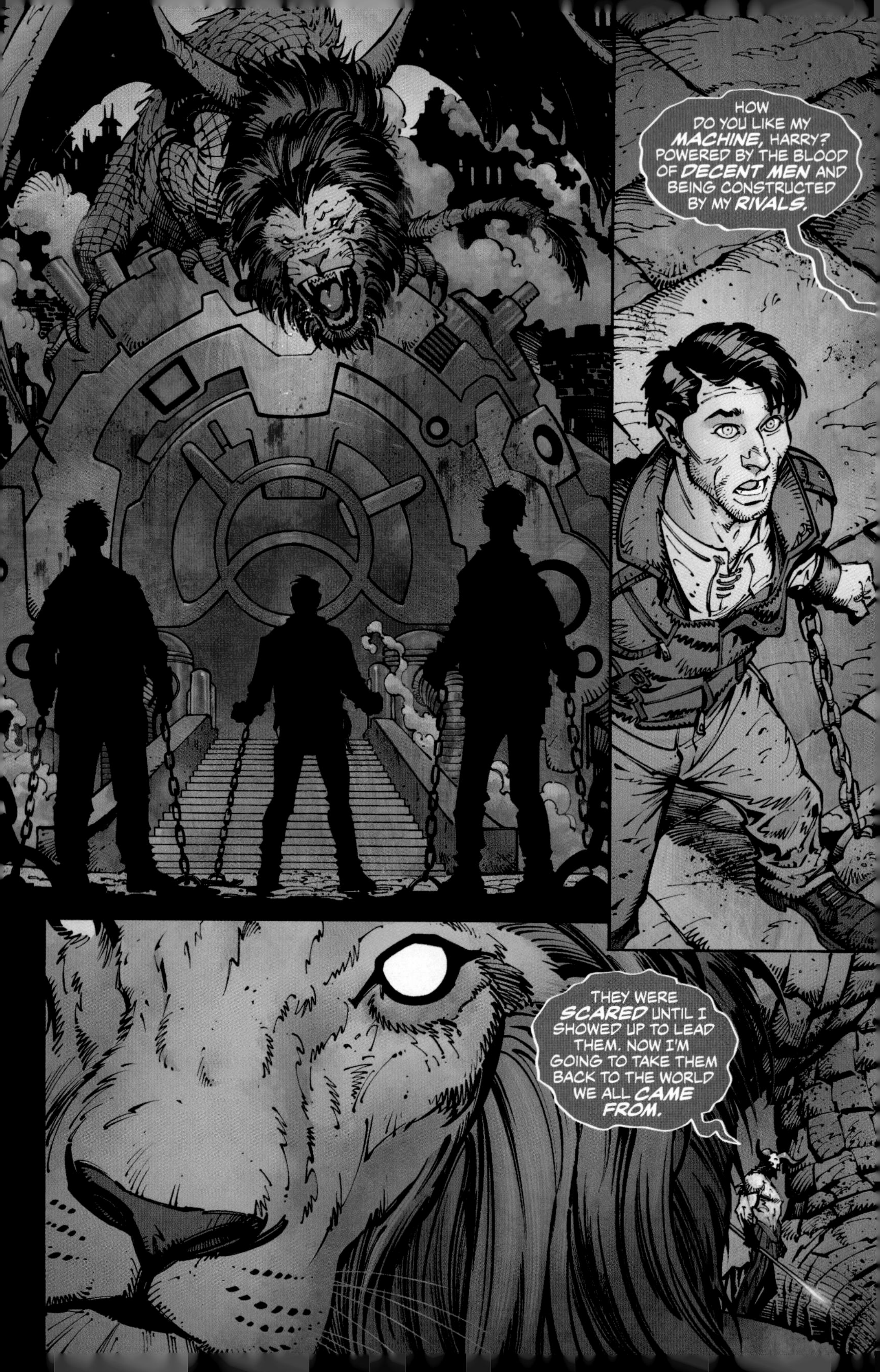
HOW DO YOU LIKE MY MACHINE, HARRY? POWERED BY THE BLOOD OF DECENT MEN AND BEING CONSTRUCTED BY MY RIVALS.
THEY WERE SCARED UNTIL I SHOWED UP TO LEAD THEM. NOW I'M GOING TO TAKE THEM BACK TO THE WORLD WE ALL CAME FROM.

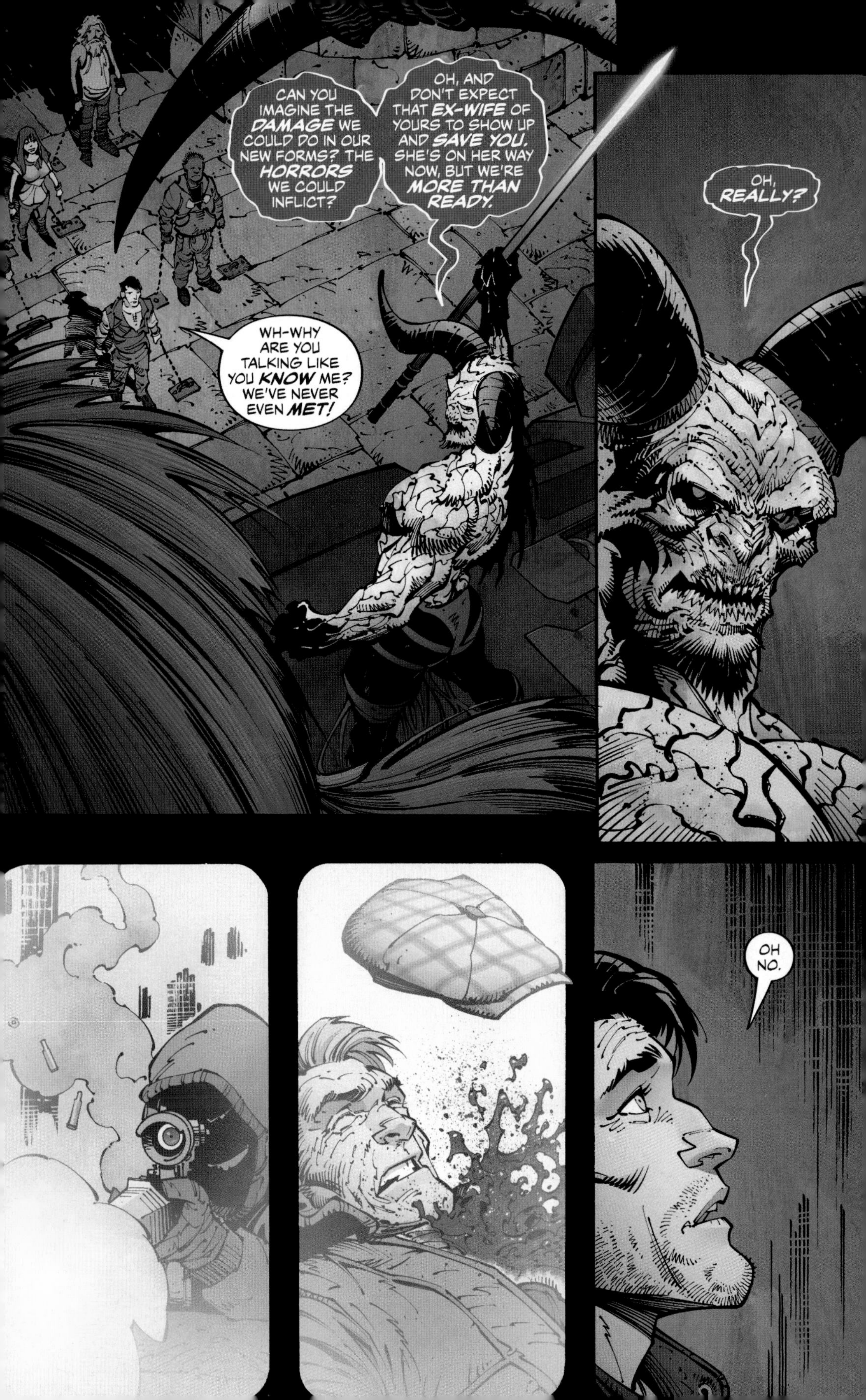
CAN YOU IMAGINE THE DAMAGE WE COULD DO IN OUR NEW FORMS? THE HORRORS WE COULD INFLICT?
OH, AND DON'T EXPECT THAT EX-WIFE OF YOURS TO SHOW UP AND SAVE YOU. SHE'S ON HER WAY NOW, BUT WE'RE MORE THAN READY.
WH-WHY ARE YOU TALKING LIKE YOU KNOW ME? WE'VE NEVER EVEN MET!
OH, REALLY?
OH NO.

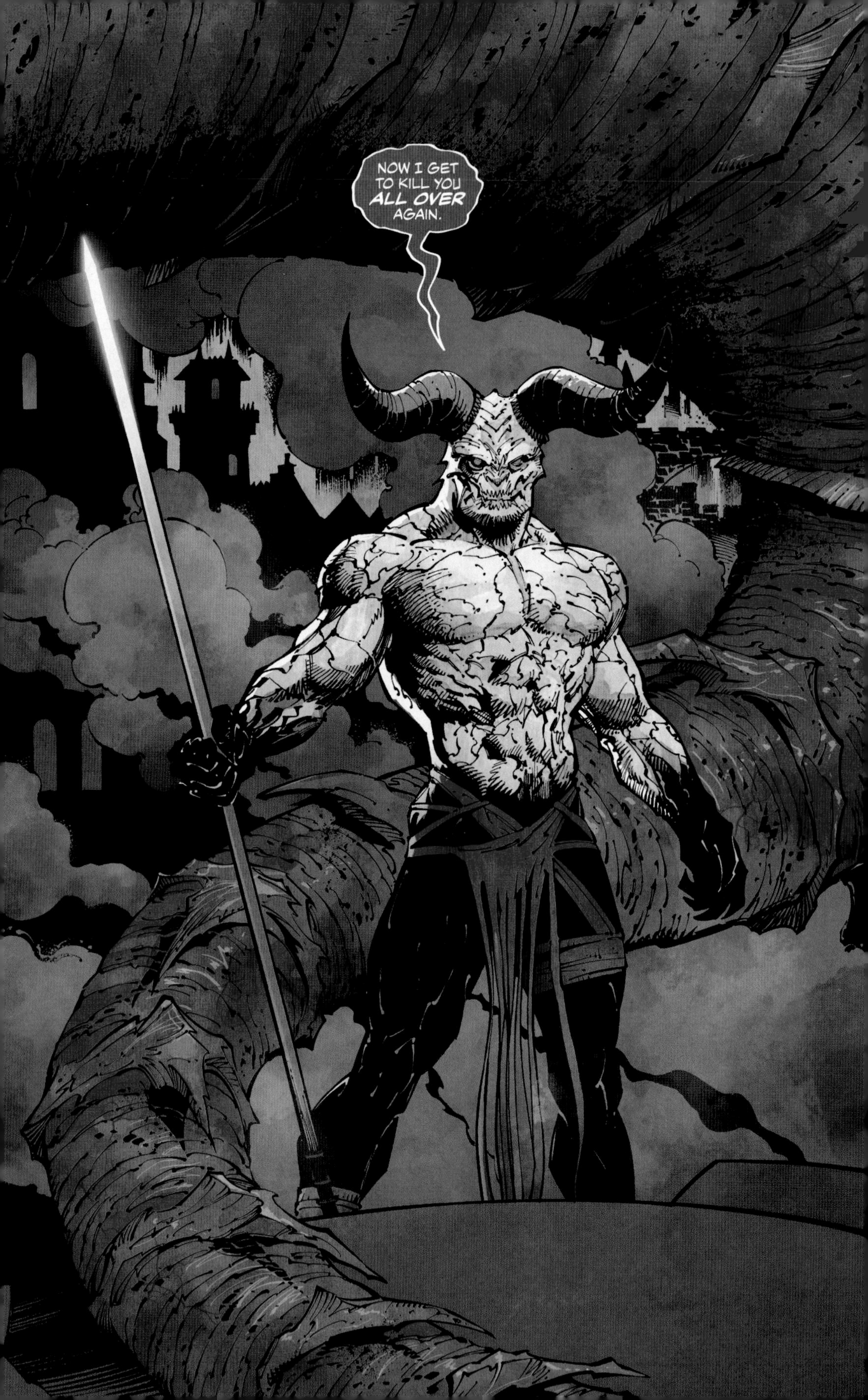
NOW I GET TO KILL YOU ALL OVER AGAIN.

SIX

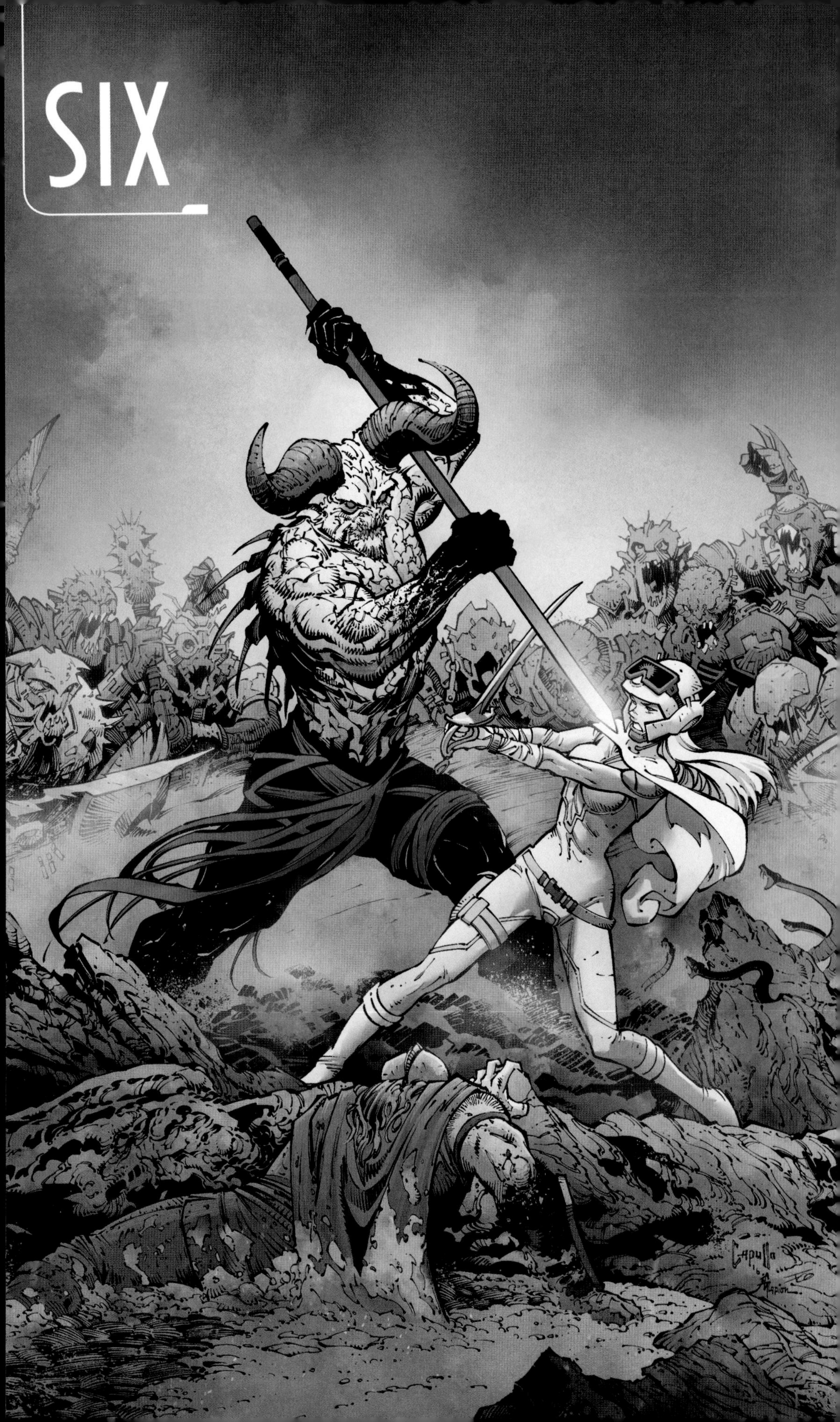

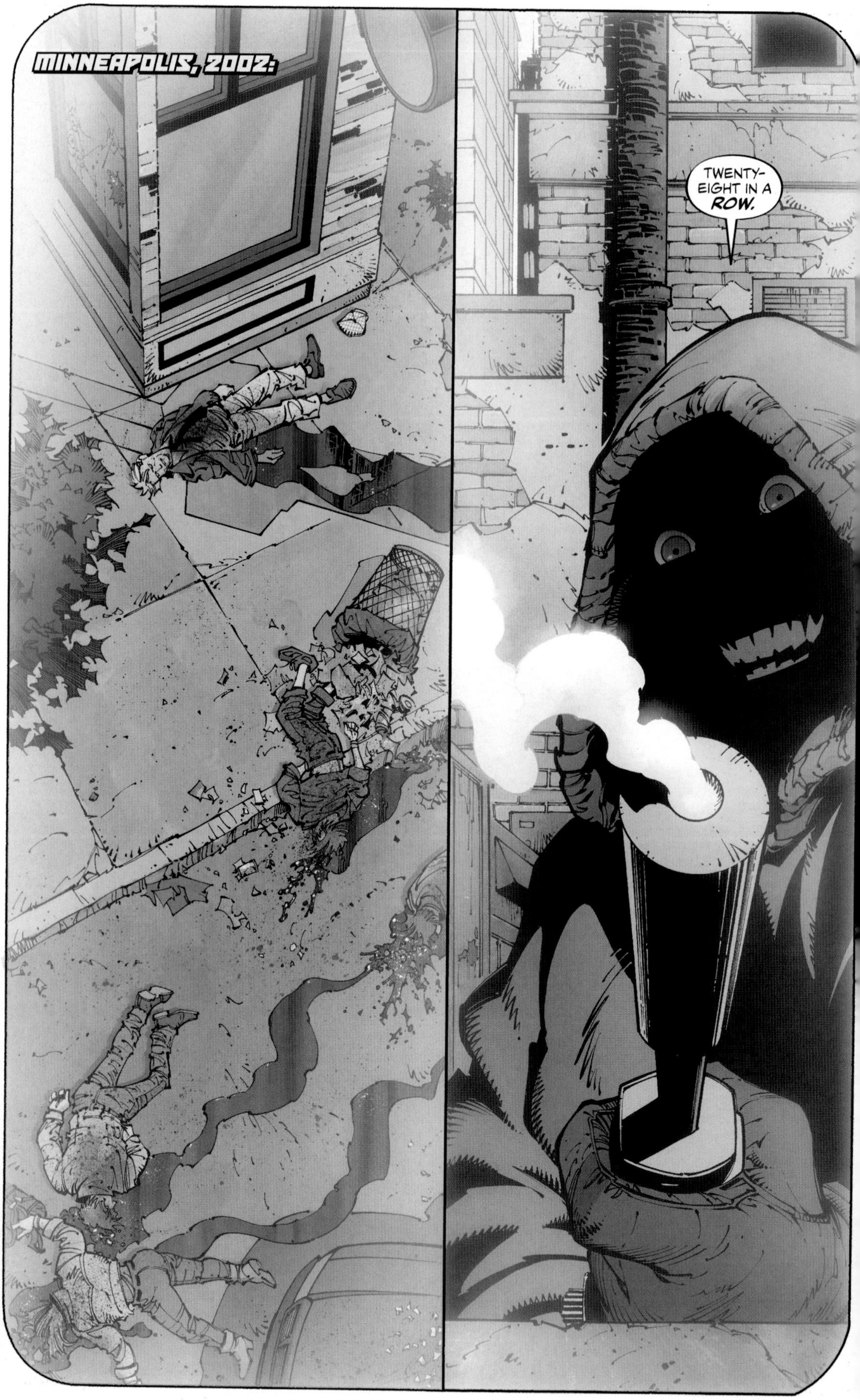
MINNEAPOLIS, 2002:
TWENTY-EIGHT IN A ROW.

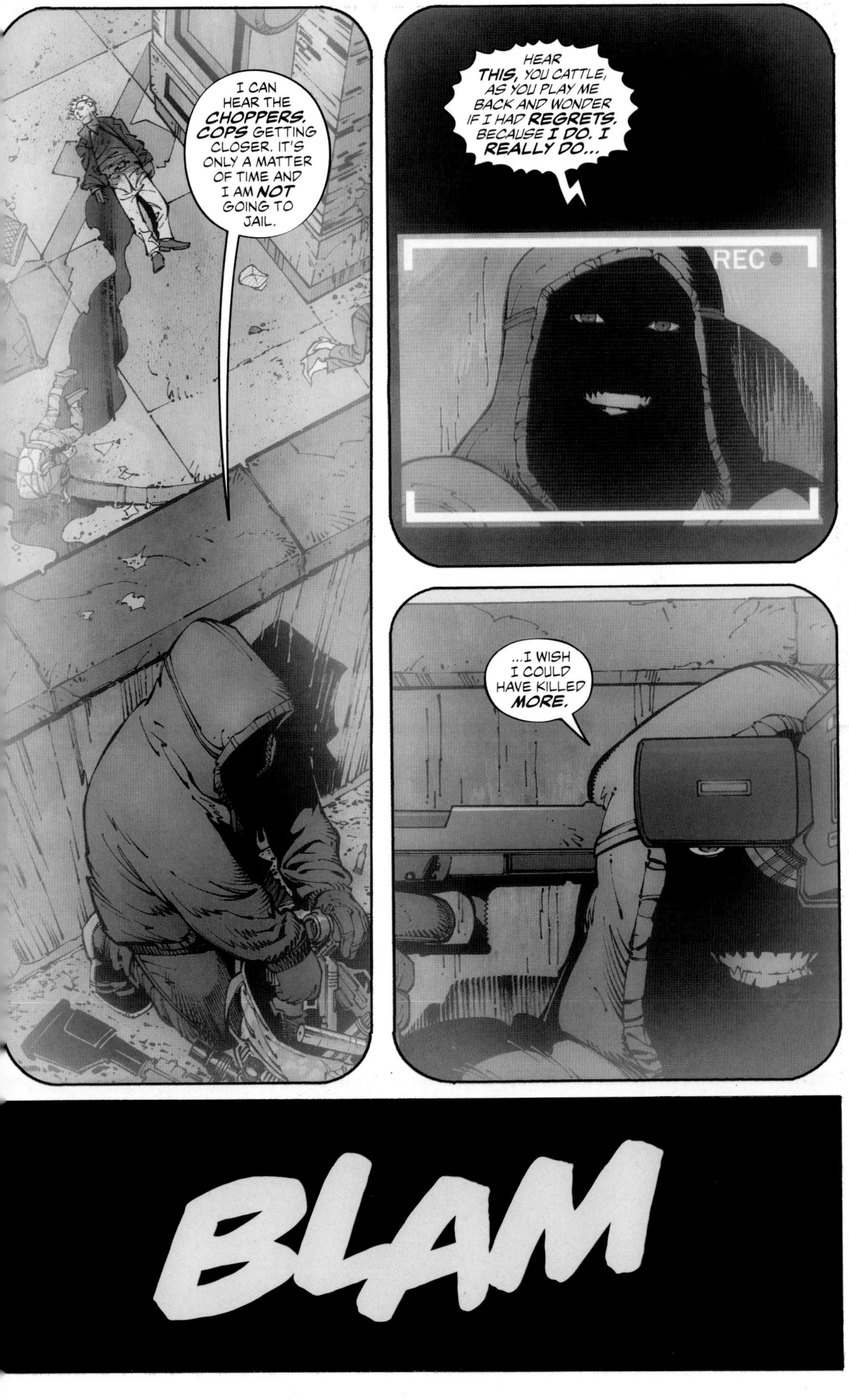
I CAN HEAR THE CHOPPERS. COPS GETTING CLOSER. IT'S ONLY A MATTER OF TIME AND I AM NOT GOING TO JAIL.
HEAR THIS, YOU CATTLE, AS YOU PLAY ME BACK AND WONDER IF I HAD REGRETS. BECAUSE I DO. I REALLY DO...
REC
...I WISH I COULD HAVE KILLED MORE.
BLAM

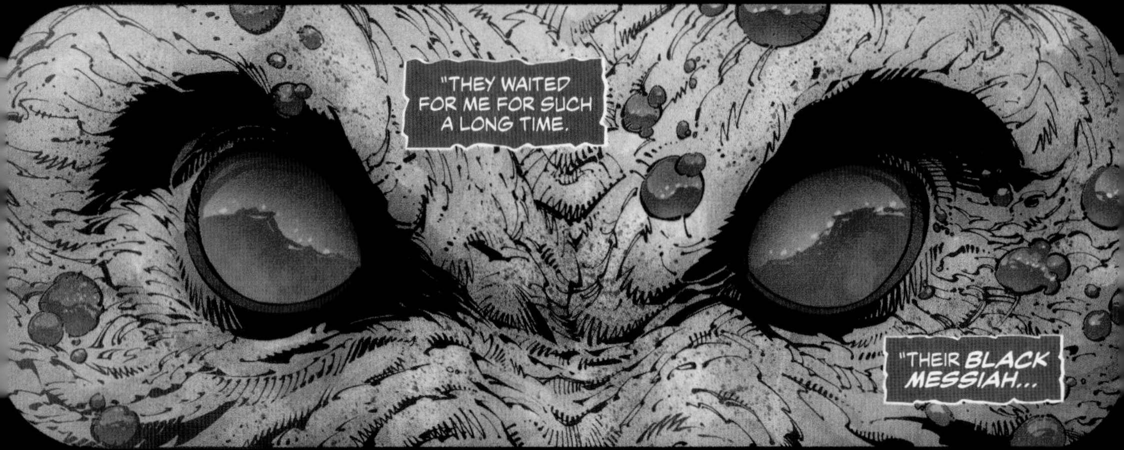
"THEY WAITED FOR ME FOR SUCH A LONG TIME.
"THEIR BLACK MESSIAH...

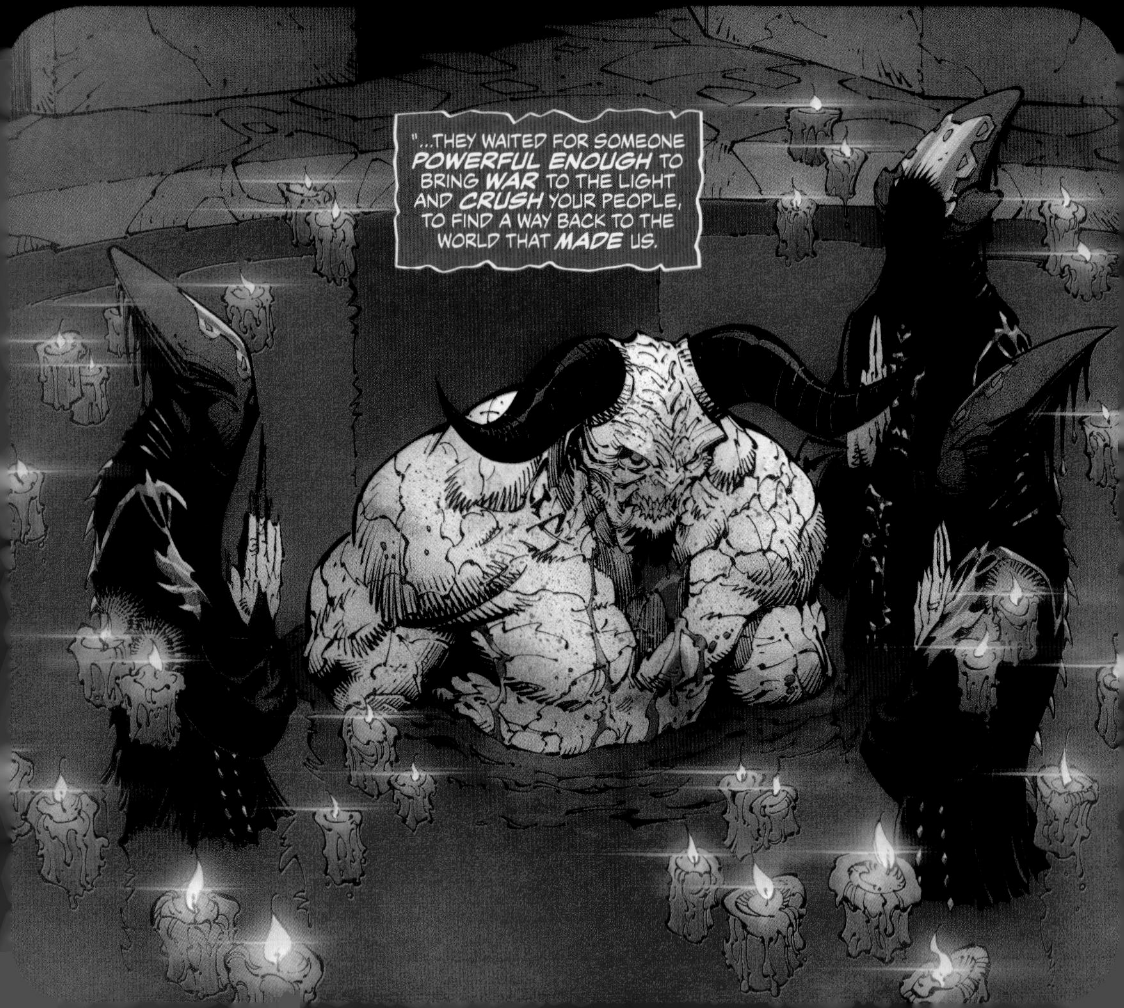
"...THEY WAITED FOR SOMEONE POWERFUL ENOUGH TO BRING WAR TO THE LIGHT AND CRUSH YOUR PEOPLE, TO FIND A WAY BACK TO THE WORLD THAT MADE US.

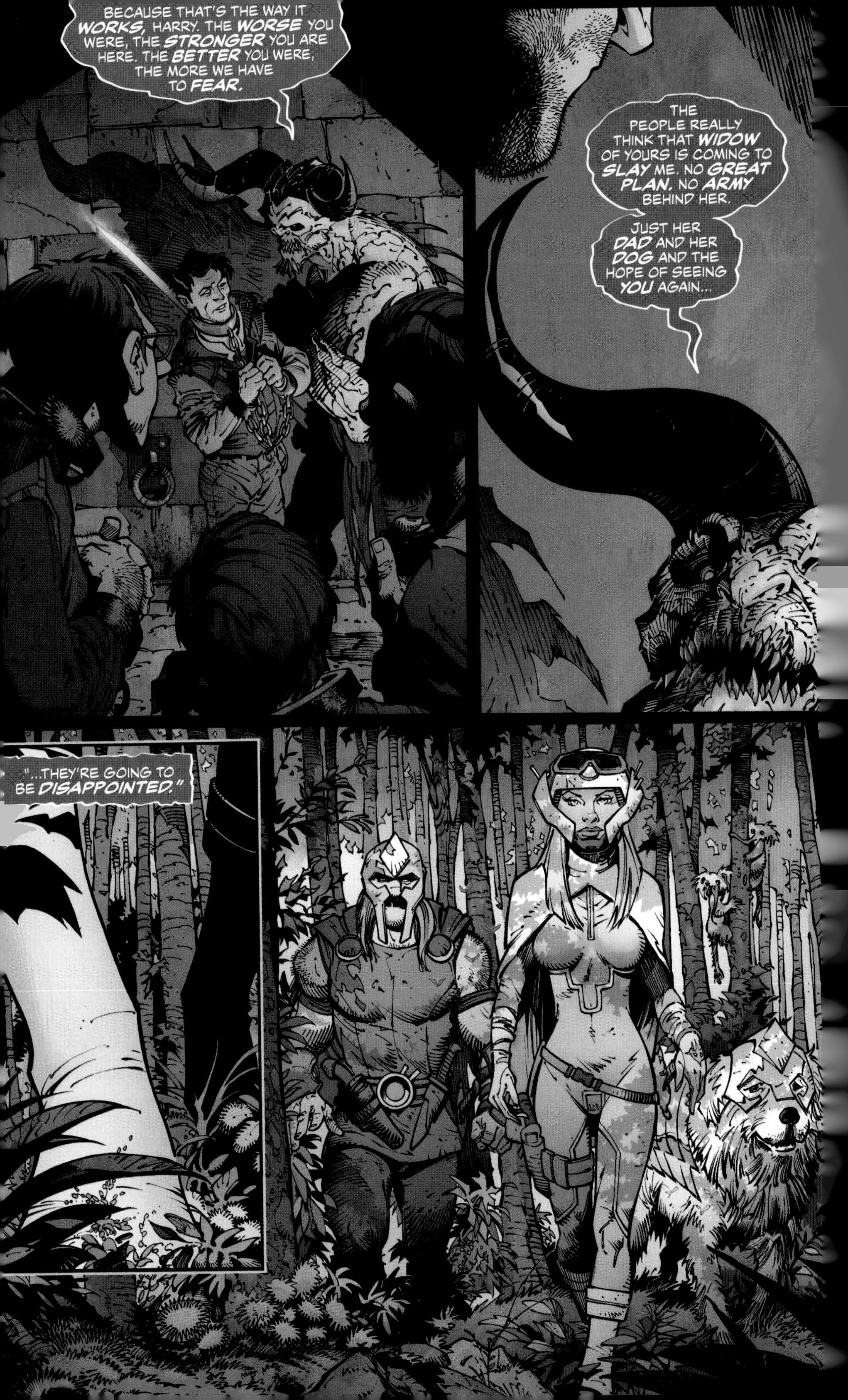
BECAUSE THAT'S THE WAY IT WORKS, HARRY. THE WORSE YOU WERE, THE STRONGER YOU ARE HERE. THE BETTER YOU WERE, THE MORE WE HAVE TO FEAR.
THE PEOPLE REALLY THINK THAT WIDOW OF YOURS IS COMING TO SLAY ME. NO GREAT PLAN. NO ARMY BEHIND HER.
JUST HER DAD AND HER DOG AND THE HOPE OF SEEING YOU AGAIN...
"...THEY'RE GOING TO BE DISAPPOINTED."

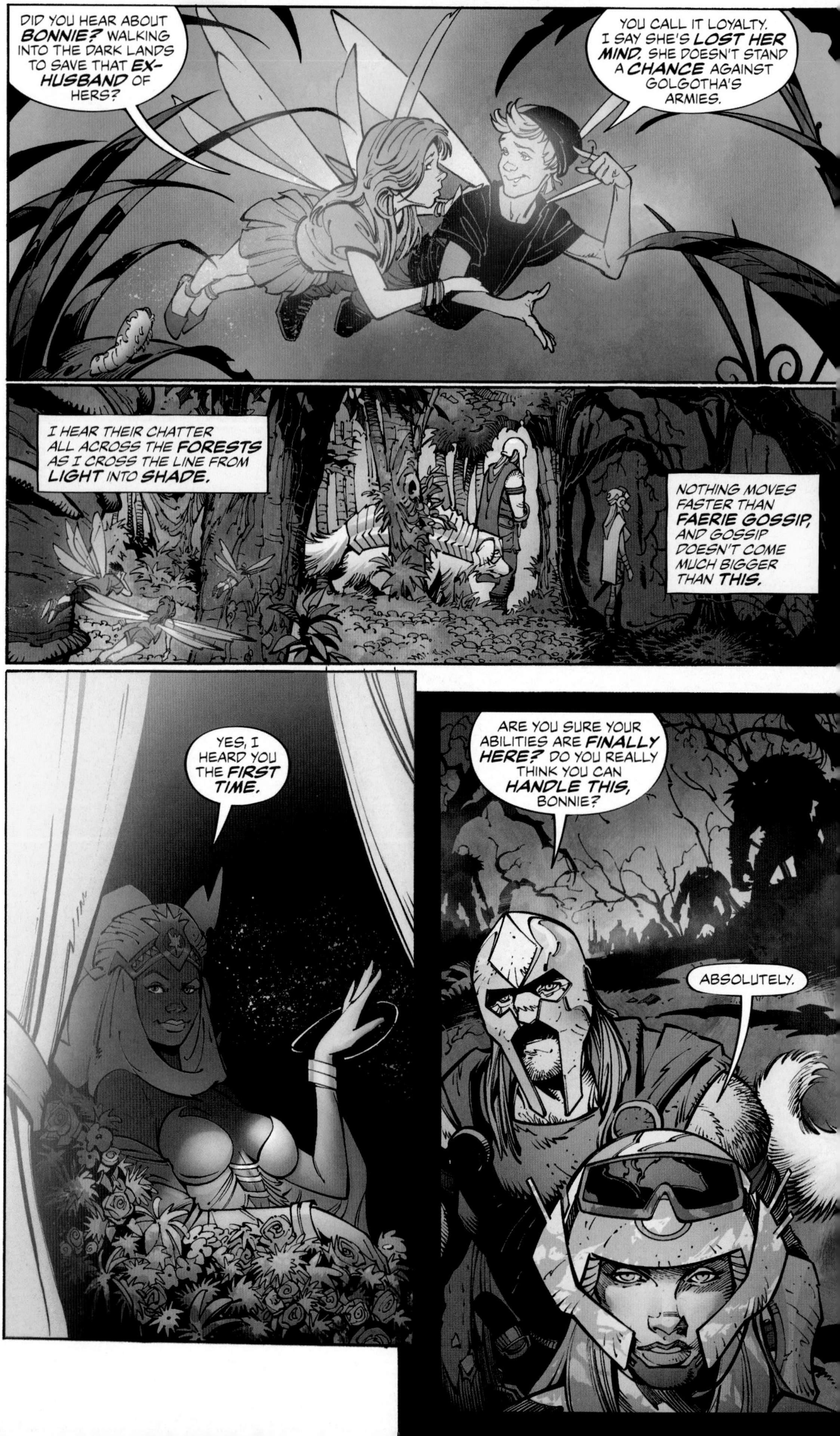
DID YOU HEAR ABOUT BONNIE? WALKING INTO THE DARK LANDS TO SAVE THAT EX-HUSBAND OF HERS?
YOU CALL IT LOYALTY. I SAY SHE'S LOST HER MIND. SHE DOESN'T STAND A CHANCE AGAINST GOLGOTHA'S ARMIES.
I HEAR THEIR CHATTER ALL ACROSS THE FORESTS AS I CROSS THE LINE FROM LIGHT INTO SHADE.
NOTHING MOVES FASTER THAN FAERIE GOSSIP, AND GOSSIP DOESN'T COME MUCH BIGGER THAN THIS.
YES, I HEARD YOU THE FIRST TIME.
ARE YOU SURE YOUR ABILITIES ARE FINALLY HERE? DO YOU REALLY THINK YOU CAN HANDLE THIS, BONNIE?
ABSOLUTELY.

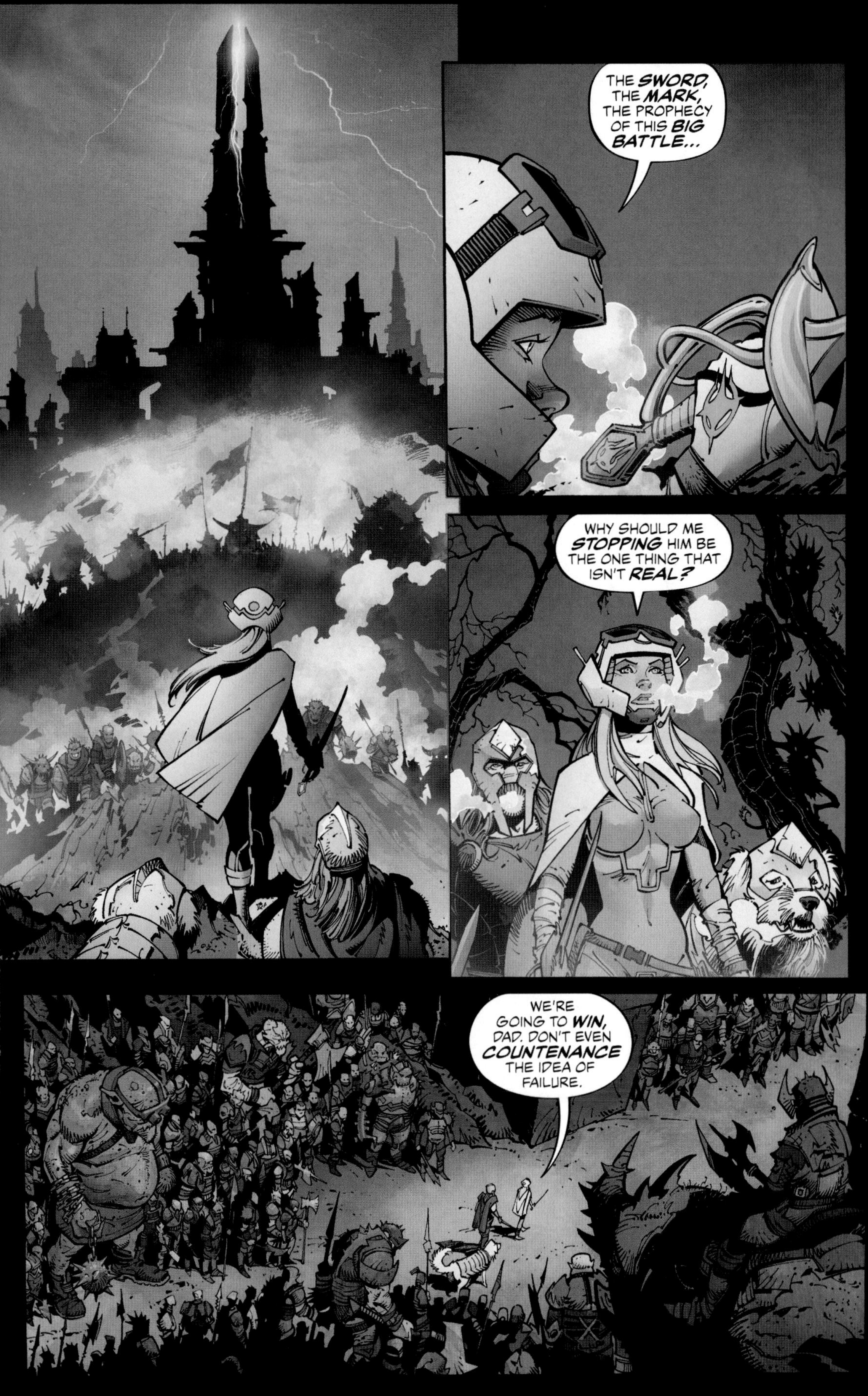
THE SWORD, THE MARK, THE PROPHECY OF THIS BIG BATTLE...
WHY SHOULD ME STOPPING HIM BE THE ONE THING THAT ISN'T REAL?
WE'RE GOING TO WIN, DAD. DON'T EVEN COUNTENANCE THE IDEA OF FAILURE.

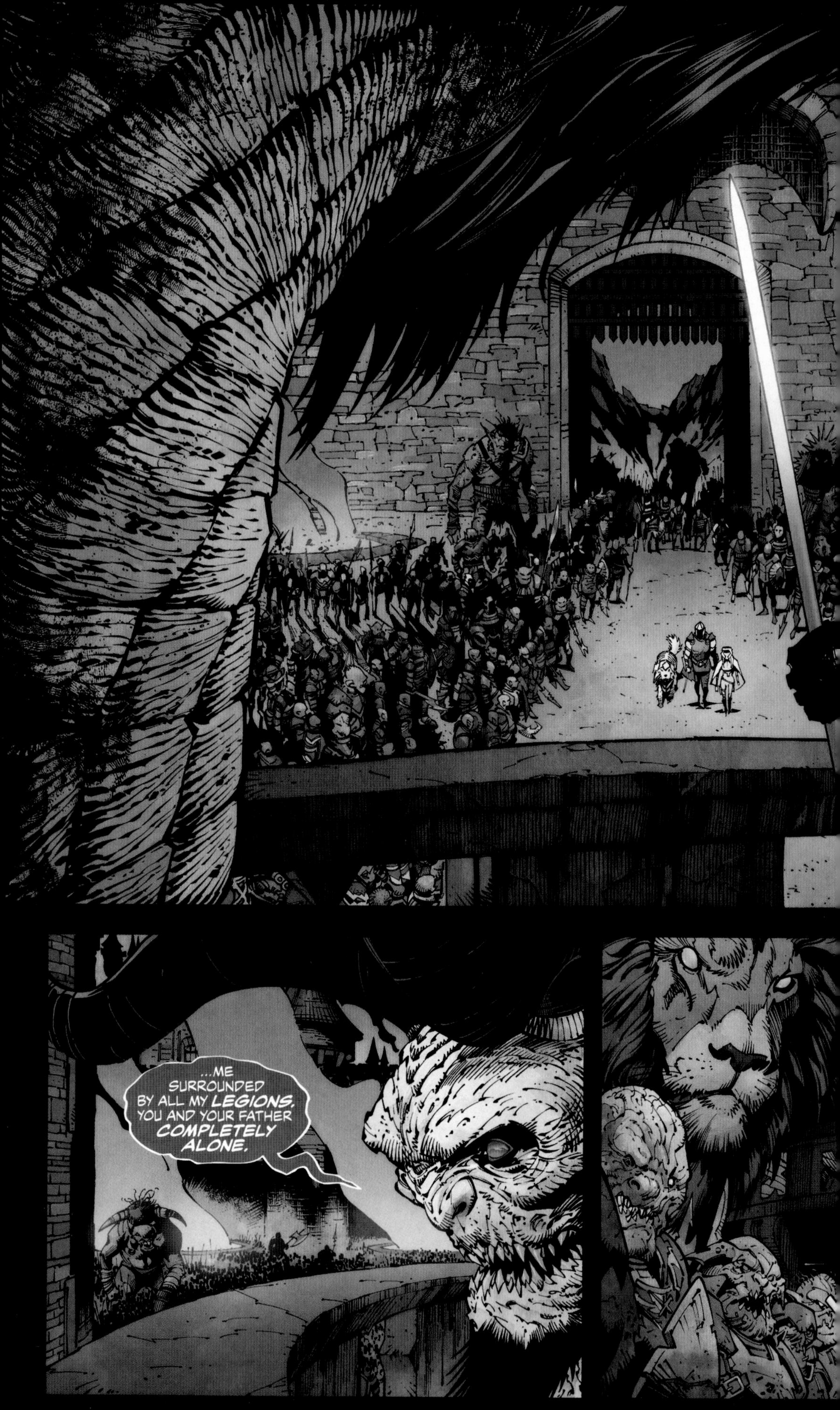
...ME SURROUNDED BY ALL MY LEGIONS, YOU AND YOUR FATHER COMPLETELY ALONE.

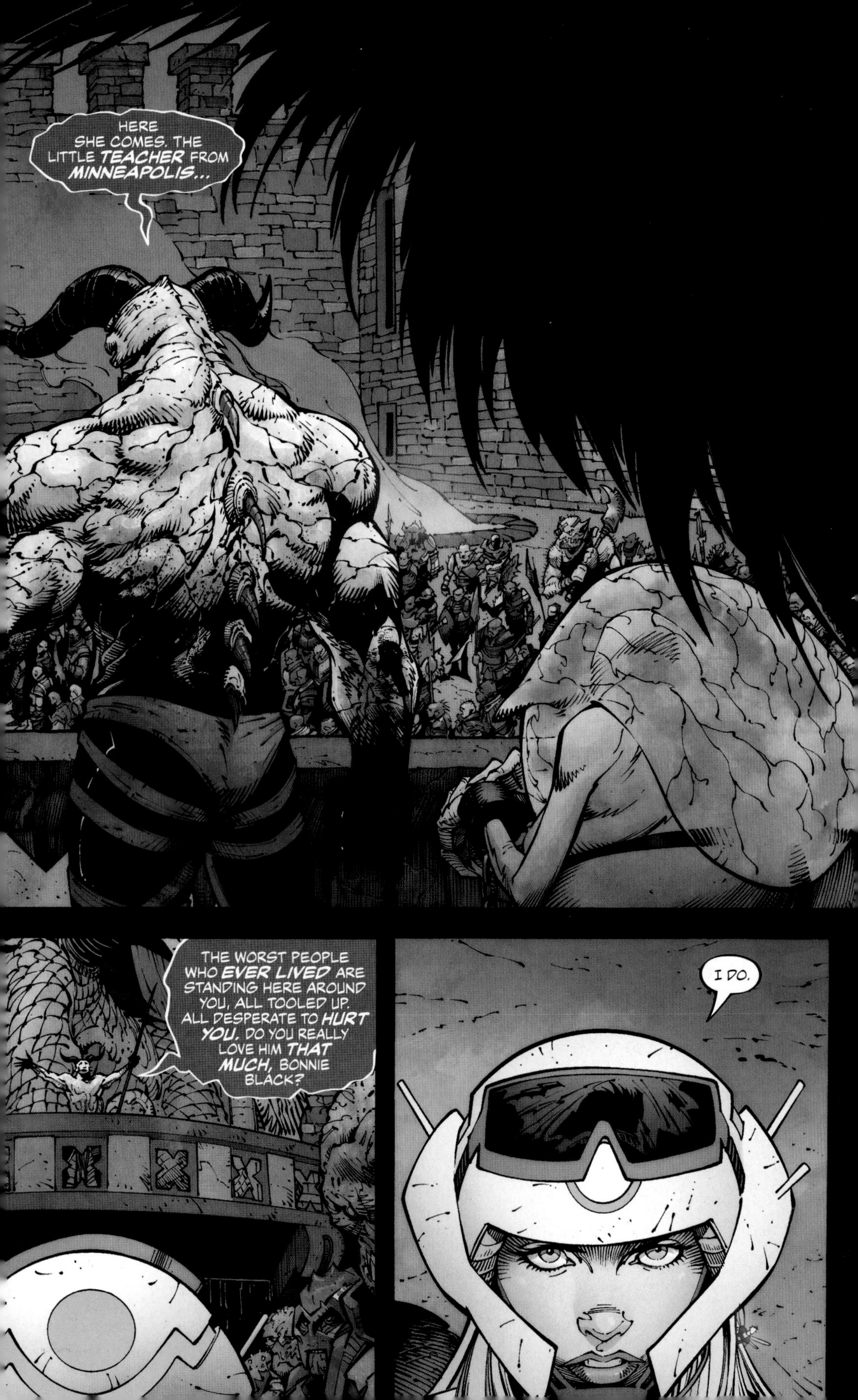
HERE SHE COMES. THE LITTLE TEACHER FROM MINNEAPOLIS...
THE WORST PEOPLE WHO EVER LIVED ARE STANDING HERE AROUND YOU, ALL TOOLED UP. ALL DESPERATE TO HURT YOU. DO YOU REALLY LOVE HIM THAT MUCH, BONNIE BLACK?
I DO.

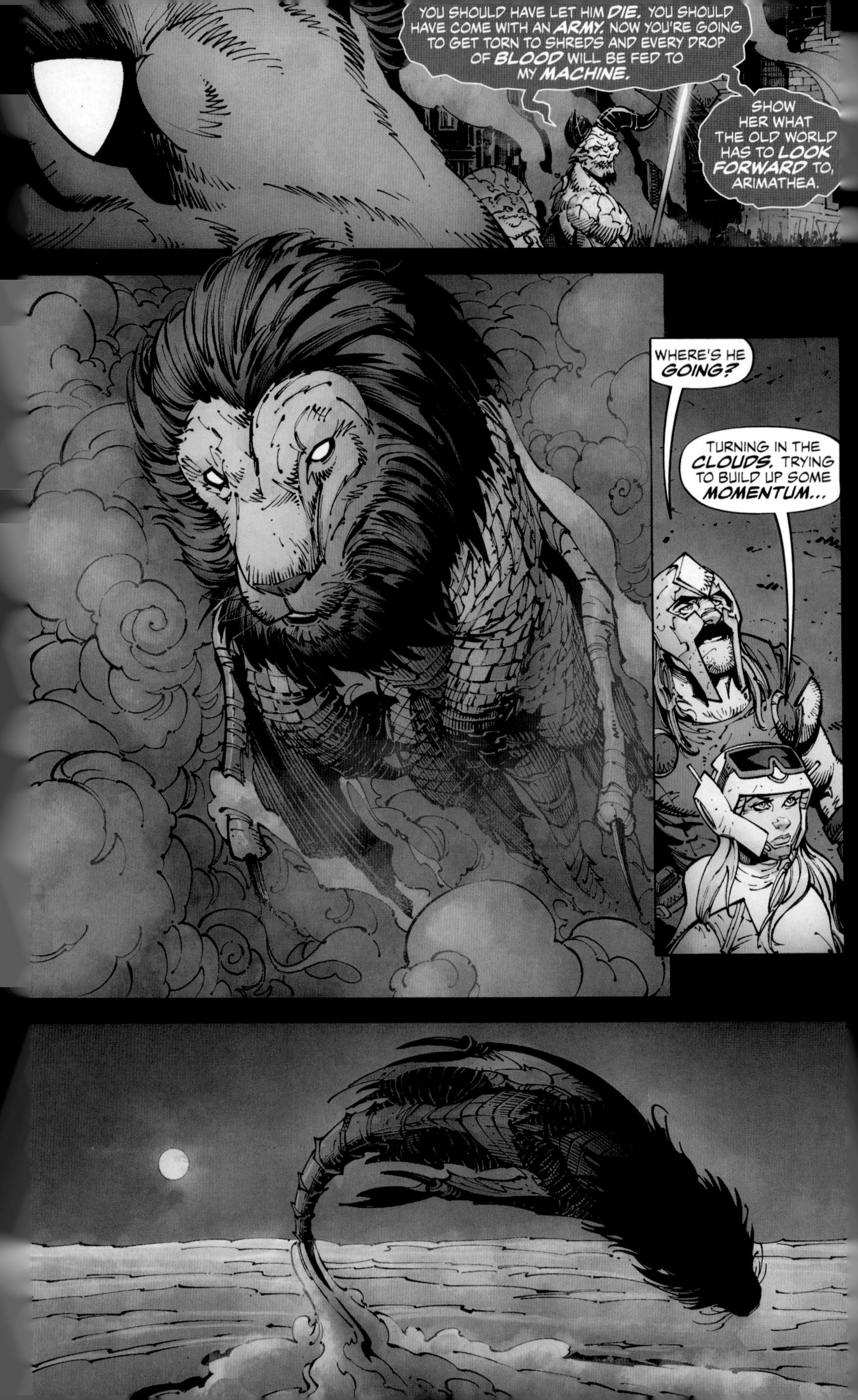
YOU SHOULD HAVE LET HIM DIE. YOU SHOULD HAVE COME WITH AN ARMY. NOW YOU'RE GOING TO GET TORN TO SHREDS AND EVERY DROP OF BLOOD WILL BE FED TO MY MACHINE.
SHOW HER WHAT THE OLD WORLD HAS TO LOOK FORWARD TO, ARIMATHEA.
WHERE'S HE GOING?
TURNING IN THE CLOUDS. TRYING TO BUILD UP SOME MOMENTUM...

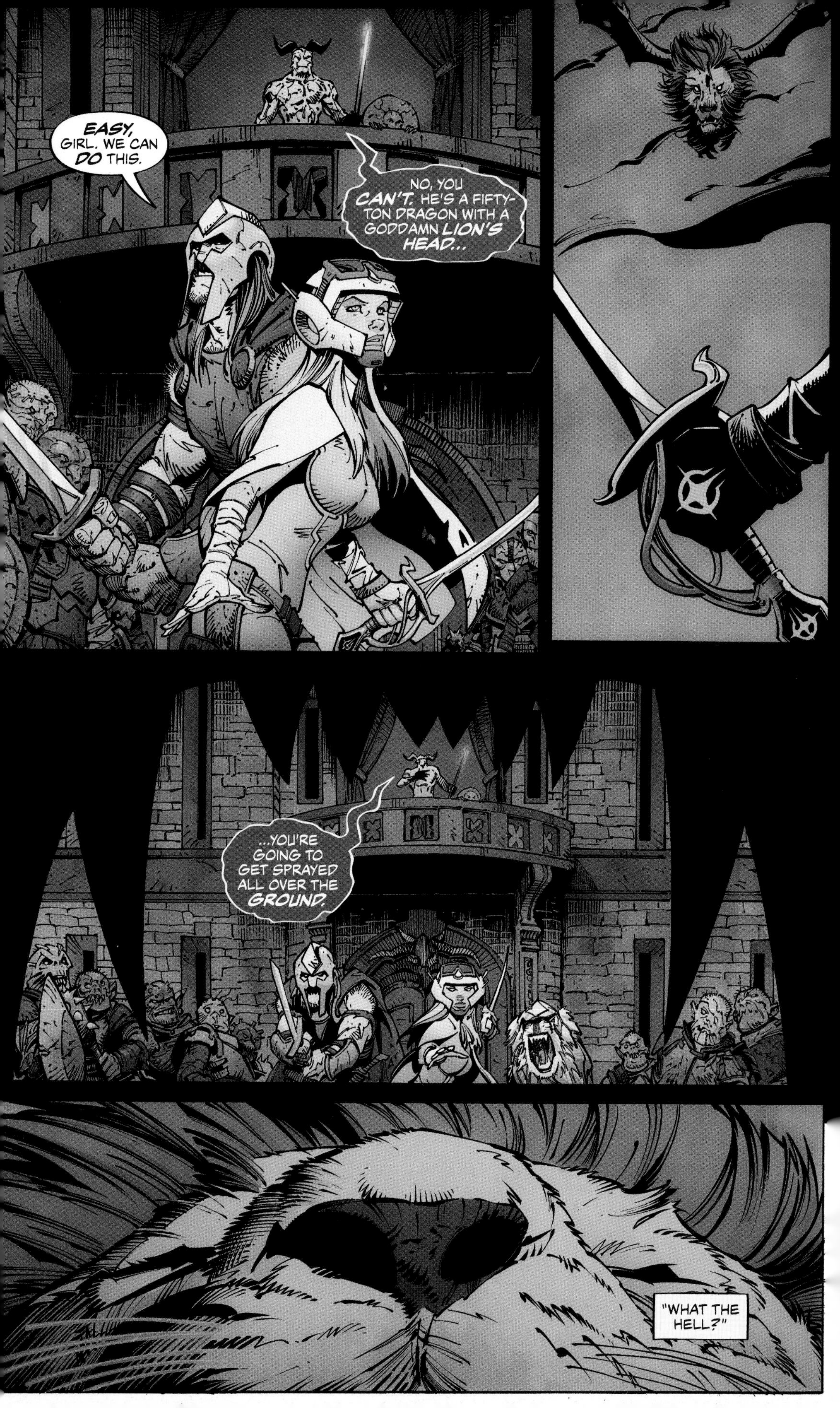
EASY, GIRL. WE CAN DO THIS.
NO, YOU CAN'T. HE'S A FIFTY-TON DRAGON WITH A GODDAMN LION'S HEAD...
...YOU'RE GOING TO GET SPRAYED ALL OVER THE GROUND.
"WHAT THE HELL?"

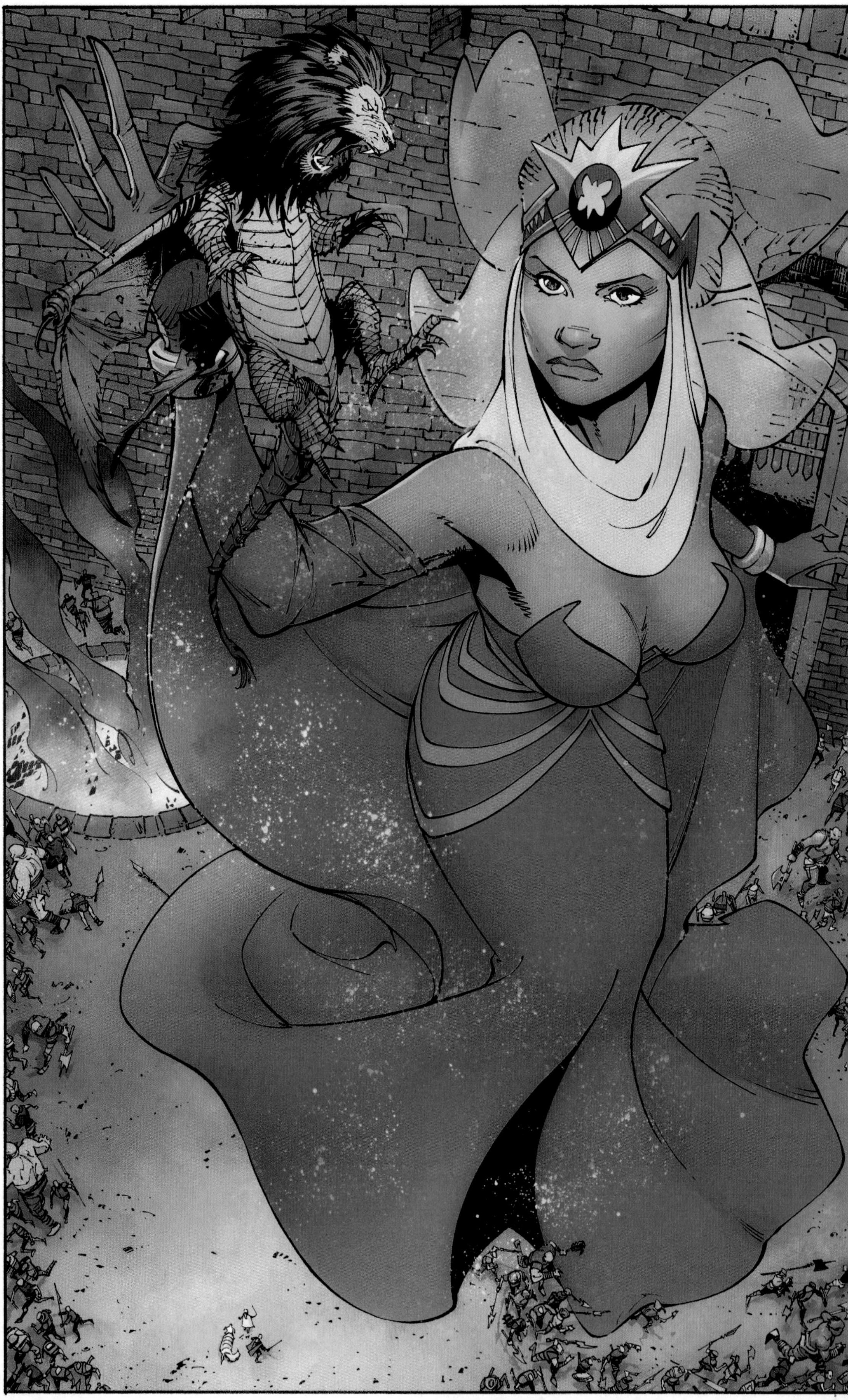

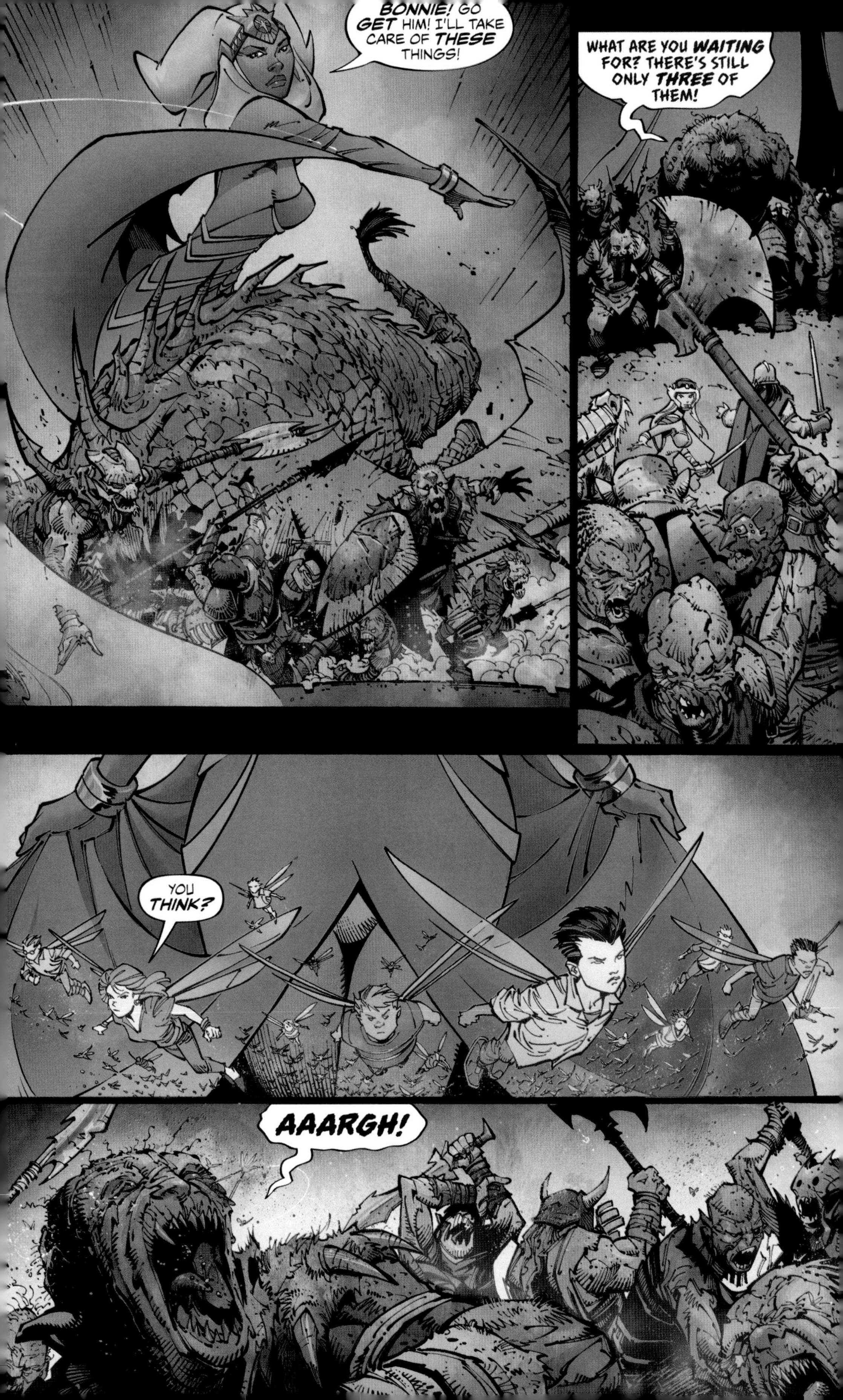
BONNIE! GO GET HIM! I'LL TAKE CARE OF THESE THINGS!
WHAT ARE YOU WAITING FOR? THERE'S STILL ONLY THREE OF THEM!
YOU THINK?
AAARGH!

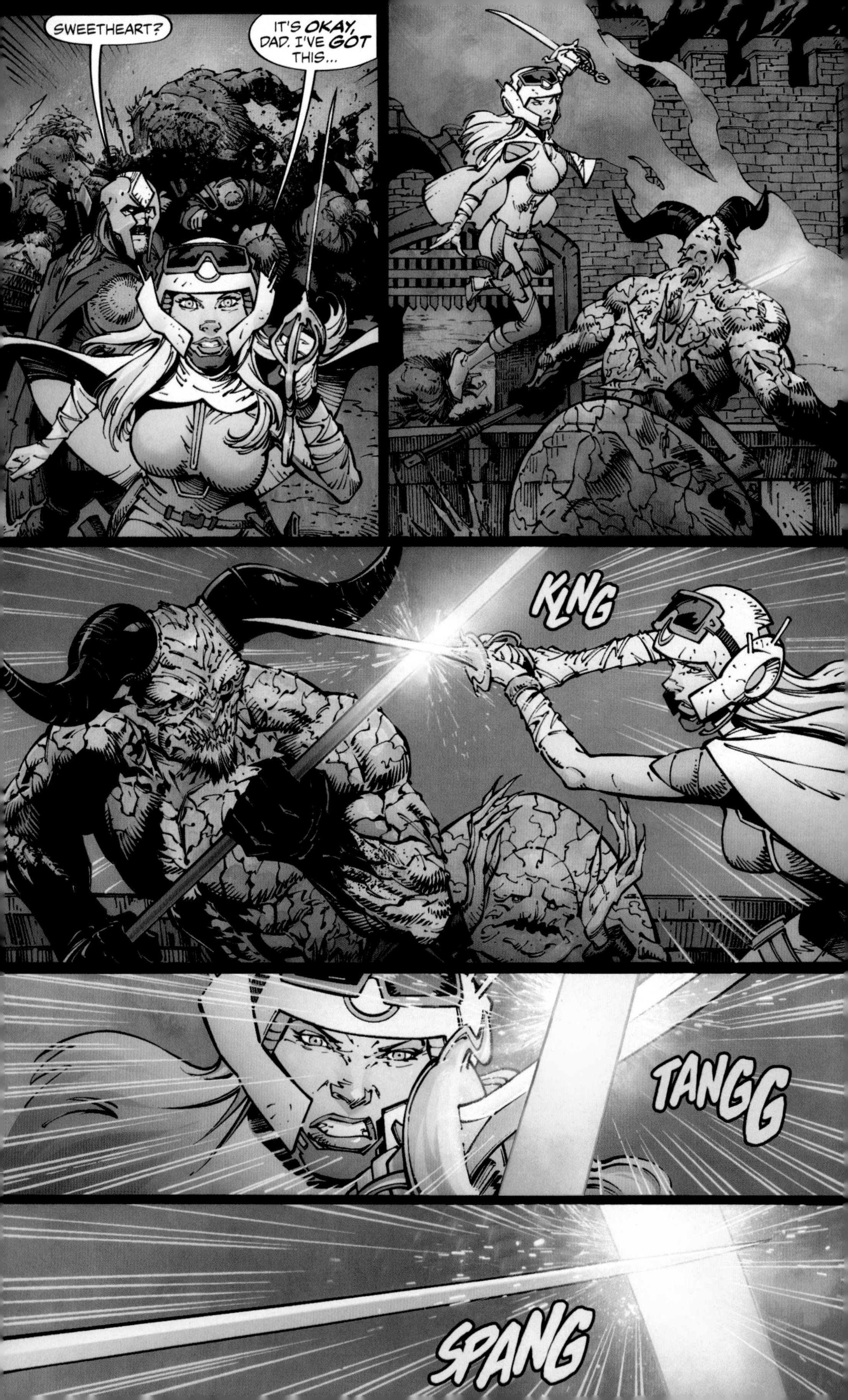
SWEETHEART?
IT'S OKAY, DAD. I'VE GOT THIS...
KLNG
TANGG
SPANG

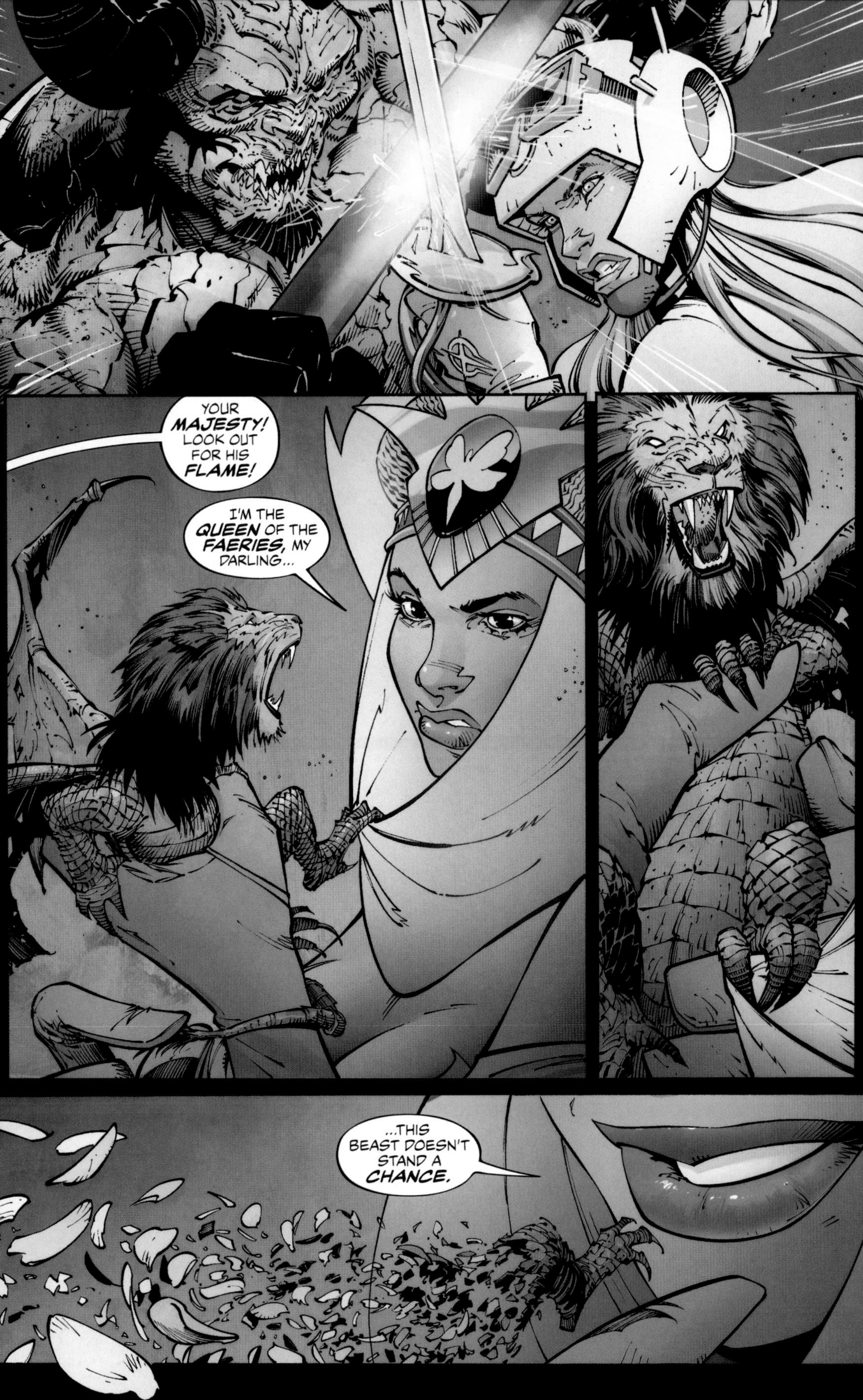
YOUR MAJESTY! LOOK OUT FOR HIS FLAME!
I'M THE QUEEN OF THE FAERIES, MY DARLING...
...THIS BEAST DOESN'T STAND A CHANCE.

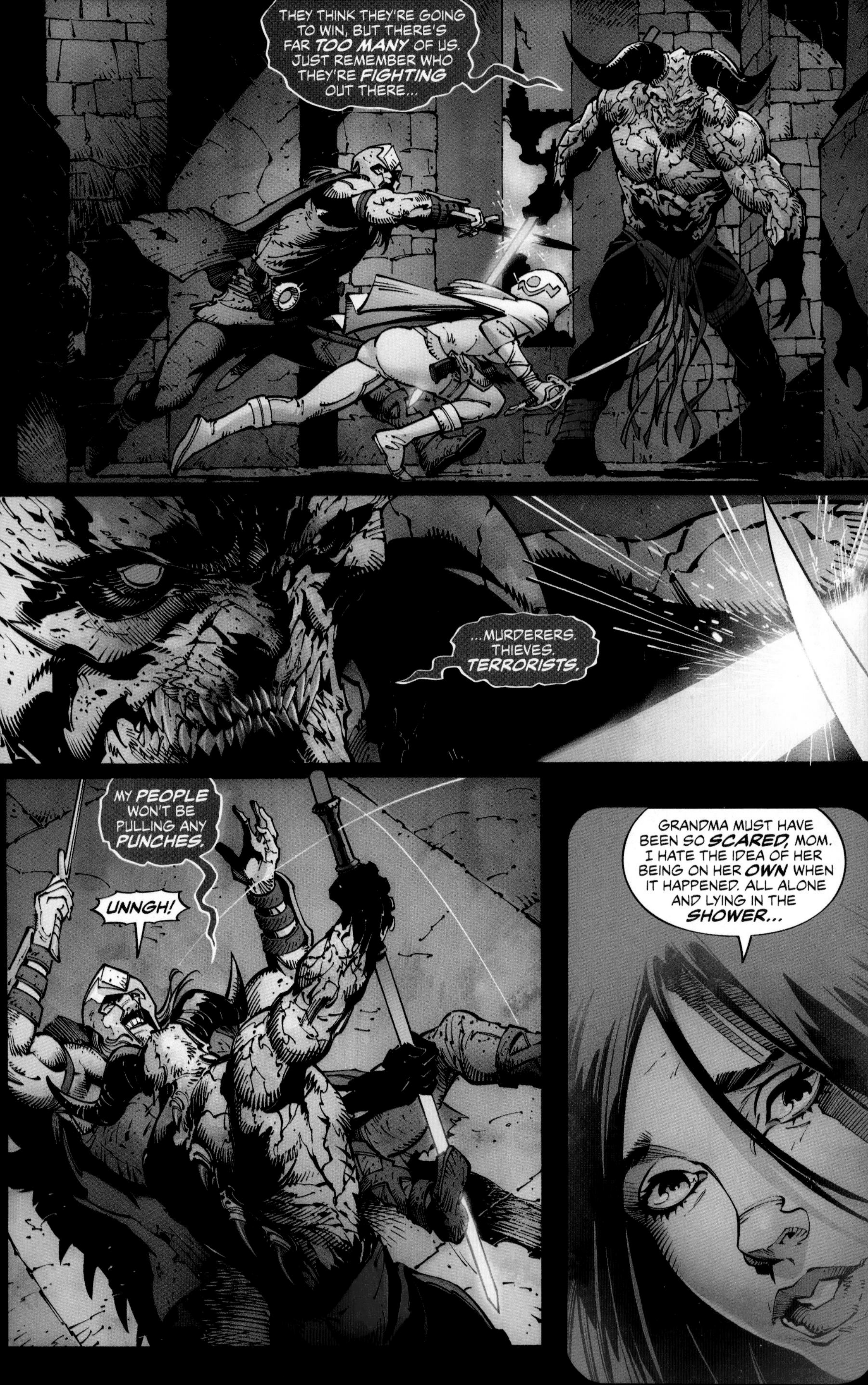
THEY THINK THEY'RE GOING TO WIN, BUT THERE'S FAR TOO MANY OF US. JUST REMEMBER WHO THEY'RE FIGHTING OUT THERE...
...MURDERERS. THIEVES. TERRORISTS.
MY PEOPLE WON'T BE PULLING ANY PUNCHES.
UNNGH!
GRANDMA MUST HAVE BEEN SO SCARED, MOM. I HATE THE IDEA OF HER BEING ON HER OWN WHEN IT HAPPENED. ALL ALONE AND LYING IN THE SHOWER...

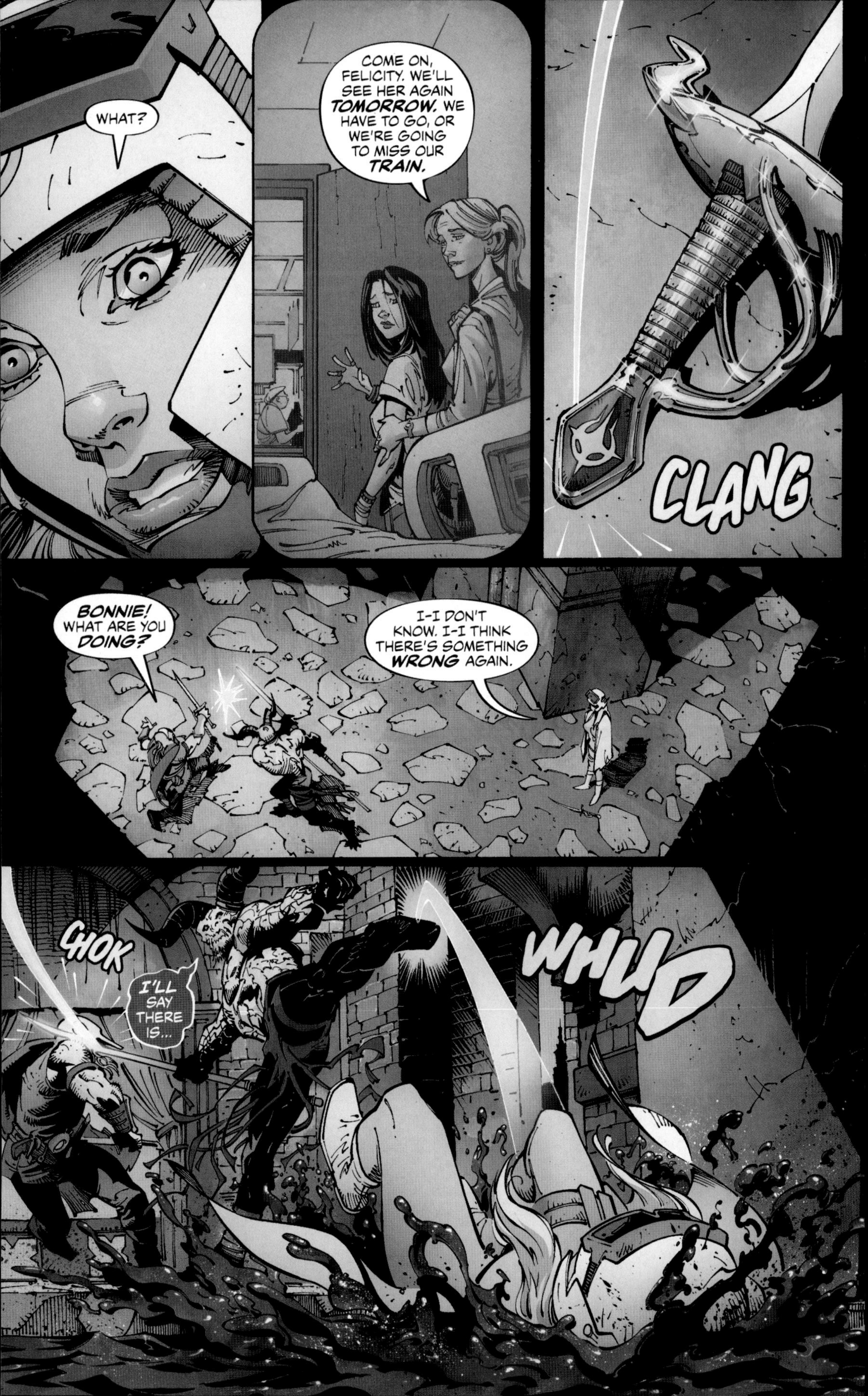
WHAT?
COME ON, FELICITY. WE'LL SEE HER AGAIN TOMORROW. WE HAVE TO GO, OR WE'RE GOING TO MISS OUR TRAIN.
CLANG
BONNIE! WHAT ARE YOU DOING?
I-I DON'T KNOW. I-I THINK THERE'S SOMETHING WRONG AGAIN.
CHOK
I'LL SAY THERE IS...
WHUD

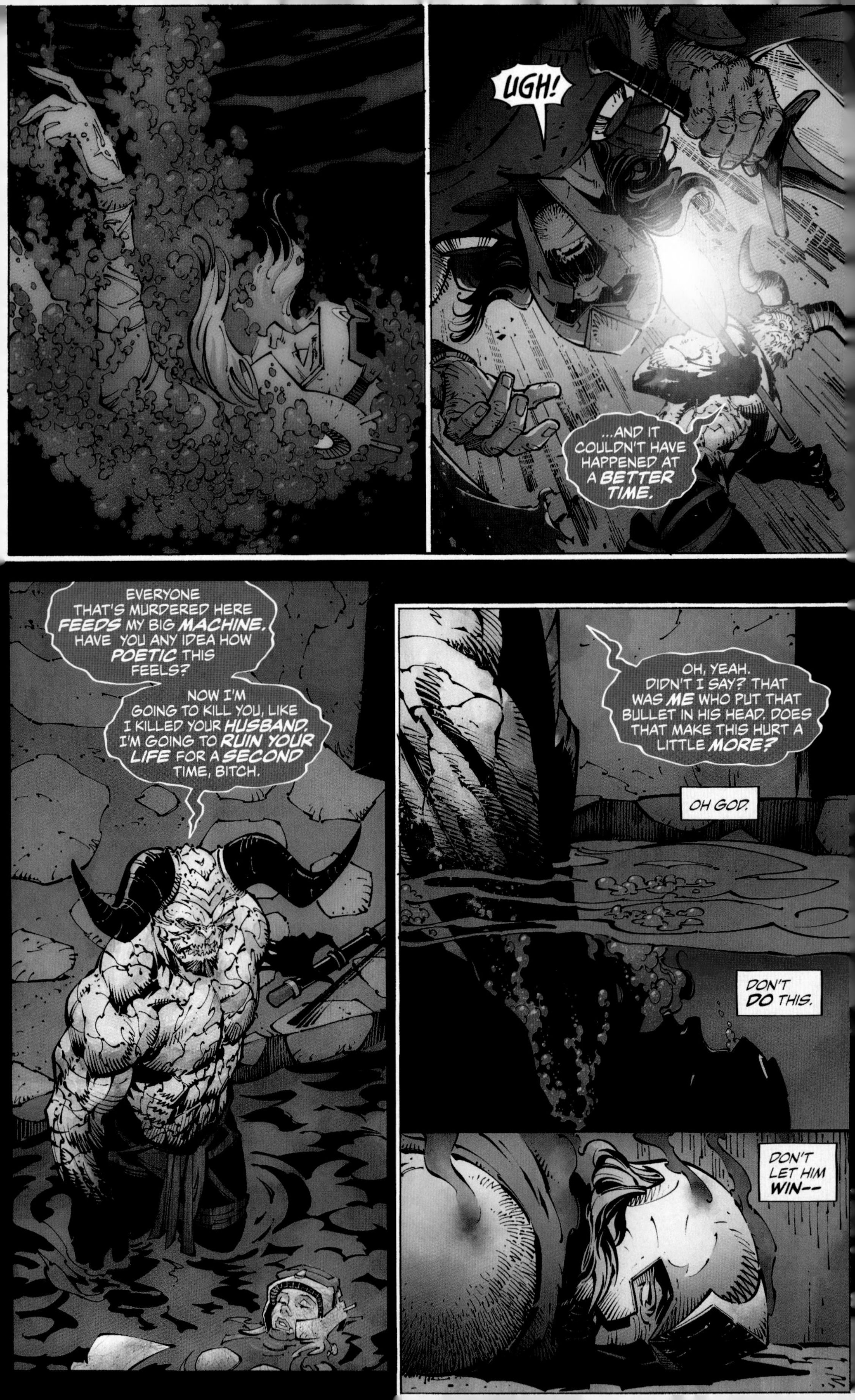
UGH!
...AND IT COULDN'T HAVE HAPPENED AT A BETTER TIME.
EVERYONE THAT'S MURDERED HERE FEEDS MY BIG MACHINE. HAVE YOU ANY IDEA HOW POETIC THIS FEELS?
NOW I'M GOING TO KILL YOU, LIKE I KILLED YOUR HUSBAND. I'M GOING TO RUIN YOUR LIFE FOR A SECOND TIME, BITCH.
OH, YEAH. DIDN'T I SAY? THAT WAS ME WHO PUT THAT BULLET IN HIS HEAD. DOES THAT MAKE THIS HURT A LITTLE MORE?
OH GOD.
DON'T DO THIS.
DON'T LET HIM WIN--

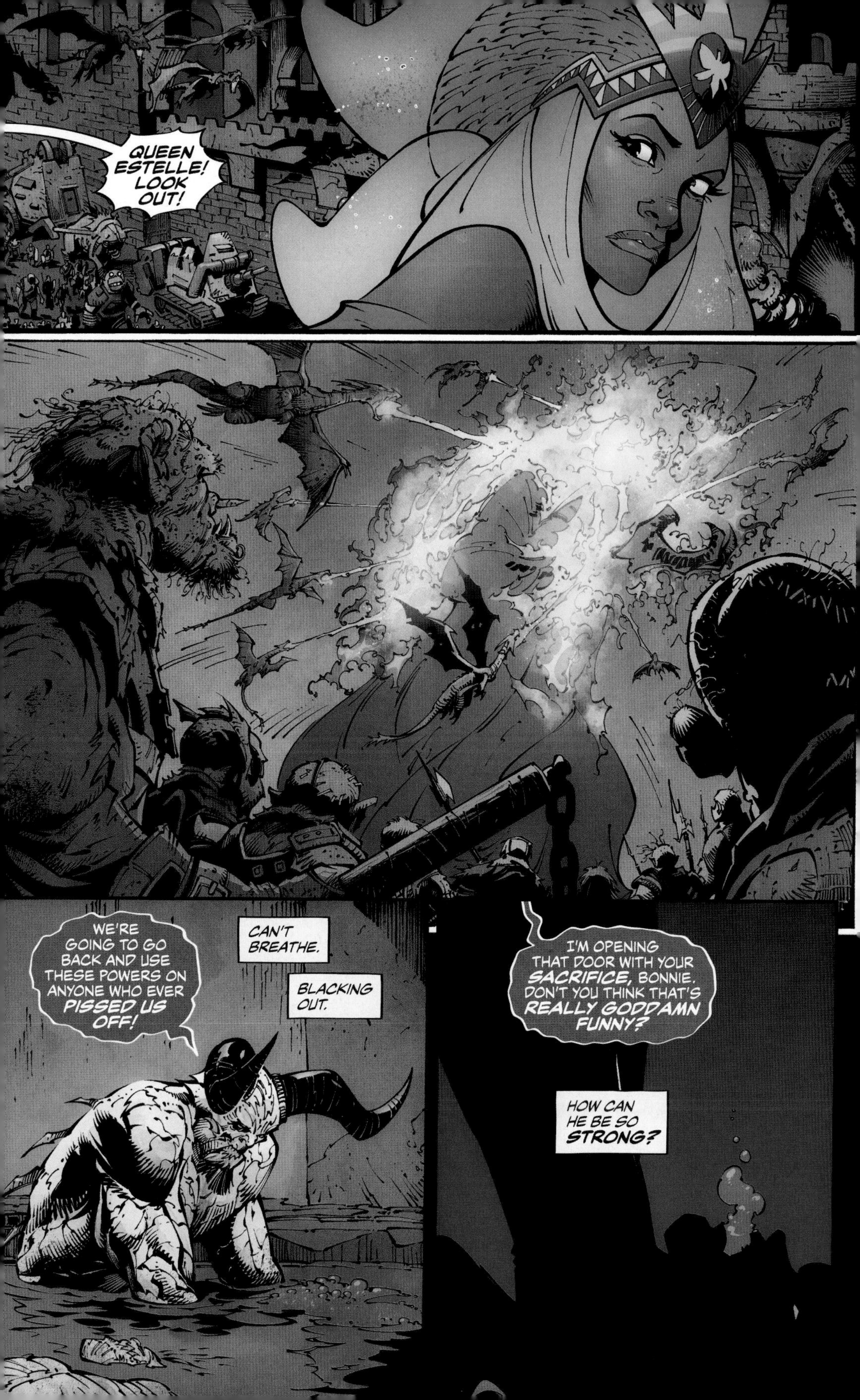
QUEEN ESTELLE! LOOK OUT!
WE'RE GOING TO GO BACK AND USE THESE POWERS ON ANYONE WHO EVER PISSED US OFF!
CAN'T BREATHE.
BLACKING OUT.
I'M OPENING THAT DOOR WITH YOUR SACRIFICE, BONNIE. DON'T YOU THINK THAT'S REALLY GODDAMN FUNNY?
HOW CAN HE BE SO STRONG?

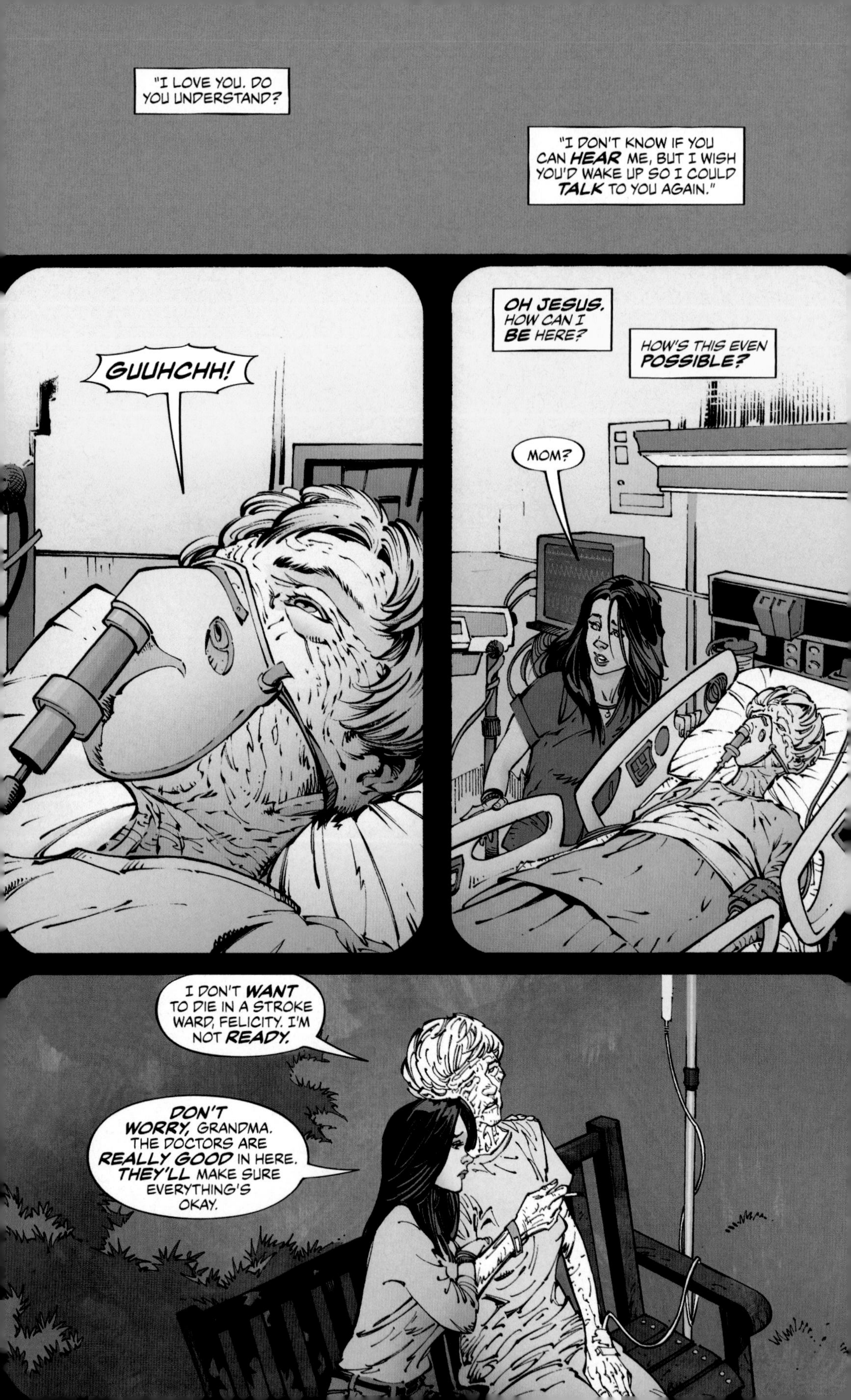
"I LOVE YOU. DO YOU UNDERSTAND?
"I DON'T KNOW IF YOU CAN HEAR ME, BUT I WISH YOU'D WAKE UP SO I COULD TALK TO YOU AGAIN."
GUUHCHH!
OH JESUS. HOW CAN I BE HERE?
HOW'S THIS EVEN POSSIBLE?
MOM?
I DON'T WANT TO DIE IN A STROKE WARD, FELICITY. I'M NOT READY.
DON'T WORRY, GRANDMA. THE DOCTORS ARE REALLY GOOD IN HERE. THEY'LL MAKE SURE EVERYTHING'S OKAY.

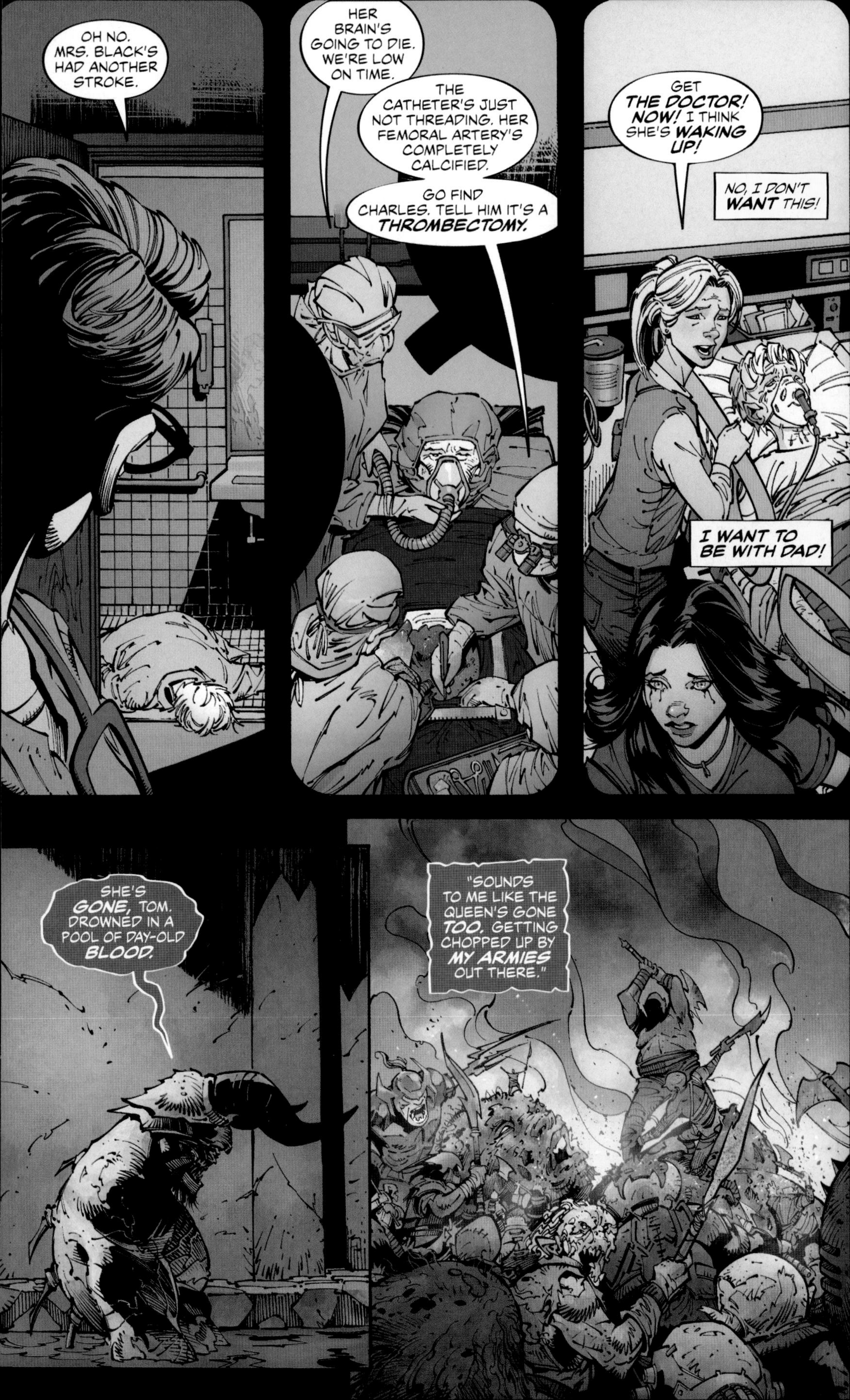
OH NO. MRS. BLACK'S HAD ANOTHER STROKE.
HER BRAIN'S GOING TO DIE. WE'RE LOW ON TIME.
THE CATHETER'S JUST NOT THREADING. HER FEMORAL ARTERY'S COMPLETELY CALCIFIED.
GO FIND CHARLES. TELL HIM IT'S A THROMBECTOMY.
GET THE DOCTOR! NOW! I THINK SHE'S WAKING UP!
NO, I DON'T WANT THIS!
I WANT TO BE WITH DAD!
SHE'S GONE, TOM. DROWNED IN A POOL OF DAY-OLD BLOOD.
"SOUNDS TO ME LIKE THE QUEEN'S GONE TOO, GETTING CHOPPED UP BY MY ARMIES OUT THERE."

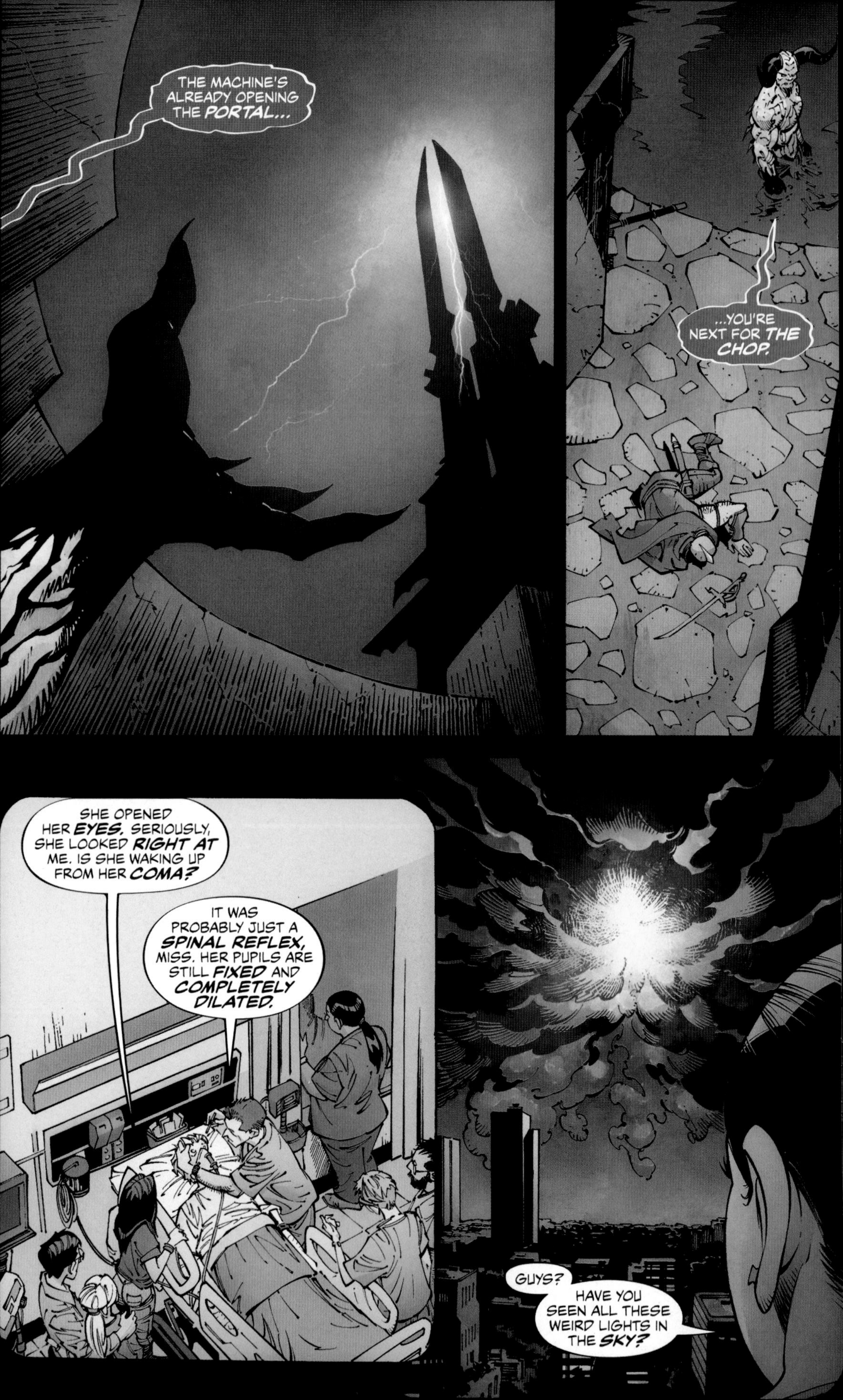
THE MACHINE'S ALREADY OPENING THE *PORTAL...*
...YOU'RE NEXT FOR *THE CHOP.*
SHE OPENED HER *EYES.* SERIOUSLY, SHE LOOKED *RIGHT AT* ME. IS SHE WAKING UP FROM HER *COMA?*
IT WAS PROBABLY JUST A *SPINAL REFLEX,* MISS. HER PUPILS ARE STILL *FIXED* AND *COMPLETELY DILATED.*
GUYS? HAVE YOU SEEN ALL THESE WEIRD LIGHTS IN THE *SKY?*

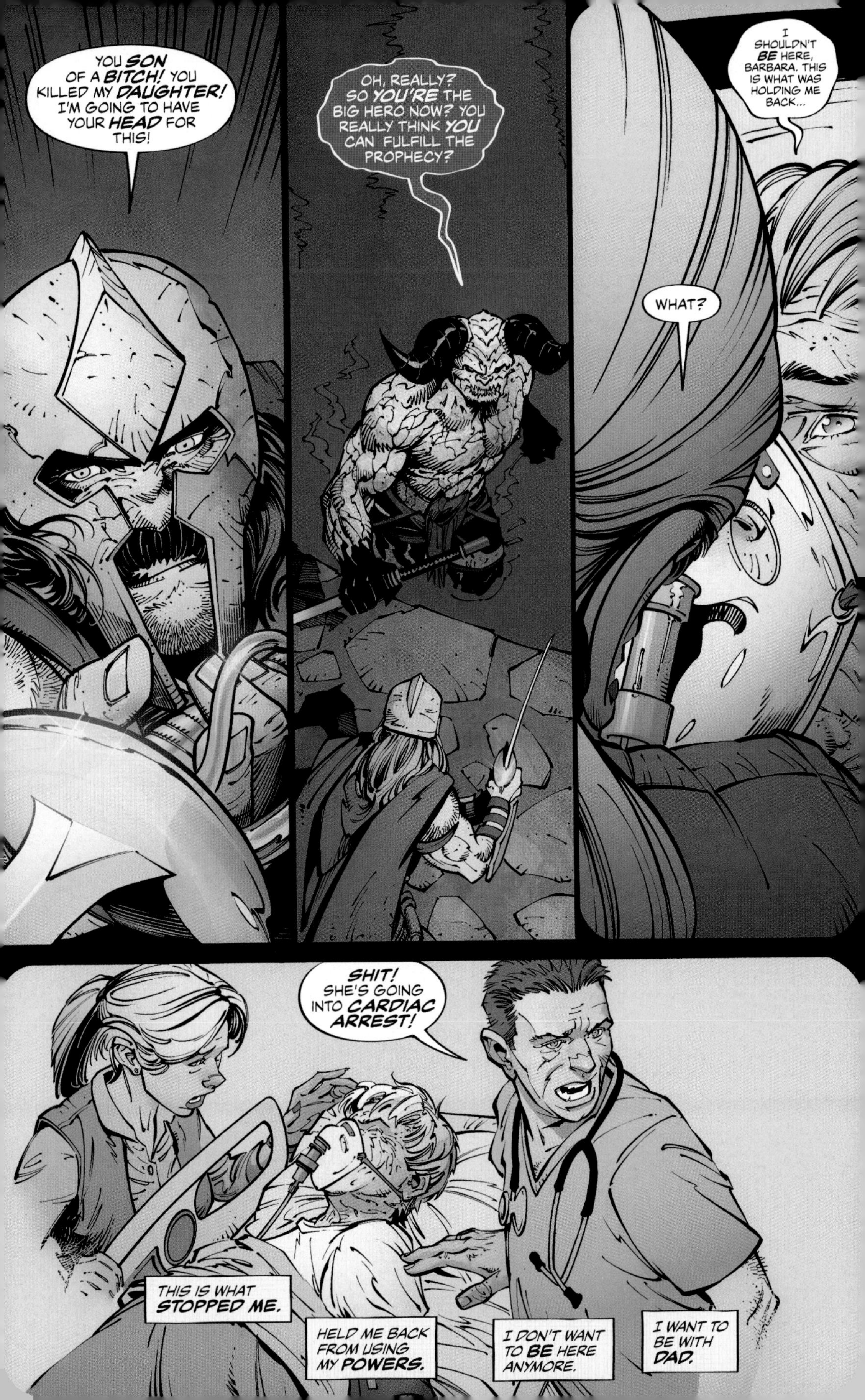
YOU SON OF A BITCH! YOU KILLED MY DAUGHTER! I'M GOING TO HAVE YOUR HEAD FOR THIS!
OH, REALLY? SO YOU'RE THE BIG HERO NOW? YOU REALLY THINK YOU CAN FULFILL THE PROPHECY?
I SHOULDN'T BE HERE, BARBARA. THIS IS WHAT WAS HOLDING ME BACK...
WHAT?
SHIT! SHE'S GOING INTO CARDIAC ARREST!
THIS IS WHAT STOPPED ME.
HELD ME BACK FROM USING MY POWERS.
I DON'T WANT TO BE HERE ANYMORE.
I WANT TO BE WITH DAD.

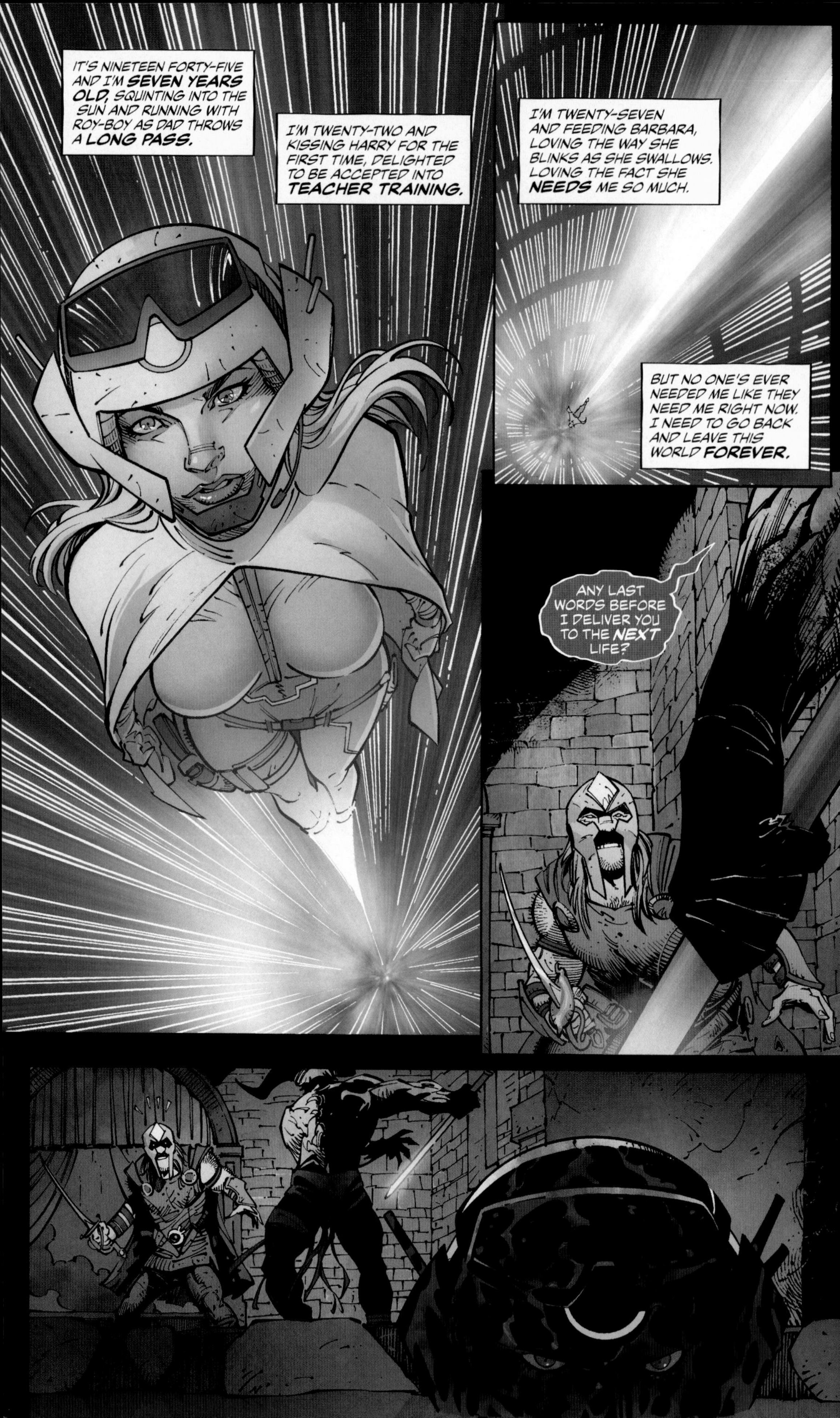

IT'S NINETEEN FORTY-FIVE AND I'M SEVEN YEARS OLD, SQUINTING INTO THE SUN AND RUNNING WITH ROY-BOY AS DAD THROWS A LONG PASS.
I'M TWENTY-TWO AND KISSING HARRY FOR THE FIRST TIME, DELIGHTED TO BE ACCEPTED INTO TEACHER TRAINING.
I'M TWENTY-SEVEN AND FEEDING BARBARA, LOVING THE WAY SHE BLINKS AS SHE SWALLOWS. LOVING THE FACT SHE NEEDS ME SO MUCH.
BUT NO ONE'S EVER NEEDED ME LIKE THEY NEED ME RIGHT NOW. I NEED TO GO BACK AND LEAVE THIS WORLD FOREVER.
ANY LAST WORDS BEFORE I DELIVER YOU TO THE NEXT LIFE?

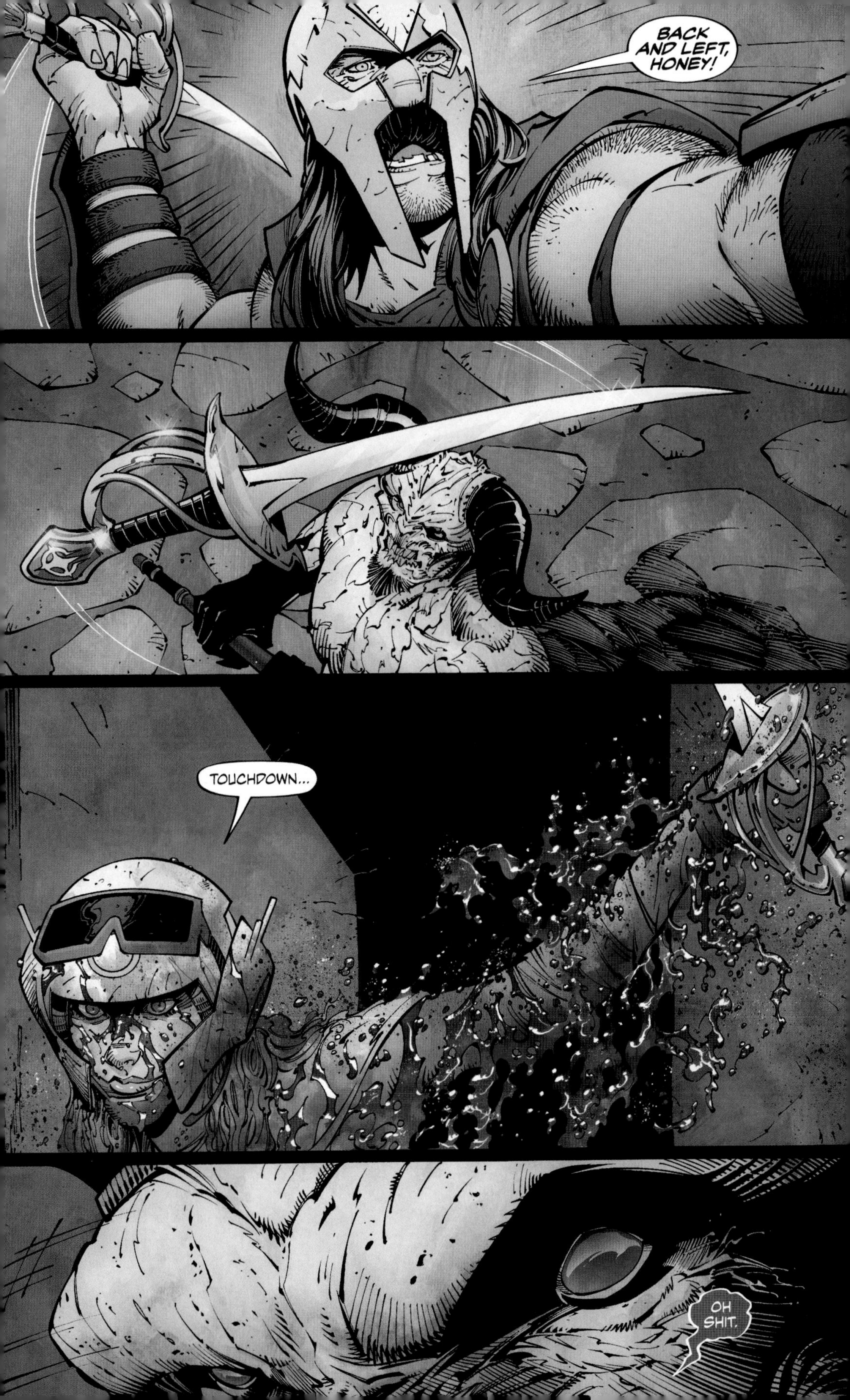
BACK AND LEFT, HONEY!
TOUCHDOWN...
OH SHIT.

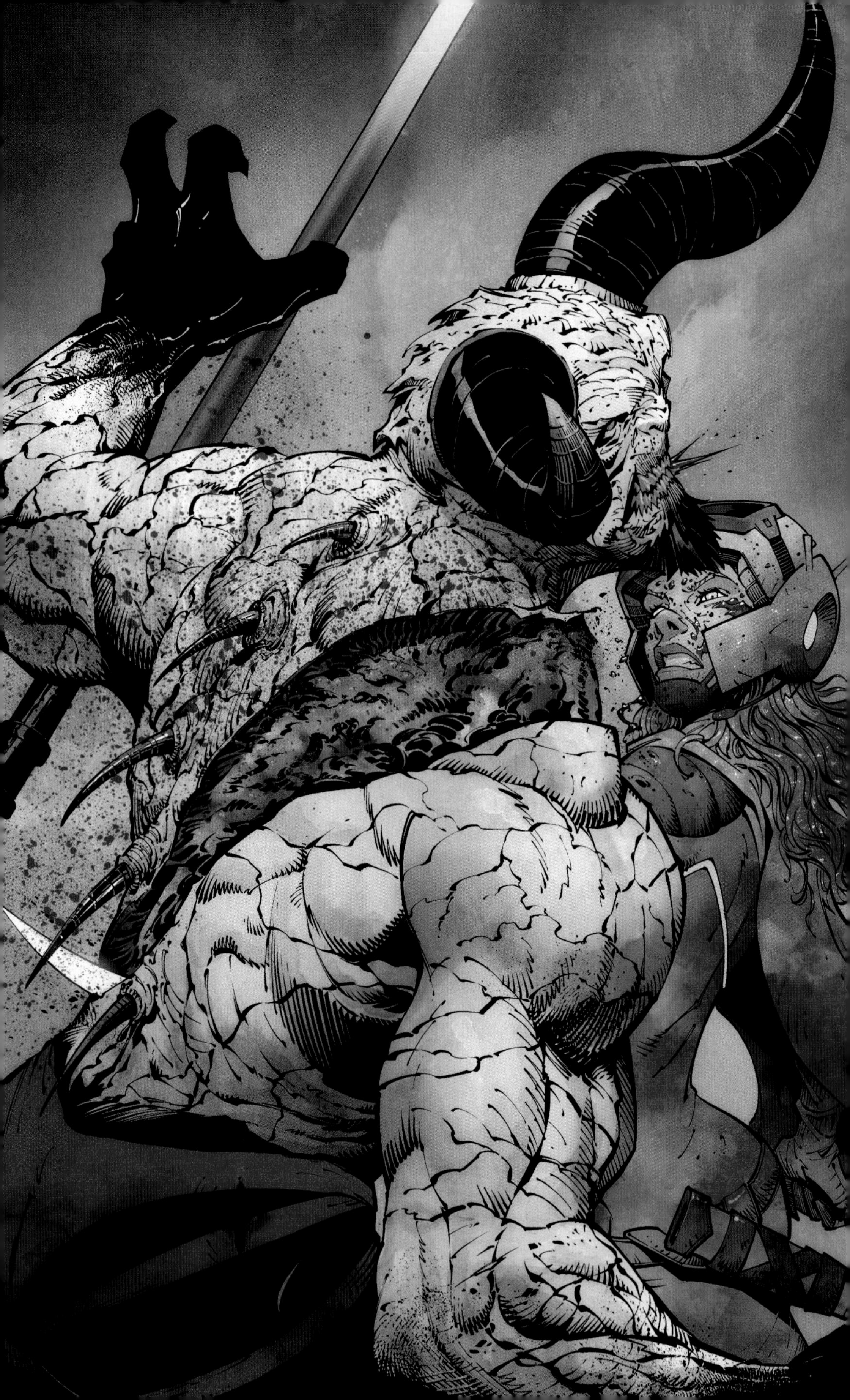

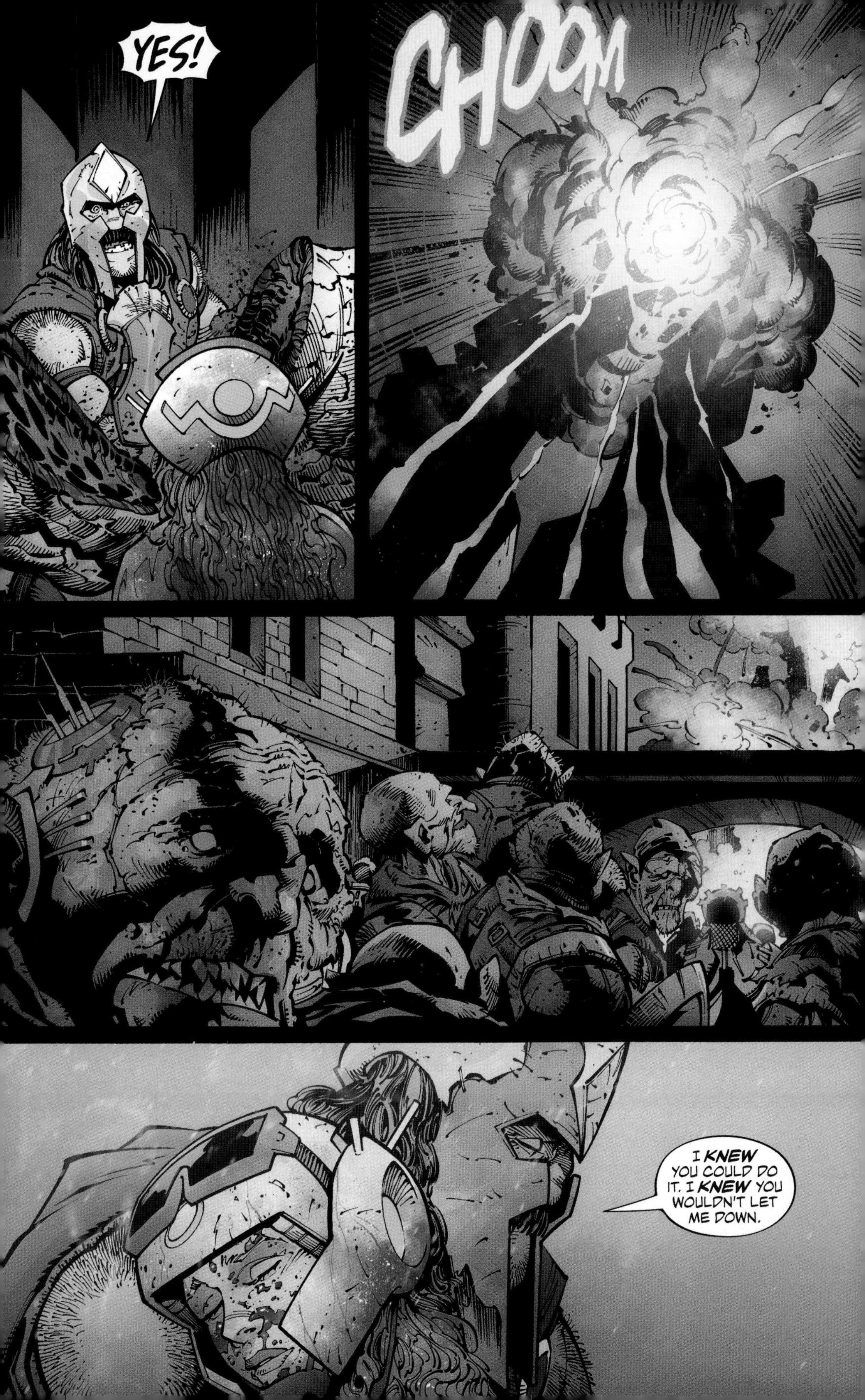
YES!
CHOOM
I KNEW YOU COULD DO IT. I KNEW YOU WOULDN'T LET ME DOWN.

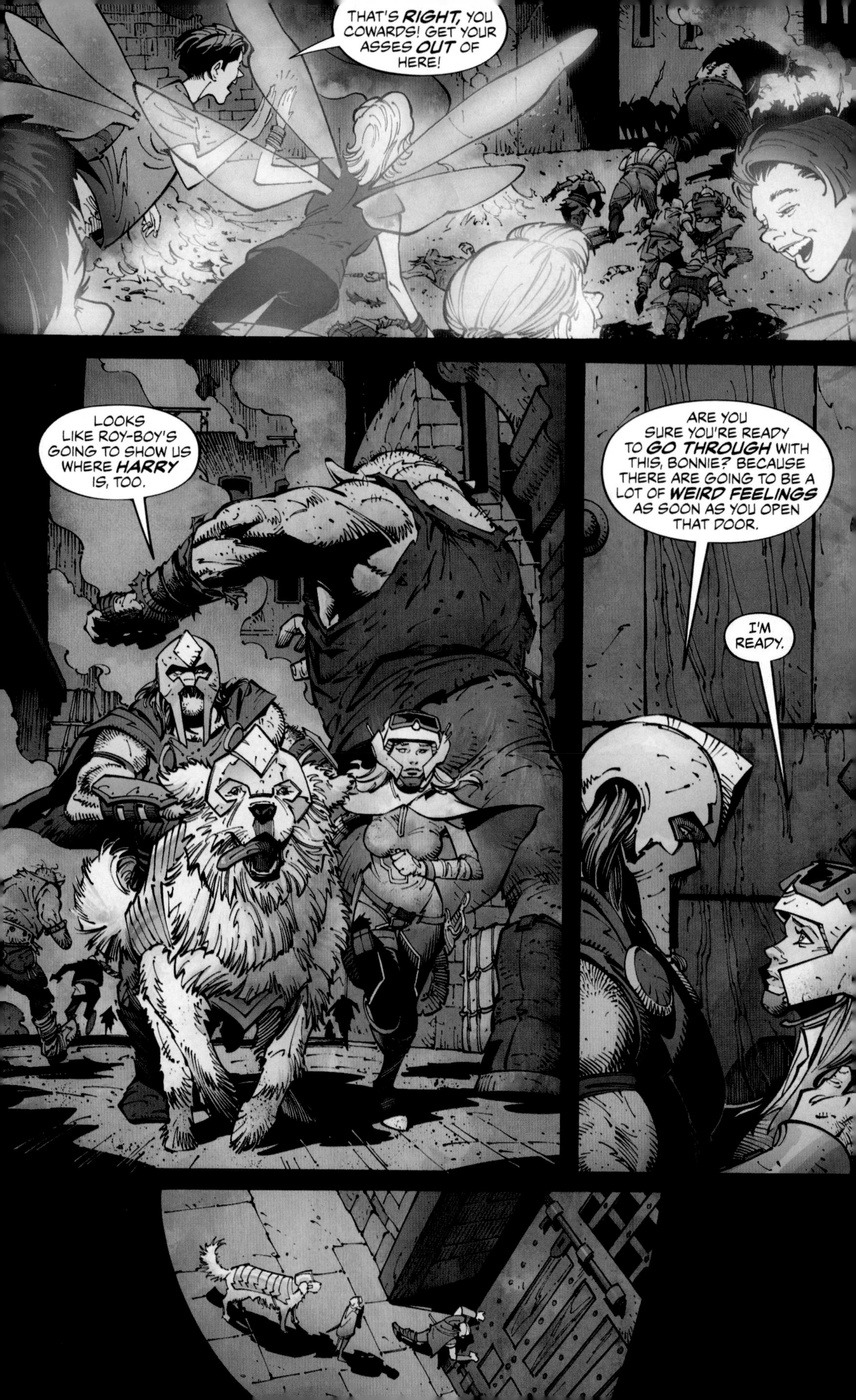
THAT'S RIGHT, YOU COWARDS! GET YOUR ASSES OUT OF HERE!
LOOKS LIKE ROY-BOY'S GOING TO SHOW US WHERE HARRY IS, TOO.
ARE YOU SURE YOU'RE READY TO GO THROUGH WITH THIS, BONNIE? BECAUSE THERE ARE GOING TO BE A LOT OF WEIRD FEELINGS AS SOON AS YOU OPEN THAT DOOR.
I'M READY.

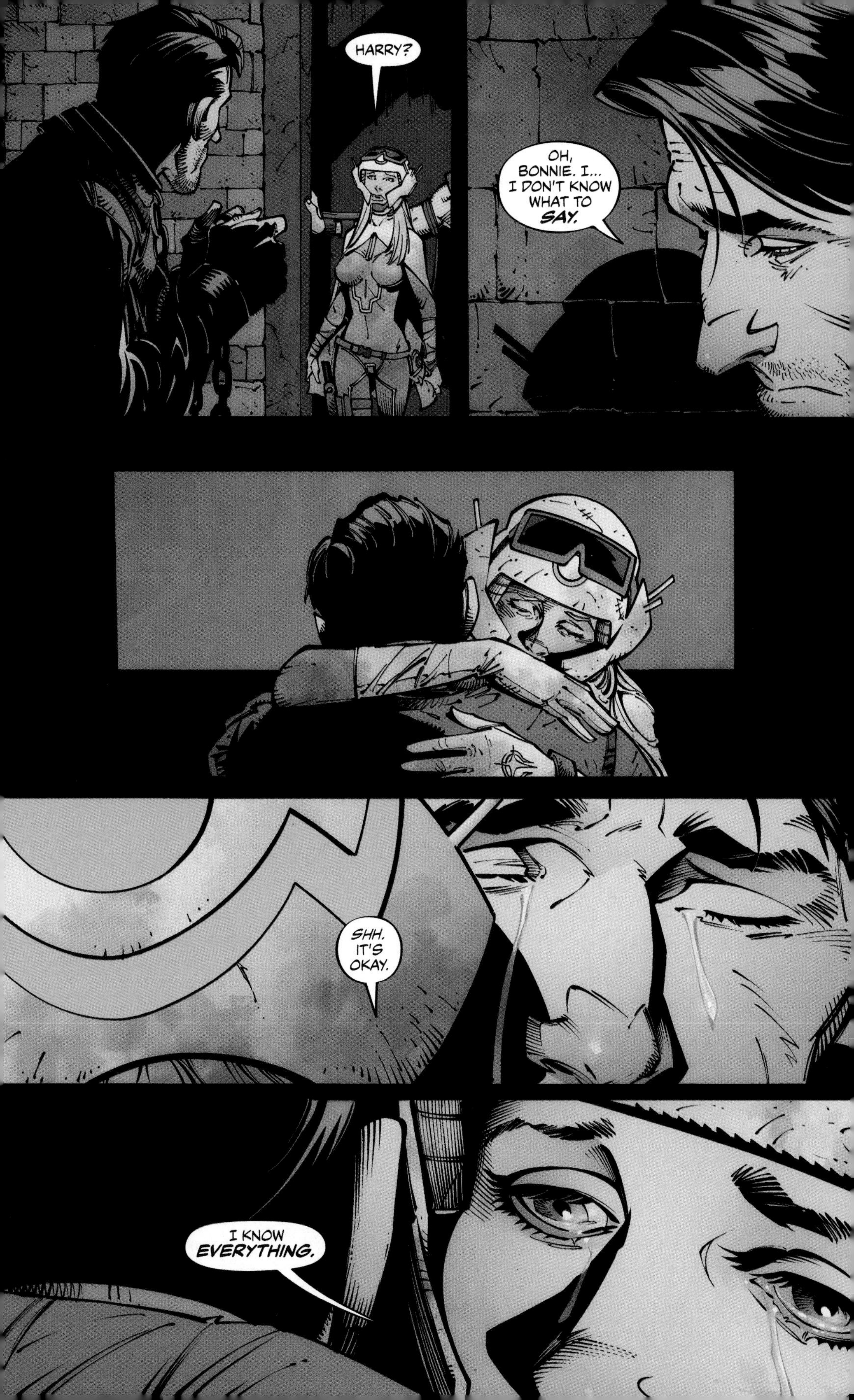
HARRY?
OH, BONNIE. I... I DON'T KNOW WHAT TO SAY.
SHH. IT'S OKAY.
I KNOW EVERYTHING.

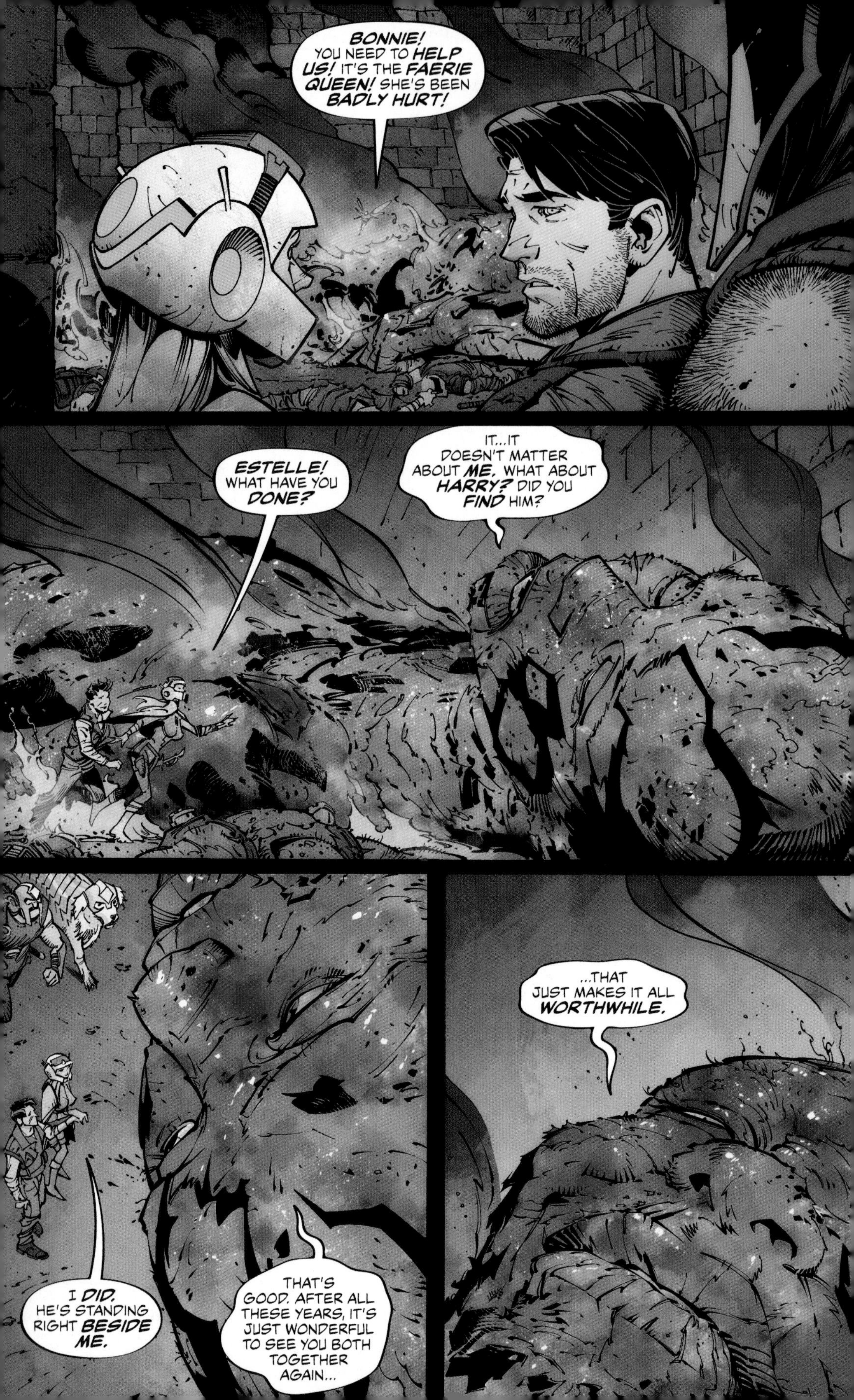
BONNIE! YOU NEED TO HELP US! IT'S THE FAERIE QUEEN! SHE'S BEEN BADLY HURT!
ESTELLE! WHAT HAVE YOU DONE?
IT...IT DOESN'T MATTER ABOUT ME. WHAT ABOUT HARRY? DID YOU FIND HIM?
I DID. HE'S STANDING RIGHT BESIDE ME.
THAT'S GOOD. AFTER ALL THESE YEARS, IT'S JUST WONDERFUL TO SEE YOU BOTH TOGETHER AGAIN...
...THAT JUST MAKES IT ALL WORTHWHILE.

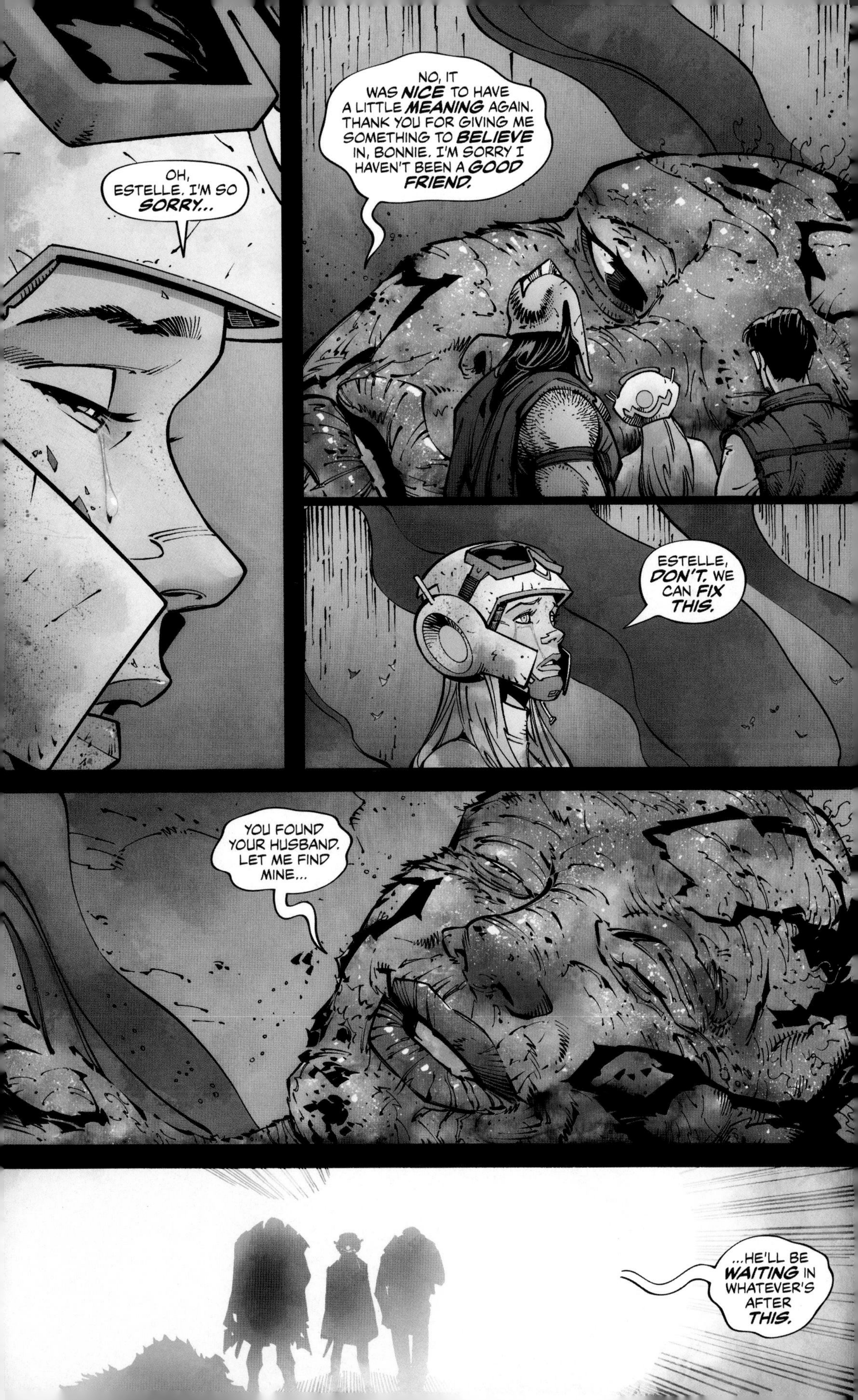
NO, IT WAS NICE TO HAVE A LITTLE MEANING AGAIN. THANK YOU FOR GIVING ME SOMETHING TO BELIEVE IN, BONNIE. I'M SORRY I HAVEN'T BEEN A GOOD FRIEND.
OH, ESTELLE. I'M SO SORRY...
ESTELLE, DON'T. WE CAN FIX THIS.
YOU FOUND YOUR HUSBAND. LET ME FIND MINE...
...HE'LL BE WAITING IN WHATEVER'S AFTER THIS.

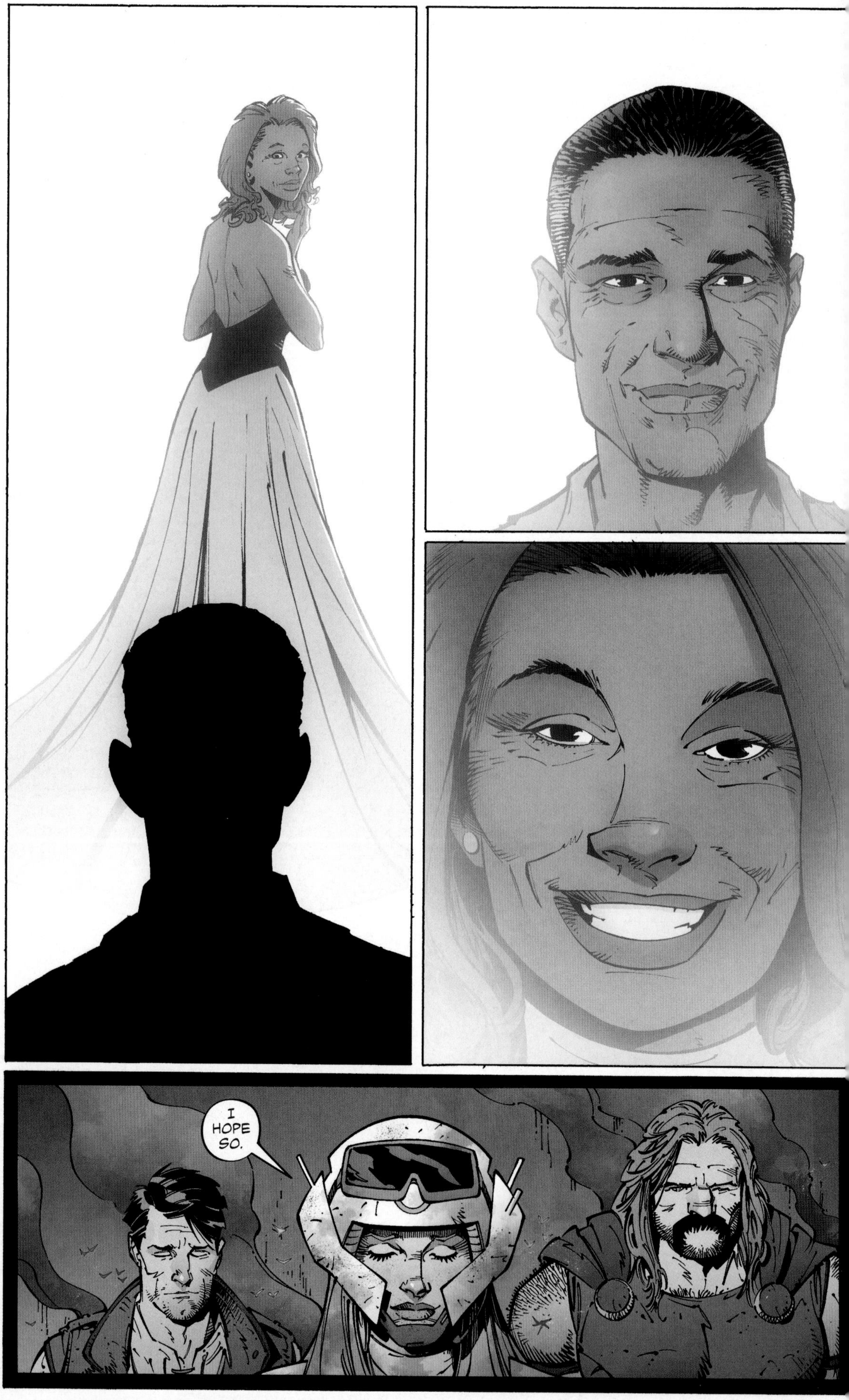
I HOPE SO.

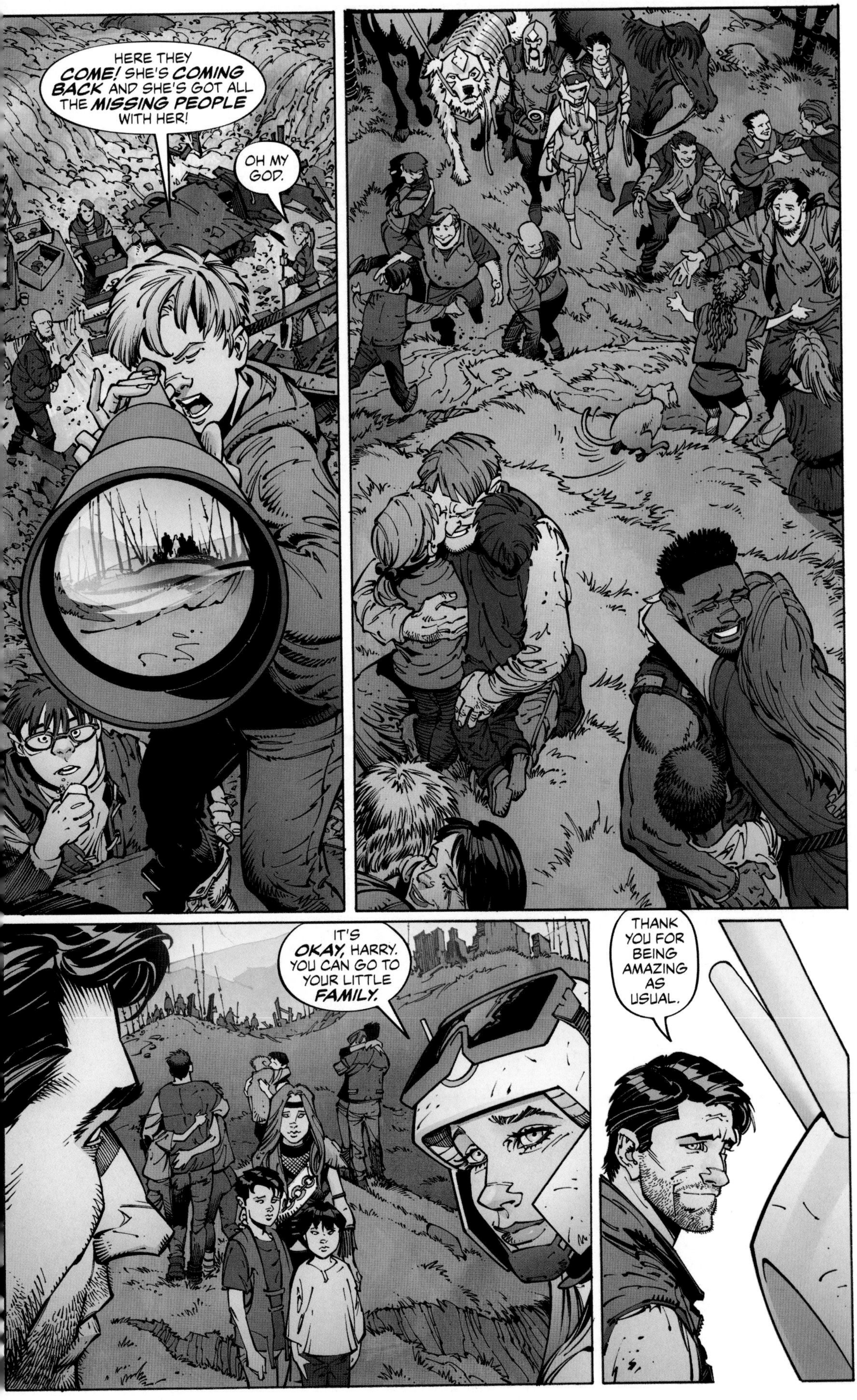
HERE THEY COME! SHE'S COMING BACK AND SHE'S GOT ALL THE MISSING PEOPLE WITH HER!
OH MY GOD.
IT'S OKAY, HARRY. YOU CAN GO TO YOUR LITTLE FAMILY.
THANK YOU FOR BEING AMAZING AS USUAL.

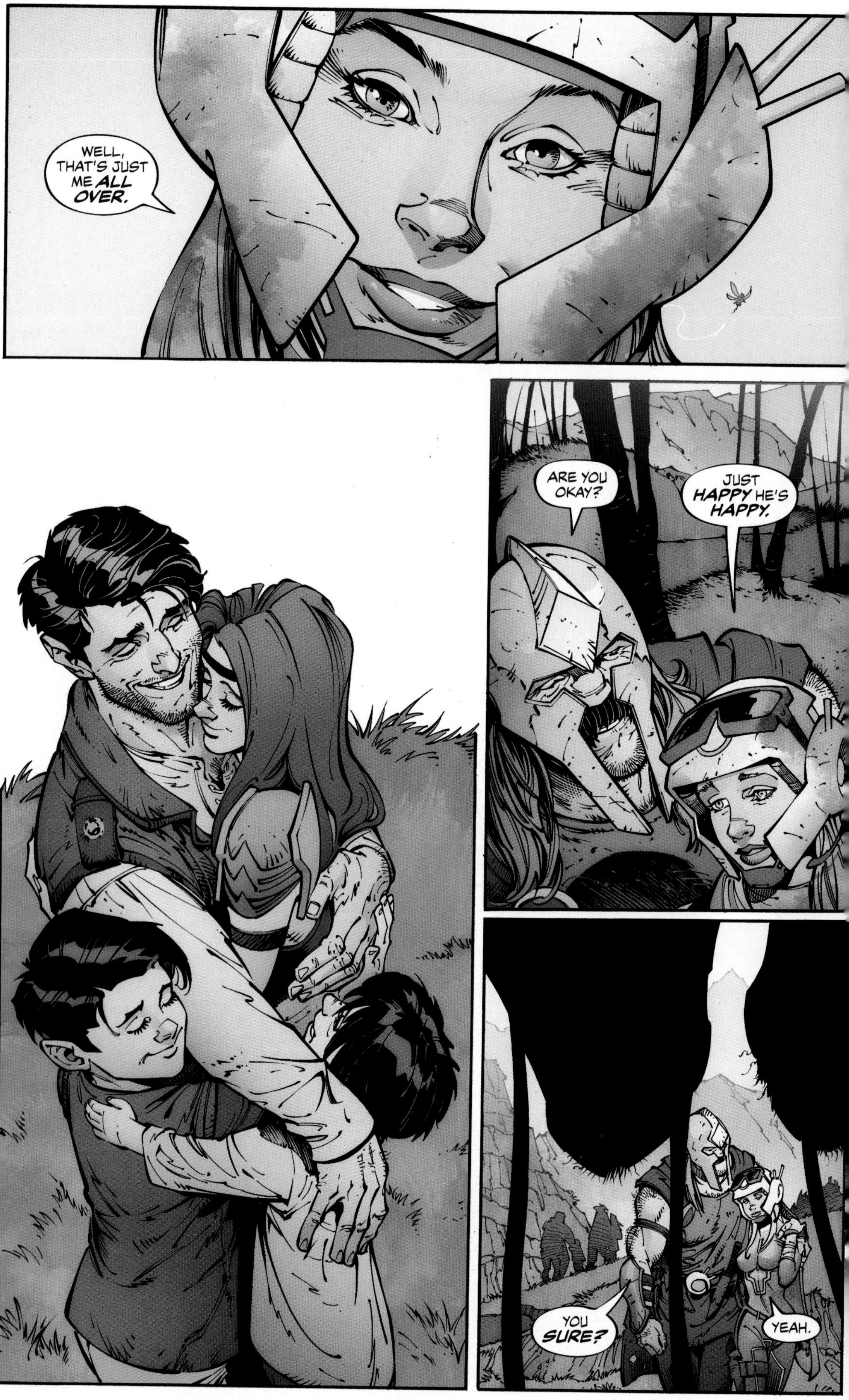
WELL, THAT'S JUST ME ALL OVER.
ARE YOU OKAY?
JUST HAPPY HE'S HAPPY.
YOU SURE?
YEAH.

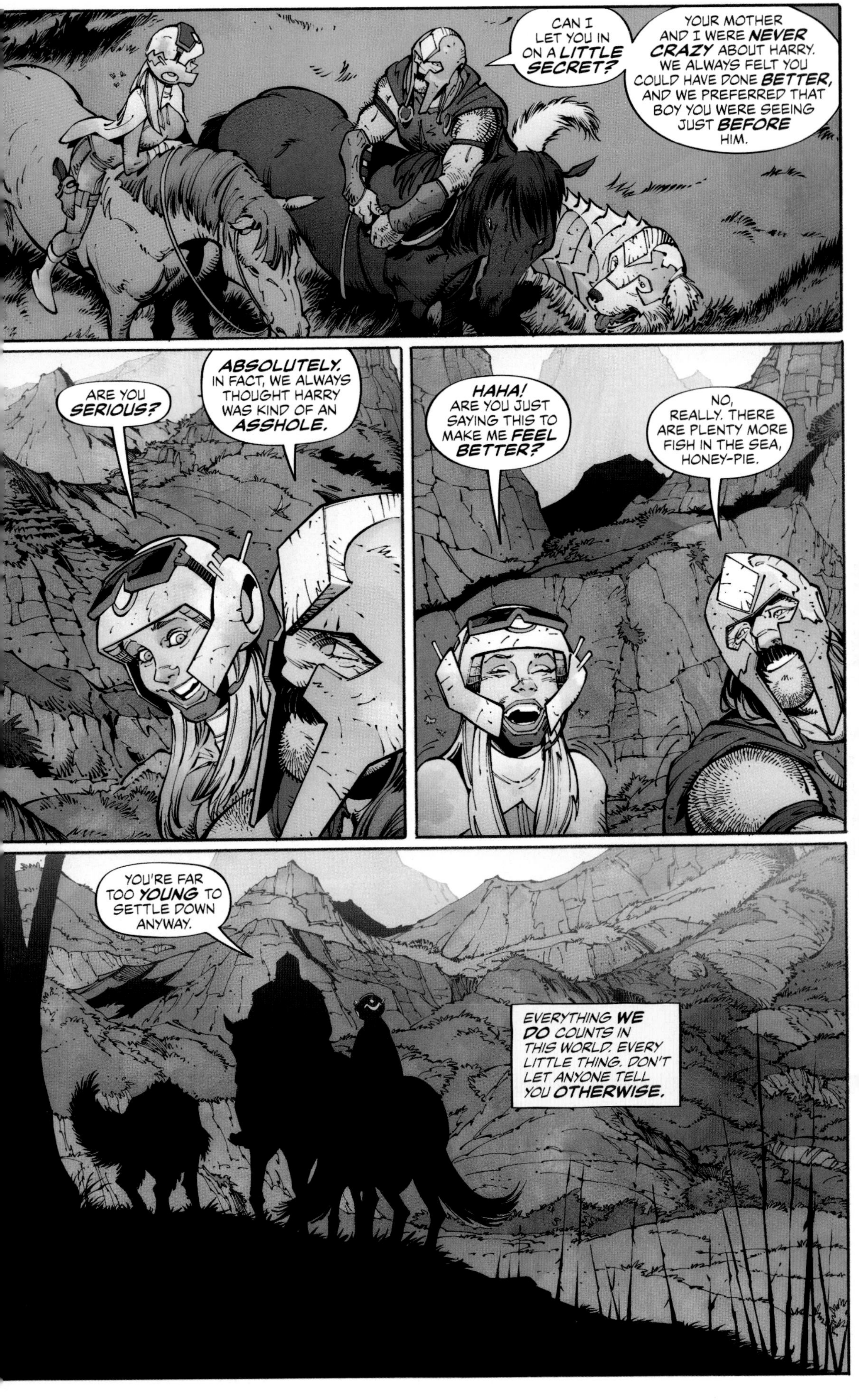
CAN I LET YOU IN ON A LITTLE SECRET?
YOUR MOTHER AND I WERE NEVER CRAZY ABOUT HARRY. WE ALWAYS FELT YOU COULD HAVE DONE BETTER, AND WE PREFERRED THAT BOY YOU WERE SEEING JUST BEFORE HIM.
ARE YOU SERIOUS?
ABSOLUTELY. IN FACT, WE ALWAYS THOUGHT HARRY WAS KIND OF AN ASSHOLE.
HAHA! ARE YOU JUST SAYING THIS TO MAKE ME FEEL BETTER?
NO, REALLY. THERE ARE PLENTY MORE FISH IN THE SEA, HONEY-PIE.
YOU'RE FAR TOO YOUNG TO SETTLE DOWN ANYWAY.
EVERYTHING WE DO COUNTS IN THIS WORLD. EVERY LITTLE THING. DON'T LET ANYONE TELL YOU OTHERWISE.

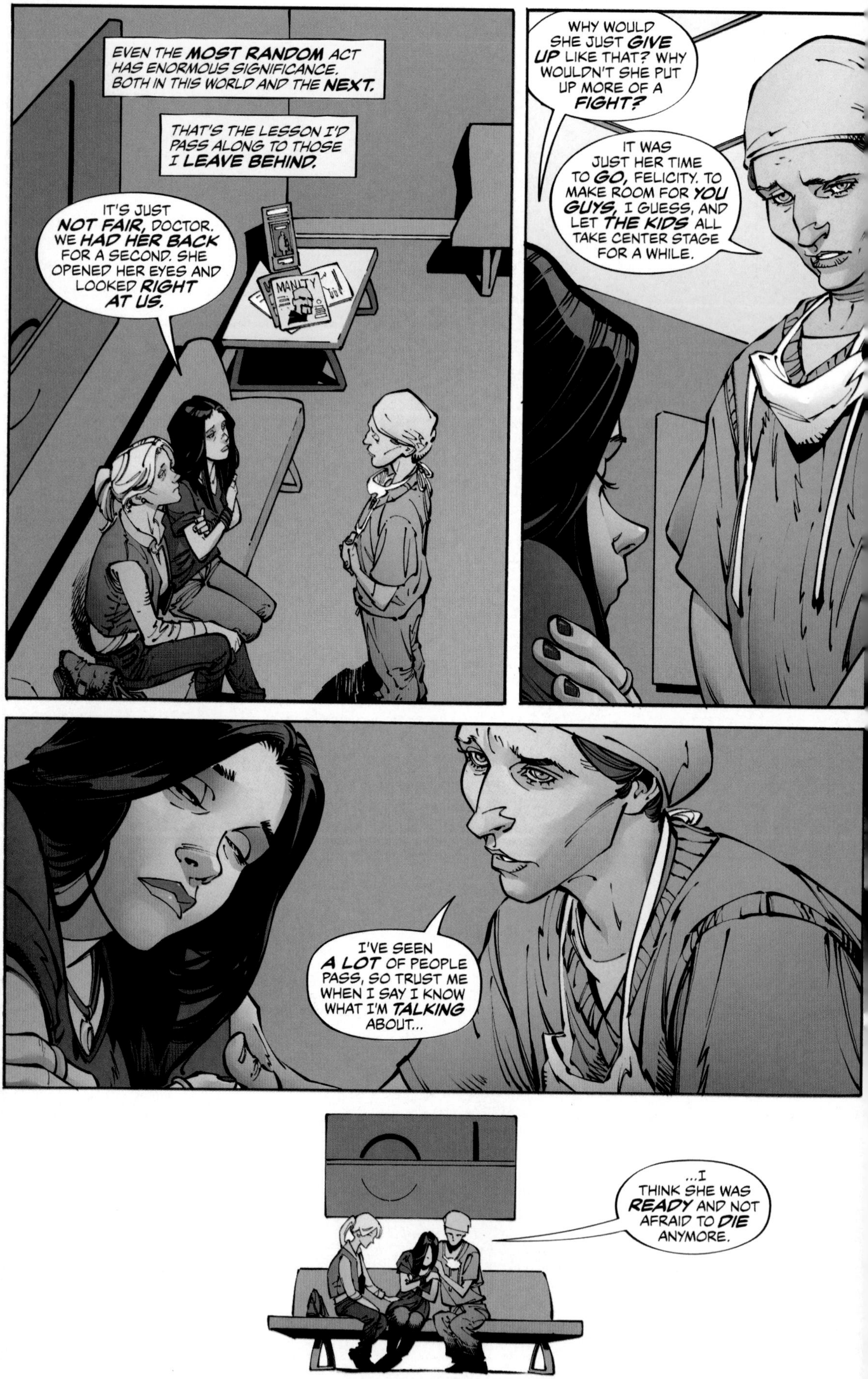
EVEN THE MOST RANDOM ACT HAS ENORMOUS SIGNIFICANCE. BOTH IN THIS WORLD AND THE NEXT.
THAT'S THE LESSON I'D PASS ALONG TO THOSE I LEAVE BEHIND.
IT'S JUST NOT FAIR, DOCTOR. WE HAD HER BACK FOR A SECOND. SHE OPENED HER EYES AND LOOKED RIGHT AT US.
MANITY
WHY WOULD SHE JUST GIVE UP LIKE THAT? WHY WOULDN'T SHE PUT UP MORE OF A FIGHT?
IT WAS JUST HER TIME TO GO, FELICITY. TO MAKE ROOM FOR YOU GUYS, I GUESS, AND LET THE KIDS ALL TAKE CENTER STAGE FOR A WHILE.
I'VE SEEN A LOT OF PEOPLE PASS, SO TRUST ME WHEN I SAY I KNOW WHAT I'M TALKING ABOUT...
...I THINK SHE WAS READY AND NOT AFRAID TO DIE ANYMORE.

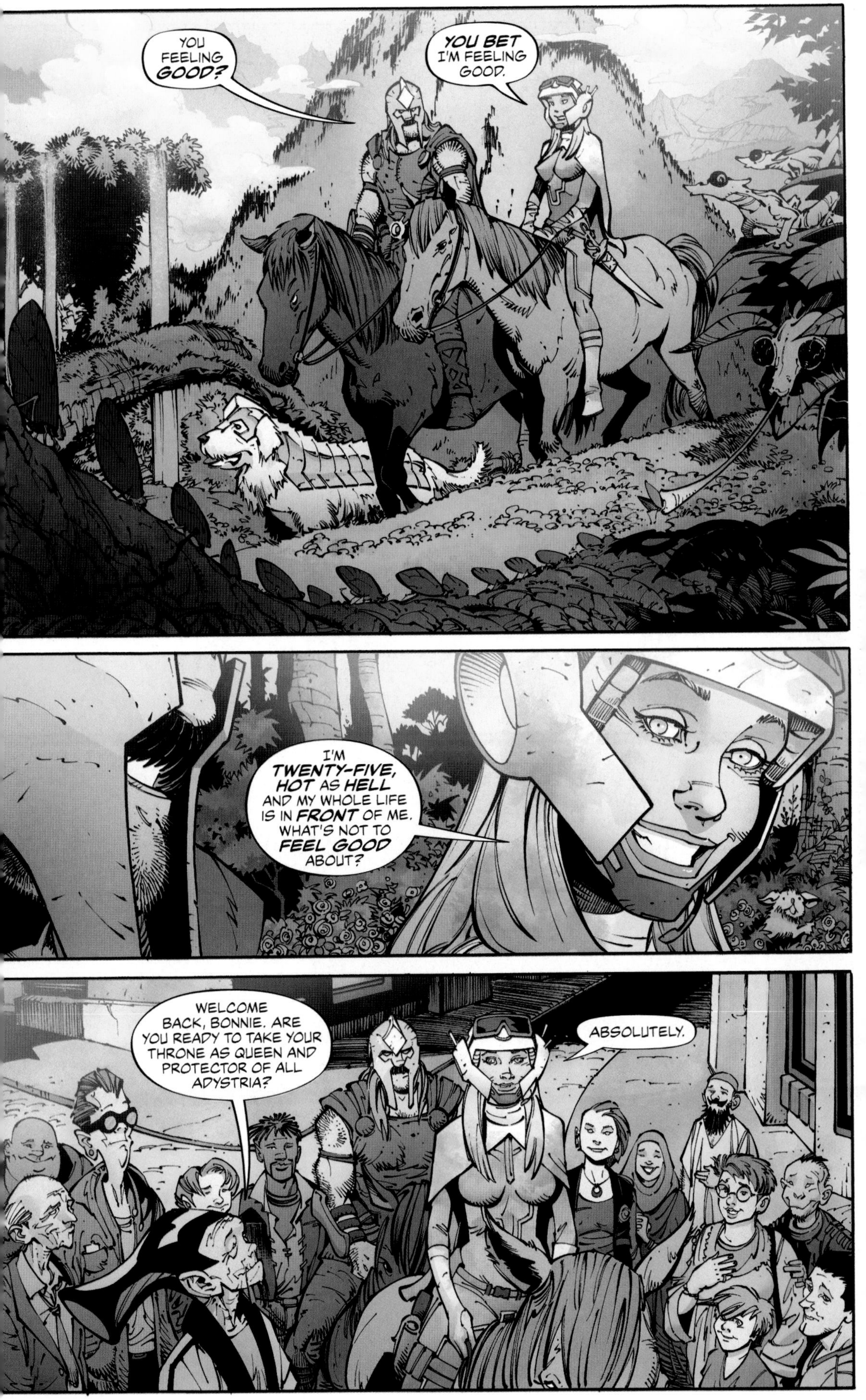
YOU FEELING GOOD?
YOU BET I'M FEELING GOOD.
I'M TWENTY-FIVE, HOT AS HELL AND MY WHOLE LIFE IS IN FRONT OF ME. WHAT'S NOT TO FEEL GOOD ABOUT?
WELCOME BACK, BONNIE. ARE YOU READY TO TAKE YOUR THRONE AS QUEEN AND PROTECTOR OF ALL ADYSTRIA?
ABSOLUTELY.

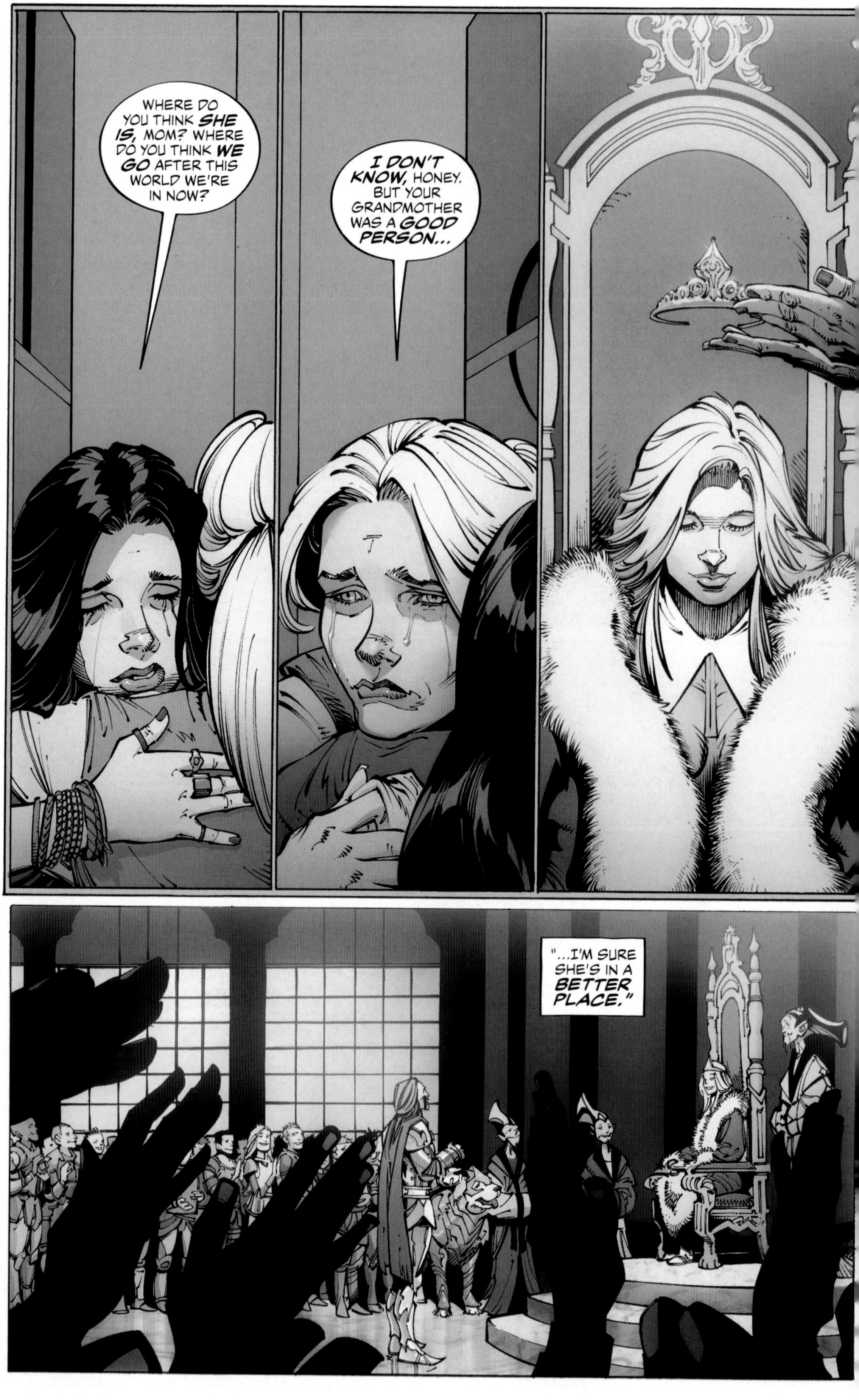
WHERE DO YOU THINK SHE IS, MOM? WHERE DO YOU THINK WE GO AFTER THIS WORLD WE'RE IN NOW?
I DON'T KNOW, HONEY. BUT YOUR GRANDMOTHER WAS A GOOD PERSON...
"...I'M SURE SHE'S IN A BETTER PLACE."

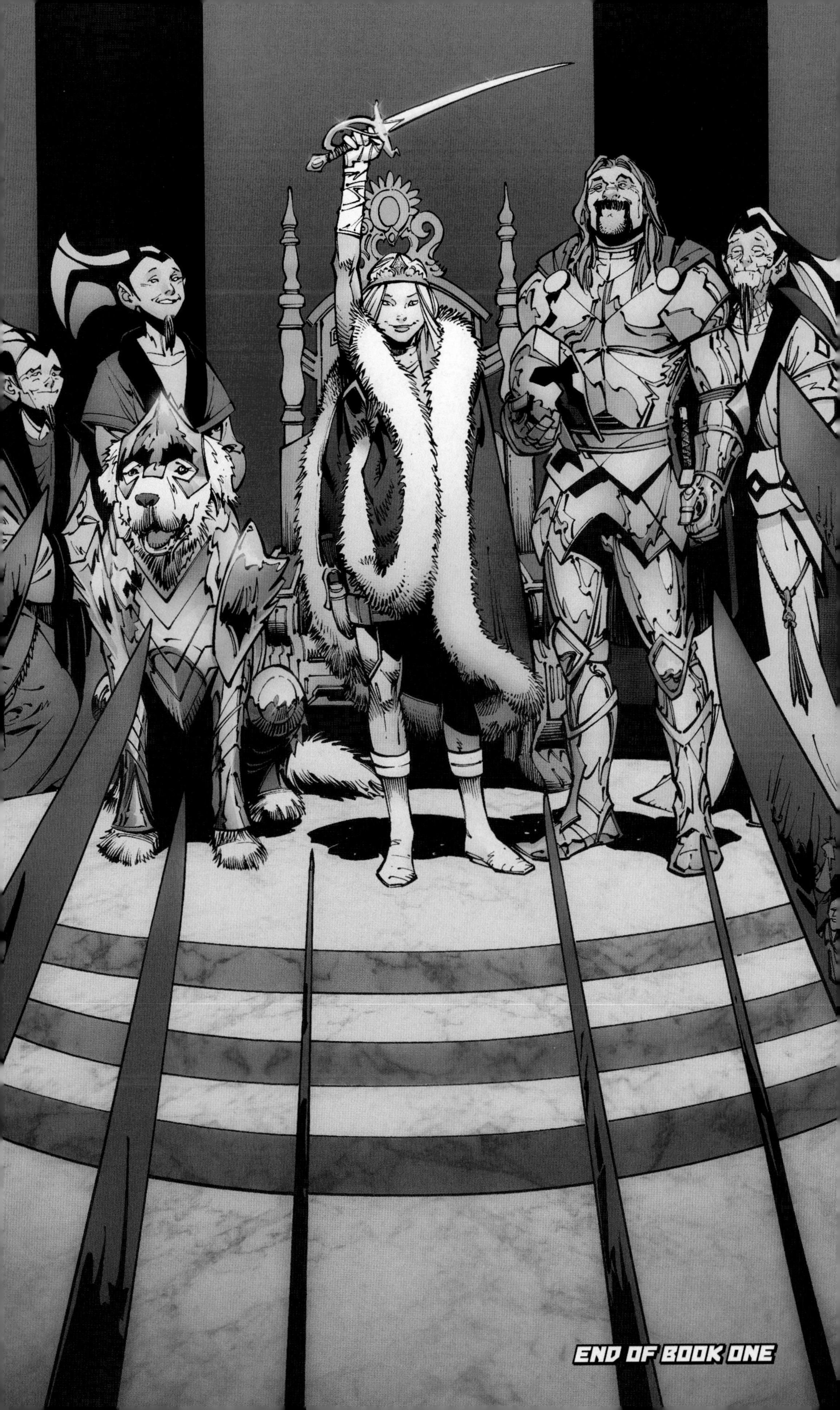
END OF BOOK ONE

CONCEPT SKETCHES BY **GREG CAPULLO**

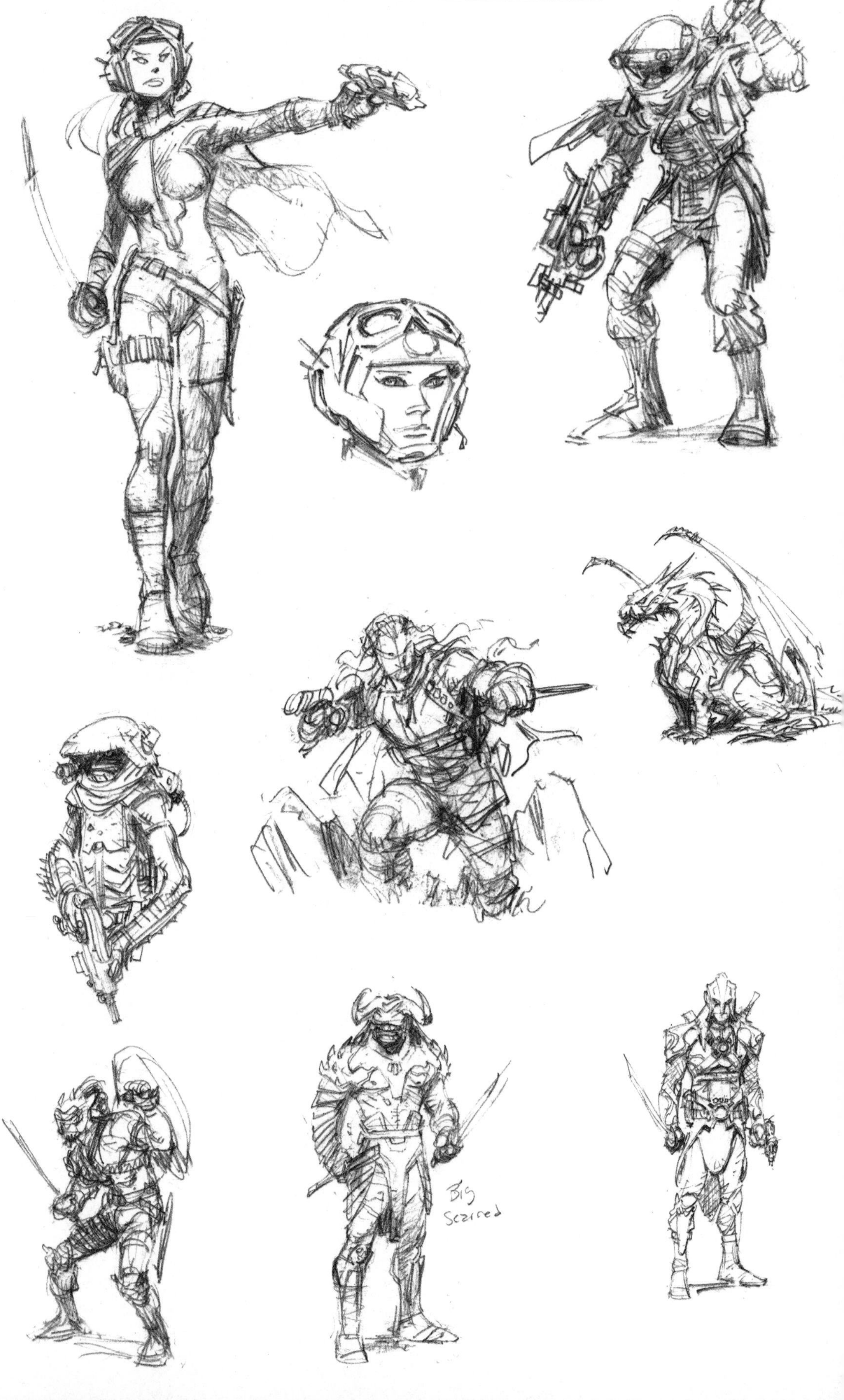

Big
Scarred

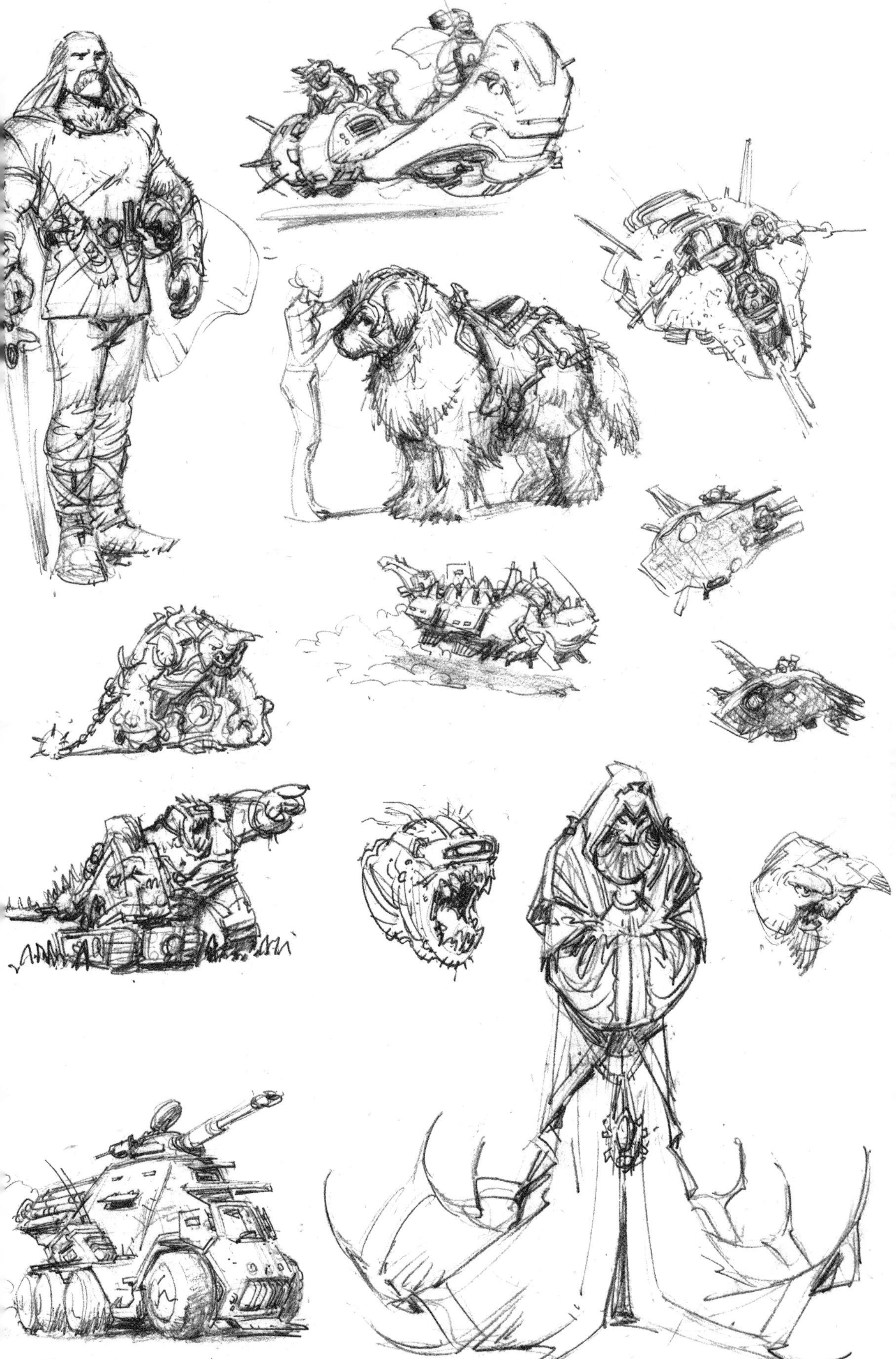

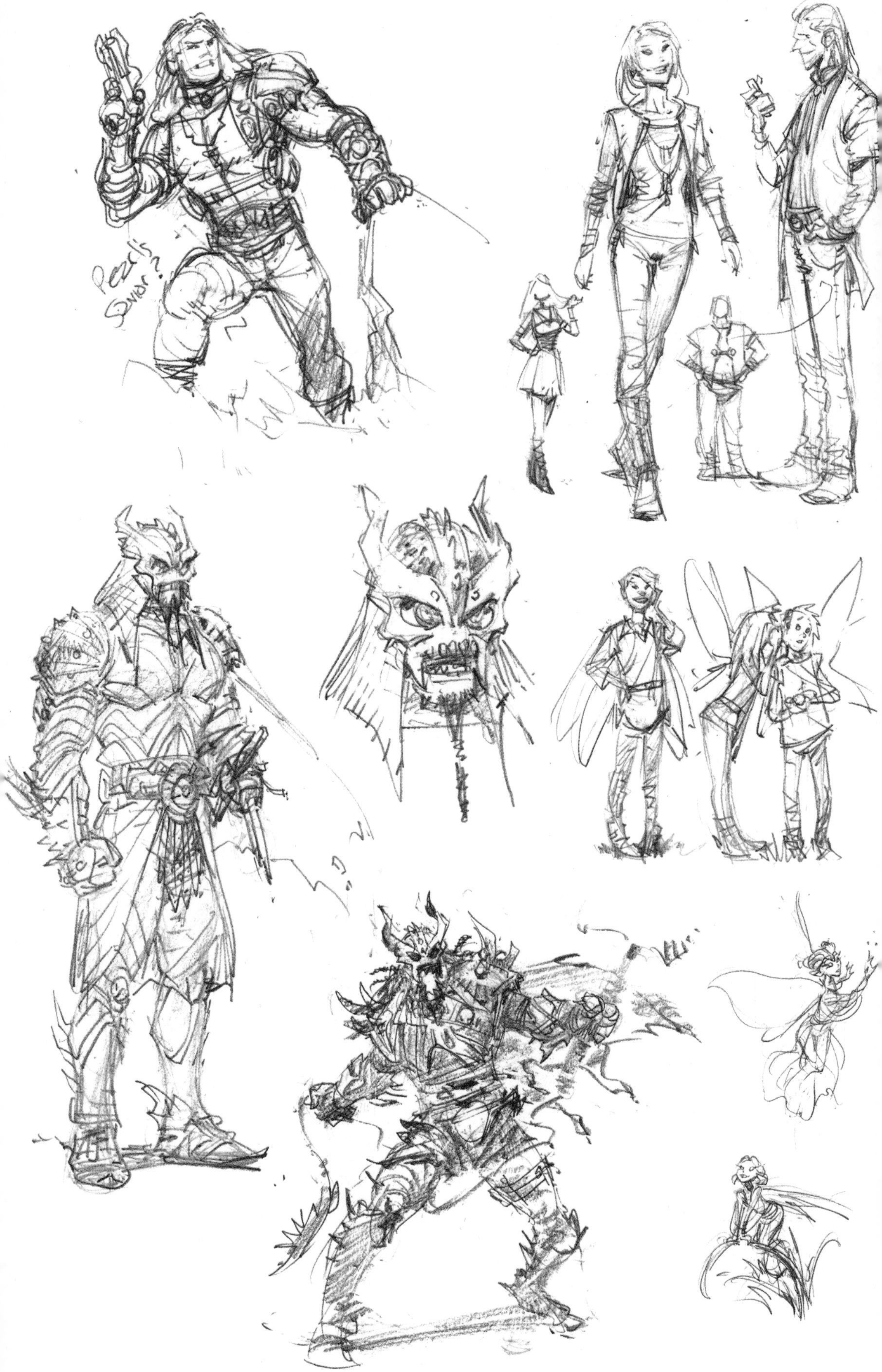
Pezzi's

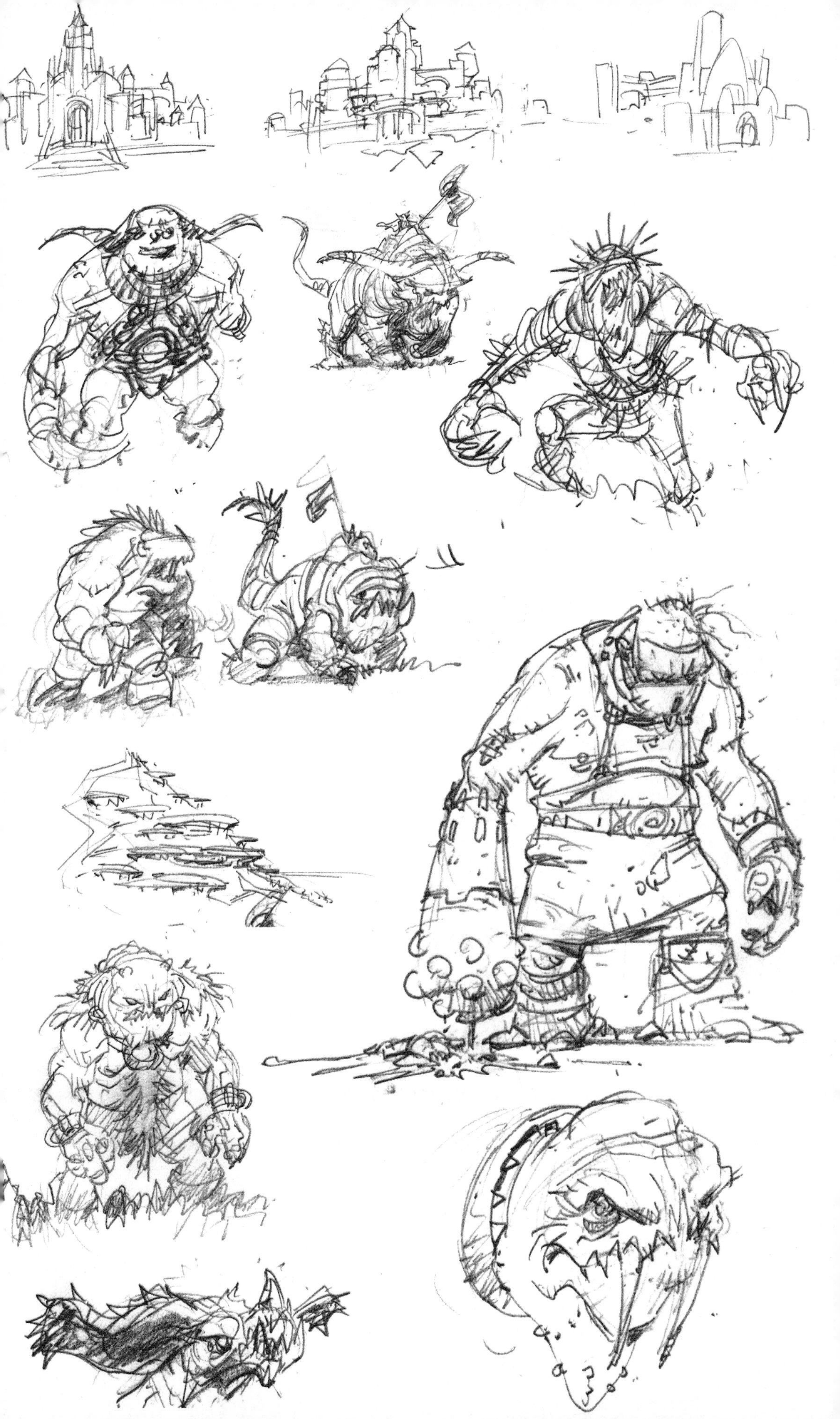

MEET THE CREATORS OF *REBORN*

MARK MILLAR

Mark Millar is the *New York Times* bestselling author of *Kick-Ass*, *Wanted* and *Kingsman: The Secret Service*, all of which have been adapted into Hollywood franchises.

His DC Comics work includes the seminal *Superman: Red Son*. At Marvel Comics he created *The Ultimates*, selected by *Time* magazine as the comic book of the decade, and described by screenwriter Zak Penn as his major inspiration for *The Avengers* movie. Millar also created *Wolverine: Old Man Logan* and *Civil War*, Marvel's two biggest-selling graphic novels ever. *Civil War* was the basis of the *Captain America: Civil War* movie and *Old Man Logan* was the inspiration for Fox's *Logan* movie in 2017.

Mark has been an executive producer on all his movies, and for four years worked as a creative consultant to Fox Studios on their Marvel slate of movies. In 2017, Netflix bought Millarworld in the company's first ever acquisition and employed Mark as President to continue creating comics, TV shows, and movies in a new division. His much-anticipated autobiography, *How To Bulletproof Your Horse*, will be published next year.

GREG CAPULLO

A self-taught illustrator, Greg Capullo began his comics career for Marvel on one of their flagship books, *X-Force*, before soon moving over to Image Comics to work for Todd McFarlane, taking over as penciller on *SPAWN*. Since that time, Greg has worked for the past seven years for DC Comics as artist on the *New York Times* highly acclaimed *Batman* series and most recently on *Dark Nights: Metal*. Greg's creator-owned properties include *The Creech*, a sci-fi horror comic, and *Reborn*, which was acquired by Netflix. Greg has provided art for Blizzard Entertainment's *World of Warcraft* and was the cover artist for many popular musical groups including Five Finger Death Punch, Korn, and Disturbed.

JONATHAN GLAPION

Jonathan Glapion began his comics career in 1998 at Image, where he contributed inks to such titles as *Curse of the Spawn*, *Sam and Twitch*, and *Universe*. After spending several years at Marvel inking *Elektra: The Hand*, *Gravity*, and *Ultimate X-Men*, he shifted his focus to their distinguished competition. Since 2007, he has worked on a wide variety of DC titles, including The New 52 *Batman*, *Batgirl*, *Suicide Squad: Rebirth*, *Batman and Superman*, *New Super-Man*, and *Action Comics*, as well as *Wonder Woman*. He has received awards such as: the Inkwell Awards 2010, The Props Award and The Most-Adaptable Inker Award 2013, the 2013 Harvey Awards for Best Inker Nominee, and the Inkwell Awards 2017 Small Press and Mainstream Independent Award. Most recently, Jonathan worked on *Reborn* with Greg Capullo, and is currently working on *DC's Dark Nights: Metal*.

FCO PLASCENCIA

FCO Plascencia is a professional comic book colorist based in Mexico. He studied graphic design, and was fortunate enough to work on animation and comics right after school. His previous projects include *Spawn*, *Batman*, *Invincible*, and *Wolverines* among others. He enjoys drawing, oil painting and technology.

NATE PIEKOS

Nate Piekos graduated with a Bachelor of Arts degree in graphic design from Rhode Island College in 1998. Since founding *Blambot.com*, he has created some of the industry's most popular fonts and has used them to letter comic books for Marvel Comics, DC Comics, Dark Horse Comics, and Image Comics, as well as dozens of independent publishers. He is a nominee and winner of several industry awards, and his design work has not only been utilized in comics, but in product packaging, video games, on television, and in feature films.

RACHAEL FULTON

Rachael Fulton is series editor of Mark Millar and John Romita Jr's monthly ongoing *Kick-Ass* series, as well as the monthly ongoing *Hit-Girl* series, working with talent such as Eduardo Risso, Rafael Albuquerque, and Goran Parlov. She is editor of Netflix's Millarworld division, where she is currently producing *The Magic Order* with Mark Millar and Olivier Coipel. Her past credits as series editor include *Empress*, *Jupiter's Legacy 2*, *Reborn*, and *Kingsman: The Red Diamond*. She is collections editor for the most recent editions of *Kingsman: The Secret Service* and all volumes of *Kick-Ass: The Dave Lizewski Years*. She tweets about feminism and cats from the handle @Rachael_Fulton.

NET

OTHER BOOKS BY

EMPRESS
MARK MILLAR
STUART IMMONEN
with WADE VONGRAWBADGER & IVE SVORCINA

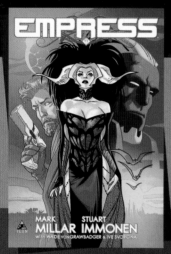

EMPRESS
Art by Stuart Immonen

Huck
MARK MILLAR
RAFAEL ALBUQUERQUE
DAVE McCAIG
BOOK 1:
ALL-AMERICAN

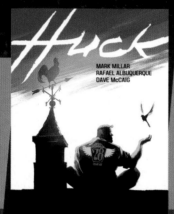

HUCK
Art by Rafael Albuquerque

MILLAR MURPHY
CHRONONAUTS
#1
$3.50

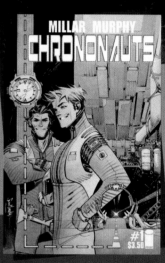

CHRONONAUTS
Art by Sean Gordon Murphy

MARK MILLAR DUNCAN FEGREDO
MPH

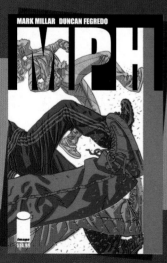

MPH
Art by Duncan Fegredo

MARK MILLAR · FRANK QUITELY
JUPITER'S
LEGACY
BOOK ONE

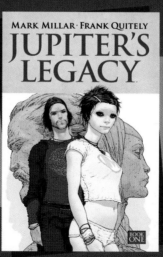

JUPITER'S CIRCLE 1 & 2
Art by Wilfredo Torres

MILLAR · TORRES · GIANFELICE
JUPITER'S
CIRCLE
BOOK ONE

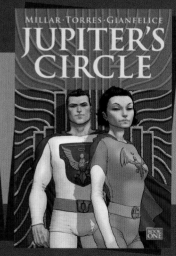

JUPITER'S LEGACY
Art by Frank Quitely